THEY WERE BOTH TOO PROUD
TO BACK DOWN. . . .

As Waco turned to walk away from her, Dixie caught his arm. She could taste the sweet flavor of rebellion as she asked, "I got the impression that you aren't afraid of anybody. Are you? Afraid?"

"No," he drawled slowly. "Are you?"

Dixie worried her bottom lip with her front teeth. "I've never crossed my father."

"Daddy's little darlin'?" he taunted. His fingers wrapped around Dixie's arms and lifted her until her lips were only a fraction of an inch away from his. "Listen carefully, gorgeous. Nobody calls me a coward."

"Nobody calls me 'Daddy's darlin' daughter!"

"I'm not scared of your old man or you," he countered. His lips grazed hers with each word he spoke. He meant to intimidate her, to make her back off gracefully.

Her chin raised. "Neither am I."

"Prove it." He gave her the opportunity by letting her be the aggressor. If she wanted his kiss, she'd have to meet him more than halfway. He watched the dark pupils of her eyes expand. He inhaled the honeysuckle fragrance of her shampoo.

She wasn't afraid of him, she told herself. Her eyelids drooped and she stood on tiptoe. Her soft lips whispered against his mouth. He wanted aggression. He got shy, sweet seduction. It was more than enough.

ANNA HUDSON

SOMEDAY

PINNACLE BOOKS
KENSINGTON PUBLISHING CORP.

PINNACLE BOOKS are published by

Kensington Publishing Corp.
850 Third Avenue
New York, NY 10022

First Printing: April, 1995

Printed in the United States of America

At one time or another, we are all confronted by life's stumbling blocks. I am proud to dedicate this novel to five ladies who find a way over, under, around or through difficult times, and manage to keep a broad smile on their faces. I admire their "Texas grit."

To Lesley Chaney, a special young lady who continues to grow by leaps and bounds. At twenty, you have more insights into the true meaning of love, loyalty and integrity than most women twice your age. Being your friend gives me great joy.

To Kathy Payson, who has the best mental health of any woman I've ever met. Two hours of playing cards with you helps me "get my head on straight." Your zest for life is inspirational.

To Debbie Macomber, a dear friend and fellow writer, who is a blessing, an angel in disguise. Your generosity, kindness, and wit brighten my darkest days.

To Linda Lael Miller, a much deserved New York Times *bestselling author, who graciously encourages her writer friends that haven't made it . . . yet. Someday, we'll all have "grass in the front yard."*

To Denise Little, editor extraordinary. Talented and knowledgeable, you have devoted hours to making me understand why all authors aren't millionaires, and yet, at the same time you've given me hope and instilled determination. May our association be long and fruitful.

What is a dedication that doesn't mention the mainstays in an author's life? To Henry, Jane and Scott, Hank, my eternal gratitude for loving me, unconditionally.

And to Jack Hudson and his new bride, Rita. Congratulations! May your marriage hold all the happily-ever-afters found in each romance I've written.

Love you all!

One

April, 1985
Pearwood, Texas

"You promised you'd sign my yearbook today," Dixie said in a scolding tone. Her voice echoed off the tiled walls of the boys' locker room. For modesty's sake, she squeezed her eyelids shut. The pen between her fingers trembled, as did her hand. She took a deep breath to steady her nerves. The locker-room odor assaulted her nose as though she'd pulled a grungy sweat sock over her head. She wanted to cut and run, but pure, cussed stubbornness prevailed. "Do it!"

Chad Armstrong's face blanched white with shock; then a red tide of embarrassment crept up his neck to his blond hairline. Reflexively, one of the hands he'd crossed over the front of his jockstrap reached for the object Dixie held out to him.

Stunned into silence by the invasion of a woman into their sacred male domain, a dozen sets of astonished eyes watched while the pen teetered on the side of Dixie Mayson's forefinger. In suspended animation, it slid, toppling end over end until it crashed against the white tiled floor.

Dixie's eyes flew open.

The faint noise sounded louder than the firing of a starting gun, and had the same effect on the track team. One boy grabbed a towel to cover himself, another opened his locker door to block her view, and a third climbed inside his locker. The remaining boys scrambled into their clothes.

Over disparaging shouts and snickers, Dixie heard the team's captain, Pete Saunders, yell, "Dammit, Armstrong, sign it and get Dixie out of the locker room."

Chad stooped to retrieve the pen, as did Dixie. Her hard head collided with his. For several seconds Dixie had real stars in her blue eyes each time she gazed at Chad. She heard a mild expletive cross his lips. He grabbed the pen while she straightened up. To quell her dizziness she bit her lip. Chad was one of the few boys in the senior class taller than Dixie.

She'd gloried in the fact that she'd had to raise her face to look up at his blond hair and blue eyes. A lump of unrequited love lodged in her throat, strangling her, making it impossible for her to speak. She held the yearbook open to the place where a picture of him jumping for a basketball rebound dominated the page.

Quicker than a slam dunk, he scrawled his name beneath it. "Go!"

"Aren't you going to write something else?" she dared to ask, pushing her luck to the hilt.

Her yearbook snapped shut beneath her nose in reply.

"Dixie, *please* . . ." Chad implored, making shooing motions with his hands. "Leave. Now!"

A triumphant gleam shone in her eyes as she pivoted on one foot and marched to the door. "A promise is a promise. You made it. I kept it."

The razzing tones of Chad's teammates were muffled as the locker-room door swung closed behind her. What did she care if they thought she had "brass balls bigger than a thrower's disk"— whatever that meant.

In first period English class, she'd vowed to her best friend, Sara Fairchild, that she'd get Chad's autograph or die trying. Chad should have cooperated, instead of avoiding her and promising to catch her later. Then, she wouldn't have been forced to go to such extremes.

"Shoot fire," she whispered, hugging her yearbook to her chest and bounding up the steps two at a time, thinking of the sequel. Without a doubt, Pearwood's cutesy-butts would spread the story all over school by lunch the next day.

She didn't care. Like it or not, Chad had paid attention to her. When it came time for him to decide who he was going to ask to the prom, her name would be foremost in his thoughts.

"It was worth it."

The impulse to hold her yearbook high, like a championship trophy, and gleefully skip and twirl down the wide corridor between the classrooms, coursed through her veins. She'd noticed several teachers in their classrooms. Without a doubt, she mused silently, they'd come rushing into the hallway to investigate any commotion.

"No point in making a spectacle out of myself for nothing," she reasoned silently.

She counted on the thick wall of silence between teenagers and adults, to keep her father from finding out about the minor infraction of school rules it had taken to get Chad's autograph. Nobody ever snitched on her because they knew John Mayson had one hell of a temper. He could raise the school roof six inches off-center without working up a sweat.

Dixie lengthened her stride, but not enough to be conspicuous. The outside chance that the local grapevine might carry tales to John had her worrying her bottom lip. She'd heard John spout his code of behavior so often, she could recite it by heart: fairness, respect and integrity.

Unfortunately, none of these had crossed her mind before she had crossed the threshold of the boys' locker room.

Grounded for life, again, Dixie silently predicted. That's after he gives me a thorough asschewing.

She shifted her yearbook to one arm, pushed open the door below the red exit sign and stepped into the spring sunshine. Dixie paused, momentarily weighing the slight chance of facing the consequences of her actions, against the prize in her hand, then she let out a rip-roaring, "Whooooeee! Yes! I got it!"

An hour later, Dixie and Sara were sprawled across a bed comparing autographs. "To a sweet girl with a great sense of humor," Dixie read aloud, grimacing at the signature in her yearbook. "Hank."

"He wrote in mine, too." Sara flipped to the picture of the president of their senior class. "Roses are red, daisies are yellow, dump Todd and I'll be your fellow."

"Sissy will beat you to death with her pom-poms if she reads what he wrote. Just yesterday, she was moaning and groaning in chemistry class about Hank not asking her to the prom, yet."

Dixie perused the short autographs peppered with "sweet," "smart," and "funny" in her yearbook, to the lengthy prose scribbled in her best friend's book. She'd have gladly traded half her brains and a barrel of laughs for Sara's yearbook. Or a date to the prom.

". . . I can hardly wait until graduation night. I ache for you," Sara read from her yearbook. "Look how Todd signed it."

"U R 2 QT WRDS," Dixie read silently. Todd had drawn a heart, with X's and O's in it to symbolize kisses and hugs. Trite, but terrific.

Momentarily, a flash of pure envy changed Dixie's turquoise blue eyes to emerald green. It wasn't that she wanted Todd Lang to write something sappy in her yearbook, she assured herself, smiling tightly. After all, at five feet six, Sara's boyfriend barely reached her Adam's apple. But, according to Sara, what Todd lacked in height he made up for by being the best kisser in Galveston County.

Her smile drooped slightly. What little, Dixie knew about kissing had been acquired at a spin-the-bottle game at Sara's tenth birthday party. Wet lips and slobbery tongues, she recalled, wondering what it would be like to kiss Chad. Vastly different, she decided, tucking a pillow under her head. Chad's kisses would be tender, loving, gentle—a man's kiss.

As though Sara had heard Dixie's last thought, she asked, "Did Chad sign your yearbook?"

"Uh-huh." Dixie Mayson flipped to the section devoted to sports. Scrawled across the picture of two basketball players leaping for a rebound was Chad Armstrong's illegible signature. "See?"

Sara Fairchild glanced at the picture and scowled at Dixie. "This is it? He didn't write anything?"

There were times when Sara's insensitivity made Dixie want to cheerfully throttle her best friend. This was one of them. It had taken Dixie the entire day to garner enough courage to corner Pearwood High's most popular athlete inside the boys' locker room.

"He smiled at me," Dixie lied boldly. Sara's minimizing the value of her trophy autograph sparked Dixie's temper. "That's something, considering I had to chase Chad into the boys' locker room!"

Giggling behind her hand, Sara gasped, "You didn't!"

"I had to or I wouldn't have gotten it."

Sara flopped back on the bed. "Holy moly, Dixie.

If I had the guts to go in there, I wouldn't be asking for autographs. Just think, me surrounded by twenty guys clad only in jockstraps!" She rubbed her hands together, then made pinching motions with her fingers. "Imagine, all those buns and me the only baker!"

Dixie laughed. "A part-time job at the doughnut shop hardly qualifies you as a baker." Nudging Sara's arm she reminded, "You're wild about Todd. Remember?"

"Love ain't blind!" Sara drawled. Her Texas accent was thick with denial. She flipped her yearbook closed and opened the fashion magazine she'd hidden in her notebook. Pointing to a sexy, red satin evening gown that had a slit from the hem to midthigh, she said, "That's me, six inches taller."

Dixie's eyes were drawn to the opposite page where the model wore a strapless, powder blue gown with ruffles cascading from the waist to the floor. A gorgeous male held a nosegay of forget-me-nots toward the petite model. "That's me, six inches shorter."

And with a date, Dixie thought wistfully.

"I wish I had your legs," Sara groaned. She grabbed the magazine and bounded off the bed. Rising on her toes, she slapped the nonexistent saddlebags on her upper thighs.

Chuckling, Dixie asked, "How would you like being a skyscraper in a subdivision of one-story homes?"

"How'd you like being the butt end of the short people jokes?" Sara countered.

"That would be better than being called a carpenter's dream . . . flat as a board."

"Better than boom-boom?" Sara scoffed, pointing toward her well-endowed bustline.

"Guys like short women with big boobs. You drive them wild. Me, I couldn't get s-e-x if I was the sole resident in a house of ill-repute."

For once in their crib-to-high-school friendship, Dixie shocked Sara into complete silence.

"Just take a good look at me, Sara. I'm still growing and I'm taller than the Jolly Green Giant!" She pulled her thick braid of hair over her shoulder, snatched off the rubber band, and began to uncoil it. "My hair is this gawd-awful orange, not to mention it being straight as a poker. Do you know what my father calls me?"

Sara shook her curly blond head. "What?"

"Coppertop," Dixie groaned. "Do you know what they use copper pipe for in the mansions he builds? The plumbing! My hair reminds my father of the pipe."

"I don't think he means his nickname as an insult," Sara protested. "It's kinda cute."

"Cute is one word that no one uses to describe me."

"C'mon, Dixie, you know what they say. Beauty comes from within."

"Great! A coppertop with beautiful guts. That bolsters my confidence."

"Yeah, right," Sara scoffed. "Who did the class vote as Girl Most Likely to Succeed?"

Under her breath Dixie murmured, "I'd trade my future success for a date with Chad to the Pearwood Senior Prom."

Dixie snapped her lips closed, feeling as though she'd blown out the candles on her birthday cake and blabbed her wish. She hadn't meant to divulge her heart's secret desire, just in case it would jinx any chance she'd had of Chad asking her to the prom.

Surprised, Sara gasped, "You told me you didn't give a damn whether you had a date or not."

"I care," she admitted, with a weak smile. Dixie swung her long legs off the bed. "Nobody wants to be the only girl at Pearwood High that's too unattractive for a guy to ask her to the prom. Face it, Sara. I have been a complete social flop."

"Have been?" She crossed to be bed and stood in front of Dixie. "I see that gleam in your eyes, Dixie Mayson. What else are you holding back from me?"

"I'm going to change. I can't simper and flutter my eyelashes, but there are things I can do." Grinning, she added, "I have a plan."

"Uh-oh," Sara groaned. "Now I am worried. I hope Chad's parents paid their hospitalization premiums."

Giving Sara an amused glance, Dixie admonished, "You won't let me live that little mistake down, will you?"

"Nope." Sara grinned angelically. "Would you, if I'd been the one who . . ."

"You should," Dixie interrupted. "That fiasco was your brainy idea, not mine."

"My idea was for you to casually bump into Chad in the hallway. While he picked up your books, you were supposed to invite him to my Christmas party."

"So? I did exactly what you said to do." Tongue in cheek, she added, "I bumped into him."

"Bumped?" Sara squealed. "The ambulance attendants carted Chad out of the junior-high building on a stretcher!"

"It was not my fault that he rebounded off me and fell down a flight of steps."

"And broke his arm in three places."

"That happened in eighth grade, for heaven's sake."

"Now that we're older, you have something bigger and better planned for poor Chad? Something better than trapping him in the boys' locker room?"

"He isn't poor," Dixie refuted, latching on to the one error in Sara's tirade. "The Armstrong family owns the land where the new shopping center is being built."

"I didn't mean 'poor' literally. Stop trying to change the subject. What's your plan?"

Dixie took a deep breath and spilled her secret plan to Sara as though presenting her with a sack of uncut diamonds. "I'm going to fix the hole in Chad's muffler."

"Fix it? With what? Bubble gum?" Sara squeaked, shaking her head in disbelief.

"Solder." The blank look she received reminded Dixie that her friend had no mechanical aptitude whatsoever. "What guy wouldn't like to have a girlfriend who is also a *free* mechanic?"

"Forget his muffler." Sara rolled her eyes heavenward when Dixie shook her head. "Stick to flirting, would you? Use those gorgeous blue eyes of yours. Bat your eyelashes at Chad. Wink. Swing your hips. Feminine wiles have worked for centuries."

"Welcome to the dawn of the twenty-first century, Sara. Today's man appreciates a woman who can . . ."

"Make him feel ten feet tall and hung like a horse," Sara injected bluntly. "Times change. Men don't."

Dixie clenched her hands in frustration. "I've tried feminine wiles. We both know the end results—no date to the prom." When her best friend didn't argue the point, she said quickly, "Lately, I've been asking myself why I've failed, and I've come up with the answer. I detest the pretense of being a not-too-bright redhead. Why should I be ashamed of having a brain? A strong mechanical aptitude? Face it Sara, I'm good with my hands."

When Sara covered her ears, Dixie caught her wrists and pulled her hands down.

"Listen to me. What I'm saying is logical. In grade school, the guys thought I was terrific. They always wanted me on their team."

"Yeah, because you could throw, hit or kick a ball farther than most of them."

From the dry tone of her voice Dixie realized Sara hadn't made the connection yet. "Remember how they'd show up at my house on Saturday mornings? How I designed and made copper guns for their G.I. Joe war games? Hell's bells, Sara, in third grade they'd have elected me Prom Queen!"

That made Sara smile. "I can just see you, dressed in your Ninja outfit. Face and hands blackened with charcoal. Gracefully wielding a samurai sword in one hand and carrying a dozen long-stemmed roses in the other . . . as you silently stalk the Prom King around the crepe-paper decorated gymnasium."

Much as Dixie liked the fanciful image, she had to be realistic. "Chad won't escort Madame Ninja to the dance. But, I can use the same mechanical skills it took to make the copper guns to fix his car."

Sara paused, then shook her head. "Chad won't be attracted to a woman with black grease under the fingernails."

"I'm not giving him a lube job. I'm going to silver solder the hole in his muffler. Nice, clean, neat work. No muss, no fuss, and *no* grease."

Sara paused, considering the possibilities. She raised one carefully plucked eyebrow and asked, "Are both of you going to be flat on your backs underneath his car?"

"I suppose so."

"That's a start in the right direction."

"Sara . . ."

"Don't Sara me. Men have sexual thoughts every fifteen seconds. At eighteen, they're at their sexual peak." She lowered her voice. "Saturday night Todd told me he was in agony and would die if I didn't let him make love to me."

Since Sara lacked enthusiasm over her brilliant idea, Dixie was glad Sara had changed the topic. Her eyes followed Sara as she crossed to her dresser. "What did you do?"

Sara picked up a comb and fluffed the ends of her naturally curly blond hair.

"C'mon, Sara, spill it. Remember the pact we made back in grade school? No secrets!"

"You've been keeping secrets." Sara was tormenting her as she grinned mischievously at her reflection. She couldn't compete with Dixie when it came to math and science or auto mechanics, but when it came to guys, she was the expert. Unable to contain herself, she said glibly, "Todd was at school today. Unless you believe in reincarnation or ghosts . . ."

Dixie's jaw dropped. It took several seconds for her to realize Sara was serious as a heart attack. "You lost your virginity?"

"I didn't lose it." With a regal toss of her blond hair and a slow sexy wink at Dixie, she replied, "I bestowed it on Todd."

Curiosity rounded Dixie's eyes. The amused condescension on Sara's face made Dixie feel as though her feet had grown another two inches in length. She sat up, folded her legs Indian-style and tucked her size elevens under her knees. Uncertain of what to say or do, she kept her facial expression neutral and she said, "You didn't tell me that you loved Todd."

"Do I have to love him to make love?" Sara teased.

Yes! Dixie shouted silently.

Aloud she said, "You wouldn't do it if you didn't love him."

"Wouldn't I?"

"Of course not. Sex between a man and a woman is special. It's the glue that holds a marriage together. Dad says . . ."

Sara stiffened her arms and shook her hands at Dixie. "Spare me from listening to one of John's stick-in-the-mud morality lectures, *please!"*

"Are you saying you don't love Todd?"

"I'm saying I wanted to have fun like all the other girls in our class. Everybody's doing it!" Her hands went to her slender hips. "Aren't you sick and tired of being one of the last virgins at Pearwood High?"

Dixie felt ill. Unworthy. Unwanted. Unloved. Was she really and truly the only virgin in the senior class, she wondered. Sara never lied to her, but she did stretch the truth.

Picking up her yearbook, Dixie turned to the senior class pictures and began pointing at her classmates. Each place her finger stopped, Sara nodded.

"What about Maxine Faust?" Maxine was as

wide as Dixie was tall. "You aren't going to tell me . . ."

"Ninth grade. After the school picnic."

"You're kidding."

"Not according to her."

Dixie's finger slid over her own picture. "What about Dorothy? I've never seen her even speak to a guy!"

"Talking isn't a prerequisite. I overheard Michael telling Todd that last year at the prom he saw . . ."

"At the junior prom!" Dixie recoiled as though struck by lightning. "No way. Marcy Tilton fixed Dorothy up with a blind date."

Sara chuckled at Dixie's naïveté. "Afterward. Michael saw them parked on the oilpatch road."

"That doesn't mean . . ."

"The car looked like a Mexican jumping bean," Sara drily interrupted. With a giggle she added, "I can imagine what Todd's Pathfinder looked like with us bouncing up and down in it."

Closing the yearbook, Dixie indulged in a moment of self-pity and heaved a huge sigh.

"What's wrong with you?" Sara plopped beside Dixie and poked her in the ribs. "You're supposed to be asking a million questions. Don't you want to know the nitty-gritty details?"

Aware that she was reacting like a wet blanket at a beach party, Dixie forced herself to smile. "Did you like it?"

"Sure. It was great. Just like in the movies."

Wanting more details, but slightly embarrassed, Dixie cautiously asked, "Which movie?"

"None your father would let you watch," Sara replied drolly.

Dixie nodded. Not only was she strictly forbidden from attending movies, their house was the only one in Pearwood without cable television. Her father was another prime reason why none of the guys showed up on the Maysons' front porch. "Amen."

Sara wrinkled her nose and pretended to shiver. "His blood must have changed to ice water the night your mother died in childbirth. But, don't let me get sidetracked on him. Where was I?"

"About to tell me about doing it."

"Oh, yeah." Sara tapped her finger against her lips. "Well, there was lots of frantic grabbing and groping, huffing and puffing, stroking and poking."

Blushing, Dixie ducked her head. "You make it sound like the two of you were stringing copper pipe through wooden studs."

"What?"

Dixie was the recipient of another blank look.

"Never mind." There was no point in explaining to Sara that each descriptive word she'd chosen could aptly be used to describe the sounds and motions a top-out plumbing crew made while installing pipe in a house. Deciding she'd heard enough explicit details of Sara's deflowering, Dixie unfolded her long legs and started toward the bedroom door. "I just remembered that Dad told me to sweep up at the warehouse this afternoon."

"Now?" Sara cocked her head to one side and glared at Dixie's taut shoulders. This uptight reaction to her profound news wasn't what she'd expected. Sighing, she reluctantly followed Dixie down the hall corridor. "Don't you have to fix dinner for your father?"

"He won't be home until dark."

"But you said you'd go to the mall with me," Sara complained. "Todd is going to meet us there and take both of us to the movies tonight."

"Maybe I'll catch up with the two of you later." Dixie didn't want to say or do anything to hurt Sara's feelings, but knowing Sara and Todd were lovers changed everything. She needed time alone. "Okay?"

"Uh-uh." Sara crossed the polished oak floor to the front door ahead of Dixie. "I know what happens when you go to the warehouse. You start puttering around and forget what time it is. You'd better watch it or you'll end up married to Texas Proud Construction Company, just like your old man."

Dixie faked a shudder as she closed the front door behind them and locked it. Although Pearwood had one of the best police departments in the state of Texas, the town was close to Houston, and everyone took the precaution of locking their doors.

She heard Sara lightly treading down the wooden porch steps. She hoped Sara wasn't miffed. "See you later?"

"I won't count on it. You have fun at the warehouse. Todd and I will . . . alone, together, . . . know what I mean?"

Dixie frowned. Maybe she should tag along with Sara and Todd. Better to suffer the humiliation of being a third wheel than for the two of them to be cavorting in the back of Todd's Pathfinder.

On the heels of her disturbing afterthought, she called, "Be good."

"I'm always good," Sara called over her shoulder, with a naughty flounce of her hips. "Sometimes I'm just better than others."

"Be careful."

With a jaunty thumbs-up sign, Sara teased, "If not, we'll name it after you."

"Great, just great," Dixie groaned and shot her a thumbs-down gesture.

As she watched Sara follow the worn path through the shoulder-high hedges between their two houses and disappear from sight, a feeling of abandonment swamped Dixie. She'd often felt alone inside herself, but never more than now.

Feet dragging, Dixie trudged toward the driveway where she'd parked her black pickup truck. No date to the prom, she reflected, with a sinking heart, and the last virgin in the senior class. Unless she did something drastic, nothing would change. Sara's prediction would come true. She would die an old maid with DATELESS VIRGIN carved in her tombstone.

Lost in her dire thoughts, she climbed in her truck, started the engine and began the short drive to TPC's warehouse. Chad has to invite me to the prom, she mused. For damned certain she wasn't going alone like she had last year.

Dixie strummed her fingers impatiently on the steering wheel while she waited for a red light to change. She had to get Chad's attention and hold it. The muffler idea still seemed workable to her. Once she had Chad underneath his car, thinking male thoughts, he'd find her . . . irresistible?

"Irresistible," she repeated firmly, not allowing self-doubt to enter her mind.

Mentally, she rehearsed what she hoped would happen. She'd squeeze the striker to light the torch. Sparks would light her eyes. While she passed the silver solder over the damaged muffler, she'd seductively let her bare forearm brush against his sleeve. She'd purse her lips, pretending to concentrate. She'd will him to kiss her. Between kisses, he'd beg to take her . . .

A honking horn shattered her daydream. The light had turned green.

Frowning, she glared in the rear-view mirror at the truck behind her and gunned the gas pedal. "Couldn't you have waited to honk your horn until after Chad asked me to the prom?"

The driver continued to lay on his horn as he pulled alongside her. "Hey! Gorgeous! Pull over!"

She recognized the carpenter's logo painted on the side of the rusted-out truck as belonging to one of the crews her father had recently hired. A smile twitched the corners of her mouth as she turned in the grocery store's parking lot.

John Mayson would blow a gasket if he heard

one of the carpenters speak to his daughter. Driving down the main street of town, blowing his horn and calling me gorgeous would earn this guy a pink slip.

His brakes squealed louder than his horn. Dixie halfway expected the driver to stick a leg out and drag a foot on the pavement to get his damned truck stopped. She heard him whack the door to get it loose from the frame. Expecting the driver to be as dilapidated as his truck, she felt her breath catch in her chest when she saw two extremely long muscular legs encased in pressed jeans come into view. A wide, leather carpenter's tool belt hung loosely on his narrow hips. Her eyes quickly traveled across the blue chambray shirt stretched tautly across the stranger's broad shoulders to his face. His features looked as if they had been hewn from oak by a master woodcarver who'd sought to portray the perfect image of the American outdoorsman. His square chin, straight nose, high cheekbones, all combined to make him look arrogant and tough. His hair and eyes were as dark as sin; his smile every bit as inviting.

He fitted the description of the type of man her father had warned her to avoid. Cocky ne'er-do-wells, that's what John called them. They drifted from job site to job site, earning enough money to buy beer and raise hell until they wound up in jail. John hired and fired his type on a regular basis.

If the stranger hadn't caught her at a weak moment and called her gorgeous, she would have followed John's strict instructions to turn up her nose and get away from this type of guy as fast as she could.

Instead, she smiled warmly at the carpenter.

"Thanks for pulling over." The stranger hooked one thumb in his back pocket and gestured toward the TPC, Inc. painted on her tailgate. "You work for Texas Proud?"

Dixie started to nod, but decided this drop-dead handsome stranger who thought she was gorgeous was the perfect man for her to practice Sara's feminine wiles on. She couldn't bring herself to flutter her eyelashes, but she did flip a thick skein of hair from her face and gazed intently into his eyes with a come-hither look.

"No. I borrowed their truck for a joyride," Dixie teased in a low, sultry voice.

Waco Stone felt a double whammy in his gut. First, she belted him with her blue eyes and then walloped him with her sexy voice. Raised on the wrong side of the tracks, he could hear the whistle blow on the freight train to Hell when trouble came his way. A man with half the sense God gave a rock would have moseyed on down the train tracks, without a backward glance. But, after the ass-chewing he'd received in front of his crew from old man Mayson, Waco savored the heady rush of adrenaline pumping through his veins. A woman's eager lips and soft body would go a long way to restore the blows his pride had taken, not to mention the poetic justice of making out in one of TPC's trucks.

Trouble was always a tempting alternative to walking the straight and narrow.

"Want some company?" he drawled, leaning his arm on the chrome rim of her window.

With his elbow scant inches from her breast, and a dangerous glint in his eyes as they trekked down the neckline of her blouse, Dixie realized she'd bitten off more than she could chew.

Better to spit out the truth now, she decided, than try to swallow a string of lies.

"This is my truck," she blurted. She watched his dark eyes slowly climb up the V of her blouse, across her neck and cheeks before she added, "I'm Dixie Mayson."

"Figures," Stone replied. Automatically, his arm dropped to his side. Office help was fair game for a temporary fling, but Mayson's daughter was strictly off limits. Within minutes of signing a subcontractor's contract, the riding boss at TPC had informed him of John's unwritten mandate: Keep your eyes and hands off Mayson's daughter or the old man will drill holes in your hide with a dull screwdriver. At the time, he'd laughed. He wasn't laughing now.

"Your old man owns Texas Proud?"

His rhetorical question didn't require a response, but Dixie nodded. Her affirmation lowered the warmth in his eyes to subzero temperature as his eyes narrowed. Dixie noticed that his dark lashes were incredibly long and curly. "What's your name?"

"Waco. Waco Stone."

"Are you working on one of the new crews out at Sage Meadows?"

"Yeah."

Estimating that Waco was close to her own age, she asked, "A carpenter's helper?"

Waco grinned. It had been years since he'd been that low on the totem pole. "No."

"Framer?"

"Finish carpenter," Waco replied, certain his status in the carpentry trade would elevate her opinion of him by several notches.

Dixie raised one eyebrow skeptically. Bullshit, she thought, using one of her father's barnyard phrases. It took years of practice to hone the skills necessary to be hired by John Mayson as a finish carpenter. Waco was either older than he looked or a damned liar.

Or . . . her smile returned when she realized he must be trying to impress her.

Like father like daughter, Waco mused, closely watching her facial expressions. She had no way of knowing he'd seen the same disbelief on her father's face when Mayson had read his application form.

Weeks ago, he'd proven his skill by installing a difficult piece of triple-crown molding in the Sage Meadow display house. Swiftly and accurately he'd accomplished the task. Had Mayson praised him for the perfect fit? Hell, no. Mayson had grunted noncommittally, then ordered him to match the molding's finish with the pickled oak cabinets installed in the kitchen. A trick assignment since the molding he'd installed was made of pecan wood. He'd refused, saying the task was impossible. Like a ray of sunshine on an overcast day, a hint of admiration gleamed in Mayson's eyes. He'd offered Ted a contract, with a thirty-day probationary clause. One slip-up and the contract was null and void.

There hadn't been any, and wouldn't be, not if Waco could stop his male hormones from exploding like popcorn. This job was a stepping stone to bigger and better contracts. He'd be a shithead to let a woman mess up his prospects.

With that thought firmly in mind, he gave Dixie a mock salute and stepped away from her truck. A second coat of varnish applied to the mantelpiece today would have put him another twenty-four hours ahead of schedule, but it wasn't worth the risk of being caught with Mayson's daughter. "See you around, gorgeous."

"Wait a minute!" Oddly dismayed by the idea of his abruptly departing, she asked, "Is there some reason why you stopped me?"

"I need a gallon of varnish from the warehouse."

Dixie glanced at her watch. "Burt Simmons has locked up and gone home by now." She lifted the spare key ring off the turn signal lever and held it in the open palm of her hand. "I could let you in."

As Waco reached for the tarnished brass key he could almost hear Zeke—the hard-fisted, Bible-thumping uncle who'd raised him—spouting the story about Eve beckoning Adam to eternal damnation by holding a polished apple in the palm of her hand.

Before he could pluck the key from her palm, Dixie curled her fingers tightly around it. "I'll have to let you in and out of the warehouse. Nobody gets this key but me."

"Suit yourself." It stung his pride to know he wasn't considered trustworthy. What the hell, he mused. At twenty-three, he'd grown accustomed to having things he needed snatched from under his nose. His eyes glittered with hot defiance as he sauntered back to his truck. "I'll lead. You follow."

Dixie twirled the key's chain around her index finger and grinned. Waco Stone thought she was gorgeous! He'd hardly been able to take his eyes off her! As she followed his junker-truck down the back road leading to the warehouse, she ignored the small inner voice in her head that warned her that John Mayson would think Waco Stone was completely unsuitable for her.

Two

Waco Stone drove as cautiously down the back road that led to the warehouse as his noisy truck would allow. With one eye on the road and the other on his rear-view mirror, he expected Dixie Mayson to change her mind. Being John Mayson's daughter, she didn't strike him as the type of woman who'd sedately tag along behind any man.

And yet, he noticed her truck was close enough to play bumper tag.

God, she's a looker, Stone mused, grinning as he wondered how his boss had sired such a beauty. Now he understood why John's riding boss had issued the no-trespassing warning. Hell, if Dixie was his, he'd put her up on a pedestal surrounded by barbed wire, and never let her out of his sight.

"Best you keep your eyes glued to the road," Stone coached to himself. He could pull himself up by his bootstraps until they resembled a bow tie and he'd still be lower than the cuff of her designer jeans. "She'll cost you your job."

A year ago he'd have reached out and grabbed Dixie. He'd have taken what he wanted from her, consequences be damned. When his uncle had fallen off a three-story roof, it had drastically changed his take-your-job-and-shove-it attitude. That wasn't to say he had any great love for the man who'd grudgingly raised him after his parents took off for parts unknown, but by the same token, Waco couldn't thumb his nose at the old man either.

Uncle Zeke had his good points; even if they were few and far between. He'd kept food in Waco's belly, clothes on his back, and taught him a trade. Conversely, Zeke had marched him to the woodshed for the slightest infraction of his rules—until Waco had turned thirteen. When Waco was six inches taller and fifty pounds heavier than Zeke, the days of physical abuse ceased. After the accident that left his uncle with multiple leg fractures and several broken ribs, their roles had reversed. For the past year, Waco had financially supported both of them.

"Carpenter by day, housewife at night," Stone grumbled as his eyes strayed to the rear-view mirror.

According to Zeke, what Waco needed was some sweet, young thing to cook and clean for both of them. Sage advice coming from a man who took his pleasures from a woman and dumped her the minute she mentioned getting hitched. Zeke cared more about his daily six-pack than he'd ever cared about a woman. Nevertheless, the idea of having a woman to do the chores did have a certain appeal.

Waco smirked at the bizarre notion of Dixie Mayson parading around his one-bedroom travel home, picking up Zeke's empty cans and dirty socks, then slaving over a propane gas stove to prepare a meal for them.

Fat chance!

She'd take one look at where he lived, and her pert nose would skyrocket toward the heavens.

"Someday," he vowed. His fingers tightened on the steering wheel. Someday he'd be rich. He'd own a fancy house, a fleet of pickups, and marry a super-fine lady. When that day arrived, he'd sink his roots so deep into the ground he'd forget what it was like roaming from job site to job site, like a tumbleweed blown by a restless wind.

Waco didn't know how or when he'd strike it rich, but deep in his gut he felt positive he'd instinctively recognize the opportunity to get rich when he saw it. Until then, he'd keep his nose to the grindstone. Physically, in that position he should be able to avoid trouble.

As he pumped the brakes and gradually stopped in front of Texas Proud's warehouse, his mind backtracked to the present. After he'd slapped a base coat of varnish on that mantel, he had to fix his damned brakes. As Zeke aptly phrased it, "No rest for the wicked."

Deliciously wicked thoughts sprang to mind as he watched Dixie sashay to the warehouse door. A bona fide leg-man, he appreciated the sight of her long slender legs encased in faded denim. The curve of her heart-shaped backside was enough to make the palms of his hands itch. Were she anyone else's daughter, he'd have let his eyes drop to half-mast and allow a sensuous image of his hands cupping her derrière, of having those shapely limbs wrapped around his waist, her sleek calves squeezing him closer . . .

Whoa, he silently chastised, rapidly blinking his eyelids. That puppy don't hunt, and you can't afford a pedigreed lapdog.

Dixie plunged the key into the lock and simultaneously glanced over her shoulder. "You coming?"

No, but I'm breathing hard. The thought crossed his mind; he stowed the bawdy remark, and replied, "Yes, ma'am."

Automatically, he shoved his wide-brimmed Stetson on his head. He needed to keep his horns from showing. And he didn't mean the ones on his head. With his door blocking her view of him, he adjusted his britches to accommodate his swollen member.

"Wait a second." Dixie pushed the button inside the office that activated the opener. "You can come through the double door."

His hat dipped, hiding his grimace as he glanced downward. Turned sideways, he might need the space. He grinned at his mental exaggeration. Everything born and raised in Texas was big, but not that big. He'd have been able to make it through the office door. Just barely, he amended, proud of his manhood.

Dixie flipped on the lights. Although the sun was hours away from setting, the windowless warehouse had been as dark as a tomb. Long rows of fluorescent lights, hung high in the forty-foot ceiling, blinked on. Deep shadows were cast by the racks holding lumber, pipe, and various items used to build a subdivision of houses. The pleasant fragrance of pine hovered close to the concrete floor.

"Do you know where to look for what you need?"

Her innocent inquiry held a wealth of innuendo. Oh, yeah. He knew exactly where to look . . . and it wasn't anywhere close to the gallon pails of varnish stacked on the back row of shelves. Only a few zipper teeth below the silver belt buckle of her jeans. One quick glance at her face had him tugging the brim of his hat lower. An inch more and his headband would circle his eyeballs.

Son-of-a-bitch, he silently cursed. *She's got me blushing like a schoolboy!*

Dixie mimicked Sara's gesture of pushing her hair back from her face. Her fledgling smile wilted as he strode briskly away from her.

"Yes, ma'am." He cleared away the husky quality of his voice. "I'll be out of your hair in a minute."

"You don't have to call me ma'am. It sounds like you're talking to a crotchety old lady." She'd liked it far better when he'd called her gorgeous; she'd settle for her first name. She traipsed closely behind him. "Dixie is fine with me."

"I don't think so." He had to get something in its proper perspective. Her name was a good starting point. He added, "Ms. Mayson."

"Ms. Mayson? That's worse! Makes me sound like a decrepit old algebra teacher."

Her mentioning school made him wonder if he'd been lusting after jailbait. "How old are you?"

With his back to her, unable to see her face, she was tempted to flat-out lie. She guessed him to be in his early twenties. "Would you believe twenty-five?"

"No."

"Twenty-three?"

"Sixteen, going on a divorced thirty-five?" he retorted, smiling at her.

"What does that mean?"

He turned. Brushing back his hat he gave her a long, sizzling, calculating look. "It means you're flirting with trouble, gorgeous."

If he hadn't called her a gorgeous flirt and if she hadn't noticed the appreciative gleam in his sinfully black eyes, she'd have bluntly told him the truth. She felt feminine and desirable. These were new feelings to the last virgin in Pearwood.

Her confidence soared.

Like a kitten testing its claws, she trailed one finger down the side of his face. His jaw clenched. The rasp of his whiskers against her nail sent goosebumps skittering up her arm.

"Let's say I'm old enough to know better, but young enough to be curious?"

For half a millisecond, Waco was tempted to remove the questioning lilt of her voice by slanting his lips across hers.

She's the boss's daughter.

In the blink of an eye, he turned his back on temptation.

"There's the ladder. Excuse me, ma'am. I'll get that gallon of varnish and be out of here."

"Dixie," she corrected through clenched teeth. "Everybody calls me Dixie."

A frown marred her smooth forehead as she watched him stride toward the far corner of the warehouse. For an instant, she'd thought he wanted to kiss her. Had she been too flirty? Too bold? Too coy? His eyes had drifted toward her lips, hadn't they? What stopped him? It wasn't lack of willingness on her part!

She moved aside while he angled the cumbersome ladder in place.

He touched the brim of his hat. "Okay, Dixie it is," he conceded, "if that's what your father allows."

Suddenly, the answers to her questions dawned on her. Waco Stone did not want to antagonize his boss, who happened to be her father. From the way he carried himself, she sensed a streak of rebellion against authority figures. "Do you only do what my father allows?"

"He signs my paychecks." Waco hiked one boot to the first rung. Pausing, curious about her relationship with John, he asked, "How about you?"

She steadied the ladder for his climb. "When John roars a command the clouds pass over the sun, strong oaks sway, and the tide changes directions—other than implicitly following his orders, I do as I please."

"Any orders from John about flirting with one of his subcontractors?"

Dixie lifted one shoulder. She blurted honestly, "You're the first . . ." She bit her tongue to keep *man who has paid attention to me* from passing through her lips.

"First what?"

"Employee I've flirted with," Dixie substituted in a hushed voice.

That might sound snobbish to Waco, but it was better than the truth. The older men John employed treated her as though she still wore pigtails; the younger men acted as though she had the plague. All of them were polite, but they rarely spoke to her when they could avoid it.

Her quiet confession made Waco feel tall enough not to need the ten-foot ladder. There were plenty of well-built, good-looking men collecting Texas Proud paychecks once a week. She'd made an exception to her own rules by flirting with him.

He lifted the container of varnish off the shelf, slowly retreating down each rung until his knee lightly brushed against her knuckles. Her accidental touch set him afire as he looked down at her upturned face, and yet, her eyes held a silent appeal that banked the flames, and profoundly squeezed the untouched softness of his soul.

Compelled to explore this new feeling, for long seconds, he stared into the blue depths of her eyes. A man could get lost in them . . . or find himself, Waco mused. Her dreamy look made him feel as though he was capable of being a better man than he'd been. With her encouragement, he could hang the moon and touch the stars—build skyscrapers from toothpicks.

Waco broke eye contact by shaking his head. Goddamned foolishness, he berated himself silently.

"You're off limits," he spat, with his feet firmly planted on the concrete floor. "Anyone who courts John's daughter gets fired."

Her eyes widened. Granted, she did consider her father a benevolent dictator, but she couldn't imagine him actually building a wall between her and his men. That was archaic!

"Says who?" she demanded.

"Bill Anderson, the riding boss."

As Waco turned to stride away from her, she caught his arm. She could taste the sweet flavor of rebellion as she asked, "I got the impression that you aren't afraid of anybody. Are you? Afraid?"

"No," he drawled slowly. "Not of Bill Anderson. Your father is a grey horse of a different color though." He saw the all-too-familiar gleam of defiance shoot from her eyes at him. "Are you afraid of him?"

Dixie worried her bottom lip with her front teeth. "I've never crossed my father."

"Daddy's little darlin'?" Waco taunted. He smiled, but it didn't reach his eyes. He squared his shoulders; his pelvis struck forward into a cocky stance.

"Stop it!" She coiled her fingers into a tight fist. Although she abhorred physical violence, she wanted to pop Waco Stone right in his smirking mouth. "Who are you to make fun of me? You're the yellow-livered-coward that's afraid of losing your job because you spoke to me!"

Waco dropped the sealed bucket of varnish. His arms reached forward; his fingers wrapped around Dixie's upper arms and he lifted her until her lips were only a fraction of an inch away from his.

"Listen carefully, gorgeous." Only a sugar-coating of huskiness in his voice covered the heat of his temper. "Nobody calls me a coward."

"Nobody calls me 'Daddy's darling daughter'!"

"I'm not scared of your old man or you," he countered.

His lips grazed hers with each word he spoke. He meant to intimidate her, to make her back off gracefully.

Her chin raised, then slightly tilted to one side. "Neither am I."

"Prove it." Waco gave her an opportunity to show her spunk by letting her be the aggressor. If she dared to want his kiss, she'd have to meet him more than halfway because his risk was greater than hers. He watched the dark pupils of her eyes expand, felt her nipples bud through her cotton shirt against the muscular wall of his chest. His nostrils widened to smell the scent of fear; he inhaled only the honeysuckle fragrance of her shampoo.

She wasn't afraid of him, she told herself, or her father.

Her eyelids drooped; her arms broke free of his hold and circled his shoulders as she stood on tiptoe. Her soft lips whispered against his mouth. He wanted aggression; he got shy, sweet seduction.

The tip of his tongue slowly traversed from one corner of her sealed lips to the other. Dixie quivered under that light touch. Her lashes swooped down, then up as she gazed at him. His expression hadn't changed, but his skin seemed to be pulled tighter across his fierce cheekbones; his lips were redder, a bit fuller; his tan darker. His body heat lured her, pulling her closer. He projected a raw, steamy sensuality that was unlike anything the boys at Pearwood High exuded. He made her ache, as if the film of moisture she felt clinging to her lips had anointed her, made her a woman.

From what seemed a hazy distance, she heard a steady beep, beep, beep.

"You're being paged," Waco whispered lazily against her mouth. His hand rested lightly on the small of her back as she lowered one arm and fumbled with the off switch. "Your father?"

"He beeps me when he leaves the office."

"You'd better go."

He bent his head and covered her lips with his mouth, and feeling them tremble and part, he kissed her harder, tilting her head back so he could deepen the kiss.

Dixie felt the prongs of his wide carpenter's belt buckle nip her waist as he pulled her closer. She opened her mouth to the tip of his tongue. He tasted sweet and heady and dangerous. A pang of regret pierced her heart when he sealed the breach he'd parted by lightly rubbing the pad of his thumb across her lips.

"Will I see you again?" she whispered, afraid her first kiss would be their last.

"I'll call you."

He wouldn't, not with odds in favor of John picking up the phone, but with her looking up at him with her heart in her eyes and his own heart pounding like an automatic nail hammer with the safety switch removed, he couldn't say no.

"Tonight?" she pressed, her anxiety plain on her face for him to see. Her palms scrubbed the side seam of her jeans. "I have my own separate line."

He pulled a marker from his shirt pocket. "What's your number?"

She recited it and watched while he wrote it in the palm of his hand. "I'll talk to Dad about what Bill Anderson said to you."

"Don't."

"Why not?"

"Because that would be like poking a stick in a hornet's nest." He snapped the cap back on his marker and returned it to his pocket. Maybe Dixie had John wrapped around her finger, but he doubted it. "From what I've heard about your old man, he gives the subcontractors two choices——his way or the highway."

"That sounds like him. I can be just as stubborn as he is." Dixie grinned. "Must be hereditary."

Picking up the can of varnish, Waco crossed toward the warehouse door. Thoughts of dating a woman like her put a spring in his step. "Do you like to dance—Western?"

"Yes." She two-stepped in front of him, gracefully spinning around on one foot. "I do a wicked Tush Push."

"I'll bet you do." A mental image of her heart-shaped fanny swaying to the rhythm of a country tune made his throat parched. He placed the can in the bed of his truck. "Have you been to Desperados?"

"No, but I've heard it's fun." She'd also heard it took a twenty-one-year-old Texas ID to get inside the front door. Mentally choosing a club she'd heard didn't have an age requirement, she suggested, "The Frontier Room has live music on Saturday night."

"I've been there." Back inside his truck, he added, "Too many high-school kids with fake ID's trying to buy pitchers of beer."

"They can be a pain," she agreed loftily while inwardly shrinking an inch. Skip the dancing, she thought, searching for another option. "There's always the movies."

"Sounds good to me. Pick one you'd like to see."

Fairly certain that meant he'd call her later tonight, Dixie beamed him a wide smile. "Later?"

"Yeah. Later." He touched the brim of his hat, floored the clutch pedal and ground the gears until his truck shifted into reverse. "Needs a new clutch."

"I could help you put one in," she offered. His look of surprise, one that gradually changed to one of delight made her laugh. It didn't take a fake ID to install a clutch. "I'm good with my hands."

"A woman after my heart. I could use a second pair of hands. Sunday is the only day I'm not working though."

"Sunday? Great!"

With his truck rolling in reverse, Waco stuck his head out the window and called, "I'll call you tonight."

Dixie waved until he'd driven out of sight. Exhilarated, she jumped, clicking her bootheels. It wasn't a date to the prom. It wasn't even a date to go dancing or to the movies. But that didn't bother her.

Her fingers fluttered across her smiling lips. He'd kissed her, a real soul-searching kiss, for heaven's sake. As far as she was concerned Chad Armstrong could stick a wad of bubble gum up his muffler. She had a date with a man, a real hunk of a man, one who made Chad seem like a kid.

Dixie shut off the lights and pulled the cord that manually lowered the door. The Texas Proud logo painted across the front of it reminded her of the one fly in the ointment—her father being Waco's employer.

While she locked the office door, she mulled around in her mind exactly how she'd make John change this policy she'd never heard of before today. Just broaching the subject would be difficult. What could she say? Oh, by the way, I hear you'll fire anyone who so much as looks at me? Isn't that rather feudalistic? Or, I met this terrific guy that asked me out, but he needs an ironclad contract stating you won't fire him? Or, something drastic like, I've cooked your last meal unless . . .

Dixie glanced at her watch, then at her pager where she saw 911, her father's code that meant he was on his way home. It's after six! With a hop and a skip, she rushed to her truck. One guaranteed way to put her father in a foul mood would be to serve dinner late.

Southern-fried chicken, mashed potatoes, green peas, and red-eye gravy would put him in an agreeable frame of mind, she thought, laying a strip of rubber on the parking lot. She looked at her watch and willed the small hand to move back an hour. In twenty-five minutes, all she could whip up would be a big batch of crispy-on-the-outside raw-on-the-inside chicken and a bowl of unpeeled, half-cooked potatoes.

"Better stick to our usual Friday-night hamburger and French fries."

Quite honestly, whether her father was well-fed or ravenous, Dixie had to admit she was terrified of a showdown with him.

Aside from a couple of minor rebellious escapades, she'd followed his rules to the letter. Granted, she often dotted the i's and crossed the t's with a quirky flourish, but she never crossed out a direct order.

Dixie pulled the corner of her lip between her teeth and worried it. She could avoid the whole issue by not mentioning having met Waco Stone.

Her keen sense of fairness ruled out sneaking around behind John's back.

He'll have to change the rule or make an exception, she resolved silently. She'd point out to him that he only hired the best men in the trades. His craftsmen were skilled, reliable and trustworthy. Therefore his rule was unnecessary, dictatorial and just plain old dumb.

"Scratch the last part," she mumbled. Calling her father's edicts dumb wouldn't keep Waco on TP's payroll.

As though her truck had automatic pilot, she found herself parked in the driveway before she realized she was home. A couple of feet more and she'd have rammed the back of John's Suburban.

Speedily, she exited her truck and glanced at the wide porch that gracefully skirted the front of the house. Her father stood at the top of the steps, feet spread, his arms folded across his massive chest, waiting for her. Dressed in a dark navy blue suit, a starched white shirt, with a striped tie knotted at his throat, the only concession John gave to comfort were the polished boots on his feet.

"You beat me home!" she called, pretending to ignore his forbidding expression. She took the steps two at a time. "Have a good day?"

"Marginal," he replied succinctly.

"Hungry?" She gave him a lame smile and scooted around him and through the door. "I'll have dinner ready in a jif."

"No rush. The call I received from your calculus teacher caused me to lose my appetite."

Keeping ten paces ahead of John, she strode into the kitchen, opened the refrigerator and grabbed the package of hamburger. All the while, she silently cursed Miss Abigail Schuster for having a nose ten feet long supported by a mouth equally as wide.

"I made an A on her last test. She says I ought to be a math major when I go to college."

Not a man easily diverted from his goal, John said, "What's this I hear about you visiting the boys' locker room?"

"There's nothing much to tell, Dad. Chad Armstrong promised to sign my yearbook. I had to remind him to keep his word." She glanced up in time to see her father's lips twitch as he suppressed a smile. His reaction prompted her to add, "A man's word is his honor. Correct?"

John made a noise that Dixie placed somewhere between being a cough and clearing his throat.

Quick to recover, he boomed, "Ladies don't belong in men's locker rooms."

"You didn't say anything Monday night, after the Oiler game when that female reporter interviewed your favorite quarterback."

"Football players expect reporters. They were clothed."

Dixie peeled the cellophane wrapper off the meat and began shaping their hamburgers. "I didn't see anything."

"Why not?" John circled the center work counter,

stopping when he towered over his daughter. The flat of his hand slammed against the cutting board. "Did God strike you blind?"

"I shut my eyes," she confessed, with a small but sassy smile.

"Mine are wide open and I don't think I like what I see, young lady. I know for certain I didn't like having Kate stifle her giggles while she read Abigail's message."

God bless Kate's sense of humor, Dixie thought, rolling her eyes to the ceiling. Fearless of her father's tirades, Kate had worked for him as long as Dixie could remember.

In fact, now that Dixie gave it a second thought, Kate was the only person in the company who could make the boss lean back in his chair while she shook her small fist in his face.

"Kate giggled?"

"She has a misplaced sense of humor. I didn't think your antics were the least bit funny. I expect my daughter to conduct herself in a manner befitting the Mayson name. We have a reputation to uphold in this community."

Dixie tuned John out as she seasoned the meat and began peeling the potatoes. She knew this lecture by heart. Each pause required a nod; each rise of a decibel of volume required a pained expression. No interruptions. Backtalk would get her sent to her room. Without dinner. Grounded, for life. Again.

While she alternately nodded and winced, silently, she began to wonder if her father realized she was no longer a six-year-old. He'd made his point. Did he have to keep going on and on and on? So what if she'd trespassed into the male locker room? It wasn't something that would be carved on her tombstone. St. Peter wasn't going to thumb through his list of mortal sins and cast her into hell for this minor transgression.

Several minutes later, she dropped slivers of potato into a skillet of hot oil. They sizzled; Dixie did, too. To hell with him dictating the rules around here, she thought defiantly. She wasn't an imbecile; she could think for herself. Dammit, she knew right from wrong, and she would be willing to pay the price for any indiscretions, if only her father would let her make her own decisions!

Grease popped from the skillet at the same moment it occurred to Dixie that she didn't have to beg permission to make decisions. She didn't have to justify her behavior. As she examined the tiny burn on her arm, she realized that her father could protect her, but only to a point.

She brushed past John to get to the sink where she ran cold water across her arm.

"Are you hurt?" John asked, his voice laced with concern.

"No."

"Let me see."

She refused to hold her arm up for his inspection. "I'm fine."

"You should be more careful. You tossed those potatoes in the skillet without testing to see if the oil was too hot."

His mild criticism burst the bonds of constraint that she'd held on her temper during his monotonous lecture. "Stop treating me like a child," she blurted. She heard John suck wind, but she couldn't hold her errant tongue. "And stop making a big deal out of nothing. Over half the senior girls have seen one helluva lot more naked skin than I saw today!"

"Don't you speak to me with that disrespectful tone in your voice."

"Disrespectful? Me? Your darling daughter?" She wiped the water off her arm with a dishtowel and flung it into the sink. "How can Miss Goody-Two-Shoes be a disgrace to the Mayson name? What does being *good* get me? Does it get me a date to the prom? Or a boyfriend? Or even Chad's autograph? No!"

Tears of pent-up rage surged up the back of her throat. She'd shot off her mouth; she instantly regretted it, but she wouldn't give her father the satisfaction of seeing her cry like the baby she'd proclaimed not to be.

She swallowed, hard. Twice. "I respect you. But it's time for you to show me a little respect. You can begin by pitching your canned speeches into the trash can."

She watched him bloat like a toad in danger.

"Daughter, you'd best go to your room and reconsider your actions."

Starting toward the door, she huffed, "I'm going. But not to my room. And not to reconsider what I said." Storming from the kitchen, she shouted, "Why don't you take your own advice for a change!"

Three

"Your phone rang last night while you were out asserting your independence." John greeted her coldly, turning the page of the morning *Houston Post* and glaring over his bifocals. "Perhaps I should have the line disconnected. It's rude for Sara to call after nine."

Dixie bit her tongue to keep from informing her father that Sara couldn't have called. They'd gone to the movies.

Afterwards, when she told Sara what had happened at home, she'd been congratulated by her, then warned that the Texans at the Alamo had a just cause, but lost the battle. Independence didn't come easily; it took grit, determination, and stamina. Under no circumstances was Dixie to grovel for what she'd said.

Mutely, Dixie started her normal daily routine by refilling his coffee cup. She wanted to serve him crow, feathers and all, but settled for fixing his usual bacon, eggs, and toast. While she scrambled a half-dozen eggs, a secretive smile curved her lips.

It had been Waco who'd called at midnight.

Wouldn't her father have had the surprise of his life if he'd picked up the receiver, and instead of hearing Sara's, "What's up?" heard a sexy, male voice croon, "Hi, gorgeous."

Afterward, she'd drifted to sleep remembering the sound of his husky voice. In her dreams, Waco—tall, tanned, and handsome in his black tuxedo—led her from a chauffeured limousine, up the steps of the high school, into the gymnasium decorated with crepe paper from ceiling to floor. She imagined the looks of stunned surprise on her friends' faces.

A couple of the cheerleaders had cupped their hands across their mouths and began asking, "Who is he?!"

Whispers, louder than the sounds of silks and taffeta moving in unison with the music, would circle the room. Envious glances followed them; the crowd parted like the Red Sea as Waco held her hand and led her to the dance floor.

Waco's black eyes gazed at her, seemingly bedazzled by glamour. Reflected from their mirror depths, Dixie envisioned herself dressed in a strapless gown of shimmering gold. Her breasts appeared full and round, which created a shadow of cleavage, but Waco was too mature, too much a gentleman to gawk down the front of her dress. When he took her in his arms, slowly waltzing her around the room, she could hear the faculty *ahhh*ing in unison, "Such a gorgeous couple."

The memory of the dream was so alive, so lifelike, John startled her when he folded the newspaper, and dropped it on the table. She glared at the eggs she'd cracked, wishing she were snuggled under the covers continuing her heart's fantasy.

John sipped his coffee and said casually, "I arranged for Phil Armstrong's boy to invite you to the prom."

The dreamy expression on Dixie's face changed to mortification. She wheeled around from the counter to face her father. "You discussed me with Chad's father? Like I was a piece of undeveloped property?"

"Don't get upset. I subtly mentioned . . ."

Dixie covered her ears. Subtlety? Knowing John, he'd been as subtle as a jackhammer.

It took every ounce of restraint she possessed to keep from lobbing the bowl of raw eggs at him. Her throat constricted, lowering her voice to nearly a whisper as she said, "Call Mr. Armstrong and tell him it was all a mistake. I will not go to the prom with someone my father had to bribe."

"No cash swapped palms," John defended, his integrity impugned. "Just friends helping friends."

Her hands shook with anger as she poured the contents of the bowl into the pan. How could her own father lecture her on disgracing the Mayson name, then do an about-face, and completely humiliate her? Being the last virgin in Pearwood was an honor when compared to being such a hideous geek that her father felt obligated to arrange her dates. Knowing how John was partial to killing two birds with one stone, she wouldn't be the least surprised to learn he'd also drawn Chad a map of the oilpatch roads, with a big, red X on the perfect place to park his truck.

"Call Mr. Armstrong," she ordered between clenched teeth. "Tell him you were misinformed, that I have a date."

"Do you?"

"No," she admitted. Was this the best time to bring up the subject of Waco Stone? Her head shook involuntarily. She was too distraught to argue logically on his behalf. "Just call Mr. Armstrong, *please.*"

"Women," John scoffed under his breath. "They tell a man their problem and when he solves it, they get upset." Louder, he cautioned, "Don't blame me if you sit at home, alone, the night of the prom."

"I won't blame you," she promised, in a state of angry, defiant rebellion. "I'm looking forward to the day you start treating me like I am a woman. In case you didn't notice, I've grown up."

"I have noticed." John grinned. "You're almost as tall as I am."

"Then why don't you treat me like a grown woman?"

"I do."

"Not," she argued stubbornly, pointing at her pager on the counter. "See that? It's an electronic babysitter."

"It's a convenience. A means of communication."

"Right," she replied sarcastically. "To the rest of the world 911 means an emergency, but to me it means get home before the lord and master arrives. It's a digital tyrant!"

"Lower your voice, young lady," John warned. "You're shouting."

Dixie whipped the eggs feverishly, scared to continue the fight, and yet, too frustrated to control her mouth. She poured the eggs into the skillet and bellowed, "It's time someone did. You never listen!"

"I hear you," he yelled. "I'll call Phil!"

"That's what I mean." She turned from the stove, pointing the spatula at him. "You think this is over your arranging a date for me."

"Isn't it?"

"No! Don't you understand? It's about your dominating my entire life! I can't go anywhere, say anything, do anything without your permission!"

"You've got that right," he agreed. "As long as you're in my house, eating my food, sleeping under my roof, you'll follow my rules. Period."

Dixie took two steps toward him. "And if I don't?"

"You'd better, if you know what's good for you."

"And you're the one who determines what's good for me? Right?"

"You damned betchum, daughter. When I say 'jump,' I expect your feet off the ground, as though you'd been goosed by a cattle prod."

Infuriated, Dixie turned her back on him. The sound of her father scraping his chair across the tiled floor as the stench of scorched eggs assailed her nose made her stomach coil into a knot. John had never hit her; he'd shaken the stuffing out of her once or twice, but then, she'd never openly defied him. The floor seemed to shake beneath her feet as she heard his footsteps approaching her.

"Did you burn my eggs?"

Burned was a mild description; charred was more accurate, Dixie mused triumphantly, not the least bit apologetic. She skimmed the top part off and dumped it on the plate between two wedges of toast. "You gripe when they're gooey."

Displeased and irate, he noticed she'd only fixed one plate. "Aren't you eating breakfast?"

"Not today."

John took a second glance at his eggs and said, "Can't say as I blame you."

"I didn't burn your eggs intentionally."

"Passive aggression instead of open defiance?"

"I didn't burn them *un*intentionally, either," she snapped.

His shaggy grey eyebrows beetled together as he took a third look, then glared at his daughter's face. "I'll pick up doughnuts on the way to the office. A man could starve to death around here."

Automatically, Dixie's lips parted to apologize for her behavior. Obstinately, she clamped them shut. He hadn't begged her forgiveness for being overbearing or for meddling in her social life. Mimicking his stance and facial expression, she lifted her chin arrogantly and made eye contact.

Quick-tempered, his face contorted with fury as he grabbed her wrist in a viselike grip and hissed, "Get down off your high horse, missy. I've had enough of your silly nonsense. I won't tolerate willful insubordination. Do you understand me?"

Dixie twisted her wrist free of his hold on her. Only their eyes clashed. She refused to submissively drop her gaze. "I hear you."

"You'd damned well better," he roared. "I'm going to work, and when I get back, I expect you to display an attitude adjustment."

Not waiting for her reply, John spun on his heel. His back ramrod straight, he left the kitchen. Seconds later, she heard the front door slam.

Dixie rubbed her wrist; her vision was blurred by futile rage.

He wanted a change of attitude; she'd give him one. Without a backward glance, she left the mess in the kitchen. She'd cooked and cleaned and taken care of his clothes as long as she could remember. Did she get a thank-you? Did John praise her? Pat her on the shoulder? He expressed more gratitude to the man who swept the warehouse than he showed her.

"Let him mop and dust," she snapped as she briskly strode down the corridor to her room. "Let him wash his charred eggs out of the skillet for a change!"

She stripped off the grubby grey sweatsuit she wore on Saturdays to clean house, letting it fall on the carpet. She stooped to pick it up, changed her mind and kicked it under the bed.

Let him dig under my bed to collect the dirty clothes, she thought. She'd spent plenty of time retrieving his socks from under his bed.

She yanked a pair of pressed jeans off a coat hanger. In the future, she'd iron hers, but his trousers could go to the cleaners or he could wear them rumpled. Same for his shirts, she vowed. He could take care of his clothes or pay someone else to do them.

The days of free laundry service had terminated!

Selecting her favorite white Western shirt, with coyote conchos decorating the yolk, she rammed her arms into the sleeves. Six snaps later, she shoved the tail into her jeans, zipped the fly shut and threaded a buckskin belt through the loops.

Earlier, she'd French braided her hair to keep it from falling in her face while she did her chores. Her fingers nimbly tore the rubber band from the tip of the braid. Vigorously she rubbed her scalp until her hair tumbled down her back, wild and free.

While she changed clothes, she considered how she'd spend the day. She considered calling Sara, but a day shopping with her wouldn't satisfy the reckless adrenaline pumping through her body. Too tame. She wanted to do something exciting, something daring, something that would curl her father's toes when he heard about it.

She couldn't decide on what or where; she did decide on who: Waco Stone.

Unless she was mistaken, he had a wild streak as wide as a two-by-four supporting his spine. Last night, he told her he'd be finishing the custom cabinetry at the display house in Bayou Creek Estates. All she had to do was drive there, lure him away from his hammer and nails, and let him take it from there.

Within the hour, she parked her truck directly in front of the Texas Proud Homes sign. Family pride began gnawing a hole in her anger and resentment as her experienced eye noted the details that set her father's company apart from other builders: spacious lot, curved sidewalk, multi-gabled roof, exquisite brickwork, beveled glass entry, wide arched windows, and triple-layered landscaping. Quality design and workmanship made this a house a buyer would be proud to call home.

Other builders stuck to the tried-and-true two-story. Prospective buyers entered the foyer and predictably found the dining room on the left/living room on the right. Straight back, they'd pass a half bath and enter the kitchen on the left/family room on the right.

Texas Proud drastically altered the ho-hum, conventional floor plan. As Dixie unlocked the front door with a passkey, a tingle of anticipation made her eyes sparkle. John had cast aside the concept of two living areas, in favor of a sunken great room. Curved walls flanked the foyer, with steps nestled against them that led to the upper level. Across the wide expanse of living area, the entire back of the house was glass. Because the sliding doors opened to a screened pool, landscaped with tropical plants, Dixie felt as though she'd crossed the Texas border and entered an exotic paradise.

"Want a glass of champagne?" Waco teased her, as he saw her eyes widen with wonderment.

"There's a complimentary bottle of bubbly in the icebox."

Her mouth felt dry, not caused by what she'd seen, but the cozy image of coming home and hearing Waco offer her a drink. When she turned and saw him, her tongue clove to the roof of her mouth.

Unable to speak, she watched Waco's loose-limbed swagger as he ambled toward her. He wore the same thigh-hugging jeans and low-slung carpenter's belt, but he'd removed his shirt. Whorls of dark hair sparsely covered his manly chest, descending in a V to his stomach. The urge to reach out and feel the contrasting texture of sleek skin and hair made her slide her hands into the back pockets of her jeans.

"I'll have mine on the rocks, with an olive," she answered, trying to appear sophisticated while she slowly recovered her powers of speech.

"Champagne on ice, with an olive?"

Waco's chuckle did strange things to her insides. Realizing that she must have requested something abnormal, she added, "I don't like straining chunks of ice through my teeth. It makes me brain-crazy."

"Brain-crazy?"

Dixie nodded; her red hair glistened in the sun pouring through the sky-lights. "Like when you drink a slurpy, fast, and it freezes your throat and makes your brain numb. Hasn't that ever happened to you?"

"Late yesterday afternoon, as a matter of fact."

No dummy, Dixie realized she'd had that effect

on him when he'd met her. A wild blush painted her cheeks a rosy pink.

"And again around midnight." He lifted a strand of saffron-colored hair off her cheek and tucked it behind her ear. Leaning down, his lips close to his fingertips, in a hushed tone he said, "You have a very, very sexy telephone voice."

Shivering with delight as his warm breath blew against her ear, she searched her mind for an equally extravagant compliment, but had settled for a quiet, "Thank you."

Waco trailed his forefinger under her jaw until he reached her chin. Lifting it, he asked, "Did you set things straight with your father?"

"Sort of," she replied evasively. When he arched one eyebrow, she added, "We had a major fight."

"Who won?"

"Well, let's just say John knows I'm no longer a child and that I plan on doing what I please, for a change."

"What about his hands-off-my-daughter rule?"

Dixie jerked her chin away from his hand. She couldn't look into his eyes and spout a glib lie. "Even the U.S. Constitution has amendments."

"Yeah, but they weren't chiseled in concrete." Waco plowed his fingers through his wavy hair and sighed heavily. "I thought about you and me and your father all night, Dixie. From John's reputation, I figured he wouldn't change his policy."

"Guess that means no Tush Push for us?" she asked lightly, as she valiantly tried to keep her chin from wobbling.

"I pounded the street looking for a job when I knocked on John's office door." Waco tucked his thumbs beneath his belt and smiled at her. "Nothing's changed. There are other doors. Texas Proud isn't the only builder in Houston."

"Meaning?"

She held her breath, not daring to hope he'd risk losing his job because he wanted to be with her.

His grin widened. "We'll both be in trouble if John finds out we're Tush Pushing in the same dance line."

Dixie flung herself into his arms, giving him a mighty hug. Her feet left the floor as he held her close and swung her around in a big circle. Laughing, feeling light as a feather and utterly gorgeous, she knew she'd fallen in love with Waco—a secret love that would endure forever, in spite of her father's archaic rules.

"Someday, we won't have to sneak around," Waco promised, setting Dixie on her feet. "I won't be a subcontract carpenter all my life."

"What's wrong with what you do? It's honest work." Her arms gestured toward the triple-crown molding and bookcases. "You take pride in your work, don't you?"

Capturing her hand, Waco pulled her toward the kitchen. "I want to build custom houses that will make this one look like a bungalow."

"Mansions?"

"Yep. And eventually I want my own showplace, with a pool, and stables, and a couple of lakes stocked with fish . . ."

"And a dozen servants to take care of it," Dixie supplemented, remembering the mess she'd left in the kitchen.

"But today, I have to put the finish trim on those cabinets. One small step at a time until I can make a giant leap to fame and fortune."

"I can help," Dixie offered. She picked up a piece of rounded trim. "Do you want me to measure and miter, while you tack them in place?"

Astonished that she knew how to cut wood, much less able to fit corners, he asked, "Did John teach you how?"

"Nope. Dad's too busy wheeling and dealing at the Westheimer office to teach me anything." She scanned the area looking for his miter box or electric saw. "When I was a kid, he let me tag along with one of the riding superintendents."

"My equipment is set up in the laundry room. I've measured and cut most of the strips I need." He held out a small can of wood putty. His eyes ran an appreciative bead down the length of Dixie. Conchos, tied with dangling strips of rawhide, were hazardous. One wrong move and she'd ruin those fancy clothes. Or worse, she could hurt herself. "Why don't you help by holding the strip of molding while I put it in place, then you can follow behind me, filling the holes with putty."

"Afraid I don't know what I'm doing?" she teased.

"I don't doubt that you're smart. I just don't want you hurt." He removed the molding from her hand, staring pointedly at the turquoise stone set in elaborate silver on her ring finger. "Carpenters don't wear jewelry, not if they're partial to having five fingers."

She slid it off and dropped it in his palm. "Keep it for me? I don't want to lose it."

"It looks expensive. You'd better put it in your jeans pocket."

"I would if I could." She flattened her stomach and could only slide her fingers knuckle-deep into her pocket. "They're a little tighter than usual."

"I noticed," he replied, his lips quirked as he wiggled his eyebrows at her. "You have great legs, ma'am, and the sweetest tush this side of the Mason-Dixon Line."

Laughing at his comical antics, she smoothed her hands over her slender hips. "I'm too tall, too flat, and . . ."

"Gorgeous. Simply gorgeous." He slid the ring on his smallest finger; it only went to the first joint. "You have such slender fingers. My hands make two of yours."

"Not quite," she denied, placing the heel of her hand against his to measure their fingers. His were calloused; hers were soft. His were deeply tanned; hers were nearly white. His were longer; hers the shortest by an inch.

Neither of them noticed or made the comparison. She looked into his dark eyes deeply and saw herself through his eyes. She wasn't a teenage reject. She was smart and beautiful and sexy. At least, that's how he saw her.

"You're just right for me." He tucked the ring

in the pouch on his belt, stooped down to pick up the appropriate piece of molding for the center island cabinet, and began hammering finishing nails into the molding. "There's nobody better."

Wanting to clear up any half-truths she'd told him yesterday, she said, "I'm eighteen, Waco."

"That's a relief." He wiped imaginary perspiration from his forehead.

She pinched a tiny amount of putty from the can and poked it into the nail hole. "Why?"

"You're not jailbait. My 'somedays' would end abruptly if John had me thrown in the slammer for corrupting his underage daughter."

"You don't have to worry about that, either. He already thinks I need an attitude adjustment. I'd have to rip off my sassy mouth to satisfy him."

"Five years ago, Zeke felt the same way about me," Waco added. He estimated a measurement eight inches from the last nail. Lightly, so as not to split the trim, he pecked in another nail. "He claimed I was a rip-roarin' hellion with a death wish."

"Were you?"

"Probably," he conceded, remembering how angry and frustrated he'd been. "I dropped out of high school to help keep a roof over our heads. Back then, I thought the world owed me a living because I could cut a relatively straight line and bang a few nails into a two-by-eight without smacking my thumb."

Dismayed, she wrinkled her nose. "Your father let you drop out of school?"

"Zeke is my uncle." He whacked another nail, then countersank it by gently tapping the small head with the sharp point of another nail. "He couldn't say much since he didn't make it beyond sixth grade."

"What about your parents? Didn't they object?"

"They split for parts unknown before I was potty-trained."

Her dismay changed to sadness. She couldn't imagine growing up without *either* parent. There were times when she'd wallowed in self-pity because her mother had died shortly after she'd been born. Frilly dresses, hair-bows, and birthday parties the other girls had, she'd envied. Temporary housekeepers pretended to care, but they weren't the same as having a real mother.

"Have you tried to find them?"

"Fifteen or so years ago Zeke got a pittance from them. The note said they were living in a commune in California." Waco laughed harshly. "Some con artist sold them a 'gen-u-ine' treasure map. Soon as they struck it rich, they were going to send for us. Needless to say, we never heard from them again."

Sympathetically, she touched his shoulder; he shrugged her hand off him.

"I don't need your pity. Zeke and I have managed to scratch out a living without them."

"Zeke must be proud of you," she replied. That comment earned her a hard look. "What I meant is, hellions aren't steady, reliable, skilled craftsmen. And they sure as heck aren't employed by

Texas Proud." She grinned and jabbed his muscular bicep. "You might still have a death wish though."

"Hard work never killed anybody, has it?"

She chuckled. "No, but hanging around with the boss's only daughter could be dangerous."

"Trust me to be careful, real careful, and I want you to be the same. Don't stir up any trouble with John. Let him think you've reconsidered. Make peace with him."

"Be Daddy's sweet little darlin'?" she teased, quoting him.

"Uh-uh." Waco raised upright and looped his arm around her waist. "I'd much rather you be my darlin'."

Idly, John rotated the pencil end over end as he listened to the Saturday-morning reports from Texas Proud's department heads. Six men and one woman comprised the executive staff, and all listened intently as the computer specialist, Blake Jergins, explained the advantages of using the software he'd recently added to the computer system. Everyone seated at the conference table was computer literate, except John. His mind functioned faster than the latest Pentium chip.

Not a bald or greying head in the room other than mine, John noted, feeling older than his fifty years. He suspected Dirk Stallman, vice-president in charge of finances, of dabbing Grecian Formula on his roots, but he didn't begrudge Dirk his determination to appear as vital and youthful as the other elite members of the organization.

His own head of thick, pure white hair set him apart from the others, like a crown born from experience and wisdom.

Fidgety, he narrowed his eyes and circumnavigated the faces focused on Blake Jergins' overhead projection. Integrity, ambition, and expertise had been the prime attributes he'd utilized as criteria when he'd chosen his right-hand men. He'd trust any of them with his life. More importantly, he trusted them with his money.

Those were the same values he'd instilled in his only child. One day in the not-so-distant future, he mused, Dixie would take her place at the table as senior vice-president in charge of operations.

He scowled, recalling the minor rebellion that had taken place earlier. He'd spent eighteen years with her, building a strong foundation for success. It would take the precision of a highly calibrated transit for him to walk the thin chalk line between genius and insanity. His male ego warned him that insurrection was intolerable; nip it in the bud, prune back her willfulness until it was eradicated. But, his analytical mind refuted those impulses, asking how he expected to prime her for greatness when he'd broken her high spirit? God knew, his own inner being had the strength of a steel I-beam combined with the resilience of a reinforcement rod. Hell, until this morning, he'd been concerned that she was too placid, too submissive, too . . . feminine.

Maybe it's time to switch stratagems, he contemplated, as he was watching Dirk demonstrate how the best architectural renditions were worthless when the plumber's toilet mysteriously wound up in the center of the living room. In May, Dixie would graduate. Instead of bringing her to TP's headquarters as planned, he could put her in charge of a special project, one that pulled together the infinite bits and pieces of knowledge she'd acquired under his various superintendents' tutelage.

John sat forward in his chair as his idea formed. Years ago, he'd bought a sweet little piece of property and had Tom Thorpe, his architect, sketch a blueprint for his dream home. The plan had been put on hold because the acreage was outside the Pearwood School District, where Dixie had attended school since kindergarten. His eyes circled back to Gil Albertson, his man in charge of land procurement and Walter Block, projects manager. They'd tried to convince him to develop the land for a subdivision, but he'd refused. Back in the corner of his mind, he'd envisioned his own house, a state-of-the-art showplace.

Why not combine his plans? Kill a flock of birds with one stone?

"Are there any questions?" Blake asked, directing his attention toward John.

When no hands were raised, John asked, "Can Tom's architects scan a preliminary set of drawings into the computer to get a cost printout within the hour?"

"Yes, sir. That's the beauty of this software. Everything from the foundation to the roof shingles, in one cost-estimation package."

"Tom, pull out the designs for the Mayson Lane house. Have Blake do a work-up." John narrowed his gaze and turned to Dirk. "Would this expense be detrimental to the cash flow? Any tax write-offs if I reside in a display home?"

"I'll have to check into it," Dirk hedged, poking wire-framed glasses up the bridge of his blade-thin nose. "With proper documentation, there may be a couple of loopholes you could take advantage of. As to the availability of capital, Texas Proud is solid financially. As long as Houston is the oil-refining capital of the world, this area is a growth magnet. My annual report projects an increase of housing starts to be approximately seventy percent over the next decade."

"What about the weekly reports, sir?" Kate Williams dared to ask. These once-a-month Saturday morning meetings generally ended at noon. She'd planned on having a good eight hours to wade through the blueprints littering her desk. As interior-design coordinator, she required all custom houses to have her stamp of approval before local permits were issued.

Rubbing his hands together in anticipation, John said, "Have Phyllis order lunch and give Dixie a call. Since she'll be coordinating this project, I want her in on the ground-floor operations. Each of you will continue your normal operating procedures, with my daughter as your protegée." He stood up and walked over to the computer terminal and gave

Blake a pat on the back. "Good presentation. Can I rely on you to teach her this cost-estimating package?"

Before Blake replied, he quickly turned, catching each member of the staff casting baffled looks at each other.

"Dixie graduates in May. She's learned the basics. I want to see how she applies them."

"Might I suggest she begin with a tract home?" Walter suggested. He stood. Equal in height and breadth, and approximately the same age, he and Kate alternated being spokesman for those vice-presidents who were less bold. "Success breeds success. Why overwhelm her?"

John flattened his hands on the table and leaned forward. "Hogwash! You were a superintendent and she still wore her hair in pigtails when TP contracted tract homes. Give her that assignment and she'd be bored spitless!"

"What about college?" Kate asked shortly.

Deliberately misunderstanding the question, he replied, "You think she's prepared for that massive a project?"

As though on cue, the men chuckled while Kate glared at John.

"She mentioned the University of Texas, in Austin," Kate persisted tenaciously.

"Too big, too far away. Out-of-town expenses would eat up the profit."

"I think what Kate means is . . ." Walter began, coming to Kate's assistance.

"I'm not obtuse," John interrupted, verbally

showing the doubting Thomases that he was in command. He picked up the pencil he'd fiddled with and considered adding dramatic flair by hurling it across the conference room. "Texas Proud will educate my daughter." The eraser singled out each person one by one. "Each of you has advanced degrees. You'll be her professors. She'll learn more in the year it takes to build Mayson Manor than a college student learns with a Master's degree in construction engineering."

Only Kate possessed the nerve to argue and the sense to do it privately. "Could we discuss this in my office?"

"This isn't up for discussion. I've made my decision!"

"In that case, I'd like to be on the record as officially opposed to bringing Dixie Mayson aboard with little experience and no university background."

"Dammit, Kathryn, you're the last person I expected to object."

"Why? Because I'm forty, single, and shattered the glass ceiling that oppresses other midmanagement females? Will I be required to sing a rousing rendition of 'I Am Woman' while I tutor Dixie?"

Silence invaded the room; only the muted buzz of the fluorescent light fixture could be heard for several seconds.

John stared at Kate as though they'd just been formally introduced. When had she exchanged gracious tact for militant feminism, he wondered, completely astounded.

"Gentlemen, you'll excuse us, won't you?" He pivoted on one well-shod foot and strode toward the door and held it open. "Ms. Williams, if you please . . ."

Head held high, Kathryn flipped the end of the designer scarf she wore loosely draped around her neck over her shoulder. Strong men quaked when John roared; smart cookies didn't crumble.

"My pleasure, Mr. Mayson. Perhaps you'd best assign lunch duty to another member of your staff," she suggested softly.

"I'll make arrangements with Phyllis," Dirk volunteered. He gave Kate a silent thumbs-up signal, as did three other men in the conference room.

Behind John's back, Kate knew she had their support. In the construction business most employees consider an authority figure a son-of-a-bitch. But, when it came to a final showdown, she also knew she'd be the single voice of reason singing in an all-male choir.

Rejecting their kiss-ass mentality, she skirted through the door John held open for her.

Four

"Sit down," John commanded, settling into his burgundy, leather desk chair. The combative tilt of Kate's chin fortified his resolve to include Dixie in future executive sessions. His daughter could learn a thing or two from this statuesque, dark-haired, brown-eyed woman. Kathryn epitomized the legendary southern "steel butterfly," from her soft drawl to the edge of her lacy lingerie that John saw as she gracefully crossed her legs. "Who appointed you my daughter's fairy godmother?"

"I did."

"Who delegated that authority to you?"

"You did."

"Bullshit."

Kate wrinkled her nose and flicked an imaginary dust mote off the long sleeve of her cashmere dress. Men in the construction business had a penchant for foul language. She seldom voiced her distaste; a withered-rose look generally sufficed to quell the most ardent redneck's foul mouth.

"Then let's call my meddling in your personal business part of our silent agreement," she countered softly.

"A silent agreement?" John raised his voice. "As in blackmail?"

Smiling at him to blunt the cutting edge off her sharp tongue she added, "I'd say fifteen years as your mistress entitles me to far more than merely voicing my opinion."

"Things aren't over between us, merely put on hold."

Kate shook her head. "I say it is."

The current status of their tumultuous relationship wasn't up for debate. A year ago she'd removed the key to her condominium from his key chain. She'd awakened from her romantic haze and realized the difference between living together and loving together was one important letter: *I,* as in identity. She'd become everything John desired, but that left nothing for herself. Call it a midlife crisis, or just plain coming to her senses, Kate knew the limbo lifestyle she'd led with John was no longer satisfactory.

"I'm not here to discuss what you want. Let's stick to what your daughter *needs.* Every young woman needs a college degree," Kate stated unequivocally, drawing him back to the main topic of discussion.

"Dixie is not leaving Pearwood to attend the University of Texas." John rubbed his chin thoughtfully and lifted one eyebrow. "I might consider letting her attend a community college, part-time, after Mayson Manor is completed."

"Your daughter isn't an undeveloped piece of land that you can convert into a planned community. People can't be sectioned into tidy lots and fenced in."

She could tell her analogy had fallen on deaf ears when John folded his arms across his chest and leaned back in his chair. She'd wasted her breath.

Abruptly, he inclined toward her. "Was Dixie part of our problem?" he asked starkly.

"No."

Intrigued by mysteries, John considered using his persuasive powers to pry into her reasons for ending their arrangement. For an impatient man, he'd shown remarkable restraint for the past year. To save face, he'd acted as though closing her bedroom door had been a mutual agreement.

Stoicism did not suit him.

He'd continue to bide his time, for now, but soon, very soon, he wanted some answers from the comely woman who lithely removed herself from her chair.

Kate paused at his office door. "There's more to campus life than what's found between book covers. Do you want your daughter to be socially retarded?"

That struck a raw nerve. He'd started his day arguing with Dixie over getting her a date for the prom. Rising, he circled his desk and strode to stand beside Kate. Just as he started to put his hands on her shoulders, she turned toward him, but one hand remained on the doorknob. Her troubled brown eyes pulled at his heartstrings, but his arms dropped to his sides.

Kate felt physically drawn to John; she always had. Only inches apart, she gazed into his bedroom blue eyes. His charismatic charm weakened Kate. Old fantasies of love, commitment, and walking tall beside her man began to swirl in her mind. It became more and more difficult each time she had to walk away from her heart's secret wish.

"You could teach her social graces," he suggested, his blue eyes warm with sincerity. "A teenage girl needs a woman's gentle touch."

For several seconds Kate considered being a surrogate mother to John's daughter. It took immeasurable fortitude for her to twist the doorknob. The latch clicked open.

Before she sidestepped through her escape route, she said, "Pretending to be Dixie's mother isn't part of my job description. Get yourself a wife."

John caved against the door frame as though she'd poked him in the stomach. Dammit, for a second she'd almost relented. He'd seen it in her eyes. Why did she continue to deny him what they both wanted?

He strode back to his desk feeling mean-spirited enough to fire Kate. She was the only person in the organization who hadn't the slightest qualm about saying no to him.

"Phyllis!" he shouted, not bothering to press the intercom button. "Did you get hold of my daughter?"

"No, sir," came over the speaker, timidly.

"Why not?"

"No one answers the phone. I paged her, too, but she hasn't responded. Do you want me to keep calling your house?"

"Yes. Inform her that she's to be here by one o'clock, sharp."

"I'll keep trying, sir."

"Trying my patience," John mumbled, as he thumbed through the weekly reports. Must be a full moon tonight. Or a PMS epidemic. Until today, he'd never worried about having a date to a dance, or being a social retard, or any such tomfoolery.

Why can't women think like men!

"Stop," Dixie implored. Wisps of fog curled through the leaves of the oaks lining her street. The seductive scents of gardenia, azalea and hyacinth filled the night. "He'll hear your truck."

Waco slowed to a snail's pace. "You said John plays poker till dawn on Saturday."

"He does. Usually. But that's his Suburban parked behind my truck." She prepared herself for an ugly scene. The minute her father laid eyes on Waco, John would transform into a dragon: flames would roll from his mouth and smoke would spout from his ears. "The porch light is lit. John believes all the hellin' in the world starts after midnight."

"It's after two." Concerned for Dixie's welfare, he asked, "Do you want to spend the night at my place?"

"No! He'd have a missing person squad looking for me. Drive on by the house and park down the road. I don't want you to get into trouble."

"Yes, Dixie. I'm not letting you face him alone. I've seen the man angry. His eyes bug out. He clamps his teeth on his lower lip. And then he starts bellowing like a stuck hog. Uh-uh. I'll walk you to the door. Let him take his frustration out on me."

He began to apply the brakes; she pressed the gas pedal with her left foot.

"Dixie! Stop it! You'll drop the transmission."

The aging truck backfired, loudly. Startled, Dixie mashed the pedal beneath her foot. Back wheels spinning, gravel spurting, they careened down the street several hundred yards. Waco pushed her foot aside and applied the brake.

"Let me out here." Before Waco could stop her, she'd opened the passenger's door, leaped to the curb, and slammed the door. "Bye."

"Wait a minute . . ."

"Go!" She sprinted away from his truck calling over her shoulder, "He'll fire you on the spot! I promise, I'll be okay! Go!"

Everything happened so fast, Waco didn't have time to weigh and measure their actions against the consequences. He wanted to stay, to protect Dixie from her father's ire, but he realized that confronting an irate father protecting his only daughter was like going to a gunfight with a pea-shooter.

"Shit fire," Waco cursed, worried about Dixie.

His foot ground against the brake pedal as he leaned across the front seat. He wasn't budging an inch until he felt confident Dixie was safe.

He watched Dixie dart up the steps. Waco held his breath; his stomach coiled with tension; his mouth tasted coppery. At any moment all hell could break loose. He listened for the sound of raised voices, for Dixie calling his name; he heard only the sputtering noise of the engine. A minute later, air whistled through his lips as the porch light blinked on and off, three times.

John must be asleep, he deduced silently, a small grin of relief curving his mouth. They hadn't been caught this time, but what about the next time. And the next?

Slowly, he drove down the street.

"Stop right where you are, young lady," John blustered. He stepped from the small office at the back of the house where he'd been working as Dixie lightly scampered up the steps. "Where the hell have you been until all hours of the morning?"

Dixie's heart lurched. She'd thought herself home-free. The sound of John's voice booming up the stairwell cost her a year's growth—not that she wanted to grow another inch.

"Out," she replied succinctly. Her eyes flew to the door. God, please, make him drive off, she prayed silently.

"Out where? You've been gone the entire day! Phyllis must have worn out the redial button calling here!"

Groping for a legitimate excuse, she said, "Sara . . ."

"Don't you lie to me, missy," he snapped. "I saw Sara in her bakery store uniform. That young fella she's dating brought her home and they drove off about an hour later. She came back at midnight. You weren't with her!"

"You interrupted me. I started to say that Sara and I planned to go shopping and to the movies, but she had to work."

"That accounts for Sara's activities. You march yourself down those steps and tell me where you've been since noon."

Dragging her heels, Dixie checked the impulse to cross her fingers behind her back and lie like a rug. She wasn't eight; she was eighteen. She'd learned from childhood that the consequences for getting caught in a baldfaced lie would double, no, treble whatever punishment John decided the misconduct merited.

"I didn't answer the phone or the pager because I am no longer a child that you have to keep tabs on," she bluffed. She hadn't lied, yet. Deciding to stick as close to the truth as possible, she said, "Tonight I was at the Corral, with a bunch of friends. If I hadn't been so mad at you for treating me like a baby, I'd have left a note. I didn't drive, so I couldn't leave before midnight."

Truth, fib, truth, fib, she mentally recounted, hoping the truth would somehow overshadow the fib.

"Who brought you home?" John demanded. "Why didn't he walk you to the door?"

"Because I insisted he just drop me off." She'd

managed to keep her gaze steady, but her chin rose. She knew she'd be striking a match to a short fuse as she added, "I didn't want you to embarrass me in front of my friend."

"Me? Embarrass you!"

Eyes bugged, teeth clenched, his fingers curled as he reach forward, Dixie was certain he'd wanted to throttle her. Nimbly, she climbed two steps upward. He must have realized how close he was to physically striking her. He shoved his hands in the pockets of his plaid flannel robe and turned toward the wall.

"You are not to see that young man again," John ordered, once he had his temper under control. "You said yourself that he's a new classmate. He could be some punk who transferred in from a juvenile home, for all you know."

"Dad," she protested, stringing out the three letters. "That's not fair!"

He twisted at the waist, holding up both hands. "Don't argue with me. My mind is made up."

"That's unreasonable. When are you going to start trusting me to pick my friends?"

"When you show good judgment and behave in a responsible manner," he snapped. "Now, go to bed. I don't want to discuss this any further."

That's it? He hadn't grounded her for life, or restricted her to bread and water? She detested his high-handed treatment, but felt as though she'd gotten off lightly.

Her foot struck the first landing when she heard his final decree, "Tomorrow, you're going to the

Westheimer office with me. I'll keep you too busy to be out dancing until dawn."

"What if I've made plans?" Pure contrariness prompted her to antagonize him. That, and a strong desire to be with Waco while he worked on his truck. "What if I don't want to go with you to your office?"

"Your mouth is overloading your brain. Whatever plans you made *for the next six months,* you can cancel."

"You're grounding me for six months?" Her fists ground into her hipbones. "No way."

"You'll do what I tell you to do as long as you're living under my roof, spending my money!"

"I'll get a job and earn my own money," she threatened.

"Good. You're hired. You start tomorrow, parttime."

"A free-for-nothing job? No pay? No benefits? Whoa, hold me back. I'll take two of those," she rebuked sarcastically.

John's hand sliced through the hostile air between them. "Not another word, Dixie Lee Mayson. I'll expect an apology at breakfast, when you've had time to cool off and come to your senses."

I didn't do anything wrong! she wanted to shout. She settled for an icy glare of scorn and quietly trod up the steps, silently vowing to die before he'd squeeze an apology out of her.

They hadn't done anything wrong, had they?

Was it a crime to poke putty in nail holes, to stroll through the Galleria mall, to eat dinner and go dancing? She would feel guilty if she'd been parked on a dark oilpatch road, getting it on, but Waco stuck to the superhighways. Queen Victoria would have approved of Waco's courtly behavior.

Thanks to her Neanderthal father, she hadn't even gotten a good-night kiss!

She peeled off her clothes; rebelliously, she booted them under the bed. Yanking her nightshirt over her head, she thought, he wants me to cool off? She'd give him cool. A below zero, cold-shoulder treatment, that's what he'd get from her.

Fussing and fuming, she went into the bathroom to complete her nightly routine of scrubbing her face and teeth. She returned to her bedroom, picked her brush off the nightstand and began brushing her hair a vigorous hundred strokes. For each swipe the bristles made, she plotted future icy encounters with her father. If she could hold her redheaded hot temper, she'd have him shopping for ski clothing in July!

The phone buzzed; she'd switched its bell tone to the lowest level.

"Hello?"

"Hi. Everything okay?"

Her heart beat crazily at the sound of Waco's voice. "Yes . . . I mean, no."

"No?" Waco growled. "I'll be right over to get you."

"No!" Dixie giggled nervously and clamped her fingers across her mouth. The image of Waco storming into the house to save her from her father's wrath sent sweet shivers throughout her. "Dad went ballistic, but he didn't do anything violent."

"Dammit, you should have let me take you to the door. Why did you give an all-clear signal?"

"I thought he was asleep. He caught me while I tiptoed up the steps."

"What'd he say?"

"He wanted to know where I'd gone, who I'd been with, and why I wasn't home by midnight." While she spoke, she returned the brush to its place and snuggled between the sheets. To muffle the sound of her voice, she pulled the covers over her head. "I told him I'd gone out with a new guy at school, and that we'd gone dancing with a group of friends."

"You should have told him the truth," Waco said, denying the swell of relief he felt.

Selfishly, he wanted to be with her, but responsibility for Zeke weighed heavily on him. John yelling at Dixie was nothing compared to her father's reaction at seeing a lowly carpenter kissing Dixie good-night. Instantaneous unemployment, delivered with a knuckle sandwich.

"I told half-truths," she whispered, "not lies. You are a new guy and there were some people from Pearwood at the Corral." She heard a car honk. Puzzled, she asked, "Where are you?"

"I'm at a pay phone a couple of blocks from your house."

Dixie smiled, her eyes closed as she relished the thought of him caring what happened to her. Against her will, she decided she'd better tell him the bad news. "I can't help you work on your truck tomorrow."

"He grounded you?"

"More or less. I have to go to the office with him."

"On Sunday?"

"Sundays, holidays, . . . they're all the same to him."

"I usually work seven days a week, too," he admitted.

Her smile grew wider. "You were taking a day off to be with me?"

"My brakes do need new shoes. I was looking forward to seeing if you're as good a grease-monkey as you claim to be," he teased with a deep chuckle.

"Fix the brakes by yourself and you'll have to wait another fifty thousand miles to find out, huh?"

"Not with my truck. It's glued together with baling wire and bubble gum, Mechanics see dollar signs when they hear me drive down the street." He heard her hushed laughter, then asked, "When will I see you again?"

"When eagle-eye blinks," she bantered, half-heartedly.

Waco groaned drily, "We'll both be old and grey by then."

"You could call me tomorrow night," she hinted. "I could make some arrangement with my friend Sara to cover for me."

"More lies and half-truths?" Waco sighed, rubbing his forehead. "God, I detest sneaking around like a thief in the night. It makes me feel like I'm doing something to be ashamed of."

"It isn't your fault or mine that we can't openly see each other. John is the one who is treating us unfairly."

"I've thought about approaching another general contractor, but first I have to fulfill this contract. Otherwise, John could blackball me. Hell, he could sue me for everything I *don't* have or will earn in the next decade."

"See? He's tied our hands. We don't have a choice. Trust me. It won't take long for John to get sick of playing the role of warden."

Discouraged, Waco shook his head at their dilemma. Their future looked dismal. "He could be right. Maybe I won't amount to anything. Have you thought of that?"

"No!" She twisted the receiver's coiled line around her finger. "I've seen your work. Someday you will have your own company." She paused, waiting for a response. When she heard only silence, self-doubt began niggling at her. Why risk his job when there must be hundreds of women panting after him? Why bother sneaking around when any woman would be proud to be seen with him. In a small voice, she asked, "Don't you want to see me again?"

"I shouldn't," he conceded, "but I do. You're beautiful and smart. Sweet and sexy."

"I am?" she fished.

"Uh-huh. Best of all, you make me laugh and feel good."

The soft, lyrical croon of his voice, as he said all the things Dixie thought she'd never hear from a man, was sweeter than a mother's lullaby.

"That's how you make me feel, too," she whispered. Borrowing a line from a thousand country-western ballads, she added, "I'll be heartbroken until I see you again."

"I can't allow that, now can I?"

"No. We'll think of something."

"I'll talk to you tomorrow night." He paused, reluctant to break the fragile means of communication. "Sweet dreams, gorgeous."

Silently, her lips formed a kiss. "Bye."

She returned the phone to its hook knowing sleep would be impossible. Waco's flattery had created in Dixie a new peace with herself. After listening to him, she no longer felt too tall, or gangly or ugly.

Cherished, she mouthed, that's how he makes me feel.

She crisscrossed her arms over her chest, hugging that special feeling close to her, wishing she was holding Waco in her arms.

Five

In the morning, Dixie lazed in bed later than usual, and she could hear her father in the kitchen, banging skillets, running water, rummaging in the refrigerator. John sounded like the proverbial bull in a china shop—and each clang and clatter delighted Dixie.

Since he lacked faith in her ability to pick and choose her friends, she lacked faith in her ability to fix his breakfast.

Glass shattering against the tiled floor brought a long jaw-popping yawn, then a smile from Dixie's generous heart-shaped lips.

"Dixie!" she heard bellowing up the stairwell. "Get up! Now!"

She did. Propping her elbows on the pillow, she watched the sunlight filtering through the lacy curtains, which cast a series of elaborate cobweblike shadows on her bed's coverlet. Dust motes danced to the tune of the spring breeze. From the limbs of a nearby oak, she heard the trill of a mockingbird.

From below, she heard the heavy tromp of John's boots traveling up the steps. His knuckles rapped against her door. "Come on! Early bird gets the worm."

"You eat them," she mouthed, impertinently. "I'll have cereal."

She swept the bedding aside as she renewed her vow to give her father a silent, cold-shoulder treatment. Since he took her housework for granted, she'd let him fend for himself. He could cook and clean. And if he couldn't, it was time he learned how. Or he could contact an employment agency and go through their entire list of housekeepers until he found someone who could replace her.

"At least a housekeeper would get free room and board and a paycheck," she groused quietly.

Predicting that her father would bang again, she crossed to the door. Her finger had barely finished pressing the button to lock it when she heard John knock.

Smiling grimly, she chose the opposite side of the board he'd hit and echoed the sharp raps.

The knob twisted, with futility. "Is this door locked?"

"Yes, sir." Swearing she could hear his back molars grinding, she made a mad dash for the bathroom as she pulled her nightgown over her head. "You don't object to my having privacy while I'm getting dressed, do you?"

"Far be it from me to invade your privacy," he growled, like a man who'd smacked his own thumb with a hammer. "I'm leaving in thirty minutes. You be ready."

Dixie drew an imaginary mark on the bathroom

mirror. "Chalk one up for the good guy," she gloated. "By noon, he'll be begging me to go out with Waco!"

Thirty-three minutes later, she bounded down the steps as though she were early. What she wore made grungy fashion look neat by comparison. Her knees poked through the gaping holes in her slit jeans; her big toenail could be seen through the hole in one dingy grey sneaker. A purple glue stain dribbled down the front of her T-shirt, which was six sizes too big. The crowning effect was the twin pigtails tied with fuchsia-pink, sequined ribbon.

Her stance reeked of you-treat-me-like-a-troublesome-five-year-old-brat-so-I'll-fit-the-image.

"Ready?" John asked dubiously.

Her pigtails bobbed pertly as Dixie nodded her head.

"I'll drive, otherwise we'd get a traffic ticket for having an underage driver," he commented, picking up his briefcase and holding the door for her.

Neither of them spoke during the drive; John divided his attention between the road and plans for Mayson Manor, and Dixie split her concentration between snubbing John and daydreams of Waco.

"Go into the conference room," John bade as the elevator stopped at the fourteenth floor. "I have a couple of calls to make. Why don't you glance over the architectural plans on the table? You might find them of interest."

She stood petulantly in the receptionist area. Slowly, her cantankerous, icy veneer began to thaw.

A strong sense of belonging seeped through the cracks of her fractious attitude, until the pride she always felt when she entered her father's domain sent a ripple of shame running through her.

She remembered how empty the office space had looked when John had leased it: bare white walls, construction-grade carpet, steel Formica-topped furniture. Cubicles for the executives had been formed by flimsy portable walls; secretarial workstations cluttered the remaining open area. She recalled Kate comparing the acoustics here to those in the Astrodome—when the Oilers were on the road, a whisper could be heard in the free seats; when filled to capacity, the players couldn't hear the quarterback call the play.

The day John signed the lease, Kate arrived with a roll of interior design sheets tucked under her arm. A dozen burly men began removing the old fixtures. Close on their heels, TP's best carpenters followed. Permanent walls were erected; plush carpet and padding were installed. Nature guided Kate's color palate from the loden green carpet to light blue wallcoverings to accent pieces in vibrant splashes of autumn colors. Overstuffed leather seating arrangements provided both comfort and elegance.

Ambling toward the conference room, pride in her father renewed itself. Yes, he could be tyrannical, but would this transformation have taken place without John ruling with a iron fist? Would the gallery of water-colored drawings of homes he'd completed exist? Here, at the nerve center of Texas Proud, her retaliation seemed out of place.

Her appearance only validated John's mistaken opinion that she was childish and immature.

Compelled to right that wrong impression, she untied the bows and removed the rubber bands that held her braids. She tucked her oversized shirt into the jeans' waistband. Unfortunately, the holes in her sneakers and jeans couldn't be repaired.

Concern for her appearance became secondary the instant she saw the ink drawings scattered on the conference table. The sketches looked like a home that would qualify for *Southern Architectural* magazine's Design of the Year award.

Grace and grandeur blended the rich Texas ranch heritage with the traditional southern plantation.

Notations penned beside the main floor plan drew Dixie's eyes away from the exterior view. "Double French doors with beveled glass. Twenty-two foot recessed oval ceilings. Four marble fireplaces. Mahogany-paneled library and study. Six bedrooms. Servants' quarters."

"What do you think of it?" she heard from the doorway.

"It's absolutely beautiful." Awe warmed her tone of voice. "Did Tom Thorpe design it?"

"Yes, to the owner's specifications."

"Is it under contract?"

"There are a couple of contingency clauses that have to be resolved," John hedged.

"Loan approval? Sale of their existing home?"

"No."

"Locating a lot where they want it built?"

"No. They own the land, free and clear."

"Then what's the snag?"

"It's not the buyer. It's Texas Proud. I have the right person chosen to oversee the project, but that person isn't interested."

Disbelief raised the tips of her brows. "Since when are you letting your superintendents pick and choose their jobs?"

"I'm not. Joe Cash is going to be the building super. A project of this magnitude requires a project manager." John grinned as he laid his hand on her shoulder. "You."

"Me?" she gasped.

"Why not you? You're the perfect choice since this is going to be our new home—Mayson Manor."

Stunned, she sank back in her chair. None of this made sense to her. Feeling as though she was caught in a whirlpool of ambiguity, with a manhole sucking at her heels, she sputtered, "B-b-but last night you made it clear that you don't trust my judgement . . . that I'm just a kid."

"You are when it comes to men, but not when it comes to working for Texas Proud. I've been grooming you for this project since you were in diapers. Remember how I used to put your portable crib in the bed of my truck? While I supervised a job, you watched." John chuckled and patted her shoulder. "You could read floor plans before you knew your ABC's."

"Dad . . ."

His hand squeezing her shoulder quieted her resistance.

"While other girls played with Barbie dolls, you were hammering together blocks of wood, building castles." Caught up in his memories, he went on, "And remember when I taught you how to solder? You soldered together pipe and made enough guns and rifles to arm a revolution! And what about the tree house you built when you were ten?"

"Almost built. I had it framed and was putting the sheets of plywood on the gabled roof when the tree limbs broke." Grimacing, she glanced up at John. "You were furious."

"Only because you should have checked with me, first. When you didn't, I purposely let it collapse underneath you."

"I could've broken my neck!"

John chuckled. "The limbs were too low for you to hurt yourself. My point is that you designed it, set up work schedules, organized your buddies to haul scrap lumber off another job site, and you framed it. You were only ten years old. Ninety percent of the boys graduating in your class couldn't accomplish that.

"And last year," he continued, "remember how you wired the out-of-door lighting for the country-western extravaganza your class sponsored? That was a major undertaking that would have blown the fuse of most electrical subcontractors."

"Kid stuff compared to Mayson Manor." She tapped the blueprint of Mayson Manor with her finger. "Granted, I know the how-to basics of each trade," she acceded as she bent forward and touched the drawing, "but figuratively speaking, I could break my neck, again."

"I don't want to hear that kind of talk. Why do you think you've spent every summer learning a different phase of construction?" Before she could open her mouth, he drilled his finger into his chest, and answered, "Because I was preparing you for your future. Starting this summer, you're going to be an intrinsic part of Texas Proud, proving to everyone in the construction business that you've learned everything I've taught you."

Dixie realized that from one breath to the next, he'd gone from persuading her that she'd be competent to issuing a mandate, from flattering her, to validating his own ego. He'd arbitrarily decided she'd step into his boots, and as far as he was concerned, they'd damn well better fit!

"What about college?" she asked hesitantly. She'd assumed she'd graduate and go on to college, like Sara and her other friends. "I filled out the application form to go to the University of Texas. The counselor at school said she's certain I'll be accepted because of my grade point average."

"It'd be a waste of time, money and effort."

"Is that a definite no?"

"I'm not inflexible. I wouldn't oppose your taking a few night courses at the University of Houston."

"That isn't the same as going away to college. Sara and I thought we'd room together."

"Sara has to go to college because it's a stepping stone to getting a good job. I'm offering you a job that graduate students would stand in line for blocks to get."

"It's not that I don't appreciate . . ."

"You don't appreciate anything," John snapped. "That's what's wrong with your generation. You're spoiled. I've served everything up to you on a silver platter."

"Appreciate what you've taught me," Dixie said, as though uninterrupted. "You've told me what I've done and you've lined out my future for me. There's only one thing you haven't done."

"What?"

"Ask me what I want to do."

"What do you want to do?" Waco asked, afraid she'd let John prevent her from seeing him.

Nestled under the blankets, Dixie sighed. "I want to see you. Our house is like a tomb since I told my father I didn't want to be responsible for building Mayson Manor. He hasn't spoken three civil words to me.

"And school is worse," she added miserably. With the prom only ten days in the offing, it was the main topic of discussion. She'd heard through the grapevine that Chad had asked a pint-sized, freshman cheerleader. Cradle-robber. Who Chad invited didn't make any difference to her, she'd told herself.

"Is John still insisting that you go directly from school to his office?"

"Yeah. Old eagle-eye hasn't blinked, yet."

"Dixie?"

"Ummmm?"

"I finished the model house. The drywall crew won't be ready with the one in Pasadena until Friday."

"So you'll be off tomorrow and you'll be working this weekend?"

"Yes. I was thinking . . . John will be busy down on Westheimer . . . and if he thought you were at school . . ."

Dixie grinned, following the drift of his thinking. It had been so long since she'd had anything to smile about that her face felt as though it might crack.

"And the school thought I was home sick?" she suggested with glee. "We could meet somewhere?"

"Or, I could pick you up after John leaves the house."

"Better," Dixie agreed. "I'll leave my truck in the driveway. That way everyone will think I'm at home."

"Will your father call to check on you?"

"I can tell him I was asleep and didn't hear the telephone ring."

"Don't you have an answering machine?"

"Good idea. I'll record a new announcement saying I'm sick in bed and for the caller to leave their number. Uh-oh, I just thought of something. I have to have a written excuse to get back into school."

"No problem. I'll forge one for you."

Dixie chuckled. "You sound like you're an old pro at this. Did you skip school a lot?"

"Nah, Zeke never cared if I went to school." He refrained from telling her that going to school was a privilege only the wealthy could afford, as far as Zeke was concerned. His uncle wanted him at work, earning money to help pay the bills. If there had been another way to see her, he wouldn't have suggested she play hooky. Frowning, he asked, "Missing one day won't hurt your grades, will it?"

"No. Besides, I need a mental health day."

"A mental health day?" Waco chuckled. "You'll go crazy if you don't get out of there?"

"You've got the picture. Me, stark-raving mad!"

"We can't have that happen. Where would you like for me to take you?"

Dixie thought for several seconds before coming up with the perfect answer. "Galveston. Let's go to the beach."

"It's supposed to be eighty and sunny tomorrow."

"Sounds heavenly."

"Sounds dangerous to me."

"Why?"

"What's the school going to say when you show up suntanned?"

"I'll wear sun block."

"You'd better wear a swimsuit, too," he teased. "Can't have your picture plastered on the front of the newspaper for skinny-dipping on a public beach."

Blushing, she laughed softly. "Can you imagine

John picking us up at the police station? He'd be livid!"

"Don't get any bright ideas, gorgeous. He'd leave me there. Permanently."

Dixie felt her toes curl. His pet name for her never failed to cause the same response. "I'd bail you out."

"With what? Your good looks? Or do you have a purse that matches your birthday suit?"

Over the telephone lines their quiet laughter met and mingled, blending into mutual happiness. The moroseness that blighted her hours at school and the hours with John vanished with the sound of his voice. Waco's midnight call had become the bright spot in an otherwise dreary existence.

"It seems like months since I've seen you," she whispered.

"You haven't forgotten what I look like, have you?"

Dixie shut her eyes. A crystal clear image of him—tall, tanned, and handsome—lazily walking toward her in the display house instantly came to mind. Her fingers touched the ends of her hair as she imagined them splayed across the masculine hair on his chest.

"Dixie?"

"I'm here."

"For a second I thought you'd had to hang up."

"Uh-uh. I was picturing you in my mind."

"It took that long?" he mocked good-naturedly. "Should I pin a red carnation to my shirt so you'll recognize me?"

"No. I haven't forgotten what you look like—blond, blue eyes, with a dimple in the middle of your forehead—right?"

Waco groaned, then chuckled. "At least you got the dimple in the right place."

"I have a photographic memory." Her laughter broke off when she heard John climbing the steps. "Oooops, I hear footsteps. I'd better get off the phone."

"Sleep tight, gorgeous. I'll see you tomorrow—bright and early."

"Bye."

The phone had barely been returned to the nightstand when she heard a rap on her door.

"Are you on the phone?"

Feeling feisty, she faked a sleepy voice and replied, "Uh-uh, I'd squash it."

Six

"You're going to wear the carpet out," Dixie scolded herself as she anxiously darted from the front window in the dining room to the side window in the great room.

One final check in the mirror assured her that she looked anything but sick. The pastel peach top made her cheeks appear rosier than usual; the matching shorts exposed her long legs to advantage. Bending at the waist, she ran her fingers through her hair, then straightened, tossing it back to relax the curls and make it appear fuller.

She fussed with it, glancing at her watch and willing the long hand to move faster. "He'll be here."

Early, she pleaded silently, plopping her sunglasses on her nose. *Very early.*

Her heart did a little jig when she saw Waco's beat-up truck coasting down the street. Grabbing her beach bag, she hurried through the door and down the sidewalk. His vehicle had scarcely stopped before she jumped inside it.

Her heart went wild when she looked at Waco. The dreamy image she conjured up each night didn't hold a candle to how handsome Waco really was. She thought it impossible for her heart to pick up its pace, but when he shot her a slow, sexy wink, she put her hand over her heart and actually felt it pump.

"Hi." He bracketed her jaw with one hand and brushed his thumb across her bottom lip as his dark eyes drank down her image. "You look beautiful."

Dixie pressed her palm against the back of his hand, letting her eyelids slide closed for a second while she caught her breath. *He thinks I'm beautiful.* Joy, such as she'd never known, coursed through her. With him, she wasn't the ugly duckling who hadn't been invited to the prom. He made her feel beautiful.

"Thanks," she whispered, still breathless as she opened her eyes. "You do, too."

Waco chuckled and teased, "Thanks. I don't think anyone has ever told me I'm beautiful. Cute, once or twice when I was a little tyke, but never beautiful."

"The world must be full of blind people," Dixie said softly.

"Or those glasses you wear are tinted rose-colored." His hand dropped to the gear stick. Accelerating, he shifted into second and then third. "Notice anything different?"

"No noise?"

Nodding, he said, "Sunday, after I fixed the brakes, I decided to install a new exhaust system. Can't have a loud racket causing the neighbors to gawk out their windows. Somebody might snitch on you."

"I'm not worried. I've lived there my entire life, so nobody notices when I come and go."

"Good. Where I live everybody has a nose four feet long."

From their lengthy late-night telephone conversations, she should have known where he lived, but she'd never thought to ask him. As he turned south on Highway 45 toward Galveston, she did. "Do you live in an apartment?"

"A trailer park in Alvin." He glanced at her, gauging her reaction. She appeared interested, but he noted thankfully that she wasn't peering down her nose at him. Undoubtedly, he could fit his entire trailer, including the collapsible awning, into her living room. When she didn't volunteer a comment, he wondered what she thought of his gypsy lifestyle. "A home on wheels suited the here-today-gone-tomorrow way that Zeke wanted to live."

"Past tense?" she asked, hopefully. "Has he changed his mind?"

"No. We've been here less than six months and he's wistfully gazing at the highway, with maps of California spread on the kitchen table. He has itchy feet, I guess."

"What about you?"

"I want to sink roots and stay here."

Relieved to know Waco wasn't one of those here-today-gone-tomorrow carpenters her father abhorred, she said, "In a way, I sort of envy you."

"You do?"

Amused by how he raised his eyebrow skeptically, she asked, "Why so surprised?"

"Because I hated being a human tumbleweed," he replied fervently. "We've moved so often, a magazine I subscribed to three years ago in New Mexico still hasn't caught up with me!"

"But think of all the places you've been and the people you've met. I've never set foot across the Texas border. From what I have seen, Texas could be an island!"

Waco laughed and reassured her. "It isn't. What's that saying? If God owned heaven and Texas, he'd rent out heaven and live in Texas. Whoever coined that saying must have been to the places where I lived."

"That bad?"

"Not good," Waco replied dismissively. He pointed to the bridge arching over Galveston Bay. "Any preference when it comes to beaches?"

Dixie deliberated her options for several seconds. Stuart Beach, on the east end of the island, had carnival rides and concession stands. The west end of the island would be practically deserted this time of year. Miles and miles of beach, with only the sea gulls to distract them from each other. The choice of people versus privacy made the decision easy. "The west end, near Pocket Beach."

"You must be a mind reader." When he came to the seawall, that had been built shortly after the Great Hurricane of 1903, he turned right. "The surf is calm, but we'll have to be careful of the undertow."

As though she could read his mind, she knew exactly what he meant as his eyes roamed from her face, across the bodice of her blouse, down her slender legs. Dixie rubbed her palms across her bare knees, glorying in the exquisite feel of anticipation and excitement as they tingled and danced down her spine; they made her feel alive, vivacious, effervescent.

Innocuous banter flowed between them, but her awareness of him made the things unsaid, the silent undercurrent that could be dangerous.

Kissless days had gone between the afternoon they'd met and today. But at night, as she lay awake waiting for his phone call, Dixie had thought about little else.

Often, during the short drive to the beach, her eyes had lingered hungrily on his lips; she'd felt his eyes on her, but she'd carefully refrained from returning his gaze. He'd know too much if she allowed him to see into her soul—the yearning, the frustration, the desire to be held in his arms with his lips slanted across her mouth.

"Someday I'll own a house on the beach," Waco said, pointing to a large, blue-grey, two-storied home perched on stilts. He made a sharp left off the paved highway onto a sandy ribbon of road. He drove past several tiers of pastel-colored houses, each built higher than the one in front of it, until they'd reached the ones overlooking the gulf, most of which were shuttered. "Pick out the one you like best."

Hunching forward, Dixie looked through the

windshield's greenish sun-strip. "There—the one at the end, secluded from the others."

"ESP, again?"

"Great minds have similar thoughts?"

Waco smiled at her, glad she wanted to be on a deserted strip of beach with him. "It's for sale," he observed, parking next to the realtor's sign. "Let's use their boardwalk to cross the dunes."

"Private. No trespassing," she read, gesturing to the warped sign posted on the cross-over. Her nose wrinkled as she cast him an impish grin. "But then again, you could be a prospective buyer."

"Could be," he agreed, pocketing his keys. "I'd qualify for a no-money-down-and-fifty-year-no-interest-loan."

Too anxious to wait while he shouldered his door open, Dixie gathered her beach bag and dismounted. She inhaled, invigorated by the smell of saltwater. The wind blew skeins of russet red curls across her face. She wished she'd brought a rubber band until she noticed Waco staring transfixed as the threads of hair caught in her lashes. His hand reached for her face, hung suspended in midair for a tense moment, then turned palm upwards, for her to take his hand.

Hand-holding should be such a simple thing, she mused, as she placed her hand in his. But the roughness of his skin abraded against the soft pads of her fingers; his strong fingers twined their fingers together until she felt the calluses on his palm. The light tug on her hand seemed connected directly to her heart.

Her yearning quadrupled tenfold.

"Wait a sec," he said after a thoughtful pause. "There's a beach blanket and a cooler in the bed of the truck." Still holding her hand, he picked what looked like a bedroll from the back of the truck. "I brought sun block, too, just in case you forgot."

"I didn't. Along with a year's supply of sun cream, I brought enough food to feed an army." She grinned up at him. "Between what the two of us brought, we could camp out for weeks."

Once they'd crossed the boardwalk over the undulating dunes covered with sea oats, and spread his crazy-patch quilt on the sand, Dixie wondered how to get Waco to make the first move. With miles of water in front of them, long stretches of empty beach on each side of them, and empty vacation homes behind the dunes, they were isolated in privacy.

As if by mutual consent, they kicked off their sandals and sat on the blanket, facing the waves of blue-grey water that rhythmically washed the sand. Close, she thought, measuring the inches between them, but not close enough. Accidentally on purpose, she spilled the contents of her beach bag, and when he bent forward to see what she'd brought, their shoulders touched.

Their eyes met—his filled with curiosity, and hers with wonder.

Waco cleared his throat and hesitated. "Wanna go for a swim?"

"I'm not hot enough yet to go swimming." Her

eyes followed the tip of his tongue as he moistened his lips. "We could . . . uh, search for seashells?"

"Or build sand castles?" he suggested. He gave in to the urge he'd had earlier and captured an errant strand of hair that had woven between her lashes; it entangled between the webs of his fingers, causing her to tilt her head to one side. Slowly, so as to not harm a hair on her head, he rested the side of his hand on her bare shoulder while he untangled the strands of silk from his fingers. What should have been a simple task grew complicated when he accidentally brushed the back of his hand across the fullness of her breast. He heard her draw a deep breath, and realized his own lungs were starved for oxygen. How long had he been holding his breath without realizing it? He gulped in air, broke eye contact, and began searching the littered coverlet for a means of quieting the downward surge of blood rushing to his loins. "Or play cards?"

"Strip poker?" The risqué suggestion slipped between her lips before she could halt it. Couldn't help it, she excused silently. Without his hand lingering, she felt her nipple tighten. Slightly embarrassed by her boldness and her body's response to his slightest touch, she dropped her eyes and nibbled her lower lip. "I have to warn you. I'm wearing my swimsuit under my clothes."

"That makes you a four-to-three odds-on favorite, not including your sandals or my shoes."

"Shoes count," she blurted, slipping her toes into the leather straps.

Suddenly fearful he'd take her up on her outlandish suggestion, she picked up the deck of cards and removed the rubber band that bound them. Holding her shaky hands ten inches apart, she attempted to fan the cards from one hand to the other. She would have caught them, should have caught them, since she'd done this trick hundreds of times, but she chose the wrong time to glance up at him. His lopsided grin utterly destroyed her concentration. Cards catapulted everywhere.

"Fifty-two pick-up is the name of the game," he said, then recited the rule, "The person who gets the fewest cards pays a forfeit."

Welcoming a challenge that would take her mind off the myriad sensations he caused, Dixie dropped on all fours and began collecting cards.

"Mine," she claimed, when they both grabbed for the same big pile.

While she tugged at the corners, his large hand encircled the center. He settled the dispute by pinching his thumb and fingers together; the pasteboards flew into the air, landing off the coverlet.

"Foul—ten-yard penalty!" she whooped, pushing her shoulder squarely against the center of his chest to knock him backward as she scrambled on hands and knees after them.

Laughing, Waco landed on his backside, but grabbed her ankle. "Twenty-five-yard penalty for the illegal body block!"

"No holding!" Her fingers were within inches of snagging them. In her haste to get the biggest pile, she'd sprawled across most of the remaining cards. "Let go or you'll make me kick you!"

"No kicking." She squealed as he tunneled in the sand under her hips and flipped her over, simultaneously releasing her ankle. "No burying them, either!"

"Got 'em!" she crowed as her arms circled the pile like Indians surrounding a wagon train. "These are mine!"

He picked up the corner of the blanket; the remaining cards slid into a haphazard pile that appeared to be more than half the deck.

"Yeah, but I've got more than you do," he gloated, giving her leg a little love-pat. "Count and weep, sweetheart."

"You'll be the one doing the bawling," she boasted, certain she'd won. Rolling to her side in the sand, she counted, "Two, four, six . . ."

"Hey," Waco protested, "you're putting the cards down one at a time. No counting by twos."

"Okay." She shot him a cheeky grin. "Five, ten, fifteen."

"Ten, twenty, thirty," he countered, laughing with her.

"Three hundred, four hundred . . ."

Louder, Waco counted, "Four thousand, five thousand . . ."

"Five million, six million . . ." she shouted.

With mock ferocity, he countered, "Six billion, seven billion . . ."

"Seven trillion, eight trillion . . .

"Wait a minute," Dixie protested as she sat up,

her arms forming an X as she crossed them and joked, "We're beginning to sound like legislators cutting the federal budget."

"You're right," he agreed with a chuckle. "Let's be fair. I'm willing to compromise."

"Now you are sounding like a politician," she groaned, holding up her stack for him to see. "I don't want to be compromised, thank-you-very-kindly. I won. Fair and square."

"With that little-bitty pile." He shook his head. "No way. You lost. You owe me a forfeit."

Confident she had the most cards, she handed hers to him. "You count mine and I'll count that measly stack you have."

"Don't have to," Waco said with a wicked grin. Quicker than she could skitter across the sand to stop him, he shuffled the stacks together. "They're all mine!"

"That was a rotten trick, Waco Stone." With him on his knees holding the deck over his head like a trophy, and her standing over him, she could easily have attempted to snatch the cards. Only the daredevil twinkle she saw in his eyes prevented her from doing what he expected. She lifted one shoulder, as though winning didn't matter to her. "Too bad. Guess you'll never be able to prove that you won. No forfeit prize for you."

His arm dropped to his side and he hung his head in repentance. "Damn, I really wanted to kiss you, too."

"Too?"

"T-w-o," he spelled. She was an innocent, but

he wasn't. He'd seen the hungry look in her eyes during the drive to Galveston, when she thought he was concentrating on the road. His suspicions were confirmed when he saw her toes curl into the sand. Refusing to look up at her, he tormented, "That's how many it takes to kiss."

Not bothering to hide her grin, but fully aware of his trying to pull another hoax on her, she pretended true remorse by sighing, "Pity."

"Yeah."

"Maybe next time you won't be so greedy."

"And let you win?" He lifted his face; his eyes were full of mirth. "My forfeit would have been a kiss?"

Yes, she thought, looking at his ill-concealed smirk. Not for a zillion cards would she admit it. "No."

"No?"

"No." Her imagination whirred into top speed. What would have been as good or better than a kiss? "I was going to make you dust the sand off me." She had the pleasure of watching his throat constrict. "With your tongue."

Quicker than a seagull nose-diving for a shrimp, he snagged his arm around her waist, dropping the cards. As he rose to his feet, he lifted her off the sand. Playfully, he dusted her rear end, then the backs of her bare thighs.

"Forfeiture rendered, ma'am, minus the grit in my spit."

With her arms she hugged his shoulder to keep her balance, and she wiggled against him with

each swipe. "Should I feel honor-bound to reciprocate?"

"That would be nice."

"Kisses should be better than just nice," she
said, prolonging the ecstasy of slowly gliding down
the length of him until her toes touched the coverlet. "They should be . . ."

He took the words right out of her mouth by
kissing her, fiercely, passionately, with wild aban-
don. What she'd thought, he did. What little sand
had been left on her clothing was shaken free as
his hands roamed down her spine, over the flare
of her hips, until she pressed tightly against him.

Only the inquisitive gulls hopping along the
frothy water's edge observed the first time Dixie
felt a man intentionally cup the underside of her
breast, then ever-so-lightly circle her nipple until
it hardened beneath his touch.

While her tongue mimicked the probing of his,
he began unbuttoning her blouse, promising himself that just touching her through her swimsuit
would be enough to satisfy him.

Then, he'd have to stop.

Dixie is a good woman, he reminded himself,
not the type who'd enjoy a lusty romp on a beach
in broad daylight.

He'd have to stop.

Soon.

As her shirttail parted and he gained access to
her bare midriff, his determination to respect her
slipped a notch. Her skin felt like satin, sleek and
warm, almost hot against his hand. Only a tiny,

tiny pull of a drawstring knotted at the back of her suit was between him and near sublimity.

He suckled the tip of her tongue, drawing her inside of him, then followed her retreat, deep into the honeyed recesses of her mouth.

One little tug, he thought, tempted, very tempted to go beyond his self-imposed limit.

Nothing wrong with light petting, he tried to assure himself.

Or heavy petting. Or going all the way. Wrong? Quite the opposite. Having sex with her would be fantastic. Feeling himself grow hard as the hickory handle on his favorite hammer, he imagined those long legs of hers wrapped around his waist, holding him deep inside her where no other man had been.

Aware he'd halfway convinced himself to seduce her, he broke off the kiss, turned and stalked away from her.

Bewildered, not being able to read his mind as she'd claimed, Dixie called after him. "Waco?"

"I'll be back in a minute. Stay there."

His walk changed to a lope, then a run. Straight for the water? He leaped over the first three waves; he lunged into the fourth. Why had he kissed her, fondled her, and taken off like a scalded dog? What had she done wrong? She must have done something drastically wrong!

For several seconds, she couldn't see him. When those seconds stretched beyond a minute and she still didn't see him, she raced to the edge of the water. The sand felt hot on the soles of her feet, until she splashed into the saltwater.

Damn, this water is freezing!

As his head popped from beneath the water's surface, it dawned on her why he'd taken his running leap into the frigid gulf.

Was this mad dash into the gulf the equivalent of a cold shower?

"Was he as hot and bothered as I was?" she whispered in awe, wondering why he'd stopped.

He'd touched her breast. For an instant, she worried that they were too small, that she was too flat. But she hadn't flinched away from him; she'd melted closer than base coat on bare wood. She'd wanted him to touch her. If it hadn't been so damned awkward, she'd have reached back and untied the top of her suit.

Her brow wrinkled into a deep scowl. Wasn't it supposed to be the woman's prerogative to say, "No, no, no . . . or go, go, go!"

We're going to have to talk about this, she decided emphatically. Hands on her hips, toe tapping, splashing droplets of water on her ankles, she waited impatiently for him to wade back to shore.

"Why'd you run off like that?" she demanded without preamble. "The way you hot-lapped off the beach, I thought you were swimming to Florida. Underwater!"

Perplexed by her reaction, Waco thought about a reply as he peeled off his shirt. "Are you mad?"

"Your darned-tootin' I'm mad. You stayed under for ten minutes. I thought you were drowning."

He grinned, pleased to know she cared enough to be worried. Nobody else did, or had during his entire life.

"Don't laugh at me," she warned, wanting to pelt him in the arm. "You scared me."

"I'm not laughing. I promise." He folded his soggy shirt, wrung it out, and shook it in the wind. "I didn't mean to scare you."

"Why did you run off?"

"Because I needed to cool off," he stated simply.

While he'd been submerged, shouting salty expletives at Neptune, he'd come to the profound conclusion that he'd done the *right* thing. In fact, while he'd clenched his teeth to keep them from chattering, he'd felt damned proud of himself.

"Isn't the woman the one who says when to stop?"

"Sometimes, yes, and sometimes, no."

"Could you be a little more explicit, please?"

Waco tried to think of an analogy to fit the situation, but couldn't think of one. Little wonder, he mused, watching the breeze blow her shirt open and shut was enough to distract a saint, which he wasn't by any means.

He flopped his damp shirt over his shoulder, took her hand, and ambled down the beach. "A person has to do what they can live with."

"Could you be a little more specific?"

"A blunt answer?"

"Yes!"

"Okay." He stopped, took her by the shoulders and looked her in the eyes. "I'd feel guilty as hell if I'd thrown you down on the blanket and screwed your brains out. Blunt enough?"

Dixie felt her cheeks turn flaming red. Instinctively, she wanted to duck her head, but her curiosity refused to let her break eye contact. "Is that what you wanted to do?"

"It's what I would have done a year ago, without giving a damn about how the woman felt."

"You'd have . . ." She stumbled over the phrase he'd used and substituted, "Made love to me?"

"I'd have tried my damnedest."

"So what stopped you today?"

"Respect."

"For me?"

"And me. Both of us." His hands slid up her neck until they framed her face. "You're special, Dixie. And you make me feel special, too. When I'm just talking to you on the phone, I forget that I'm Mr. Nobody from Nowhere, Texas."

"Don't talk that way about yourself."

"It's the truth."

"Was maybe . . . I didn't know you then."

"You wouldn't have wanted to." He took a deep breath, when he spoke his voice was pulled from deep in his gut. "I grew up hellbent on proving to the world that my parents were right—that I wasn't worth a shit—pardon my language."

His thumbs smoothed the twin lines that formed between her brows. She wasn't offended by his language, only by what had been done to him. She held his wrists, feeling his life's blood pumping through him.

"But you'd changed, before I met you," she said, not wanting to take credit for the man he'd become.

"Only my work ethic." He pinched the bridge of his nose between his thumb and forefinger as he tried to think of a way to make her understand. "My respectability is like a thin veneer of polished oak laminated over cheap pressboard. It scares the hell out of me to know that at any minute the veneer could crack and you'll see the real me."

"You need to look at yourself through my eyes. I see you for what you are, Waco. Solid oak, through and through."

"Maybe." He paused in dubious thought; his hands dropped to his sides. A carpenter by trade, he knew a good veneer could fool even the most experienced eye. Slowly, thoughtfully, he began walking, following the line of flotsam that had washed up on the beach. "Maybe."

His vulnerability made her heart ache for him. She wanted to reach out and touch him, but she kept her hands to herself. The explosive chemistry between them could reignite instantaneously. Much as she needed his kisses to reaffirm her newfound femininity, he needed her to bolster his flagging confidence.

"No maybes between you and me," she stated unequivocally. "You're a good man, Waco Stone." Apologies didn't come any easier for her than they did for her father, but she felt compelled to give him one. She'd castigated him when he'd only wanted to do right by her. Hanging her head, she said sincerely, "I'm sorry for getting mad at you. You were right to stop us."

"Apology accepted." He draped his arm over her shoulders and hugged her. "Someday, I'll make you proud of me. Maybe then, I won't have these hang-ups about my past."

"No maybes," she said, looping her arm around his waist. "The best is yet to come."

Seven

"Where were you today?"

By the skin of her teeth, Dixie had made it home and safely in her bedroom, before her father arrived. Her dreamy thoughts of Waco and their day at the beach were shattered. She peeked from under the sheet to where he stood at her doorway. He wasn't red-faced, and the vein on his forehead wasn't throbbing; that was a good sign. Did he know for certain she'd skipped school? As she watched him jerk his tie loose, she decided, he must.

"At the beach." Guilt set her lightly sunburned cheeks aflame. "How'd you find out?"

"The school's attendance office called me when they got a recording here."

As John strolled to her bedside, she heard his silk tie slide from beneath his starched shirt collar. Why wasn't he yelling? She scooted her legs over when he sat on the corner of her bed. Confused by his calmness, Dixie wasn't certain if she was going to get a lecture or catch holy hell.

"Miss Leicht said the school board ought to

cancel classes until after the prom—for lack of student interest."

"They might as well," she agreed with a nervous giggle. "Nobody's learning anything."

"Why didn't you tell me it was Senior Skip Day?"

Because it wasn't, she replied silently, letting the lace-trimmed sheet drop below her neck. Sara said the whole class planned on walking out Friday, the day before the prom. Since it appeared as though he wasn't upset, Dixie decided to stick closely to the truth.

"That's Friday."

Mild censorship in his eyes forewarned her that he was displeased, but not irate. "You aren't going to the prom, so you took off today?"

"I don't need a final dress fitting or a hair appointment on Friday," glibly tripped off her tongue.

"You could have had a date."

"Chad Armstrong?" While he nodded, she pushed up until her back leaned against the walnut headboard. "He invited a *freshman*."

"Is that a cradle-robber tone I hear in your voice?" he asked, apparently amused.

Glad they were off the subject of her skipping school, she twisted her mouth into a wry grin. "At the last class meeting, one of the girls made a motion to only let seniors attend the Senior Prom. That sounded logical to the females, but the guys hissed and booed the idea."

"I could arrange for someone else to take you."

"Who?"

"There are a couple of men at the office who'd be suitable."

"Blake Jergins? Paul Getz? They're single, but ancient!" She rolled her eyes disparagingly at the ceiling. "Talk about robbing the cradle."

"Kate mentioned that we need a mail clerk . . ."

"Great, Dad. I can just hear the interview. You're how old? Oh, and by the way, your first duty is to escort my gruesome daughter to her Senior Prom." She slapped both palms into the thick coverlet. "Give it a rest, would you? I won't croak if I don't have a date."

"Every girl thinks it's a life-and-death matter. You can tell me that it doesn't make any difference whether you go or not, but I know better." Exasperation creased his forehead. "Why won't you stop being mule-headed and let me make some arrangements?"

While John's voice grew louder and louder, Dixie recalled how Waco believed no one cared about him. She had the opposite problem: John cared too much. He bullied and coerced her until he drove her batty, but only because he did care.

"Neighhhh . . ." was her best mule-braying imitation.

Her mulish reply halted John's tirade, dead cold. "Is that all you have to say? Nay!"

She watched his grey eyebrows raise. Winning a fight was inbred in both of them; he couldn't allow her to have the last word and she was not going to do what he wanted. With thoughts of

Waco uppermost in her mind, a date to the prom had lost significance.

"Thank you for caring, but no thanks," she pacified.

His brows gradually lowered as he gave her a thoughtful look. He'd lost. Resignation to that fact could be seen in his eyes.

He neatly folded the tie he'd been holding in his hands, rose to his feet, and started toward the door. After a couple of steps, he said, "Don't you skip school on Friday, young lady, or you'll have to reckon with me. I expect you out of bed, downstairs cooking dinner in no more than ten minutes."

"You simply have to skip school on Friday," Sara said, with a pout, adding her usual flair for drama. She'd arrived shortly after dinner to drop off. Dixie's homework and tell her the latest gossip. "I made a hair appointment with Linda for you right after mine."

"I'll call and cancel it."

"She's been turning down appointments left and right. She'll kill you!"

"She'll have to get in line," Dixie commented drolly. "Dad will kill me if I do skip. Besides, why should I skip school to have my hair fixed when I'm not going to the dance?"

"Not going?" The appalled expression on her face was almost comical to Dixie. "You're a senior. You don't have to have a date to go."

Dixie gave her a bland look. Her friend couldn't

comprehend how humiliated she felt at not having a date. Surely, out of a hundred boys in the class, one of them should consider her company worthy of a corsage. Some of girls had several guys ask them. Why couldn't one of those rejects have come to her? Before she'd met Waco, she'd have gratefully accepted an invitation from the Elephant Man!

"You make it sound as though I'm committing a mortal sin," Dixie replied drily.

"It *would* be sinful to miss your Senior Prom."

"God will forgive me," Dixie predicted with complete faith. "Dad did, when I refused to let him buy me a date."

"I won't! I can understand why you don't want your father to fix you up, but you went stag last year and had a good time."

"Yeah, a blast." Dixie plucked a loose thread on her bedspread. "Do you know how many streamers of crepe paper were strung on the south end of the gym? Eight-hundred-fifty-seven. I counted them while you were dancing with Todd."

"Only because you didn't dance with him."

Dixie groaned loudly. "Sara, I'm six inches taller than he is. The only reason he asked me to dance is because you had your sharp elbow stuck between his third and fourth rib."

"You're going," Sara announced, flouncing over to Dixie's closet. "The prom is like . . . a rite of passage, from being a child to being a woman. Not going to it would be like not attending graduation. Dammit, I won't let you miss it!" She reached back to the far recesses of Dixie's closet and pulled out a plastic garment sack that contained a collection of evening dresses. "You can wear your homecoming dress from last year. Nobody'll remember it."

In a tone as dry as seasoned wood, Dixie replied, "With good reason. I look like a scarecrow in black chiffon."

"You looked sophisticated," Sara corrected, flattering Dixie shamelessly. "Linda can fix your hair up, with a few kiss-curls dangling by your ears, and I'll let you borrow my rhinestone earrings. You'll look terrific!"

Dixie swung her legs off the bed, removed the garment bag from Sara's fingers and returned it to where it belonged. "Arguing with you is pointless."

"Tell me that you honestly and sincerely don't want to go to the prom and I'll shut up."

"I honestly and sincerely don't want to go to the Senior Prom." Dixie repeated the words. They lacked conviction. Where was the heady confidence she'd felt while she'd been with Waco? Less than three hours ago, she'd felt beautiful and sexy. She could have filled those bra cups of that strapless evening dress without a padded bra! Now, as she glowered at it, she felt as ugly and gawky as she had the day before she'd met Waco.

Turning up her pert nose, Sara declared, "That fish-tale don't swim. You want to go. Admit it!"

"Okay, you're right." Dixie shoved her fingers in her back pocket and glared at her big feet. "The

Senior Prom is the biggest dance of the year. I'd be abnormal if I didn't want to go."

Deeply sorry for her friend, Sara looked crest-fallen. "Maybe it's my fault Chad didn't invite you."

"How could it be your fault?"

"He asked that underdeveloped twelve-year-old to the prom while she helped him fix a flat tire," Sara confided. "Maybe your muffler idea would have worked."

"Brains and brawn won out over simpering and flirting?" Giggling at Sara's melancholy face, Dixie gave her a sisterly hug. Chad's not being a complete nincompoop when it came to choosing a date, delighted her. There was hope for the male species when a few of them, like Waco, picked brains and personality over beauty and bust size.

"That's the exception that proves the rule," Sara replied, relentless in her belief that every man wanted a woman who would make him believe he was Sylvester Stallone's closest rival. "Trust me, the eyelashes fluttering created enough hot air to inflate every male ego to the size of the Goodyear blimp."

"Makes me want to trade my mascara for a paper of pins," Dixie said in a tone that warned Sara to drop the subject.

"Okay, no more lectures on trapping the elusive male. Hunting season is over. The trophy bucks have been tagged. But, that doesn't mean you can't go to the dance."

"I'll tell you what," Dixie arbitrated, "you talk

Dad into letting me skip school Friday and I'll have Linda fix my hair. That way, if I do change my mind at the last minute and decide to go, all I have to do is slip into my dress."

Sara looked stricken at the idea of clashing with John, but thoughtfully nodded her head in agreement. With grave solemnness she trekked to the door, and said, "If he drills holes through me with his eyes, I hereby bequeath my date to the prom to you."

"He likes you," Dixie reassured, following her into the hall, planning on eavesdropping at the top the stairs. "And he wants me to go to the prom, too. I just can't ask because he warned me not to think about taking another day off."

"You shouldn't have played sick today," Sara scolded.

Smiling, Dixie kept her secret. Later, much later, she'd tell Sara about Waco. For now, the thrill of having a clandestine relationship with an older man would be spoiled if she shared her reason for not being at school.

"Wish me luck," Sara bade, lightly treading down the steps. "I'll need it."

Dixie sank to her heels and peered through the rails of the balustrade. Feeling somewhat cowardly, she offered, "Do you want me to ask him?"

"He'd say no to you." She pointed her finger at Dixie, cocked her thumb as though she held a six-shooter, and whispered, "If you don't go . . . *pow-eee.*"

Dixie grinned when Sara blew imaginary smoke

from her blazing pistol. She came close to promising she'd go, but she still had reservations. A day spent helping Sara fuss over her dress, hair and makeup was part of being her friend; a night spent gawking at blue-and-gold streamers while Sara mooned over Todd, was above and beyond friendship.

The problem is, Dixie mused, I can't have what I want.

In her dreams, she walked into the dance on Waco's arm. Unfortunately, there were mile-high barriers between fantasy and reality. She couldn't justify a dance being more important than his contract with Texas Proud. How could she persuade Waco? And if she could, how could she prevent John from passing a brick when Waco arrived at the door?

She could hear herself saying casually, "Oh, by the way Dad, I wouldn't go with the mail clerk you wanted to hire, but I just happened to bump into Waco Stone, so I invited him. You don't mind, do you?"

Mind? He'd think she'd lost hers. Her fingers tightened their hold on the rails.

After her father fired Waco and booted him off the front porch, she'd be making some mighty tall explanations. Compared to the questions her father would ask, the Spanish Inquisition would be like a Fourth of July celebration.

Disheartened, Dixie considered her final option: going alone. Again.

It isn't fair, she silently denounced. One man in

the world thought she was special, but he was unsuitable to take her to the most important event in her life. And there wasn't a damned thing she could do about it. It just wasn't fair.

"Fair?" John boomed loudly. "Don't tell me it isn't fair for Dixie to have to go to school on Senior Skip Day!"

"But it isn't," Sara wailed on Dixie's behalf. "I think you're the meanest father in town!"

A sharp pang of guilt, caused by asking Sara to do her dirty work, prodded Dixie from her hiding place. She rushed down the steps, into her father's study. She collided with Sara, who'd made a rash accusation and was attempting to bolt from the room before her father climbed across his desk and shook her by the scruff of the neck.

"Don't yell at Sara," Dixie snapped, wrapping one arm protectively around her friend's shoulder. "You act like missing a couple of days of school is a federal crime."

"Watch your mouth or you'll be hanging yourself with your own tongue," he bellowed, pushing his chair back from the desk.

"I'm making straight A's. Missing a couple of days of class won't drop my grades."

John roared his frustration, "Go ahead! Skip school! Get kicked out before graduation! See if I care!"

Equally annoyed, but hurt by hearing him imply he didn't care about her, Dixie lowered her voice to a sarcastic whisper, "Thank you. C'mon Sara, I'll walk you home."

Once they were outside, Sara looked up at her and said, "You can sleep over at my house if you want to. Maybe your father will cool off by morning."

"I shouldn't have sent you to talk to him. I'm sorry." She pushed back the branches of the hedge that separated their yards. "I can't seem to do anything lately that doesn't displease him."

"Guess I'm not the only one who doesn't know about the good-looking guy you went to the beach with today, huh?"

Startled, Dixie audibly gasped. "Who told you?"

"A little bird," Sara heckled, cawing and flapping her arms like a seagull and circling Dixie.

"Shhhhh! That's not funny."

"You're having a boyfriend and not telling me the *gritty* details isn't funny, either."

Dixie glanced over her shoulder to see if her father was standing on the porch or watching them out of the dining room window. "Why didn't you ask me about him while we were up in my room?"

"Because I thought you'd tell me you invited him to the prom. That's why I picked the black dress and said that nobody would remember it. I meant him."

"He isn't a nobody," Dixie defended overly sensitive. "He's somebody special."

"So? Why haven't you invited Mr. Somebody Special to the prom?"

"He works for my father," she explained in a hushed tone.

Sara groaned as though she'd been stabbed. "You can't bring one of those guys to the dance."

"What do you mean . . . those guys? He's perfectly respectable. You sound like a snob!"

"I am not a snob!" On second thought, she shrugged and added, "Maybe I am. I just can't see you dating one of those loud-mouthed guys that swagger into the bakery like they built the place."

"Maybe they did," Dixie argued, pointing out the flaw in Sara's logic.

"Maybe, but they don't own it. That's the difference between you and them."

"I suppose you think it would be okay for me to bring a guy to the prom who wears a white collar and tie and works in Dad's office?"

"Yeah," Sara agreed, her blond curly locks bobbing as she nodded her head. "A junior-executive type, like Chad will be when he graduates from college. Your mystery man probably dropped out of grade school."

"No, he didn't."

"Where'd he graduate from? Harris County Juvenile Center?"

"That's ugly, Sara. All the men who work in the trades aren't delinquents."

"Was yours?"

Dixie bowed her head, reluctant to lie but not wanting to divulge what Waco had told her. He'd admitted to being a hell-raiser. He'd changed. As biased as Sara was, she wouldn't believe it.

"Being valedictorian of his class didn't come up

in our conversation," she answered drily. "Who cares?"

"You should."

"I don't." Dixie stopped at the foot of the front porch steps. "He's a nice guy."

"Yeah, well, you know what they say about nice guys coming in last. Last place would probably be a move up for him."

"How can you say that?" Dixie wanted to shake Sara until her teeth rattled. "You haven't even met him?"

"Your dad hired him. What would he say?"

"Dad has this silly rule about men who work for him even glancing in my direction. I can't ask Waco to the prom because Dad would fire him."

"Good for him." Sara slapped her forehead in disgust and mumbled, "God, I can't believe your father and I finally agree on something."

"I can't either." Dixie sighed heavily. "I'd better go home before he comes looking for me."

"Dixie?"

"Yeah?"

Confusion plainly written on her scrubbed face, Sara asked, "Aside from sex, isn't admiration and respect the biggest part of loving a guy? You know what I mean? Don't you have to look up to him?"

"While you're busy looking up at Todd, does that mean he's looking down his nose at you? The same way you look down on Waco?"

Selectively listening to only what pertained to her, Sara replied, "Todd isn't better than me. He's smarter than I am, but my family has more money than his family."

"You missed my point."

"What? That I shouldn't look up to Todd?"

"That you shouldn't feel inferior to Todd or superior to Waco."

Sara mounted a couple of steps until she stood taller than Dixie. "At least I'm not ashamed to be seen with Todd."

"Are you implying that I am ashamed to be seen with Waco?"

Retreating to the porch, Sara hissed, "Yes. Otherwise, you wouldn't be sneaking around, keeping him a big secret. I think he's a bad influence on you."

Infuriated, Dixie started up the steps. Sara darted inside her house.

"Wait a minute!"

The front door slammed; she heard the deadbolt lock slide into place. Typical Sara stunt, Dixie thought, stomping down the steps. Since she'd been old enough to walk, any time they had a disagreement Sara would grab her toys, run inside her house, and lock the door.

Right or wrong, Sara's parting shots never failed to nick Dixie's conscience.

"I am not ashamed of Waco and he isn't a bad influence!" she stated steadfastly.

Shoulders squared, she tromped back to her house. Snob! Just because Waco wasn't born and raised in Pearwood and earned his living with his hands, that didn't make him a low-life. They weren't sneaking around by choice. Circumstances beyond their control prevented them from being seen together. She didn't make the damned rules! And as long as she lived under her father's roof, she didn't have any choice but to follow them.

She swung open the screen door, practically tearing it off its hinges, and barged through the front door.

"I'm going up to my room to do my homework," she called to her father, mentally daring him to reprimand her for going with Sara to the beauty parlor on Friday.

"Night," came from his den.

As she climbed the steps, thoroughly peeved at Sara, she spitefully wished Linda would fry Sara's blond locks until they frizzled. Better yet, until they fell out. Todd would take one look at Sara's chrome-dome and she'd be stuck at home on prom night, too.

She entered her bedroom and crossed to the desk where Sara had placed her catch-up assignments. The taste of sour grapes on her tongue caused her to swallow her anger. Sara's hair falling out and missing the prom would break her heart. She wouldn't wish that on her worst enemy.

Slumping into the desk chair, she propped her feet up on her desk and tilted the chair on its back legs. Closing her eyes, she pictured Waco standing ankle-deep in seawater, with the sun highlighting blue streaks in his dark hair. He was smiling at her, telling her how good she made him feel about himself.

Then, she recalled the little things he'd told her about his background that validated Sara's accusations. He'd openly admitted to being a hell-raiser and dropping out of school. Was it his fault that his parents were irresponsible? Or that his uncle had put Waco to work to help pay the bills? Those weren't excuses; they were valid reasons for his behavior.

The front legs of the chair thudded into the carpet as the phone ringing interrupted her thoughts. She scrambled across the bed to reach it before the second ring.

"Hello?"

"How's the prettiest woman in Texas?"

Recognizing the rough timbre of Waco's voice, Dixie scrunched the pillow under her head, rolled over and stared up at the ceiling. "Better, now that you called."

"Same here, sweetheart. I called before midnight because I forgot to write your note for the attendance office. Do you want me to put it in your mailbox?"

"The office called Dad at work."

"Jeez, Dixie, I guess I shouldn't have asked you to take off with me today." Waco paused, mentally kicking himself for getting Dixie into trouble. "I guess I'm a bad influence on you, huh?"

Dixie frowned. His voicing Sara's opinion distressed her. "You don't really believe that, do you?"

"I don't want to believe it."

"I don't believe it," she said softly, but with

strong conviction. "Today was one of the best days of my life. You made me laugh so often my cheeks are sore."

"Maybe I should give up carpentry work and audition for a stand-up comedy job?"

"That, or a riverboat gambler. You have phenomenal luck at gin rummy. It's a good thing I didn't play strip poker with you."

"You would only have lost one hand. From then on I'd have been too distracted to concentrate on the cards." Waco chuckled, knowing her cheeks had turned fire-engine red. "I'd have sunburned buns."

"Uh-uh." Dixie gave a wicked little chuckle. "I had an extra bottle of sun block."

Waco adjusted his jeans at the thought of her applying lotion to his backside. As it was, with her just massaging lotion on his shoulders, he'd spent half the day running back and forth from the frigid water to the beach towel.

"Waco?"

"Yeah?"

"I did have a great time today."

"It was worth getting into trouble at school?"

"And here at home."

"You didn't tell me. Did John raise hell?"

"Let's say he wasn't pleased with his one and only daughter. He left scratch marks on the ceiling when Sara asked him if I could take off with her Friday . . . Senior Skip Day." She paused, hesitant to talk about the prom. "The prom is Saturday night."

An unsettling quiet fell between them.

Dixie hesitated, too ashamed to tell him no one had asked her to the prom.

Jealousy prevented Waco from asking the name of the snot-nosed kid that would be her escort.

"I guess you'll be busy both Friday and Saturday night," was the closest he'd let himself come to asking for specific information. She'd probably accepted the date long before he'd met her, he rationalized silently. "Now I won't mind working until after dark."

"I wish you were going with me to the prom," was as close as she could come to saying she'd rather be with him than home alone.

"Yeah, well, I'd be like a square peg in a round hole."

"You'd look fantastic in a black tuxedo. I'd have to carry a fly swatter to keep the pesky girls away from you."

Flattered, he promised, "Someday I'll rent one and take you someplace special."

"It's a date," she readily agreed happily.

"Any chance we could get together Sunday?"

Dixie nibbled on her bottom lip. Sunday was the only day of the week her father stayed home. It would be tricky, but she'd think of an excuse to get out of the house.

"Sure. What do you have in mind?"

"A movie. Maybe a pizza, if you can get away from the house that long."

Drawing a deep breath to steel her nerves, Dixie asked, "Would you mind if we doubled?"

"With who?"

"Sara—the friend I told you about—I'd like for her to meet you."

After a short pause, during which he weighed and measured the risk of their seeing each other becoming neighborhood gossip, he said, "I'd like to meet Sara, but doubling might not be a good idea. She might slip and mention it to her parents, who might say something to your father."

"I hate sneaking around as though we're doing something wrong," Dixie complained. "Sara has the mistaken notion that I'm ashamed to be seen with you."

Doubting his worthiness, he had to ask, "You aren't, are you?"

"Of course not!"

"Then don't worry about what Sara thinks. You and I know your father's policy is the only thing that keeps you from being seen with me. Frankly, I felt like Judas when I picked up my paycheck."

"You haven't betrayed him." Her scowl inverted into a saucy grin. Chuckling, she added, "Inadvertently he's financing our dates. Isn't that ironic?"

"More like a weird form of poetic justice?"

"Where good is properly rewarded and evil is punished, " Dixie said, reciting the definition she'd memorized for a test in Senior English. Momentarily, she wondered how Waco knew so much, for being so poorly educated.

"I wouldn't peg your father's policy as evil."

"Maybe not, but it's damned inconvenient." Without it, she'd have a date to the prom, and she could spike Sara's guns by suggesting they double-date. "I'd like to edit his rule book!"

Instead of his laughing response, she heard a jaw-popping yawn.

" 'Scuse me. You'd think since I work in the heat every day that being out-of-doors in the sun wouldn't wear me out, but it does. Lordy, I dread getting up with the roosters tomorrow morning."

"At least you don't have tons of makeup work to do."

"That's the price you pay for a day at the beach with me," he teased, without sympathy.

"It was worth it. I don't mind burning the midnight oil."

"I'll let you go so you can get busy. I'll call you tomorrow night."

"I'll be here. Bye."

"Bye."

She replaced the receiver on the hook and sank back into the pillows, vowing that the whole world could be against her falling in love, but nothing could stop her.

Eight

"Would you hand me that lift-em-up-squeeze-em-together bra?" From the bathroom, Sara pointed to the Fredericks of Hollywood sack on the dresser. "How much time do I have?"

Dixie glanced at her watch. "Twenty-two minutes."

"I'll never make it! Rip the price tags off and hand it to me, would you, please?"

Following orders, Dixie silently bemoaned their spending hours combing the mall looking for the perfect pair of high heels to match Sara's white sequined dress. Too low, too high, too pointy, too rounded, too plain, too tacky—Sara's objections had been unlimited. Cinderella would have missed the ball if she'd gone shopping with Sara!

Caught up in the rush, Dixie's hands trembled as she popped the tags off the bra. "Here."

"Ohmygawd," Sara groaned seconds later. She wiggled from the bathroom to where her dress lay across the bed. "I won't be able to breathe! Help me."

Dixie inhaled deeply. To her surprise, she felt her breasts nearly spill over the lacy edge of the black strapless bra Sara had insisted that she buy. Flustered, but pleased, she exhaled noisily.

"Very funny, Groucho. I meant, help me with my dress. But first, see if my makeup is okay. No chin lines? No globs of mascara?"

Straight-faced, Sara replied, "Your blue eye-shadow matches the toilet paper. Classy touch."

"This is not the time to be funny! I had to wrap my hair so the bubble bath wouldn't relax my curls!" Gingerly, she unwrapped the turban of tissue, then lightly shook her head. "Yours looks fabulous. How's mine?"

"Super-fabulous," Dixie replied, meaning it.

Linda had outdone her reputation of being the finest hairstylist in Clear Lake. Her own hair had been swept up high on the crown of her head, teased and curled, until it cascaded artfully to her nape, with tendrils softly framing her face, making her eyes appear larger, bluer than usual.

"I'll slide into this oven-fresh bun," Sara joked, reciting a hot-dog commercial as she shimmied into her evening gown, "and I'm ready for your eating fun! Zipper me, would you?"

Dixie pulled the tab; the dress molded to Sara's svelte figure. Excitement must be contagious, she thought, almost overcoming the dread of going to the dance by herself.

Almost.

The closer it came to actually driving her father's Lexus to the high school, the closer Dixie came to tears of frustration. Lipstick could paint a smile on her face, but inside, where it counted, her heart ached.

"What do you think?" Sara asked, spinning on her toe and cocking her knee through the floor to thigh slit. "Is this dress as sexy as the one in the magazine that I picked out?"

"Sexier."

Sara preened in front of the mirror as she clipped on her earrings, a dangling collage of pearls, rhinestones and beads. "You aren't wearing the shoulder-duster earrings I set out for you. How come?"

"They're a bit . . ." Dixie had to think of a nice word for gaudy, ". . . ostentatious."

"Put them on, Dixie. Rhinestones make a girl's eyes sparkle."

She moved off the bed where she'd been perched and crossed to stand beside Sara at the mirror. Layers of black chiffon swirled several inches above her knees. Hesitantly, she took the glamorous earrings from Sara's extended hand.

"I've never worn earrings longer than a crystal chandelier."

"It's time you did." Sara opened her top drawer. "And wear my black satin belt with the rhinestone buckle. Those extra clips are for your shoes."

Dixie tightened the belt at her waist while she glanced down at the pointed high-heeled slippers pinching her toes. "I'll go for the earrings and the belt, but I draw the line at attracting attention to my feet."

"Stop fussing. You look like an exotic, high-fashion model."

For some unexplainable reason, Dixie felt almost exotic.

Almost.

The doorbell was pealing to herald Todd's early arrival. Dixie's buoyant spirits sank straight to her toes. Sara's parents were chaperons at the dance, so Dixie knew she'd have to answer the door. Sara would want to make a grand entrance.

"I'll get it," she offered before Sara told her what to do.

"Thanks. I'll be ready in a minute or two."

"Or three, or five, or ten," Dixie joked.

Sara winked. "Tell him I'm deciding what underwear *not* to wear, then call me when he starts panting."

"You're a cruel woman, Sara."

Closing the bedroom door behind her, Dixie sauntered down the hallway, hoping her first pair of high heels wouldn't cause her to teeter awkwardly down the steps. She envisioned the possibility of pitching down the stairs head first. Not a bad idea. An ambulance could whisk her off to the hospital and Sara and Todd . . . would ruin the evening sitting at her bedside.

She grabbed hold of the rail and called, "Be right there, Todd."

"I let myself in," Todd replied, from the living room. "Sara's never on time. WOW! Is that you Dixie?"

His enthusiastic comment halted her progression

down the steps. She felt a blush creeping up her neck, but couldn't stop it.

"How come I haven't noticed what great legs you have?"

"Because you never see me in anything but jeans?" Dixie supplied, traversing the last few steps.

"Or a strapless dress." His eyes bobbed from her slender ankles to the shadow of cleavage. "God, make me taller," he mumbled, raising his eyes toward the ceiling.

"Sara!" Todd wasn't panting, yet, but Dixie wasn't taking any chances. "Sara!"

"You can ride with us," Todd offered, his eyes gleaming, apparently enjoying where they landed when he didn't look up at her face.

Remembering where and what he and Sara did after the prom, Dixie mutely shook her head.

"A *ménage de tramp?*" Sara scolded from the top of the steps.

Todd grinned from ear to ear and corrected her French pronunciation, *"A trois."*

"That, too," Sara reproached. "Lecher."

"Jezebel." He pulled his hand from behind his back. "For you."

Sara completely forgot to be angry when she saw the spray of baby orchids. "Ooooh! They're exquisite."

"Exquisite flowers for an exquisite lady," Todd glibly complimented. "May I?"

Dixie felt like a Peeping Tom as she watched him pin the orchid corsage on the bodice of Sara's low-cut gown. Todd thought he was being suave, but Sara had giggled and cast Dixie a superior glance as he copped a feel.

"We're off," Sara said, giving Todd a slight hug. "See you there."

Dixie's lips felt tight; she managed a weak grin. A lump of chagrin lodged in her throat, which made speaking physically impossible. Tears clogged behind the lump.

Slowly, she closed the door, not able to bear watching them walk down the steps arm-in-arm.

Sara's air of superiority had clinched her decision.

They'd have to rope and hogtie her to drag her to the prom.

The thought of sitting on the sidelines, having the girls in the class lift their noses, as though she'd ridden in on the back of a polecat was just too damned much to endure.

She waited until she heard Todd's car depart, then picked up her satin evening bag, and stepped out on the porch. Her father was at home. She didn't want to go there and listen to him say, "I told you so."

She wanted to be alone, to lick her wounded pride in privacy.

But where?

Deciding she'd better get into the Lexus to maintain the illusion of going to the prom, she headed toward the driveway. Mentally, she ticked off a list of places she couldn't go: mall, restaurant, movies, TP's office.

Tears brimmed in her eyes as she blindly searched for the car key on John's key chain. The shiniest key caught and held her attention; it was the builder's key for the display house.

Why not? She recalled Waco saying he had to finish the trim work so the carpet men would have their installation completed before the furniture arrived. Kate had probably accomplished that feat because the grand opening would take place next weekend.

Feeling a trifle better, she climbed in the Lexus and started the engine.

Yes, she'd go there, but first . . .

Parked on the slight hill in the grove of pine trees that overlooked the parking lot of the high school gymnasium, Dixie watched the couples being dropped off in limousines and cars at the side entrance. Aside from knowing that her father would question her about who went with whom, Dixie wanted in some small way to be a part of the "rite of passage."

Hunched over the steering wheel, she alternately castigated herself for being foolish and commended herself for getting to see, without being seen.

It's my prom, she reasoned. If she'd been born a boy, she'd have been inside the decorated gymnasium, with some sweet young thing making goo-goo eyes at her.

But you're not one of the guys. Where's your pride? Your dignity?

It's not like I'm hurting anyone.

Other than myself.

She heard the faint sounds of music and laughter, mingling with the gentle sough of pine needles rubbing together, each being blown by the spring breeze. She yearned to be a part of the growing-up ritual.

Closing her eyes, she swayed to the music, picturing herself being held in Waco's arms, effortlessly skimming across the dance floor. A change in the music's tempo had her strumming her fingernails on the dashboard. Her toe tapped to the rhythm of the drums.

She loved to dance. When a band played, her inhibitions vanished, replaced by poise and grace. She wasn't being conceited; that's simply how she felt. Caught in the mood, she could almost smell Waco's after-shave lotion, almost feel the wall of his muscular chest pressed against her, almost taste the saltiness of his skin as she imagined herself boldly nibbling his ear while they danced.

As the music faded, she opened her eyes and stared into the near darkness.

Cars no longer dropped off their precious cargos. Only a few guys clustered outside the door, laughing, slapping each other on their backs. One stood alone, in front of the low Indian Hawthorn bushes, in the classic, macho-male Texan I'm-taking-a-leak pose.

The anger Dixie had kept locked deep inside her soul came to the surface. He who had everything was out peeing in the bushes? It was a sacrilege. She quelled the urge to hike down there and give that heretic a good swift kick between the legs with her pointed toe shoe.

She started the engine, pressing the accelerator

until the engine roared loudly. She'd have gladly given Sara's fake diamond earrings to have had a red light to slap on the roof of the Lexus. But she did have the satisfaction of watching the guy who defiled her dream hurriedly zip up his tuxedo britches and scoot back into the building.

"What am I doing here?" Dixie asked in disgust, for the umpteenth time.

She didn't belong inside the gym, and she certainly didn't belong outside it, with the guys. She'd go where she did belong—Texas Proud's display house.

Waco twisted the screwdriver until the hinge rose a fraction of an inch. This house had to be perfect for the grand opening. It simply wouldn't be acceptable for John Mayson to make his infamous "244 Test," where his clipboard held a list of 244 items to be inspected, and for Waco Stone to have a minus mark beside the finish carpentry work. He placed a level beside the cabinet door to make certain it hung straight.

"One room left," he murmured, picking up his toolbox and striding toward the library.

He had to doublecheck to make certain each shelf, drawer, and cabinet would pass inspection. Pride in workmanship was only part of the reason he'd returned to Bayou Creek Estates, after normal dawn-to-dusk working hours. This was the house where Dixie had helped him install the trim.

He felt close to her here. The muscle along his

jaw flexed as his teeth clenched. He needed that feeling while she was off gallivanting around at her high-school dance—with another guy. As long as he kept his mind and hands busy, he wouldn't be distracted by the whistle of that freight train leading him straight into trouble.

Last night, during their nightly telephone conversation, he'd gone so far as to try and badger Dixie into giving him the son-of-a-bitch's name. Finding out where he lived and making a little social call would have been a cinch. The only thing that stopped him was knowing how much this dance meant to Dixie.

She'd reassured him that her plans had been made long before she'd met him. And, she'd wondered out loud what he'd have said if she'd invited him.

"Right back to square one," Waco muttered, striding into the study and flicking the light switch to the on position.

He would have had to refuse her invitation.

Why had he fallen in love with the boss's daughter? Why couldn't she have been older? Lived on her own? Away from her father's influence?

What the hell, he cursed silently. He'd been born with bad luck; it continuing to plague him was no great mystery. He'd dared to believe meeting Dixie was a sign that his luck had changed. He must have had rocks in his head.

Asinine fool!

She made him feel like he was worth a million bucks, but in reality, he lived hand-to-mouth, paycheck to paycheck. One minor disaster and he'd be shuffling down the road, looking for a better job that paid more money.

The problem was—there wasn't anything better than working for Texas Proud. John Mayson was considered a nit-picking son-of-a-bitch by everyone in the trades, but he paid a premium wage for quality work.

Tired of trying to solve an insurmountable problem, Waco quickly moved down the row of cabinets. The slick, familiar feel of varnished wood beneath his fingertips went a long way toward soothing the jealous beast raging inside of him.

He liked how the lady decorator, Kate what's-her-name, had filled the floor-to-ceiling bookcases with leather-bound books, greenery, and small sculptures of wild birds. On the desk she'd left open several wildlife magazines, as though the owner of the house had stepped out for a moment, but would return shortly. She'd carried out that idea by leaving a pair of running shoes under the desk, not neatly placed, but with one toppled on its side and the other on top of it. A green plaid wing chair held two balls of yellow yarn pierced by twin knitting needles that held a half-completed garment. On the game table, a checkerboard resided, with red and black plastic checkers stacked as though the kids had tagged along with their father and mother, but would return also to finish the game.

He especially liked the wide leather sofas and chairs, big enough for a large man to sit comfortably, without having his knees touch his chin. The only thing he didn't like was the deer's head hanging over the fireplace. Having a couple of hats whimsically perched on the antlers did not lend any saving grace.

"Why would anybody want two beady glass eyes staring down at them?" Dixie asked softly from the doorway.

She'd seen his truck parked in the drive and thanked God for answering one of her many prayers.

Startled, for a second Waco thought his mind had conjured her up. He'd imagined Dixie as the mother of the kids, hadn't he? His kids. His home.

"I vote we take it down," he answered, quickly recovering his composure.

"It's a fake." Dixie crossed to the fireplace, pushed the brass plate with Missouri White Tail engraved on it, and the entire head swung outward, revealing a wall safe. "Burglars wouldn't expect a safe to be here because of the chimney. Clever?"

"Very." He stooped to return his torpedo level to his toolbox. She looked like something out of a dream, with her hair curled up and those beautiful legs of hers wearing silk stockings. Perplexed, he wondered what she was doing here. "Where's your date?"

"Here."

He saw the mischief in her eyes and jumped to the only reasonable conclusion. He scowled ferociously. "Sorry if I ruined your private party."

"You haven't. Yet."

"Yet?"

"You will if you pick up your toolbox and march out of here in a snit."

"Threesomes are boresome," he replied succinctly.

"I agree." She closed the hidden safe and crossed to the couch. "That's what I told Todd and Sara."

"Why do I feel as though I came in at the end of a movie?" He straightened up, just as she sat down and gave the cushion beside her a pat. The cloak of doubt that had weighed heavily on his shoulders the entire week began to lift as she smiled at him. "You don't have a date for the prom?"

She should have felt ashamed, but the hope igniting his smile made her confession easy. "No."

"You don't look broken-hearted." If she had, he'd have wanted to give the guy who'd broken the date a major face alteration. "Did you get stood up?"

"No."

"Would it be too much to ask for a simple explanation? Or do I have to pull it out of you?"

"Nobody asked me," she replied, her chin lifting up as her eyes followed him moving toward her. He wore a blue chambray shirt and denim jeans, and yet, he looked more handsome than the guys in formal tuxedos. He unbuckled his wide tool belt, carelessly letting it drop before dusting his britches and sitting beside her. "I was going to the dance by myself."

"Why didn't you tell me?"

"Pride." She cuddled up to him when his arm

pulled her close to his side. "I thought you'd think less of me."

"Me?" He shook his head. "I could have attended three proms and didn't."

"Three?"

"At least three. There was the senior class I might have graduated with in Waco. The class I could have graduated with in El Paso, and the class I should have graduated with in Phoenix. That's not counting schools I attended for less than six months."

Smiling wanly at him, she said, "Did you want to go to one of them?"

"Hell, yes," he divulged freely. "Why do you think our telephone conversations have been punctuated with long pauses?"

"I thought maybe you were a little jealous of my imaginary date."

"That, too, but most of all I wanted to be your escort."

"I'm glad I'm here with you," she confided. "It makes the hurt less painful."

"Zeke has a home remedy for wanting the impossible. He asks me if it hurts to want. I say yes. Then he tells me to rub my hurtin' place, 'cuz eventually the hurt will go away." He watched Dixie's hand cover her heart. "Is that where it hurts?"

"Mostly." Her curly auburn lashes lowered. "I'd rub my soul if I could locate it."

He covered her hand, linking their fingers together, desperately wanting to absorb her pain and disappointment. His forehead touched her temple. "I'm not wearing a tuxedo . . ."

"You look wonderful to me," she broke in as her heart began to race beneath his light touch.

"And I'm not the star quarterback on the football team, but . . . we could have a private dance—the Bayou Creek Independent School District prom. Yours and mine combined into one gala affair."

Tears collected in the corners of her eyes. Waco Stone, the man her best friend and only parent looked down on, had to be the sweetest, most understanding man on the planet. If she hadn't fallen in love with him on the Galveston beach, without a doubt, she loved him now.

Unchecked, a tear slid down her cheek, dropping off her chin, landing on his knuckles.

"Aw, hell, Dixie. I didn't mean to make you cry." Her tears totally unmanned him. Uncertain of what to do, he pulled her on his lap and rocked her in his arms. "Shhhh, shhhhh, don't cry, gorgeous, please. It was a dumb idea."

"No!". Dixie sniffled, trying to dam the flow of tears. "I don't know why I'm blubbering. I never cry. Never." She took a deep breath; her breasts inched from her bra, but she was too distraught to notice. Dabbing her eyes with the back of her hand, she whispered, "You're just so damned sweet . . ." *and so maligned!*

"No, I've been incredibly stupid," he castigated as his hands roamed restlessly across her bare back until they reached her cinched waist. His large hands spanned her small waist, pushing her back on his lap until he could see her face. "Tell me what to do, Dixie. Anything. And I'll do it."

Call it fate, or fortune, or destiny, or flimsy chiffon—the skirt of her dress clung to his jeans and her bodice lowered another inch; her breasts spilled free from their confining restraint.

She should have felt a blush blazing across her cheeks; she didn't.

She should have covered her exposed flesh; she didn't.

Her bright blue eyes met his, unsure and tentative, then led his dark eyes downward as she drew a long quavering breath and softly coaxed, "Love me, Waco?"

Nine

John Mayson laid his hand on the horn, blasting it in short staccato bursts. Traffic stood still, unmoved by his imperial command to get the hell out of his way. He swung open the door of his pickup and stepped out on the running board. Three cars in front of him, he spotted Sara's parents.

Gloria, her voice close to hysterics, had called him as he'd been about to leave for his Friday-night poker game, to tell him to turn on the ten o'clock news. He'd grabbed the remote control while he'd hung up the phone. Instantly, a parent's worst nightmare unfolded before his very eyes: policemen loading teenagers in police cars, shouting, kids running, batons waving, chaos and confusion. The news commentator soberly announced that the Pearwood cops had busted the prom, arresting seniors left and right for possession of alcohol and controlled substances.

Alcohol hadn't surprised John. Back in his day, he recalled staggering home from the prom, three sheets to the wind, and being violently ill the next morning with a hangover from hell. But drugs? Dope! That was a grey horse of a different color!

John had hunched closer to the television set. He wasn't certain, but he thought he saw Sara and Dixie in the crowd, loudly protesting the unwarranted seizure of their classmates. He'd thrown the remote control against the wall, and rushed through the front door.

"Goddamn, son-of-a-bitch!" In the distance, he could see the revolving blue lights of a dozen police cars. Couldn't one of those cops start directing traffic, for crissake!

A month ago, he wouldn't have worried about Dixie getting into trouble. She'd been his sweet, docile, darling daughter, cooking and cleaning and helping out where she was needed. The last two weeks, she'd been a rebellious little hellion!

Drastic mood swings were a symptom of drug usage.

That could account for her antagonistic attitude, he thought, grinding his back teeth. Dammit, she knew better than to experiment with drugs! He'd pointed out a dozen laborers who'd fried their brains with dope. Young, able-bodied men who couldn't think beyond where to get their next score. Crack-heads that couldn't pour piss out of a boot if the directions were written on the heel!

Dixie knows better, he chanted silently, in an effort to make himself believe his daughter wouldn't be involved with drugs. He'd raised her to keep one eye on the ball and her toes pointed straightforward on a narrow chalk line!

Enraged, he slammed his palm on the horn; other parents followed his example. A chorus of hostility and anxiety blared as John hoped and prayed that Dixie would be at the gymnasium, not hauled off in a paddy wagon to the police station.

"Get the hell moving!" John roared impatiently. "Get out of my way!"

Waco unzipped the back of her gown and pushed it out of the way of his hands. Doing what's right or wrong never crossed Waco's mind. His agile fingers quickly unbuttoned the front on his shirt. She pulled the tail out of his jeans while he stretched full length on the couch, taking her with him. Her arms encircled his shoulders, her breasts touching his hot flesh as he kissed her for the first time. With an expertise born from years of practice, he lightly pinched the long row of hooks and eyes until her bra fell by the wayside.

"You're so beautiful. So sweet and innocent," he crooned huskily between kisses.

She felt him use his tongue to part her lips; his calloused hand covered one breast, cupping it with infinite gentleness, barely caressing the sensitized nipple.

A new beginning, she thought silently, one in which she was cherished, gorgeous, adept at making love.

With that thought boldly imprinted in her mind, unafraid, she courageously stroked him, from his collarbone to his waist, excited by the contrasting rough-sleek texture of his masculine chest. He could have pressed tightly against her, but Waco seemed content to slowly kiss her, while slowly exploring, massaging, squeezing each of her breasts, until they seemed as hard as ripe summer apples.

He raised his head, seemingly unhurried, but felt the familiar tightness in the crotch of his jeans. She was hot for him. He could see desire beckon to him in the limpid blue color of her eyes. Beneath his palm he felt her heart beat furiously, faster than a hummingbird's wings, fanning the flames of her passion.

She was his for the taking.

And damn his treacherous, libidinous soul, he wanted her as he'd never wanted any woman. And yet, she was the one woman he held in such high esteem that he couldn't take.

Dixie felt his muscles tense, watched his eyes close, felt his hands slide to her ribs, and instinctively knew he was about to make a dreadful decision: He wanted to stop.

"Don't stop," she blurted, speaking her mind as her hands moved to frame his face, thus preventing him from shaking his head.

He groaned, "Dammit, Dixie, I'm not worthy of shining your boots. Don't encourage me . . . I'm fighting to control myself . . . I can't fight you, too."

"Oh, Waco," she breathed, cupping his ears as though she could deafen the voices coming from within him. She drew his head to her shoulder until her lips rested against his dark hair.

Momentarily, she thought of the pictures she and Sara had gone through in the yearbook. Behind each face that smiled at the camera was the secret knowledge they'd gained immediately after last year's prom.

Virginity wasn't a virtue; it was a handicap. It set her apart from being like other young women in her class.

"I've waited for this moment all my life. I want to share it with you, only you," she whispered, enticing him to claim her as his woman by arching her hips against him. "I love you."

For several long seconds Waco remained motionless. Then his lips touched the kiss-curl tangled in her diamondlike earrings. "Dixie-love, I don't want you to regret this, later."

"No regrets," she promised rashly. Her hand covered the back of his; she navigated it upward until both their hands covered her breast. She could almost hear his smile. "I promise."

Gently, he tilted her to face him and kissed her long and hard on the mouth. She returned his kiss, silently communicating how much she needed him, loved him, wanted him. His hand responded by relearning the size and shape of her breasts, with her hand absorbing the circular motion.

She hooked her leg across his thigh and rolled him from his side into the V of her inner thighs. Her dress bunched between them, but through the layers and layers of silky chiffon, she felt him, hard and strong against her. He slanted his mouth across hers in one direction, then the other; his tongue thrust inside her, hungry for complete intimacy.

"Too damned many clothes," he bemoaned, then shifted to his side and peeled the bodice of her gown below her waist. "Lift your hips, sweetheart."

Along with her dress, he swiftly removed her pantyhose and shoes, until she lay beside him donned only in the wispiest of black lace panties. His lower extremities felt a harsh jolt of male hormones.

With an experienced woman, he'd have stretched the flimsy elastic at the legs aside, to make room to accommodate his swelling manhood while he unzipped his jeans. While he tested her for readiness with one hand, he'd have freed himself from his undershorts with the other. A second later, he'd have impaled himself to the glorious hilt and begun humping his pelvis, like a automated pile driver, until he exploded.

But . . . Dixie was a virgin, his first, her first— in this they were equal.

He did shed his jeans, but not his underwear. He did move between those long luscious legs of hers, but only until his lips could capture her nipple. Her heat radiated through her fragile panties against his belly, not lower, where it could cause spontaneous combustion.

Like the hummingbird gathering nectar, he delicately sipped at her breast. He felt the humming noise she made as her strong capable hands kneaded his shoulders. Her knees cinched his waist while he suckled one dusky nipple, then the other, each appearing to pout from neglect when he momentarily left it. Each whirl of his tongue, each brush of the serrated edges of his teeth against her budding nipple elicited a spasm of desire from her in the form of an impassioned sound more expressive than anything she could have thought to say.

Through parted eyelashes, Dixie dropped her gaze to see his darkly tanned fingers stroking and shaping her soft, white flesh, with a celestial expression on his face. Immodestly, she watched, thrilled by the pleasurable sensations coursing throughout her nubile body.

It felt absolutely right to be there with his mouth consuming her and his knee riding high between her legs.

When he caught her watching him, he asked, "Change your mind?"

"No."

"I can stop," he vowed, uncertain he could keep his promise.

She arched against his thigh as she felt the backs of his knuckles brush against her stomach; she sucked it in, willing him to stop his teasing fingertips from tracing the Chantilly lace pattern of her panties. "I'll die of frustration if you quit."

"Me, too," he admitted.

She was certain he could feel her skin quivering with anticipation beneath his tantalizing touch. Mindless, her body had a will of its own. Her hips arched; he tugged the last remaining garment off her. The heel of his hand nestled against the thatch of dark auburn curls. Again, her hips rose, pushing against him, slowly grinding, creating an exquisite yearning deep within her.

She heard him take a harsh breath and slowly release it. She wanted to reciprocate, to create the same achy wooziness she felt, only she wasn't certain how to accomplish the feat. Shyly, and yet with a boldness born and nurtured by her passion, she dared to touch him.

The pictures in the health and sex education pamphlets are wrong, she mused from her foggy haze. He wasn't small or limp. Through a thin layer of white cotton, his ridge of hard male flesh rose proudly. His buttocks were clenched, the muscles taut beneath her other hand, that freely wandered to the small of his back.

"Ah, Dixie-love," she heard, his voice wrenched from his soul. "Touch me. Really touch me."

As though given permission to her silent supplication, she rolled the band of elastic at his waist downward, until it could go no farther. She had no idea how, but beneath her she felt the cushion shift, his hand brush against her arm, and the last barrier of cloth disappeared. His hand caught hers, curled it around his swollen member and he taught her a lesson every woman should know, on how to pleasure a man.

A quick study, within a few fierce heartbeats, his breathing grew ragged, and she marveled at her power to bring such a powerful, strong man to such wild bliss.

"Easy, love, easy," he gasped, struggling to retain some lucidity. He moved her hand lower, until she cupped him where he was most vulnerable, knowing her ministration would do less damage to his self-control. Now, he began to comprehend the fascination other men had with virgins. Just knowing Dixie had never fondled another man intimately made her extraordinary. She was his alone. For a man who'd never had anything he could call his own, that made her very special. Teeth clenched, he hissed, "Yes, love. Gently."

As gentle with him as he was with her, she still drew a sharp breath when his finger parted the folds of feminine flesh, like a fragile rosebud, and entered her. Involuntarily, her thighs squeezed his hand as uncontrollable ripples of ecstasy flamed upward causing a spray of goosebumps across her shoulders. He'd lit a furnace inside her; beads of perspiration dotted her upper lip and her mouth felt dry.

From what seemed a great distance, she heard his voice telling her to relax, but her knees trembled and her hands dropped to the leather cushion; her fingernails went scratching against the smooth surface as she tried to hold onto something to keep her mind from shattering into a million pieces.

Time and space lost all meaning to her. Her whole universe seemed to be centered on the erotic strokes taking place between her thighs. She heard "hot," "wet," "tight," but the words meant nothing until she felt his proud flesh enter her; she was stretching to accommodate his girth.

A momentary flash of red pain pierced her, causing her to call his name as he broke through the barrier of her virginity. Reflexively, her legs clenched around him, holding him deep within her, until an awareness of the promise of womanly fulfillment being ever so close caused a sinuous shift of her body against him. She rocked against him; instinctively raising her hips. If she felt any pain it was diminished by the greater pleasure that came from his being an intimate part of her.

What she lacked in experience, she counterbalanced with eagerness. She parried each thrust. For long golden minutes Dixie gave herself up to the incredible sensations building swiftly within her, coiling into a tight knot, until finally it burst, hurling her over the pinnacle of her passion, and his.

When Waco collapsed against her, she held him close to her heart, loving the sweet nothings he whispered in her ear. She wanted to tell him this wasn't what she'd expected, not from what Sara had told her.

Love must make the difference, she decided a trifle smugly as she peppered a string of kisses along the side of Waco's neck. She loved Waco, with all her heart and soul. She smiled, thinking how trite that sounded, but no other words perfectly described how she felt about him.

Waco felt as weak as Samson after his hair had been shorn, but he cradled Dixie close to his chest and carried her into the master suite's opulent bathroom to tend to her. He glanced at the shower, then opted for the double-sized Jacuzzi. He sat on the cold tile step, holding her across his thighs as he turned the gold-handled faucet. Water began filling the black marbleized tub.

Without protest or questions, Dixie let him pamper her. He lightly tucked the hairpins back in place that held her hair swept high on her head to keep it from getting wet, tested the water's temperature with his hand, dropped several shell-shaped scented soaps in the tub, then carefully lowered her into the warm water. He pressed the button that activated the motor and grinned at the sound of delight she made as soap bubbles whirled around her.

"This is heavenly," Dixie murmured with a smile, sliding forward until the water was neck deep, then scooting to the far side, she politely thanked him as her eyes shyly beckoned him to join her.

Foremost in his mind was one fact that prevented him from accepting her sweet invitation: She'd been a virgin. That, and being young, virile and capable of immediate recovery, he knew what would happen the minute he crawled in beside her. He couldn't allow his greediness to cause her pain a second time.

"Thirsty?" he asked, reaching for the basket the decorator had filled with rolled towels and washcloths. He visualized skimming the cloth across her breasts, dipping to the V of her thighs, but hearing a toot from his internal freight train, he dismissed that idea by giving her the cloth. "There's a bottle of champagne and two wineglasses in the icebox. Shall I get them?"

Before she could answer yea or nay, he'd wrapped a towel around his waist and hurried from the bathroom. Tonight there was cause for a champagne celebration. The night she'd dreaded for months, Waco had transformed into a night she'd remember for her entire life. Delighted, she laughed softly.

His "someday" was in the distant future; hers was here and now.

Random thoughts skittered across her mind as she closed her eyes, relaxed, and let the rose-scented bubbles wash her.

Now she was a woman.

His woman.

And he was her man.

Together, they were a magnificent couple.

In a semitrance, she heard a cork pop. Lazily, she lifted one eyelid and noted that Waco had replaced the towel with his jeans, which were unsnapped at the waist. She rose slightly, wondering if there was anything sexier than a man's bare chest, bare feet, and the knowledge there was nothing between him and his jeans.

"A toast," he announced, pouring champagne into both glasses he'd placed on the edge of the tub. Lowering himself to the tiled step, he turned off the motor and held one glass for her to take. "To happiness. Yours and mine."

"Ours." As she hesitantly sipped the effervescent wine; her eyes watched him empty his goblet in three gulps. Since drinking alcoholic beverages was forbidden by her father, she was surprised by the taste. "Is it supposed to be sour?"

"Dry," Waco corrected, with a boyish grin. He held the bottle toward her. "See? It says so on the label. Extra dry."

Being "wet" and bubbly were the only two things going for it, Dixie assessed silently. But, not wanting to appear unsophisticated, she downed the contents. She made a comical face and confided, "Soda pop tastes better."

"It is kinda bitter, like beer." Waco filled both champagne glasses to the brim. "Zeke says I have a champagne taste and a beer budget."

Dixie giggled at his small joke. The second glass does taste a tiny bit sweeter, she reassessed, beginning to feel especially glamorous, sitting in a mountain of frothy bubbles celebrating their lovemaking by sharing an expensive bottle of wine.

She crossed her legs at the knees; she lifted one leg until her big toe pointed at the shower fixture, the way she'd seen a movie star do it in an old rerun on television. A cascade of foam slithered sensuously across her shin.

Waco must have watched the same film because he raked the bubbles into his palm and blew them toward the ceiling. Some burst, others fell like iridescent snowflakes. Never having seen snow, she found the effect delightful.

Dixie sat forward and lightly smoothed her fingers over the ones nestled in his hair. Often, she wanted to push his forelock off his brow, but natural inhibition prevented the affectionate caress.

Waco mistook the appreciative gleam in her eyes as mischievousness. Grinning, he grabbed her wrist and warned, "No bubble bath fights. I have plans that don't include getting down on my hands and knees and mopping the floor."

"What do they include?" she asked dreamily, her insides feeling warm and woozy with anticipation.

"A surprise for a slightly tipsy lady." He unrolled a bath towel, stood, and held it for her. "You're going to shrivel like a sun-dried prune if you stay in the tub much longer."

"A tipsy dried prune," Dixie giggled, her hands and feet were slipping and sliding as she tried to get out of the tub. Off-balance, she came close to dunking her head. "Flattery like that will get you . . . ooops!"

Amused by her antics, Waco chuckled while lending assistance. He scooped her from the water and placed her feet on the bathmat. His laughter abruptly died in his throat as gravity worked its magic on the rose-scented lather.

Aware of how dangerously tempted he was to carry her back to the sofa and make love to her, he forced himself to concentrate on the task of burnishing her damp skin with the fluffy towel.

Aglow, Dixie murmured, "Whoever invented champagne must have gotten the recipe from an angel."

"Guess that explains the sky-high price."

"Yup," she drawled lazily. "And the reason it's called extra dry is because it doesn't quench your thirst. Whaddayathink?"

"I'll get your clothes. While you're getting

dressed I'll get you a glass of tap water." He wrapped the towel around her sarong-fashion and gave her a quick peck on the lips. "Be right back."

"Water. Ugh!" Completely confident she could solve the bothersome problem without his help, she shuffled to the tub feeling as though she walked on clouds, and drank what remained of his champagne. She held the green champagne bottle up to the light to see how much was left.

Plenty, she deduced silently.

"Waste not, want not," she recited, giggling over how suitable one of her father's truisms applied to this situation. She gulped a large swallow, liking the fizzing sensation as it hit the back of her throat. "Better to have and not need, than need and not have!"

She toasted her brilliance by raising her glass, then downed the remainder in the glass, licking the rim. "Candy's dandy, but likker's quicker!"

"What did you say?" Waco asked as he turned the corner into the master bath.

"Nothing. Just thinking out loud."

He exchanged her glass for her clothing, giving her a wry smile. "You're looped, sweetheart."

"Looped?" With a cheeky grin, she asked, "As in smasherooed?"

He nodded.

She shook her head, but stopped the motion when the room began to swim dizzily. A hiccup later, she added, "Just happy."

"Did you eat anything for dinner?"

"Nope."

"Booze on an empty stomach." That explained why a couple of glasses of wine had gone straight to her head. "I'll get the munchies from my truck. You get dressed . . ."

"I'm not hungry, Waco. Honest." She tilted her head to one side, wondering if the champagne had affected her hearing as well as her speech. "Do I hear violins?"

"I brought in my portable radio. Can't have a prom night without music and a slow dance."

She hugged her clothing to her and giggled, "Save the first dance for me. I'll be dressed in a flash."

Five minutes later, clad only in her panties and nylons, she wrestled with the hooks-and-eyes at the back of her long-line bra. The damned thing was like one of those finger-grabber toys she'd had as a kid. She couldn't get it hooked at the top, and she couldn't unhook the ones at her waist.

Oh, for a pair of scissors!

She tugged and pulled until the padded cups touched her shoulder blades and the hooks made a puckered line down her front. Exasperated, she was figuring she'd never be able to scrunch it around once she'd hooked it. She unhooked it and tossed the offending garment aside. It only took a second for the satin-lined chiffon dress to be shimmied up her hips and zipped.

As she glanced at her image in the mirror, she hoped and prayed Waco wouldn't notice any difference.

Without her purse she couldn't freshen her makeup. She studied her face, stunned by the transformation. Her eyes appeared larger, bluer, her lips fuller, and a natural pink blush tinged her cheeks.

She looked and felt . . . "Gorgeous?"

Today at the beauty parlor, Sara had promised her she'd never forget prom night. Little did Sara know how right her prediction had been.

Must be love, Dixie mused, smiling as she crossed the threshold to the living room where Waco waited, his arms open wide for her.

This night would be unforgettable.

Ten

It was after midnight when Waco walked Dixie to her front door. At her insistence, he'd circled the block to make certain John's truck wasn't parked in the driveway. Champagne had caused her mind to be fuzzy around the edges, but protecting their secret liaison had become second nature for her.

"Tonight was wonderful, Waco." Her hands climbed lethargically up the front of his shirt; his hands circled her waist. "A wish come true."

"I wish it would never end," he whispered sincerely. He lowered his lips to hers. Her lips clung sweetly to his mouth as she savored his good-night kiss. "I'll see you later this afternoon?"

The sound of tires grabbing the road behind Waco's truck frightened a hiccup from her as she said, "Oh my god, Waco. You've got to get out of here."

Startled, his arms dropped to his sides. Her hands flattened against his chest, pushing him away from her could have been the impetus to haul ass, but he was unwilling to let Dixie take the brunt of her father's anger.

A blast from his internal warning system blared

until his ears rang. He watched John rip the truck door open; heard it slam viciously.

"I'm staying," he told Dixie resolutely.

"Waco Stone?" John half-walked, half-ran, his legs quickly carrying him across the lawn. "Is that you on the porch with my daughter, you son-of-a-bitch?"

"Are you crazy?" Her eyes rounded, fearful for Waco. "Leave! You'll only make things worse!"

A steely calm settled over Waco. Dead certain his boss wanted to whup his ass, his feet automatically spread inches apart in preparation for the heavy blows he'd receive. Sizing John up, he knew he could take the older man.

But he also knew he wouldn't lift a finger to defend himself.

"Dad!" Dixie felt her stomach roll as her father took the front steps two at a time. Waco's hand captured her wrist to restrain her when she moved forward to get between the two men. "This isn't Waco's fault. I . . ."

"Shut up and get in the house, young lady!" The sight of Waco protectively stepping in front of his daughter enraged John. He sprang for Waco's throat, grabbing him by the front of his shirt. While he attempted to shake the living daylights out of Waco, he roared at Dixie, "Move! I'll deal with you after I get this low-life scum off my property."

Returning his attention to Waco, he shook Waco like a mangy, flea-bitten dog and stormed crudely, "Did you think you'd fuck your way up the ladder of success. Huh?"

Helpless and scared and nauseated by her father's accusation, Dixie covered her mouth with her hand to keep from completely disgracing all of them by spewing the contents of her stomach on both of them.

"Go inside," Waco bid, his voice austere. He wanted John to vent his spleen on him, not her. "I'll be okay."

"The hell you will!"

John doubled his fist and cocked his arm.

"No!" Dixie wailed, lunging for her father, ineffectively grabbing his forearm. In horror, she watched her father's fist smash against Waco's clenched jaw. "No!"

Waco's head snapped to the side, but he maintained his balance. Zeke had hit him harder, many times, when he hadn't deserved it. The copper taste of blood from his split lip oozed into his mouth. He blocked the next blow to his midsection. He could take whatever John Mayson dished out. Hell, he deserved every blow that connected.

The sight of Waco's blood propelled Dixie to the porch rail. Sobbing between hiccups, no longer able to control her heaving stomach, she bent at the waist and threw up. She wanted to cover her ears to stop the sounds of the two men she loved scuffling, but her stomach cramped; reflexively, her hands covered it.

"You friggin' sneak thief! I smell booze on your breath! How long have you been sneaking around with my daughter? Did you get her drunk? Seduce her?" John demanded, punctuating each question with an attempt to hit Waco. Frustrated by his inability to land another solid punch, he saw red as he pushed Waco against the wooden frame of the window. Winded, he noisily sucked air through his mouth. Between pants and shoves, he blustered, "I should have taken one look at your cocky-ass and shot it off! Should've known you were a goddamned troublemaker!"

Stoically, Waco gritted his teeth and dodged another blow. You deserve this, he kept telling himself over and over.

John swung his fist at the intense dark eyes that dared to challenge him. Waco ducked. Dixie heard bones crunch and her father's surprised yelp of pain.

John staggered backward two steps as pain reverberated up his arm, across his shoulder to his chest. "Damn you to hell, you shit-bum."

Battered and bruised, his temper frayed from the tight rein he'd held on his self-protection instincts, Waco shoved away from the window, sidestepping to where Dixie hunched against the pillar. Afraid her father would renew his attack, only this time on her, he grumbled, "Come with me."

Her eyes wild, tears blurred her vision as her glance ricocheted from Waco to her father. Other than his lip and a tear in his shirt, Waco looked relatively undamaged when compared to her father, who had blood dripping off the little finger of one hand while the other hand massaged the muscles over his heart. The defeat she saw in her father's eyes aged him by twenty years.

How could Waco ask her to choose between the two of them?

She wanted to be with Waco, but not like this—not with her father writhing in pain. He'd never forgive her if she deserted him and ran off with Waco.

She looked up at Waco. Their eyes met and communicated in a silent language only the two of them could hear.

I love you.

Do you?

Yes!

Prove it.

How?

Go with me. Now, before it's too late.

"I can't," she sobbed quietly, breaking eye contact and silently praying Waco would understand her emotional turmoil. "Go, please."

"Get off my property before I call the cops," John grunted, his chin lolling forward to his chest. "I'll have you . . . locked up. Throw . . . away . . . the key."

Waco only heard Dixie's refusal. Reeling, as though the freight train roaring in his head had sideswiped him, he turned and stumbled down the steps.

Run, his subconscious goaded him. His pride screamed silently, "Head up! Don't let them know you're hurt! Damn your rusty hide, at least swagger! Don't look back. Don't ever look back."

He was unable to think straight. His body automatically responded to the silent commands.

Dixie stared after him with her heart lodged in

her throat. Would he turn and glance over his shoulder at her? Could he give her some small signal that showed he cared? A nod? A wink? A smile?

Like a carpenter using a straightedge to measure a length of wood, Waco followed an unwavering path, neither looking right nor left, nor over his shoulder.

She gulped salty tears, but her mouth felt drier than when she'd swallowed the champagne. Ashamed of her father's behavior, and of her own for not having the guts to stand up to him, she let forlorn tears stream steadily down her cheeks.

From immediately behind her, she heard the front door squeak on its hinges and knew her father had gone inside the house. From a greater distance, she heard the sound of the truck door being shut and the grinding of a worn engine.

Abandoned by both men, alone, with only frustration, hurt, and anger as her companions, Dixie watched the red taillights until they disappeared from sight.

Fervently she prayed that Waco would circle the block, come back to talk to her. Somehow she'd square things with her father. Somehow she'd get Waco's job back for him.

She waited.

And waited.

For the entire weekend, she continued to wait. Each time the phone rang, she pounced on it. A Girl Scout delivering cookies was almost sucked to the back of the house by the speed of Dixie's swinging the front door open.

The following week at school, she listened to the scandalous prom night adventures. Half the senior class told tales of unwarranted harassment by the police department, either at the dance or on the isolated oilpatch roads. The half who hadn't attended the dance smirked, gloated, and exaggerated the stories of the downfall of the popular cliques.

According to Sara, everyone's prom night was a complete disaster. A cop patrolling the oilpatch roads in an unmarked car had hand-delivered her and her underpanties to her parents. They had exploded, then forbidden Todd from darkening their doorstep with his shadow. Sara had thrown an ear-splitting, tear-jerking tantrum, but currently only spoke monosyllabic replies to her parents' direct questions. Nor was she listening to their lectures.

"Great love would defy death, parents, or the police department" became the whispered motto of Dixie's graduating class.

Each night as the town clock struck twelve, Dixie waited for her phone to ring. Lying in bed, with her face pressed against the pillow, the memories of being with Waco brought a fresh bout of tears to her cheeks. She remembered the thrill of hearing him calling her Gorgeous—the way he'd weave their hands together until the webs touched—how his dark eyes would light up when he laughed. Mental pictures haunted her: of them walking on the beach, line dancing at the Outpost, and scuffling while they'd retrieved playing cards.

She heard the sweet endearments he'd whispered

after they'd made love, and recalled how cherished she'd felt when he'd carried her to the tub. She wondered if he thought of her, and *if* he did, why wasn't the phone ringing?

When another week passed without hearing or seeing Waco, the old doubts she'd harbored surfaced. She hadn't changed. She was still too tall, too thin, and too flat-chested. She'd been unable to hide those facts when they'd made love. Naked, she'd been unable to conceal the truth: She was unattractive, with no sex-appeal.

Or perhaps the vile accusations her father had hurled at Waco did contain elements of truth. An opportunist would believe sweet-talking the boss's daughter into bed would increase his chances of earning a gold key to the executive men's room.

Waco was ambitious. On countless occasions he'd told her he wanted to make something of himself. Being Mr. Texas Proud would certainly give him a leg up.

As Dixie examined a few distasteful home truths, her spirits sank to an all-time low. Waco hadn't loved her; he'd never told her he loved her. He hadn't deceived her; she'd deceived herself by confusing in love with making love. She couldn't blame him, only herself.

Graduation Day, diploma in her hand, Dixie crossed the raised platform in the same gym where the prom had been held, feeling older and wiser than her years. Another letdown, she thought, knowing this would be the last time she'd see many of her classmates. Most of them would be off to college, leaving her behind.

Her eyes scanned the faces of the people seated in the aluminum folding chairs. Foolishly, she'd psyched herself into believing that he'd want to be at her graduation since he regretted not reaching that goal himself. She saw familiar faces from Texas Proud's corporate headquarters, and a few distant relatives, but the one face she sought was nowhere to be seen.

He isn't here, her heart wept silently. He's gone. She had to accept that fact, painful though it was. She had to forget him, because he sure as hell had forgotten her.

After the ceremony, John attempted to breach the wall of silence erected between them by giving her a brown Texas Proud envelope and saying, "Smile, Coppertop, graduating from high school isn't a funeral procession."

Might as well be, she thought silently in her downhearted state of mind.

While her father examined her diploma and shook hands with other exuberant parents, she ripped the envelope open that contained her graduation gift. Her eyes rounded in surprise as she leafed through the official documents stating that Dixie Mayson had been accepted at Texas University in Austin. She'd be living at Doby Hall, and Sara would be one of her roommates!

"Well?" John demanded as she shoved the papers back in the envelope. "It's the college you picked, isn't it?"

"Yes." Bewildered by his radical change in plans for her, she wondered what strings were attached. "But, you said that you wanted me living at home, working at Texas Proud, attending a junior college. What changed your mind?"

"I did," Kate volunteered, stepping from behind John and giving Dixie a hug. "I've been browbeating him for months to set you free."

"Can you believe Kate-the-feminist said I'd be setting you up for failure if I had your name painted on an executive office door at Texas Proud?" He made a tsking noise. "And here I thought women wanted executive titles."

Dixie glanced from the smug, boyish grin that wreathed her father's face to Kate's proprietary hold on his arm. Was there something going on between them she'd missed?

The fleeting conjecture vanished as Kate joked, "Remember from your history classes how King George tyrannized his people for decades? He had a weak moment and signed a document that's like our Bill of Rights. Your father weakened and did the same thing."

"Yeah, and ole George lived to regret it," John replied drily. To Kate he said, "I'm not certain I like your comparing me to a tyrant."

"Why not? You act as though you have divine power," Kate sparred, winking at Dixie. "Have you ever regretted or apologized for anything you've done?"

John tucked Dixie's free hand in the crease his elbow made, looked his daughter straight in the eye, and said, "I regret not letting my daughter make her own mistakes."

Dixie squeezed his arm, accepting what was the closest thing she'd seen to an apology from her father. He wouldn't admit to the possibility of being wrong about his rules or about Waco, only to restricting her freedom to discover for herself how wrong *she'd* been.

In John's book, Waco was exactly like hundreds of other men he'd hired over the years—good at his trade, but a drifter. She couldn't argue with him. If Waco had cared, really cared, she would have heard from him by now.

Dixie hated being proven wrong, and yet in all honesty, she had to admit, albeit silently, that Waco did lack John's tenacity; he had abandoned her without a second thought. Her father always stood beside her, as he did on this very important day.

"Thanks, Dad," she murmured, accepting her fate, genuinely smiling at him for the first time in weeks. "I will make you proud of me," *someday.*

Someday.

It might have been her choosing the word Waco had often used, or the gratitude she felt for her father allowing her a new freedom, or the long term effect of sleepless nights and near starvation that caused tears to trickle down her cheeks. Whatever the reason, she could only hope the inner strength her father possessed was genetically passed down to her.

Someday, she promised silently, the pain circling

her heart would subside. She'd be able to drive by the high school and be proud of the education she'd received there. She'd pore over her yearbook with Sara and remember only the good times.

As she glanced up and down the rows of parked cars searching for a dented, yellow pickup truck, she knew that in the distant future her memories of Waco Stone would fade. He was her first love, but he wouldn't be her last.

Someday, she'd remember him without the heartache.

But not today.

Eleven

September, 1995

"Did you read this?" Sara skittered the Style section of the *Houston Chronicle* across the architectural drawing of Mayson Manor.

Dixie pushed the newspaper aside and continued to measure the distance of the main load-bearing wall. This pet project of John's would cost Texas Proud a fortune unless she could find a way to cut corners. A month ago she'd respectfully suggested they continue the ten-year-hold her father had put on this project.

John vetoed postponement.

Having graduated from the University of Texas the same year the economic crunch hit the oil business, Dixie had been a part of downsizing Texas Proud. Like other home builders, Texas Proud had suffered. Slowly, they'd recovered, but her tightening the belt had made her wary of taking unnecessary financial risks.

John had pointed out, with the Houston economy diversifying and low interest rates, that the housing market was on the verge of a boom. He'd berated her, saying Mayson Manor would be Texas Proud's showcase home.

Other members of the executive staff had agreed with John. Affluent buyers of custom-built homes expected the builder to live in the type of home he built. A grand tour of Mayson Manor would increase sales.

After she'd acquiesced to the will of the majority, the task of overseeing the construction of Mayson Manor had been delegated to her. Although she was pleased by their vote of confidence, her workload had doubled. Mountains of computer printouts crossed her desk daily for final approval.

At the time of Sara's arrival she'd been rechecking Dirk Stallman's lumber estimate. Try as she would, she could not get his figures to jibe with the calculations she'd made. Either she or he had made a costly error. Before she confronted him, she had to make certain she hadn't made any mistakes.

"Later, Sara. Dirk's estimates go out for bids this morning. I'm checking his figures."

"You don't want to read about Cinderfella?"

Dixie tried to conceal her grin, but the emphasis Sara placed on the last syllable made her smile. Since Sara and Todd's divorce two years ago, her friend religiously scoured the daily society column in search of watering holes where the rich and famous gathered. This time, Sara vowed regularly, she wasn't letting rampant sex hormones influence who she'd marry. She wanted a "rich, old geezer, with one foot in the grave and the other on a banana peel."

Shortly after graduation from high school, Sara had married Todd, her high-school sweetheart. Eight months later, she bore their son, Christopher. After seven years of living on a financial roller-coaster, Sara had taken her son and moved back into her parents' home. With no specific skills, no college degree, and little work experience, she'd been unable to obtain a job paying more than a minimum wage until she'd coerced Dixie into taking pity on her. The past year she'd worked her fingers to the bone as Dixie's secretary.

"Does the name Wade Stone mean anything to you?" Miffed by Dixie's total lack of interest, she shoved the paper under her boss's nose. "Look at the picture. Doesn't this guy look a teensy bit familiar to you?"

To pacify Sara, Dixie quickly glanced at the headline, CINDERFELLA TO BUILD CASTLES IN TEXAS and the black-and-white photograph. "Nope."

"Aw c'mon, Dixie, take a good look," Sara groaned, exasperated by her friend's lack of interest. "This man is a millionaire. Is he or isn't he your old heart-throb, the guy who broke your heart?"

"You have a memory like an elephant and the work ethics of a grasshopper," Dixie sighed, mixing her metaphors as she picked up the newspaper and tilted back in her swivel chair.

Her thick, curly eyelashes hid the flare of recognition in her blue eyes from Sara's close perusal. A pin-striped business suit and white shirt accentuated Waco's dark tan. The photographer had caught the spark in his black eyes. He carried a light-colored raincoat and a large briefcase in one hand. A petite blonde clung to his other arm and looked up at him as though he was a man with a money tree growing in his backyard.

Make that an orchard of money trees, Dixie silently amended.

"Well?" Sara leaned both hands on Dixie's desk. "Well?"

"Two wells make a double-seater outhouse," Dixie quipped, grinning at Sara.

"Is it him?"

"Could be." Dixie handed the paper back to Sara and resumed listing linear foot measurements. "The picture does look vaguely familiar."

"I swear he's the same guy you took pictures of at the beach!" Impatient with Dixie's I-don't-give-a-damn attitude, Sara folded the newspaper and lightly whacked her on the head. "Don't you want to read the article about him? It's a real rags-to-riches story."

"Don't you have something more productive to do than read fairy tales?"

Silently, she suggested, like reading the financial statement Todd filed to get the loan approved on the house we're building for him. Not that Waco's success bothered her the same way Todd's current affluence galled Sara, she told herself. Wade "Waco" Stone meant nothing to her.

"I'll read the article to you," Sara insisted. "Shut your ears if you don't want to listen."

Dixie began keying figures into her computer. "Consider them closed."

Undaunted, Sara made herself comfortable in the chair opposite the desk. After clearing her throat, she began reading, "Texan, Wade Stone, 33, recently returned to the Bayou City, where he'd been raised in near-poverty."

"He wasn't poverty-stricken when he worked for us," Dixie muttered, to set the record straight.

Sara lowered the top edge of the paper and smiled. "Your ears are closed—see if you can do the same for your mouth, please." Her blond head lowered. "Where was I? Blah-blah-blah-blah-blah. Oh yeah, . . . raised here."

"He wasn't raised here," Dixie corrected drily.

"Dixie! Hush!"

"How can you believe what you read when they made two mistakes in the first paragraph?"

"I'll skip down to the interesting part. Let's see." In a sing-song voice she paraphrased, "His parents left him in the custodial care of his uncle, Zeke Stone. Blah-blah-blah. Parents bumped from commune to commune. Oregon. Arizona. Wyoming. Ah, yes, here we go. 'After the tragic death of his parents in a skydiving accident, the California law firm of Ross, Herowitz, and Albright, had the task of finding the heir to the Stones' multimillion dollar estate.' Blah-blah. You're right—Zeke did drift from one construction job to another. It tells all the places where the Stones had lived. It took over a year for a private investigator the lawyers hired to locate the two of them."

Without realizing it, Dixie had dropped her pretense of not being curious. She'd wondered about Waco—where he was, who he worked for, how he was doing. And, she wondered if he'd fallen in love. Was the petite blonde in the picture his wife?

"Here's the juicy part. Quote, '. . . Wade Stone returns to the Bayou City as a major player in the land development on Galveston Island and in the Galveston Bay area. His firm, appropriately named Tumbleweed, Inc., will build glitzy, Hollywood-type homes overlooking the Gulf of Mexico for Houston's budding movie industry.' Tell me that was of no interest to you," she gloated, folding the paper and setting it on the corner of Dixie's desk.

"Only the part about a new developer building homes in the Bay area." Dixie jotted several numbers on the pad of paper, as though she'd been able to concentrate on her work while Sara gossiped. She'd have to erase them after Sara left.

"You can't fool me, Dixie Mayson. You're probably sitting there with that deadpan expression, secretly wishing that Waco doesn't have a sprig of hair under his hat, and his trenchcoat conceals a poochy-belly."

Dixie hid a grin behind her hand so as not to encourage Sara's inclination to male-bash.

"And . . . wishing the blond bombshell with the death grip on his arm is cross-eyed, with buck teeth and . . . and has silicone implants!"

In a pseudo-bored voice Dixie inquired, "Is the

weather forecast in the same section of the paper as the gossip column?"

"Stormy," Sara predicted without consulting the paper. "Forget the weather. You'd better read your horoscope. I think Wade Stone came back to Houston to get revenge."

"Revenge?" Dixie chuckled, then scoffed, "For heaven's sake, Sara, stop overdramatizing what happened between the two of us."

"Don't laugh. I know you think I have an overly active imagination, but just remember, I lived next door to you. I heard via the grapevine how John beat up Waco, fired him, and had the police run him out of town."

"Neighborhood gossips inflated the truth." Dixie minimized the episode, repeating the story she'd stuck to for ten years. "Waco and Dad had a disagreement and Waco departed for parts unknown, never to be heard from again." To tweak Sara's lapse of memory, she continued, "As far as police involvement? I seem to recall their being too busy at your house to notice what was going on next door."

"Ha!" She pointed her well-manicured finger at Dixie. "You can whitewash what happened, but something tells me you'll be hearing from Wade Stone."

"Houston being the fourth largest city in the nation, I doubt we'll be bumping into each other."

"Uh-huh, but the construction business is a tightly knit community. Everybody knows everybody's business." Her hand moved to her hip. "I'll bet when your dad reads this, he'll be praying for a force-ten hurricane to blow Tumbleweed out of Texas Proud's territory."

"Chances are he won't know Waco is in town, unless you read that article to him."

"Me? I may be the blondheaded bubble brain he thinks I am, but I don't have a death wish." Sara gestured to the floor-to-ceiling window directly behind Dixie, then made a pushing motion with both hands as she said, "I know what John does to bearers of bad tidings."

"You'd have to get in line. He's wrangling with the suppliers this week. That last increase in the cost of lumber has him ready to mount up an expedition to the Pacific Northwest and declare open-season on spotted owls."

Sara grinned. Tongue in cheek, she suggested, "You could extend a little Southern hospitality and call him."

"Dad is out of the office," Dixie replied, preferring to play dumb and discuss her father's whereabouts rather than return to the unsettling topic of Waco Stone. She glanced at her watch. "Your coffee break is over. Isn't it time for you to go to lunch?"

"I could dial Wade Stone's number before I go."

"How the hell did you get it?"

"That's part of the blah-blah-blahs I left out." She gave Dixie one of her cheekiest grins. "His business number is area code 407 TMBLEWD, just in case you're dying to call him."

"I'm not," Dixie stated firmly. "But I am dying

of hunger. Would you order a turkey sandwich from Frenchy's and pick it up for me?"

"You want me to drive from the Galleria to Clear Lake, for a sandwich?"

Dixie raised her eyes from the plan and glanced from Sara to the door. "You navigating the freeway and out of my office does have significant appeal at this moment. I really am too busy to gossip. And I really am starving."

"Would you settle for a burger-doodle cheeseburger?"

"Whatever. Just go. Please."

Sara rolled her eyes toward the ceiling. "That's the thanks I get for keeping you informed?"

"Please *and* thank you *and* goodbye," Dixie replied as Sara stood and crossed to the door separating her office from Sara's cubicle.

After her friend departed, Dixie struggled to keep her mind on her work, but that damned newspaper on the corner of her desk distracted her. Her hand moved, but instead of knocking it out of sight, she picked it up.

In privacy, she closely examined the picture of Wade "Waco" Stone. Her forefinger lightly outlined his silhouette as she noted the visible changes. He'd traded his Stetson for the same style hat Clark Gable had made famous, his "Texas tuxedo"—jeans and chambray shirt—for a business suit, and his carpenter's tool belt for a briefcase.

"And me for a gorgeous Hollywood starlet barely half his age," she observed drily, with a shake of her head.

Could it be that Sara's wild imagination had voiced the inner thoughts of the eighteen-year-old girl contained inside Dixie. Her serene composure had concealed her inward reaction from Sara's prying eyes, but now Dixie acknowledged that her pulse had skipped a beat when she'd recognized Waco in the picture.

"He is a handsome scoundrel," she mumbled, with a scowl as she remembered how he'd hoodwinked her into believing he loved her.

Back up, she warned herself, as she propped her elbows on the desk and rubbed her forehead to relieve the beginning pangs of a headache. You hoodwinked yourself into believing he loved you.

For her own peace of mind, she'd stopped blaming Waco years ago. While she'd been in college—figuratively, far enough away from the forest to identify the trees—her roommate, a senior majoring in psychology, had helped Dixie impartially examine her psyche to determine what had happened. After picking apart her childhood, Jenny helped her realize that, like most teenagers, she had lived in an insular world that revolved around her appearance, dates, and rebelling against parental authority.

It had been her own psychological susceptibility that had caused the disastrous affair. Not Waco.

Waco could have been any guy her father and friends considered unsuitable. To prove she was no longer a child, no longer under her domineering father's thumb, she'd tested John's confining restraints by choosing a guy who epitomized everything her father objected to: an employee, a high-school dropout, a drifter.

Jenny cited specific instances to show Dixie how she'd subconsciously wanted her father to discover the clandestine relationship: by openly defying him during their arguments, by after-hours phone calls, by skipping school and going to the beach, by going to one of Texas Proud's display homes to lose her virginity. For all intents and purposes, she'd been waving a rebellious red flag in front of her father's face.

And Waco?

Jenny thought he was a heartless son-of-a-bitch to disappear into the night without a word, but, this was an example of Waco following his own set pattern of behavior. From what Dixie told him of Waco's childhood and teenage years, it had been inevitable for him to desert her when she needed him the most. Hadn't the parents he'd loved deserted him when he was vulnerable? Jenny predicted that if Waco had stuck around long enough to convince Dixie to run off and marry him, within a year or less he'd have left her barefoot and pregnant.

Dixie could almost hear her roommate wisely advising her that time would heal a broken heart, but in the meantime, she should thank her lucky stars she hadn't become pregnant from her one sexual encounter. A daily reminder of her indiscretion would have resulted in an irreparable breach in Dixie's relationship with her father. No man could look at his daughter's baby and forget who'd fathered his grandchild.

There must have been something in the air the night of the prom, Dixie mused, because Sara's child had lots of playmates born the same month.

She had been lucky.

Hadn't she?

Dixie let her arms drop to the desk, framing the newspaper. Except for being mildly annoyed at Waco for not being baldheaded and sporting a beer-belly instead of a buxom blonde, his picture had not caused a juvenile clamoring of wild emotions.

She neatly tore the article from the newspaper and attached a note to Sara that read: "File under old business."

Once she'd uncluttered her desk by pitching the remains of the paper in the trash can, Dixie relegated Waco's picture to the out-tray and resumed her job of compiling cost figures on Mayson Manor.

Zeke ambled through the maze of boxes being organized and emptied into filing cabinets. The workers were preoccupied with their assigned tasks, so no one noticed him, least of all the arrogant young whippersnappers with their fancy nameplates hung beside their closed office doors. The urge to stick two fingers in his mouth, give a shrill whistle, and shout, "Show me the same respect you'd give my nephew," had Zeke hitching up his worn jeans and lengthening his stride to purposeful steps.

"Good afternoon, Mr. Stone," an unfamiliar

voice politely said from behind him. "Is there something I can do for you?"

Pleased that somebody in this Godforsaken catacomb must have realized he breathed the same rarified air as Waco, he spun on his heel toward the voice. A grey-haired woman three times his size in girth and several inches shorter than Zeke, stared at him over dinky little bifocals perched on her nose.

"I got important business to talk over with my nephew," he replied gruffly. "Where is he? And who are you?"

"Liz Stafford, General Office Manager." Her shoulders lifted, which made her ample bosom rise. She was not impressed by the scrawny man's loud voice or his pink-and-blue cowboy shirt and ostrich-skinned boots, or by him calling the President of Tumbleweed, Inc. a "boy." Her brows beetled together forming a straight grey line. "Mr. Stone is attending an important meeting with the building inspectors. I expect him to return shortly. If you'll follow me, I'll escort you to . . ."

"You don't hafta tell Waco nuthin, woman," Zeke informed her, turning his back to her to put her in her place. Several women he didn't know from Adam had stopped to gawk. "I'll be in his office, takin' calls. Meantime, you'd better stop lollygagging around and start doin' whatever you're supposed to doin'. This place looks like a construction site with no ridin' boss supervising the hired hands."

Before he'd taken another step, he had the satisfaction of seeing files start flying from boxes into cabinets. Yes, siree, Zeke thought, mentally giving himself a pat on the back. Waco had the book learning, but judging from how those poky women had picked up their pace, he could teach Waco a thing or two about running their business.

"Sir," Liz called, her short legs unable to match his longer stride. "I suggest you return to the reception area."

"Woman, don't you natter at me, tellin' me where I can and can't go."

"But . . ."

He charged through the freshly carpeted receptionist's area toward the double doors. Glancing over his shoulder he yelled, "I own part of Tumbleweed. I'll go where I damn well please."

"Stop . . ." Her mouth dropped open, but she knew her warning would come too late.

Zeke's howl of fury was music to Liz Stafford's ears.

"Glue," Liz said, her face stern, but with a smile in her voice. "Marble adhesive, to be precise."

Mortified, Zeke mumbled a string of curses as foul as the foul-smelling brownish-yellow goo oozing over the soles of his expensive boots. If the look he gave Liz had been loaded into a nail-gun, she'd have been crucified on the far wall of the office.

"While the adhesive is setting up and the marble is laid, Mr. Stone will temporarily be in the office immediately off the receptionist's area."

"I knew that," he blustered, his face crimson.

He heard sniggers coming from behind Liz Stafford. Stuck, he couldn't move backward or forward, or remove his boots without making a complete ass of himself.

"What's the problem?" The quiet authority heard in Wade Stone's voice sliced through the cluster of office personnel like Moses parting the Red Sea. As they stepped aside, Waco could see his uncle's predicament over Ms. Stafford's wide shoulders. Zeke's habit of landing in sticky situations usually didn't require Waco to extract him, literally. To alleviate Zeke's chagrin, he asked Liz, "Did the tile crew arrive early?"

"Yes, sir. Before eight," Liz replied. "I tried to stop your uncle, but . . ."

"Don't stand there blathering with the hired help," Zeke interrupted. "Get me out of here!"

Gladly, Waco mused, aware from the short hairs standing on Ms. Stafford's neck that his uncle must have been his usual ornery self. Last week, he'd assigned Zeke a task he'd hoped would keep the old man out of everyone's hair until he had the office operating efficiently. No such luck.

Waco encircled Zeke's waist with his arm and hoisted him straight up in the air, leaving the boots cemented in the concrete glue.

"I found a house," Zeke announced, as though dangling from his nephew's arms was standard operating procedure. With a sly look on his face, he added, "One you helped build when you were a nail-banger for Texas Proud."

Waco dropped Zeke. His jaw clenched tightly; his lips barely moved as he said, "Follow me."

"Will you be needing me?" Liz asked timidly.

"Proceed with what you were doing, Ms. Stafford. Hold my calls for the next hour." Waco quickly retraced his way back through the stacked boxes, with Zeke strutting behind him. They were inside his office with the door shut when he enlightened Zeke by saying, "Forget whatever clever scheme you've cooked up to get even with John Mayson."

"Forget it?" Zeke sank into the chair and propped his feet on Waco's desk. "He beat the hell outta you! The son-of-a-bitch tried to get both of us locked up! You want me to forget it?" He made a snorting noise. "The devil will qualify as an Olympic ice skater before I forget."

With one hand on his hip, while the other was massaging the back of his neck, Waco stared blindly through the window on the ninth floor of the tallest building on Galveston Island. His voice was as flat as the gulf's surf as he said, "I'm in Houston to make money, not dredge up an old feud."

"Bullshit. You jumped at the chance to show 'em you could buy and sell 'em, without checkin' with your banker first!"

"The housing market in California is flat. Houston is on the verge of a boom," Waco replied in denial. "Business. That's why we are here."

"So you've said. But that doesn't make it true for me." His bony finger jabbed the air. "Nobody gets away with bribin' the cops to run me out of town."

"You can't prove that."

Slowly, Waco turned to face Zeke. Self-righteous indignation must have affected his memory, he mused, vividly recalling the incident. There was little doubt in his mind that John Mayson had used his influence to sway the chief of police to threaten him, but Zeke had completely forgotten that waving a shotgun under the policeman's nose and being drunk as a skunk had complicated the problem.

"Deny those cops were in cahoots with Mayson if you can," Zeke jibed. "I'm gonna get even with the bastard. I'd sue Texas Proud and Mayson's gun-toting kiss-ass officers if it wasn't past the statue of liberations!"

"Statute of limitations," Waco corrected, silently thanking the legal system for small favors. California's courts would have been clogged from the numerous lawsuits Zeke had filed if he hadn't taken Tumbleweed's attorney aside and put an end to the embarrassment.

Zeke nodded. "Them, too. I'm like them highway signs that says, Don't mess with Texas. Anybody dumps on me and I'll make 'em pay."

Realizing the futility of butting heads with his uncle, Waco made a threat of his own. "You start messing with the Maysons and I promise, you'll be back in California quicker than you can spell Los Angeles."

Affronted by his nephew siding with the enemy, Zeke bristled. "What about the house I looked at?"

"We'll stay at the Galvestonian condo until you locate another place."

"I gave the real estate man a check. Being as I've been lookin' day and night for a suitable place for you, it seems to me you could at least look at it."

"Which house is it?" Waco asked, mildly curious.

"It's in Bayou Oaks." Zeke grinned. "You'll remember it 'cuz it used to be the display house."

Waco remembered far more than he'd revealed to his uncle. "Get the deposit back or leave it on the table. I don't care which."

"You aren't gonna look at it?"

"No."

"Why not? It's perfect! Big screened-in pool. Fireplace. Master suite and four other bedrooms. And it's empty. Just like you said you wanted."

"Find another one."

"Crystal loves it." His grin widened, exposing his tobacco-stained teeth. "She's at the condo packing up her stuff."

"You left her alone?"

"Would you stop actin' like a mother hen? With no car and no friends, she can't get into mischief. It's broad daylight outside."

Immediately, Waco grabbed the phone and dialed the condo's number. He heard it ring twice before a groggy hello traveled across the lines.

"What are you doing?" Waco spat, without exchanging social graces.

"I was bored sitting here alone, so now I'm

catching some rays out on the balcony." She must have heard Waco's sigh of relief and Zeke's chuckle, because she provocatively added, "Nude."

"Crystal!"

"Just kidding, Waco," she yawned, then made her usual complaint, "God, you're such a tight-ass. Why I agreed to live with you I'll never know."

"Zeke will be at the condo in fifteen minutes to take you to lunch." He reached in his pocket for his money clip, extracted a large-denomination bill, and motioned with it for Zeke, who'd been avidly eavesdropping, to take it and leave. "Zeke needs a new pair of boots. You can take him shopping."

For once, Zeke didn't argue.

"Joy, joy, joy," she droned sarcastically. "Should I get down on my knees and thank you?"

"That won't be necessary. Just stay out of trouble until I find something for you to do around here."

"If you really loved me, you'd let me be your secretary," she pouted. "Your office is where the action is."

"No way. We tried that, remember?"

"So I made a couple of mistakes," she answered without contrition. "All of us can't be financial wizards."

No, but with your help we can all be paupers, he thought drily. For a smart twenty-year-old woman, Crystal didn't have a lick of common sense when it came to business.

When he didn't argue, Crystal said, "I suppose

you'll be neglecting me again tonight by working late?"

"A Bay Area Chamber of Commerce dinner meeting in Clear Lake, according to the calendar on my desk. I'll see you while I change clothes."

"Can I go?"

"You'd be bored stiff."

"How could I possibly be bored when I'm with the fabulous Cinderfella?" she teased.

Waco groaned, "I'd love to throttle the reporter who thought that one up. This morning a couple of the building inspectors kept looking at my feet for glass slippers."

Laughing, she said, "I'll be dressed and ready before you get here. Bye."

The line disconnected before he could argue the point further. He hung up the receiver feeling culpable. Crystal did have a legitimate complaint. First, with her parents, who'd spoiled her by substituting cash for affection, and now, she was getting the same treatment from him. Other than Zeke, nobody had the time to give her the attention she needed.

One way or another, Waco mused, Crystal would get his attention. Of that, he was certain.

"And she doesn't give a damn how she does it."

Twelve

"Did you figure in the four-car garage?" Dirk Stallman, the man in charge of procurement asked Dixie.

Quickly, she checked the figures she'd gathered over the past week. Several emergencies had kept her from getting with Dirk as soon as she would have liked. "Yes. And the poolside cabana."

"What about the stable?"

"Stable?" Her eyes bounced from her notepad to his face. "What stable?"

"Two stalls, a tack room, and a feed room," Dirk Stallman replied blandly. "About four thousand square feet, all totaled. Of course, that doesn't include the lumber for the paddock fence John requested."

Thoroughly annoyed by Dirk's patronizing tone and her father's altering the plans without keeping her informed, she had to bite the inside of her mouth to hold her redheaded temperament in check.

He who gets angry loses the battle, she reminded herself silently.

She rolled her set of schematics off Dirk's desk and rubber-banded them with a sharp snap as she wondered why her father wanted a stable built. Neither of them rode horses, nor owned any.

"Hold the order until John and I discuss this."

"Can't."

"Can't?" His self-important smile made Dixie's palms itch. "I beg your pardon?"

"John signed the purchase order yesterday. Unless I'm misinformed, he gave Walter Block the green light to scrape the lot and start setting the foundation forms." Rapidly, he punched several keys on his computer to check his schedule. "By next week the ground work should be finished and I'll be ordering concrete for the piers."

"Download the schedule and the concrete estimate into my computer." Despite her polite smile and the calm tone of her voice, her insides squirmed with frustration and annoyance.

She hated being misinformed, hell, *un*informed. Evidently, John had started the scheduling process without her! "I'll be at the job site."

Dirk glanced at his diamond-bezel Rolex watch. "Will you have time to get there and make it to the Builder's Association meeting?"

"No. I'll have to skip the meeting." First on her priority list was resuming control of building Mayson Manor. She stood and tucked the schematics under her arm while giving Dirk another tolerant smile. "I'll get with you tomorrow on this barn business."

"John sent an interoffice communication right after lunch." He held a pink sheet of paper toward her. "This meeting is mandatory for all TP's executives."

"Why?"

"The chairman of the panel is sick. Your father is his replacement. He wants a show of strength by Texas Proud."

"What's the topic?"

"Expansion in Galveston County."

Briskly striding across his office, she said, "I'll see you there."

Considering her time restriction, she decided a confrontation with John would have to substitute for a lengthy conversation with Walter Block, the project manager at the job site. She must have looked like an Amazon on the warpath because John's secretary, Phyllis, remained seated at her desk as Dixie barged through his office door.

"We have a communication problem," she stated baldly, thumping the thick roll of plans on John's desk. "In conjunction with my responsibilities here at headquarters, am I or am I not responsible for the Mayson Manor project?"

"You are," John replied, without looking up from his notes. He waved his hand to dismiss her. "I'm putting the finishing touches on my speech for tonight."

Tenaciously, she stood her ground and ticked off her objections on the fingers of one hand. "If I'm responsible for this project, why did you make a schedule, authorize shipment, and send Walter Block over to break ground? Not to mention arbitrarily adding a stable, without consulting me. Stallman thinks I'm an incompetent idiot because you completely undermined my authority."

"He resents having his estimates scrutinized. Deal with it."

"Not with a marked deck," she snapped. Redirecting his attention to the main problem, she inquired, "Why did you change the start date?"

John looked up from his notes to see his daughter's reaction as he said, "Because I want you to concentrate your efforts on Gil Albertson's latest venture."

"In land acquisition? Why?"

"We're running short on waterfront lots." John pointed to the Galveston Bay area map hanging on the wall behind her. "You know that hundred-acre parcel of land on NASA Road One that borders Mud Gully Lake?"

"The one down from the Johnson Space Center?"

"That's the one."

"Gil and I walked it a year or so ago. We decided the low bridge that denied bigger boats access to Clear Lake prevented developers from buying it."

"A friend of ours at City Hall says there's a chance the bridge will be elevated."

"To facilitate a few waterfront estates? I doubt it."

"I do, too, but it's still a prime piece of property. Two of our clients canceled their options to build houses in the subdivision overlooking Galveston Bay because they'd heard the same rumor."

"Gil's friend at City Hall must have a ring

around his finger from dialing the phone," Dixie joked humorlessly.

"Yeah, well, Texas Proud missed a good financial shot in the arm when the back side of Clear Lake was developed." John shook his head in disbelief. "Who'd have thought those rice farms would sprout acres of houses?"

"A Yankee developer who has never seen it rain forty-two inches in two days," Dixie replied drolly, remembering Dickenson Bayou's inclination to flood. "Or been through a hurricane, like Alecia."

"A West Coast developer bought the NASA piece of land. I guess their being used to fires, mudslides, and earthquakes, makes them immune to anything as puny as gale-force winds. The odds are better here. Our disasters only happen once every twenty years. Out in California, it's a yearly occurrence."

"California?" Alarmed, Dixie settled into a chair before her knees collapsed. How many developers from California had recently relocated here? She'd only heard of one—Tumbleweed, Inc. "Are you certain the developer is from there?"

John nodded. "Gil contacted them. So far he hasn't been able to make any progress. That's why you're going to be working with him. Gil is great with Texas good-ole-boys. You have more finesse."

Since the majority of the developers were good-ole-boys, Dixie winced at his backhanded compliment. "Who did Gil contact?"

"The developer's company name is Tumbleweed."

"Tumbleweed?" she repeated, her stomach twisting into a hard knot.

"What do you know about them?"

She had long ago outgrown the need to hide information from her father. But, she had the same fear Sara had when it came to being the bearer of bad tidings. John would explode when he heard that to get the lots he needed he'd have to kiss up to a man that he'd fired.

"Wade Stone owns Tumbleweed. Stone is the developer."

"Stone?" John scratched the side of his head as though it would prod his memory. "That's a fairly common name. Should it ring a bell?"

One bigger than Big Ben!

For the past week, she'd fought the mixed feelings the name Waco Stone caused: hope and dread. Each day that passed without Waco making contact had been both a blessing and a curse.

She wanted him to remember her, and yet, she didn't. What would he say to her? The embers of their passionate one night affair were ashes. She had no desire to rake through them.

When she'd reexamined the photo in the newspaper, she decided Waco had one good reason not to call her—a beautiful blond-haired woman.

She sure as heck wasn't going to contact him, be he married or single, for business or pleasure!

"Does the name *Waco* Stone jar your memory?" she asked softly.

As the name registered in his mental computer,

John blinked, twice, and then the vein on his forehead began to throb fiercely.

"Your Waco?" he demanded in a strained voice. "The finish carpenter?"

"He isn't *mine*," she contested hotly. "You made certain of that."

John dropped his pencil then pushed back from his desk with such force his chair rammed into the credenza behind him. A bronze sculpture of a rodeo cowboy riding a bucking mustang teetered on its base; it went unnoticed. In pure disgust, John slapped his thigh. "Well I'll be a son-of-a-bitch!"

"I imagine that's the kindest name Waco would call you," Dixie said drily.

"How the hell did a finish carpenter get his hands on that kind of money?" Before Dixie could reply, he grunted, "Must have gotten it the old-fashioned way. Marriage." He pointed his finger at his daughter. "I told you he was up to no good with you."

Perversely, Dixie murmured aloud, "Texas Proud couldn't afford that strip of land at today's prices. From what I read in the newspaper, he inherited his wealth."

"Another old-fashioned way of getting money," John scoffed.

"I'd say the worm has turned, Dad. Now Waco has something you want."

"The hell he has. He's still an outsider wanting in."

She watched John rock in his chair while he reconsidered the situation. His eyes tracked over her like an appraiser's measuring tape. He wasn't uttering a word, but she knew she didn't like what he was contemplating. If her father had some misbegotten idea that Waco had returned to Houston in pursuit of her, he was in for a big disillusionment.

"I haven't seen or heard from Waco Stone since the night you kicked him off your property."

"Hmmmm," John replied noncommittally. Pride and shame kept him from revealing that he'd been physically unable to give Stone the pounding he richly deserved. "No point in bringing up a sore subject."

"I suggest you forget about dealing with Tumbleweed. There are other lots you can buy."

She watched him tug his earlobe, as though he could turn off his hearing to anything she had to say. Typical reaction, Dixie observed silently, remembering how her father had refused to discuss what had happened that evening.

It was as though he'd reduced the number of studs in a building, then covered the flaw with sheetrock, paint and wallpaper. Everything looked perfect. Only the two of them knew the structure was unsound.

At this late date, neither of them wanted to strip off the facade and examine the walls.

Finally, John sat forward on the edge of his chair and leaned his forearms on the desk. "Stone was invited to the meeting tonight. Why don't . . ."

"No." Dixie sprang from her chair and strode toward the door. "That's final."

"No?"

"No! Go bark up another tree."

"Why bark when the bird's nest is on the ground? Hear me out." Before she could twist the knob, John stalked toward her asking, "What's wrong with old acquaintances renewing a friendship?"

"You won't like it when Waco laughs in your face," she replied, deliberately misconstruing his intent.

"He won't have the opportunity. I wasn't referring to me getting reacquainted with him." Taking her by the arm, he attempted to lead her back to her chair, but she held onto the knob. "While I'm conducting the panel, you could have a friendly . . ."

"I don't believe this!" She yanked her elbow from his light hold. She held her fingers in front of his face. "For the sake of Texas Proud, I've had enough dirt under my fingernails to make an Iowa farmer jealous, but I don't do this kind of dirty work. Not for TP, not for you, not for anybody!"

". . . chat with Waco," John finished with a determined glint in his eyes. "Charm him into negotiating with Gil."

"Are you suggesting that I try to seduce him?"

"This is strictly business, Dixie," he scolded, but his face flushed a telltale red. "There's nothing immoral about you talking to him. Just let him know that you hold no hard feelings."

"That's despicable. Loyalty to you and Texas Proud does not include my charming Waco Stone."

She was spared from elaborating, since the knob was twisting beneath her hand as Phyllis opened the door.

" 'Scuse me," came through the narrow crack. "Gil is on line one. He says it's urgent."

"Don't move a muscle," John instructed, hustling to the phone. "Gil may have solved our problem."

"I don't have a problem," she clarified. "I didn't beat up Waco."

Both stubborn and inquisitive, she couldn't leave without making certain John and Gil didn't hatch up a substitute scheme to use her as bait in their trap.

"Oh yeah?" she heard her father inquire, with a scowl. "He does?"

He does what? she wondered silently. Her perspiring palm was making the brass knob slick. She hated hearing one side of a conversation and imagining the other side. Nervously, her hand dropped to her side. She rubbed the dampness on the seam of her grey skirt. From the sharp glance John gave her, she suspected that she was the topic being discussed.

"She's here in my office."

That should have been her cue to escape while she could, but she'd learned to stand firm on her convictions. No lying, no half-truths, no sneaking behind her father's back. Those were the lessons she'd learned the last time she'd been with Waco, the hard way.

"Can do," John promised, delivering another

chuckle. "You get the facts and figures together. Good job, Gil." John hung up and grinned at his daughter. "Stone won't be at the meeting tonight."

"Is that the good news?" She held her breath, anticipating the bad news.

"He's invited one or both of us to the Galvez Hotel for dinner. Seven sharp."

"Do they have crow on the menu?" she asked sweetly. "If so, I suggest you order a double serving, with a big slice of humble pie for dessert."

"I'm obligated to head up the panel discussion. I have no choice but to delegate this responsibility to you."

"And I have no choice?"

"None."

Her sense of humor saved her from a battle she'd inevitably lose.

"Life's ironic, isn't it?" she mused aloud. "You're ordering me to go out with the man you ordered off our property. And, you want to buy Waco's property from him." She paused, waiting for her father to acknowledge responsibility for his actions. When he ducked his head and riffled though the notes for his speech, Dixie had no qualms about making him worry about the evening's outcome. "Whoever it was that said war makes strange bedfellows must have been in the construction business."

Two minutes later, Dixie practically ran by Sara's desk to get to her office before she exploded with anger.

"Gil what's-his-face from land procurement just called. He wants you to . . ."

"Later, Sara."

Inside the privacy of her own office, Dixie had an uncontrollable urge to smash something, anything, to relieve her frustration. The crystal paperweight Kate had given her for Christmas would make a satisfying crash, she decided. She lifted it, mentally weighed it, drew back her arm, and had the good sense to lob it into the sumptuously padded couch across the room. The dull thud as the cushions absorbed the impact wasn't the least bit gratifying. However, expending energy on her pent-up fury did help.

Of all the short-sighted, callous, insensitive men in the world, why did her father have to take the blue ribbon? Too proud to eat crow himself, he wanted to appease Waco by making her a sacrificial lamb!

What did John expect her to say to Waco? "Hey, listen Waco, I'm sorry my father tried to separate your head from your shoulders, and when he couldn't, he fired you. He did manage to bust your bottom lip. Is that why you couldn't get in touch with me before you saddled up and rode West?"

Her hands covered her face as she realized she had forgiven Waco, but she hadn't forgotten how he'd deserted her when she had needed him.

From the door, Sara began reading from her stenographer's note pad. "Paul Getz sent the proofs over for the ad in Sunday's *Chronicle*. Anderson, the riding boss, not Andersen the window people, finished the punch-out list on 2289 Treasure Court. He says the landscaper must have used dog doo instead of cow power to fertilize the shrubs. They're wilting. And, last but not least, I'm taking off early to . . ."

Sara looked up from her note pad, saw Dixie pick up the desk lamp, dodged behind the wing chair and amended, "work late. Yes, indeed, very late. Long past my son's bedtime story."

"Relax, Sara, I'm not angry with you." Dixie returned the lamp to the faint dust circle that marked its place. "It's John I'd like to crown with this lamp."

Sara peeked from behind her hiding place, waving the pad of paper like a truce flag. "He must have really punched your button. I haven't seen you throw things since fourth grade, when you bopped Chad Armstrong in the head with your art eraser."

An idea popped into Dixie's head like she was a cartoon character. "That's it, Sara!"

"What is?"

"Chad Armstrong." She gave her bewildered friend a quick hug. "His folks were developing a strip of land on Clear Creek. The streets and sewers were in before the bust. They still own it, don't they?"

"I don't know for certain. I think it's tied up in litigation."

Excited by the prospect of locating waterfront acreage, she said, "Put through a call to Chad's office immediately. Maybe, just maybe, I'll be eating dinner at home tonight."

"Oooops. I forgot to give you the flyer your

father sent around, didn't I? Is that why you're throwing things?"

"No." Dixie unfolded the top edge of the sandwich bag, took one whiff of grilled onions, glanced at the soggy bun and pitched the sack into the trash can. "Gil arranged a meeting with Wade Stone to buy waterfront lots. John delegated it to me."

"And that pissed you off?"

"I never did like cleaning up my father's messes. What happened to the good old days when he said, 'You make a mess, you clean it up, you don't get yelled at.' Why doesn't that rule apply to him?"

"You could delegate this loathsome job my way," Sara volunteered eagerly. "Not only is Wade Stone rich, he's handsome to boot! And from the picture, he's partial to blondes!"

Dixie smoothed her hand over the long plait of auburn hair she wore in a tidy French braid. "Waco can have a truckload of blondes, for all I care. I'm calling Chad. With luck, Waco can take his parcel of land and . . ."

"Shove it where the sun don't shine?"

"And I can dine alone," Dixie said, finishing her thought. "Get Chad on the telephone, would you?"

"With you twisting his arm to get those lots, Chad'll think this is like old times," Sara teased, bustling toward her office before Dixie could heave something at her, "Try not to break it this time."

Dixie's stomach spoke for her by issuing a low growl.

Minutes later, she was at her desk when Sara buzzed through to announce, "Chad is on line three."

"Thanks." She pressed the button and smiled. "Hello, Chad. How are you?"

"Better, now that I'm talking to you. It's been a long time, Dixie. Too long. I've thought about giving you a call several times over the years."

"You have?" she blurted out, unsure that this flirty voice belonged to the same Chad she'd chased into the locker room.

"Are you calling about the tenth-year class reunion?"

"No. I hadn't heard about it."

"I received my invitation yesterday. Cocktails, a seafood dinner, then a dance."

"Mine's probably in the mail."

"I'm available, if you're still interested," he offered, with a chuckle. "I still have one good arm you haven't broken."

Dixie groaned. He hadn't forgotten either. "Actually, I'm calling about those lots your family owns on Clear Creek. Are they for sale?"

She waited several seconds before Chad replied succinctly, "No."

"You sold them?"

"They're tied up in bankruptcy court."

"Oh." Her disappointment was overshadowed by concern for the Armstrong family. The oil bust had affected everyone in Houston. The lucky ones, like

TP, had tightened their belts and put plans on hold. Financially, the Armstrongs must have been spread too thin to have spare notches in their belt. "I'm sorry to hear that."

"Don't be. It's a risk a developer takes. We'll reorganize and recuperate, eventually. It takes time."

"Sure you will," she agreed with optimism. "Meanwhile, if you hear of similar lots available, give me a shout."

"That's easy. Have you heard about Mud Gully? An outsider from California snapped it up before the local boys knew it was available. I could make a couple of calls and put you in contact with them."

"Thanks, but Gil Albertson talked to those developers."

"What are their plans?"

"I don't know, yet." Her stomach knotted. "But I will, soon."

"Waterfront lots are at a premium. Maybe we could form a limited partnership. Keep me informed, would you?"

"You, too."

"And don't forget the reunion."

"I won't. It was good talking to you, Chad."

"Call me if I can do anything for you."

"Will do."

"Bye."

Replacing the phone, Dixie had to chuckle at the way he'd said *anything*. He must have confused her with the girl who'd chased after him through junior and senior high school, to no avail. She gave the phone a little pat and said, "Sorry, Chad. I have bigger fish to fry."

Thirteen

Seven o'clock on the nose, Waco noted, watching Dixie Mayson smile warmly at two elderly women as she held the door for them to pass through in front of her. He'd been waiting, watching, wondering if he'd recognize her. When she passed by the cocktail lounge where he sat, on her way to their appointment in the dining area of the Galvez, Waco felt certain he'd have recognized those terrific long legs and her jaunty walk anywhere in the world.

Her style of dress had changed, but he really hadn't expected her to show up at a fancy hotel dining room in jeans and an oversized man's shirt, had he? Wishful thinking, he realized, knowing ten years hadn't altered how the denim fabric would fit snugly across her backside.

With his elbow on the table, his hand holding a glass of beer, he followed her progress as he leaned against the plate glass separating the bar from the corridor. He couldn't fault the pale green linen suit she wore; it made her hair appear darker, longer than he remembered, and it swayed ever so enticingly inches above her trim waist.

Waco grinned as he noted her high heels. She'd been so self-conscious about her height, he'd only seen her wear them once—that fateful night of her prom, when he'd discarded them and the sexy little black dress she'd worn. He finished his beer in one gulp. The bitter taste of hops took the edge off the flavor that particular memory caused.

"Is that her?" Crystal asked, pivoting at the waist to get a good look. "You didn't tell me she was gorgeous."

"Stop staring. It's rude."

"Can't be," she argued with a cheeky grin. "Everyone's watching her, yourself included."

His dark eyes followed the perimeter of glass. Not one pair of male eyes were on the women across the table from them. Waco motioned the waiter for the check, then removed a twenty-dollar bill from his pocket.

"Let's go."

"Afraid she'll find somebody better-looking?" Crystal was opening her purse to freshen her lipstick.

Ignoring her gibe, Waco paid the waiter. "Keep the change."

"My, my, aren't you generous tonight," Crystal commented after the waiter flashed Waco a wide smile and removed their empty glasses. She removed her lipstick.

Tersely, Waco asked, "Is that a complaint or a compliment?"

"Merely an observation." She uncapped her lipstick and removed her compact.

"Crystal, you look fine." He stood and moved to the back of her chair. "Can we go, please?"

"I have to check out the plumbing in the ladies' room."

"Now?"

"You did say for me not to do the slightest thing to embarrass you. A puddle . . ."

"Watch your mouth." Waco touched her bare shoulder to silence her. Her royal blue halter dress made her California tan and blond hair look terrific, but he was too irritated with her behavior to notice. "Go. I'll meet you in the dining room."

Turning on his heel, he buttoned his jacket and squared the Windsor knot between the points of his collar as he hurried toward the place where Dixie awaited his arrival.

He glanced over his shoulder to check on Crystal, who was nowhere in sight. His jaw clenched. Fully aware of how Crystal would say or do whatever outlandish thing crossed her mind when boredom caused one of her discontented moods, Waco began to regret empathizing with her for being in a strange city and friendless.

He knew how it felt to be lonely, but dammit, he didn't have the time or the inclination to be Crystal's playmate or her babysitter. There were times when she made him wonder why he'd felt despondent over not being part of a family.

His thoughts returned to Dixie the closer he came to the dining room. He did not share Zeke's hard feelings toward the Maysons. John believed his only daughter was secretly involved with a no-account bum, so he'd removed temptation from Dixie's path. A man protected his offspring from potential harm. That primitive instinct was as old as time itself. Under similar circumstances, he'd do the same on Crystal's behalf.

Out of sight, out of mind, Waco mused, when he began to wonder if Dixie had given him a second thought once he'd been driven out of Houston. A hundred times he'd reached for the phone, always when the clock struck midnight. And yet, he hadn't called. What could he say? Come live with me in my trailer? Live hand-to-mouth? From one paycheck to the next? He'd had nothing to offer her.

Teenage rebellion had stretched the bond between Dixie and her domineering father, but over the long haul she'd have returned to the safety and security of her father's home. For both their sakes, it had been wiser to make a swift, clean break.

As he approached the banister separating the wide corridor from the open dining area, he scanned the people seated at the tables. Twice. Dixie was nowhere to be seen.

Familiar with the business tactic of the favor-giver making the favor-getter wait anxiously, Dixie attempted to foil Waco's ploy by entering the powder room. Waco had acquired a fistful of money, she thought angrily, but he hadn't acquired the professional courtesy of a handmaid. Wealth often affected people adversely. He's probably changed into an arrogant, swaggering, . . . *snob!*

She removed a comb from her purse and feverishly pulled it through her hair, welcoming the
slight tug as it hit a snag caused by the gulf breeze.
Better for her scalp to tingle than feel her pride
stung by disappointment.

"I won't beggar myself for a few pieces of land,
no matter what my father wants," she whispered
fervently to her reflection in the mirror. "Wade
Stone doesn't own the entire coast!"

She heard a flushing sound and felt glad she
hadn't sandblasted the mirror with her scathing remark. The comb nearly fell from her hand when
she recognized the woman coming out of the stall.

For several seconds they mutely stared at each
other in the mirror.

"You're Dixie Mayson, aren't you?" the blonde
asked pertly, holding out her hand. "I'm Crystal
Stone."

In midstroke, several hairs pulled from Dixie's
head as the comb clattered against the tile floor.
Waco being an only child, the woman who shared
his name and his bed had to be his *wife*. Her eyes
widened as an unexpected pain squeezed her chest.

"Sorry." Crystal turned on the water faucet with
the hand Dixie had scorned. As she rinsed her
hands, she added, "I didn't mean to startle you."

In an attempt to quickly recover her aplomb,
Dixie stooped down to pick up her comb. Straightening, she managed a small smile. "No need for
an apology. I just came from the dining room. I
thought you all must have been delayed in traffic,
so I thought I'd freshen up while I waited."

You're babbling like a brook feeding water into the faucet washing Crystal Stone's hands, Dixie told herself, as her cheeks began turning pink. Lordy, lordy, she thought she'd outgrown being gauche. Why did the disparaging difference in their heights make her want to kick off her high heels or slouch her shoulders?

Because, she answered with unsugarcoated take-your-medicine honesty, she's married to Waco.

Crystal grinned. "You must have missed Waco. He's such a stickler for punctuality that he's probably at the table gnawing on his napkin by now." She wiped her hands on a paper towel while she leaned toward Dixie and confided, "Out at our ranch in California, Waco used to get out of bed before the crack of dawn to wake up the roosters. Heaven forbid they should crow two seconds late."

"He'll think I'm the one who's late," Dixie replied. Her mouth parched at the image forming in her mind of this beautiful young woman sharing Waco's bed.

She blinked rapidly to dispel the abhorrent image.

"He'll get over it. That dog growls, but he don't bite," Crystal joked.

With her mind clear, Dixie hastily put her comb away, not knowing what etiquette was proper. Should she leave the wife in the john while she rushed to the husband's table? Or wait for the wife and face the husband's wrath? Deciding Crystal could deflect Waco's rancor with one of her smiles, Dixie decided not to hurry.

"How do you like living in Texas?" Dixie inquired, watching the other woman meticulously apply mascara to her inch-long lashes.

"It'll be okay, I guess. Better than staying in California without my family."

"You have children?"

Crystal laughed and shook her head. "I meant Waco and Zeke. Speaking of Zeke, he said you and Waco had a hot romance way back when. Wanna tell me about it?"

Shocked by Crystal's blunt inquisitiveness, Dixie paled. She'd never met Zeke, but she wondered what sort of man would tell his nephew's wife about her husband's previous love affair.

"There's nothing of importance to tell," she responded diplomatically. "Our relationship is ancient history."

Crystal laughed. "Zeke says I ought to be an archeologist 'cause I like to shovel dirt until I dig out valuable information. You're sure you don't want to tell me anything I can use against Waco when he tries to stop me from having a little fun?"

"Having a little fun?" Dixie repeated, needing clarification of exactly what Waco's wife meant.

"You know, with guys. Waco is a terrible prude. He watches me like a hawk." She cast Dixie a sassy grin. "I'd love to have something on him, just for a change of pace."

Disliking the direction their small talk had taken, Dixie crossed to the door and held it open for Crystal. If she waited much longer, Crystal would volunteer the details of her affairs with other men. The thought of Waco being cheated on bothered her, immensely.

"I don't think that would be appropriate."

"Why not?"

"I wouldn't want you to feel ill at ease knowing Waco and I might be together negotiating contracts."

"I'm not possessive. I like you." She motioned for Dixie to precede her from the powder room. "Why should I care if the two of you get together?"

Repulsed by Crystal's permissive attitude, Dixie led the way and said pointedly, "You should care. You are his wife."

With her back to Crystal, Dixie did not see Crystal's mouth drop, or hear the soft thud of the door pushing against the blonde's backside. Like a videotape being rewound and replayed, it took a second for Crystal to realize she'd introduced herself as Crystal Stone, and neglected to add that she was Waco's sister.

A wicked smile of delight curved her lips as Crystal caught up with Dixie. She laid her hand on Dixie's arm. "You're the only woman Waco has ever arranged for me to meet," she professed urgently. "I hope I haven't offended you."

"I'm not . . . offended," Dixie replied, mentally escalating down from her high views concerning marriage. She criticized her father for having a mind as narrow as the red line on a piece of notebook paper. And here she was, being judgmental.

"I'm not wild." Crystal countered Dixie's frown

with a smile and a wink. "Not by California standards."

Dixie pondered the one question relevant to the issue. Uncertain she wanted to know the answer, she had to ask, "Do you love Waco?"

"Of course!" Crystal's dark eyes twinkled with mischief. She wanted Dixie to become her friend, but that did not cancel her intention of playing a little prank on her stick-in-the-mud brother. Sincerely, she added, "I adore Waco."

"She tolerates me," Waco contradicted drily. Concealed from their view by a silk ficus tree, he rose from the cushioned bench and signaled the maître d' to take them to their reserved table. "I see you two have met."

Dixie froze as his eyes locked on her. Again, her manners slipped into nonexistence. How was she supposed to greet the man who'd been her only lover? With a handshake? An airy kiss? A hug? How she envied Crystal for having the right to slide her arm around Waco's waist and smile up at him.

"You can kiss her," Crystal suggested impudently to her brother. "I won't mind."

Instinctively, Dixie turned her head to receive a peck on the cheek. Much to her amazement, Waco caught her chin and slanted his lips across her open mouth, taking her breath away.

"It's good to see you, gorgeous," he said huskily, for her ears only. "You haven't changed."

Completely caught off guard, she took hold of his arm to steady herself. A flash of lightning-white heat flashed from where his lips had lightly touched her to the soles of her feet.

Oh, Waco. Why did you leave me? her heart cried silently. Her eyes glistened as she thought of what they could have shared. Fortunately, the poise she'd acquired over the years saved her from blurting out the unseemly question.

"Thank you," she murmured politely.

"Good evening, ladies," the maître d' bade, smiling as he gestured toward a vacant table. "Please follow me."

"Great," Crystal enthused, her blond eyebrows raised in amused speculation at Waco. "I'm starved."

A guilty flush stained Dixie's cheeks as she glanced at Crystal. Not five minutes ago she'd been castigating the younger woman for her flighty ways, and here she was feeling like a matchstick that had been raked over a piece of emery cloth.

Get a grip on yourself, she chastised herself, when she realized she had a death grip on Waco's arm. Instantly, she dropped her hand to her side. Her knees felt weak as she followed Crystal to their table.

Why did her own body continue to betray her? She'd had a clandestine affair with this man; it had ended disastrously, for both of them. She couldn't, *would not* encourage Waco.

He's married, she told herself silently, as the waiter seated Crystal. Waco performed the same polite service for her. Inwardly, she shrank away from his fingers when they fleetingly brushed against her back.

Ashamed that he must have interpreted her involuntary response as a come-on, she blurted, "How many waterfront lots will be available?"

"Can't we order dinner before you two start talking business?" Crystal implored.

Waco smiled as he dropped his napkin into his lap. "When her blood sugar drops to zero, she's grumpy," he warned Dixie. "Why don't we enjoy dinner, then Crystal can go back to the condo while we get reacquainted?"

"Would you care for wine, sir?" the wine steward solicited, giving Waco the wine list.

"Champagne," Crystal chirped. "Please, Waco, this is sort of a celebration, isn't it?"

"Dixie? I seem to recall that you like champagne."

Another wave of memories crashed over her. Fizzy, dry liquid would completely muddle her mind. She needed to think clearly. "Just water for me, thanks. But you two go ahead and have champagne."

"A golden margarita? With sugar around the rim instead of salt?" he suggested, recalling the night they'd gone country-western dancing. Conscious of her nervously fidgeting with the silverware, he added, "It'll relax you."

"That sounds good, too," Crystal replied, flashing Dixie a wide smile. "Why don't we start with margaritas and have champagne for dessert?"

"With martinis as an entree?" Dixie quipped, forcing her lips to return Crystal's smile.

"Uh-uh." Crystal dramatically rolled her eyes. "Gin makes Waco horny."

Waco glared at his sister, who winked at Dixie, who became fascinated by the burgundy-colored polish on her fingernails.

"Ooops! *Faux pas.*" Without a hint of regret or the least bit apologetic, Crystal added, "Sorry, Waco. I guess I shouldn't repeat what I overheard you tell Zeke, huh?"

"Not unless you'd like a bar of soap for dinner," he threatened mildly. To the amused wine steward, he said, "Two golden margaritas and a longneck."

"Very good, sir."

Grateful Waco had not done the macho thing and ordered a double martini, Dixie sipped the glass of ice water that had magically been poured. It did strike her as peculiar that Waco had chastised his wife for alluding to his masculine prowess. From what she'd heard from Sara and read in magazine articles, she'd been led to believe that men liked it when wives made their husbands appear . . . as Sara aptly put it . . . *studly.*

Waco doesn't need a superficial ego boost, she decided, her gaze lingering on him. Ten years ago she wouldn't have thought it possible, but he appeared more handsome in a business suit than he had with his carpenter's belt slung low on his hips. Her eyes dropped to her silverware when Waco caught her gazing at him.

"So tell me, Dixie, did you start working for

Texas Proud after you graduated?" Waco asked benignly.

"From college, yes. I've spent the last five years at headquarters bouncing between departments learning the business. And you?"

"He got his GED and went to night school to get his degree from CalTech," Crystal volunteered proudly. "Graduated summa-alpha-omega. Ouch!" Crystal complained, giving her brother a dirty look. "That's my foot you're grinding through the floor!"

"Sorry. I thought it was the table's pedestal. What were you saying, Dixie?"

"It's natural for Crystal to brag on you," Dixie said, defending his wife.

Crystal shot Waco a so-there look. "I attended drama school at UCLA."

"You're an actress?"

"Singer-slash-songwriter-slash-actress, with the emphasis on singer. I did a couple of local commercials for car agencies. Right before we moved I had an offer to do a small singing part in a film, but Waco objected to . . ."

Waco cleared his throat to stop his sister's wayward mouth.

An irreverent giggle bubbled from between her pouty lips as she said with wicked delight, "I know the dinner table isn't the place to discuss the artistic value of nudity in films."

"I doubt anyone would have noticed your voice," Dixie commented drolly, trying to make light of her outrageous comment.

"Don't encourage her," Waco cautioned. Amusement was lighting his dark eyes as he recalled Dixie's delightful sense of humor. Her ability to make him laugh had been one of her most endearing traits. "Crystal doesn't have an inhibited bone in her body. She's liable to stand up and belt out a bawdy song."

"The only place he sings is in the shower," Crystal huffed confidentially as she nudged Dixie's arm. She gave Waco a wifely pat on the hand. "It's because he sounds like a bullfrog in a water bucket and knows it."

"Any other family secrets you'd like to spill?" he asked blandly.

Crystal appeared to give serious thought to his question, then replied, "Be sweet or I'll have to tell her about your socks."

A tuxedo-clad waiter saved Waco from further disgrace.

"The prime rib is excellent," Waco recommended before the waiter dispensed the leather-bound menus. "Is that agreeable?"

Both women nodded, neither of them was interested in food, but for different reasons. While Crystal plotted another bit of mischief, Dixie began to realize that the congenial banter had relieved her tenseness.

Waco and Crystal weren't like any married couple she'd dined with previously, but she generously attributed it to both of them having strong, diverse personalities. They squabbled, and yet, it was abundantly clear to even a casual observer that they genuinely cared for each other.

Unselfishly, Dixie was glad Waco was happy and successful. It's what she'd wanted for him all those many years ago. With one exception: she'd imagined herself being the proud wife of Waco Stone.

Fourteen

"You'd think he was still as poor as a church mouse. I swear, he works thirty hours a day," Crystal exclaimed. She stabbed her fork into a slice of rare prime rib and made a comical face at Dixie. "Can you believe that I have to wake him up to get him into bed?"

Hungry as Dixie had been when she'd buttered a cheese popover and taken the first bite, now, it tasted like sawdust. Mouth full, she shook her head and took a long drink of ice water to dissolve the wad of dough.

"You knew I was a workaholic when you begged to move in with me," Waco replied to justify his behavior.

Crystal's cheek puffed with meat as she said, "I thought you'd make time for me." Including Dixie in their tiff, she asked, "You know what they say about all work and no play."

"Makes a man wealthy?" Waco teased.

"Or a divorcee," Crystal rhymed impudently.

Waco shrugged one shoulder. "That's the one thing I don't have to worry about, do I?"

Dixie glanced from Waco to Crystal, waiting for

a snappy comeback. Crystal appeared suddenly too preoccupied with cutting the chine off her prime rib to be concerned about her marriage. That struck Dixie as odd. With one out of two marriages ending in divorce court, why was Waco absolutely certain he could neglect his wife with no consequences?

"I'm no expert," Dixie qualified hesitantly, "but, I imagine the demands of running your organization could put a strain on your marriage."

"It could, if there was a marriage to strain," Waco admitted.

Narrowing her eyes at Crystal, Dixie bluntly asked, "You're single?"

"Did you think we were married?" Crystal giggled like a mischievous child. "Waco is my brother."

"Brother?" Dixie faced Waco. "I distinctly remember you saying you were an only child."

"I thought I was." His dark eyes gleamed with amusement as he asked, "Did you think I was married to Crystal?"

"You do have the same last name," Dixie replied, feeling the assumption she'd made was valid given the information she'd had. "You don't look alike."

Thinking back, Dixie realized that Crystal had said nothing to dispel the notion of her being Waco's wife. But then again, she hadn't said they were married, only implied it. Chuckling over the mistaken identity, she recalled being horrified by Crystal's cavalier treatment of Waco. Crystal "adored" Waco, but in a sisterly manner.

Minx! Dixie should have felt angry or foolish, but instead, she felt strangely exhilarated.

"I can't get him to bleach his hair like mine," Crystal laughed. "But I do try to whittle him down to my size with my sharp tongue."

Waco nodded, in complete agreement with his sister, for a change. "You can imagine how surprised I was to learn Crystal was part of my inheritance. If I'd known then what I know now, I might still be working with the tools."

"Tell me the whole story," Dixie prompted. "I only know what Sara read to me out of the paper."

Crystal put her fork on her plate and beamed Waco a smile. "After my parents' accident, the lawyers went through their papers. Lo and behold, up popped Waco's birth certificate. It took two years of diligent detective work to finally contact him."

"After we left Houston, we moved back to a small piece of land Zeke owned outside of Waco, where I was born," Waco explained. "Shoved in the mailbox was a letter of notification from California lawyers."

"Waco and Zeke drove to California. By then, I'd been placed in a very strict Catholic boarding school. All girls!" Crystal laughed. "You can imagine how I felt when they arrived!"

"Ecstatic?" Dixie estimated.

"That's a master understatement. I was an eight-year-old basket case because one of the girls told me that orphans grow up to be nuns. Can you imagine? Me, a nun?"

"Frankly, no," Dixie acquiesced with a compassionate smile.

"Try imagining me raising a teenage girl," Waco intervened, smiling at Dixie.

Unrepentant, Crystal bragged, "I've been a royal pain in his neck ever since then."

"I wouldn't call you a pain in the *neck*," Waco argued as he rolled his tongue in the side of his cheek, and teased, "Think lower."

"But you love me anyway, huh?"

"Yeah, I do," Waco assured. "It's you and me and Zeke against the world."

By the time they'd finished their dinner and the waiter had cleared the table, Dixie decided the newspaper article Sara had given her had liberally embellished the truth. Curious about how Waco put his organization together, she'd questioned him about Tumbleweed, Inc. Crystal took credit for introducing him to her friends' parents, who built extravagant homes. Initially, Waco had coordinated everything, from locating the land to producing the final punch-out list. As word-of-mouth spread Tumbleweed's reputation, he'd learned to delegate authority. Within five years of arriving on the West Coast, financially, he could have retired. Add another five years of hard work, and Waco expanded the Stone family's inheritance to a financial empire.

While the waiter refilled their coffee cups, Waco and Dixie began fervently discussing the merits of steel construction over lumber. Crystal's jaw popped as she yawned, drawing their attention.

"Can I cut out of here?" she asked Waco.

"No dessert?"

"I had dessert while you two drank the first pot of coffee." Precociously, she added, with an elfish grin, "And all the pictures in the coloring book are finished."

Waco grinned and nodded. "Did you scribble or did you stay between the lines?"

"I never stay between the lines. Just be grateful I'm too old to stick my tongue out at you in public." She removed a set of car keys from her evening bag. Remembering her manners, she smiled at Dixie and said, "Nice meeting you, Dixie."

"My pleasure, Crystal." Despite her trick, Dixie genuinely liked Waco's sister.

"We came in my car," Waco reminded Crystal. "I'll get a cab for you."

"A cab?" Crystal groaned in protest. "Why can't I drive your car home? Can't Dixie drop you off? She won't mind."

Waco hesitated, then asked Dixie, "Do you?"

"Of course not." With a pixie grin of her own, she teased him. "How could I when you're going to sell me those lots Texas Proud needs?"

"Whoa! Stop." Crystal rose. "Before you start bargaining, give me the keys. Please?"

"I'll walk you to the parking lot."

"It's well lit." When he ignored her assertiveness by placing his napkin on the table and rising, she bemoaned, "For Pete's sake Waco, I'm not your *baby* sister. I won't disgrace you by falling down and skinning my knees."

"Remind me to tell you that story," Waco said, wanting Dixie included in their joke while he laughed with Crystal.

As Dixie watched the two of them weave through the tables, she thought how lucky they were to have found each other. Crystal had provided comic relief that made an awkward business meeting pleasant, almost fun. While Waco was reticent to brag on his accomplishments, Crystal had spewed a fountain of information.

Relaxed, Dixie sipped her coffee, feeling strangely proud of Waco's accomplishments. He wasn't the overnight success the newspaper had made him; he'd earned the respect accorded him in the building industry.

How different his life would have been if he'd stayed in Houston. Hindsight provided her with objectivity. Even without their relationship muddying the waters, she knew Waco would have been denied reaching his potential. Her father appreciated talent and ability, but he would never have allowed Waco to advance beyond construction superintendent, if that far.

Of all people, she could attest to that. John controlled and manipulated her to Texas Proud's advantage. And she let him. Otherwise, she admitted silently, she wouldn't have been sitting at this table, waiting for Waco to return. Sure, she could self-righteously shake her finger at John, but four fingers would be pointed back at herself.

Shame on him? Or shame on me?

When it came right down to it, bottom-line, they both did what was best for the company.

She held onto that thought as she observed Waco striding toward her. Texas Proud needed the waterfront lots Waco owned. John didn't have a snowball's chance in hell of getting them; she did. She had to set aside "what might have been" and stick to "what's gonna be."

Her determination would have held her in good stead, if Waco hadn't blown it away when he sat down, smiled his endearing smile, and asked, "What would it take to entice you to join my organization?"

"You're recruiting me?"

"I make it a policy to hire only the best." He flattered her brazenly. "You're experienced and intelligent, not to mention your undeniable charm. Just name the job you feel most qualified to fill, and it's yours."

Dixie grinned at his audacity. Certain he had to be joshing her, she looked him in the eye and responded, "President of the Board of Directors."

"My job."

"CEO?"

"Also my job."

With a slight lift of one shoulder, she said, "Anything less would be where I am at Texas Proud."

"With one exception."

"Which is?"

"You wouldn't be under your father's thumb."

"A thumb is a thumb is a thumb," she rattled off.

"Not necessarily."

Taking a break from his rapid-fire replies, Dixie drank from her cup and dabbed her lips with the napkin. "I appreciate your kind offer, but I'm happy where I am."

"Are you? This afternoon when I contacted Gil Albertson, I could have insisted on John facing me. I didn't. Do you know why?"

"You wanted the pleasure of my company," Dixie glibly answered.

"I'll admit to being curious about you."

"My phone number hasn't changed."

He leaned forward on his arms. "No, but, I wanted to see if your father would throw his innocent lamb to the wolf, or take me on man-to-man."

"Neither applies. I made the decision to meet with you."

"Why? For old times' sake?"

"For a very simple, direct reason. You have something Texas Proud needs. Waterfront lots. We want an option."

Doubting those were her only reasons, he settled against the back of his chair and baited her. "It's a big bay. Plenty of opportunities for land development."

"It takes a huge amount of capital investment. As you well know, we're builders, not developers."

"There are advantages to being both."

"And risks. I can give you a list of developers who lost their shirts in the real estate crash."

"The list of builders would be longer," he estimated. "Sometimes an organization has to take risks in order to grow."

The smile that reached his dark eyes clued Dixie that he wasn't speaking of professional risk. Forewarned, she prepared herself for Waco's abrupt switch of gears, by removing a plastic charge card from her purse.

"Why aren't you married, Dixie?" he asked softly. "Raising kids instead of houses?"

Smiling sweetly, she dropped the subject by placing the card on the silver tray that contained the dinner bill.

His grin widened. "That won't work with me. Asserting your feminine independence by paying the check won't provoke me."

"A trip down memory lane isn't on our business meeting's agenda."

"Isn't it? There was a time when your father would have strenuously objected to your having dinner with me." He grinned. "Strictly forbidden is closer to the truth."

"Times change," she replied curtly. She scanned the room looking for the waiter who'd hovered near their table. He was nowhere in sight. "Do you or don't you want to give TP an option on your lots?"

Waco ignored her question and responded with his own. "Have you changed?"

"I must have, otherwise you wouldn't have offered me a job."

The waiter appeared, carrying a portable phone, heading directly toward their table.

"Or plausibly, that could be why I offered it to you," Waco countered.

"Sorry to interrupt, sir," the waiter said. "There's a call for you, Mr. Stone. Would you care to take it?"

Certain it would be Crystal, he was tempted to decline. The condo was less than five miles from the restaurant. Surely she hadn't gotten into trouble that quickly. He gave Dixie a what-can-I-do look, excused himself, and picked up the receiver.

"Hello. Crystal?" His brows furrowed into a straight line when he heard a male voice. "Zeke? What's wrong?"

"I figgered since you were eatin' with Mayson's daughter that I ought to let you know what her old man did at the expansion meeting. The businessmen's association wants to block raisin' the bridge from Mud Gully Lake into Clear Lake."

"Why? Local businessmen are pro land development. Opening up that piece of land would be good for the entire area."

"Not why. Who. John Mayson."

"That doesn't make sense. Mayson wants to buy waterfront lots. Why would he oppose it?"

"Might have somethin' to do with the developer seated next to him. They'd been swappin' notes all evening. Hang on a second. I wrote his name down on a slip of paper."

While Waco waited, he turned his attention to the woman across the table eavesdropping on the conversation. Was it his imagination, or had her face blanched white?

"Here it is," Zeke said. "Armstrong. That's the young fella's name."

"According to county records the Armstrongs' land is tied up in bankruptcy court."

"There's some connection. Just thought you ought to know, bein's how you're breaking bread with the enemy."

"Meet me at the office in half an hour. I'm almost finished here. Bye."

After he'd returned the phone to the waiter, he dumped Dixie's card off the silver tray and replaced it with his own. Without insisting, Dixie picked up her card and took an inordinate amount of time returning it to her billfold.

Neither of them spoke.

Waco did a slow burn. For damned certain, time hadn't changed John Mayson's tactics. Mayson had landed the first blow of his attack while Waco had congenially wined and dined his daughter. This time, guilt wouldn't cause him to merely block Mayson's vicious blows, as he had the night of Dixie's prom. He'd fight back—an eye for an eye and a tooth for a tooth.

"I swear to you, Waco, I did not know my father's plans." Humiliation and anger made her voice shake. How could her own father deliberately send her on a fool's errand? John had no intention of letting Waco develop that property. He'd used her as a decoy to divert Waco's attention while he played an underhanded, unscrupulous trick. "Believe me, I'll get this straightened out and get back with you."

A tight smile etched the corners of Waco's mouth. "My offer stands. Name a job, other than my own, and it is yours. I'll make it worth your while."

Dixie inhaled deeply to oxidize her hot blood and purge it of anger. Waco's first offer had been genuine. Now, she suspected Waco would give her a fancy title and put her in the basement to rot. Her anger with John spilled over on Waco.

"In retaliation for John blocking your plans? Or to get even with him for firing you? Neither one is a good reason to hire me."

"Forget the past . . ."

Her eyes widened. "That's damned nice of you, considering you're the one who made passionate love to me one minute, then strode out of my life the next, without so much as a thank-you-ma'am!"

Appalled by what she'd said, she covered her mouth with her napkin. Silently she cursed her temper, her father, and the arrogant, *presumptuous* man seated across from her. She would have caused less of a scene if she'd pulled a jackhammer from her purse and begun drilling a hole in the carpet! Dixie was so embarrassed she wanted to crawl underneath the table and never have to show her face in public again!

Over the hem of the napkin, she saw the waiter try to keep a straight face while Waco scribbled his signature on the receipt, but Dixie could see the waiter's lips trembling with amusement. Not waiting for the entire staff to roll on the carpet with belly laughs, with as much dignity as she could muster, she gracefully rose from her chair and unhurriedly strolled away from the table.

She'd barely taken two steps down the corridor when she felt Waco's hand on the small of her back.

"I thought we could at least part friends this time," he said earnestly.

"With my father taking potshots at you? Trying to sabotage your company. And you trying to get even, by hiring me? Are you crazy?"

Waco smiled grimly and nodded.

"Don't you see? We're back where we started," she protested. "Do you want to sneak around like teenagers, again?"

"We've nothing to hide and nothing to fear."

He sounded so positive, so determined that Dixie gazed up at him in complete amazement. "Tumbleweed won't be the first company who has challenged Texas Proud's supremacy in the Galveston Bay area . . . *and lost.*"

Waco laughed harshly, without humor. He held the door for her. As they stepped outside into the balmy night air, over the crash of waves against the seawall, he said, "John has a thing or two to learn about fighting dirty. If he wants to throw stones, he'd better learn how to duck."

"Dammit, I can't allow you to do that!" she argued vehemently. "My world revolves around Texas Proud, too!"

"You can't stop me. It's time for you to spit out the silver spoon, or in your case, the silver nail."

"Why should I?"

Instead of going toward the parking lot, he cupped her elbow and led her across the boulevard to the sidewalk overlooking the water. The sea breeze caught her long hair, whipping it until it clung to his suit fabric, until it twined between his eyelashes, binding them together.

"Why?" He bowed his head until his lips were next to her ear. "Because your father's silver nail is holding your mouth shut. You can't think or say what you feel."

"That's not true."

"Isn't it?" he asked skeptically.

She felt the slight rasp of his five-o'clock-shadowed jaw, like a fine grain of sandpaper, against her cheek. To repress the shiver of awareness caused by his closeness and the fragrance of his masculine after-shave cologne, she turned her face away from him.

"Prove it. Tell me how you feel about me returning to Houston," he suggested. As he felt her anger relent, he pressed his advantage. "The plain and simple unvarnished truth."

In all truthfulness, she didn't know how she felt.

Physically, the allure of danger that had initially attracted her to Waco had not diminished. Unlike the young carpenter who'd been afraid of losing his job, Waco was now fearless, an inexorable adversary.

But she'd matured, too.

No longer was she a rebellious teenager batting her fledgling wings of independence against her domineering father. She could fly solo. The desperate inner need she'd always felt to earn a pat on the head from John or to acquire the stamp of approval from her peers had been replaced by confidence.

And yet, with Waco standing close to her, she grappled with emotions she'd thought were dead and buried. Why did she yearn for Waco to wrap his arms around her? Why did she still want answers to meaningless questions that should have been unimportant to her? What *did* she want from him? An explanation? An apology? Wasn't it a decade too late for that?

"Plain and simple?" she repeated. "Your return to Houston had nothing to do with me," she said implacably, sensibly setting aside her emotional turmoil. "The housing market collapsed on the West Coast. Your opportunity for expansion is here, so you're here."

"Texas is a state of mind; it's where I belong." Dissatisfied with her analysis of his situation, he nuzzled the side of her neck. Her hair was a blanket of flame-colored silk as it blew across his shoulders. "Would it help if I sincerely apologized for leaving Houston without seeing you?"

She scooped one hand behind her neck to control her hair as she looked into his eyes, looking for lies, searching for a mature reason not to accept his apology. Two words weren't sufficient to assuage the heartbreak he'd caused.

"Meet me for lunch tomorrow," he urged when she did not answer him.

"I'm busy."

"On Saturday?"

"It's my catch-up day at the office."

"Tomorrow night? Dinner and dancing? Country-western?"

"I've made plans."

Not for a wild, exhilarating evening, she admitted silently. After this hellacious week, she looked forward to a night lounging in her pajamas on the sofa, with a good book and a bottle of wine.

"Sunday?" he asked, tenaciously. With each question he'd asked, she'd retreated a step. He never lost contact. "Fifty-two pick-up at the beach?"

"No, thanks."

His hands moved to her shoulders. When she looked up at him, moonlight bathed her face in iridescence. If he hadn't been able to feel her warmth through her light suit jacket, she would have reminded him of a beautiful golden statue. Her sea-colored eyes shone brightly with antagonism. "You are still angry with me. Is it the past? The present? Or the future that bothers you?"

"All three."

Deciding he had to clear up the past, he said, "Dixie, I had no choice other than to leave. Ten minutes after I parked my truck in front of the trailer, the sheriff's department was at my door. The officer gave me one hour to get out of Pearwood or go to jail. A green and white squad car escorted Zeke and me across the county line."

Disbelief caused her eyes to widen until it occurred to her that John must have called them while she'd been upstairs crying. In a small town, elected officials paid attention to upstanding, influential citizens. Recalling how busy they'd been at the prom and later, cruising the back roads, she was surprised that her father had enough clout to demand personal service.

"There are phones in other towns," she snapped, unable to accept his excuse. "You could have called."

"And said what?"

That you loved me, her heart shouted, that you'd be back for me. Her lips clamped shut after one word, "Good-bye."

"Good-bye wouldn't have satisfied either of us. I wanted you with me."

"Maybe you didn't have a choice, but you could have given me one."

"You didn't have a choice, either," Waco rebutted, shaking his head negatively. "I couldn't let you alienate yourself from your father. If you had been crazy enough to go with me, you'd have blown graduating. I'd be the last person to recommend dropping out of high school. I had to face those facts and the fact that I had nothing to offer you. No job. No place to live. No security. Sticking around or taking you with me, either one would have caused you more heartache." His thumb caressed her lower lip. He wanted to kiss away the hurt he'd caused. "I can't blame you for being angry with me for making love to you and vanishing into thin air, but I thought I was doing the kindest thing. Why can't we start over?"

"Another hidey-hole romance?"

"It doesn't have to be that way. Your father sent you as a decoy, remember?"

Oh, did she! Her chin raised. "You've verbally declared war on my father. Do you expect me to sneak around behind his back, again?"

"I want you Dixie," he answered solemnly. "Perhaps more than I did when we were kids."

A car horn blaring immediately behind Dixie startled her.

"Hey! Waco! I came back for you," Crystal shouted through the rolled-down passenger's window. "Hop in before I get arrested for illegal parking."

Traffic began backing up behind Crystal. Horns beeped. A convertible filled with rowdy teenage boys jeered at the parked car.

"Go," Dixie mandated, grateful for his sister's arrival, which had saved Dixie from losing her pride by admitting that she wanted him, too. Ten seconds longer and she'd have revealed how heartbroken she'd been, how weak-willed she must be to seriously consider starting up where they'd left off.

Had she kept eye contact, she would have seen the steely glint in his eyes and known he wasn't going to follow her orders.

His mouth swooped down, covering hers with fierce insistence and blatant desire. Repressed yearning exploded through her like champagne shaken and uncorked. For a second, Dixie kissed him back, bracing her hands on his chest. Beneath his thin shirt, she felt the hardness of his muscles. Almost losing the frail grip she had on reality as his tongue traced the seam of her lips, Dixie clenched her teeth when the force of his kiss began to part her lips.

She pushed against his chest with both hands. Over the howls and wolf whistles coming from the convertible, she shouted, "Dammit, Waco! Sex isn't enough. I won't let you get to me that way again!"

"You can't stop me," he promised, his voice hoarse with need. "I don't make the same mistakes twice."

With that enigmatic vow, he opened the back door and propelled her inside the car. To Crystal he commanded, "Drive."

Dixie would have hugged the opposite door, but her skirt was caught under Waco's muscular thigh. His arm draped across her shoulders preventing her from wrenching it out from under him.

"Zeke sent me to get you," Crystal explained before Waco could ask why she hadn't followed his orders. She goosed the gas pedal. "Aren't you supposed to meet him at the office?"

"I'd appreciate it if you'd circle the block and take me to the parking lot," Dixie stated firmly.

"Go to the condo," Waco ordered.

"The parking lot."

Mouthing an unrefined expletive as Crystal zig-zagged from lane to lane, Waco temporarily resigned himself to postponing his confrontation with Dixie. "Make a left. Circle the block to the Galvez parking lot."

"I overheard Zeke call Dixie your enemy," Crystal said, with a impish giggle. She glanced in the rear-view mirror and taunted him, "Zeke does preach turning the other cheek. He'll be glad to know you listened to him, brother dear. That was some lip-smacking, sizzling, kisseroo you planted on Dixie. Whoooeee!"

"At midnight," Waco said softly to Dixie, "when I call you, remind me to buy a filter, would you?"

"I heard you." Crystal laughed. "It's a family joke, Dixie. He's always threatening to have a filter installed between my brain and my mouth to stop me from blabbing family secrets."

Waco watched Dixie smile in response to Crystal's explanation. Unaware of doing it, he coiled a thick strand of her coppery hair around his forefinger, rubbing the sleek texture against his thumb. Incredible, he mused, feeling aroused. Having lived in Tinsel Town, where Hollywood hopefuls were more plentiful than knots on an inferior grade of lumber, he should have been immune to a wide smile, bright eyes and long legs.

None of them made my blood rush, he thought grimly as he shifted position.

He could understand her objections to becoming involved with him. Undeniably, he'd hurt her. And equally undeniable was the fact that her father hated his guts; otherwise her father wouldn't have tried to pull the rug out from under him at the businessmen's meeting.

Most likely, he decided, a discreet affair would be the easiest path to follow.

Forget it, cowpoke, he chided silently. In Dixie's vocabulary, discreet was synonymous with sleazy, back-alley, and hidey-hole. She had unequivocally vetoed a clandestine relationship. Somehow, he'd have to placate John Mayson. Everything had to be aboveboard and on the level.

As he listened to Crystal quiz Dixie on where she'd parked, he could only hope the one minor exception she'd allow him was answering his midnight phone call.

Fifteen

"We fixed his wagon," John gloated, giving Dixie a triumphant hug when she met him at the front door of their house. "No new bridge and no new competition."

Trying to keep a civil tongue in her head, she demanded, "Why did you have me meet with Waco to buy lots?"

"Diversionary tactics, my dear daughter," he replied, chortling over his brilliant maneuver as he removed his suit jacket and hung it in the front closet. Rubbing his hands together in glee, he gestured for Dixie to join him in the kitchen. "I sent Texas Proud's top negotiator to charm the competition into submission and Stone sent an old geezer who had the finesse of a hole-hog drill to represent Tumbleweed's interests. By the end of the meeting, I taught him a thing or two about Robert's *Rules of Order*. He'd open his mouth and I'd slam the gavel down his throat."

Dixie clenched her fist and strained to hold her temper. "That old geezer is Waco's uncle. Zeke called Waco at the restaurant and told him what happened."

"How'd Stone react?"

"With animosity." Her back stiff with indignation, she crossed to the kitchen sink and leaned against it. The cold stainless-steel did little to cool her inner rage. "Tonight's victory won't run Waco out of town. He's going to fight back."

"Is that what he said?"

"He said that if you want to fight dirty, you'd better learn how to duck."

John chuckled as he perused the contents of the icebox. "He didn't win when we duked it out on the front porch."

"He didn't fight. He only blocked your blows."

"That's exactly what I've done to him. Blocked him." He reached for the six-pack. "Do you want a beer?"

"No, thanks."

Removing a longneck from the refrigerator, John opened it. After taking a thirsty swig, he said, "I'm not worried. Texas Proud has been around these parts for forty years. Our reputation is impeccable. No flash-in-the-pan newcomer is going to come in and take over our business."

"I don't appreciate your using me to divert Waco's attention," she stated bluntly. She heard her phone ringing upstairs. She glanced at her watch; Waco's midnight call? She wanted to dash up the steps, but she needed to get things straight with her father, once and for all. "Especially without informing me of your secret agenda."

"Coppertop, you can't play poker worth a damn,"

John dismissed. "You'd have shown your hand before I got to the meeting."

"I wouldn't have gone." She watched the bottle stop midway to his mouth, but continued what she had to say. "You taught me scrupulous business practices, to live by the golden rule. Where were your morals and ethics when you sent me on a wild-goose chase?"

He pointed the neck of the bottle at her. "Stone doesn't abide by the rules of fair play. In his case, I did unto him before he could do unto me."

"You didn't give him a chance to do anything to you!"

"Why should I give him a second chance. He knew the rules when I hired him as a subcontractor. He broke them."

"I broke them!"

"We aren't going to discuss your prom night. Never have and never will." He chugged the remainder of the bottle's contents and strode toward the hallway, leaving his empty beer bottle on the counter. "Tomorrow's a busy day. You'd better get some sleep."

"Dad!" she protested angrily. "I'm not eighteen. You can no longer ignore . . ."

"Can and will," he broke in adamantly. "Don't you worry your pretty little head about that humiliating incident. I forgave you for severely disappointing me. It's best forgotten."

He forgave her!

Fed up with his condescension she charged after

him. He stopped on the landing and peered down at her.

"I did not ask for your forgiveness!" she said, deliberately keeping her voice below the level of a furious whisper. "I haven't forgotten what happened or how I felt about Waco! You treated Waco unfairly then, and you're doing the same thing now! I want you to call your friends. Take another vote at the next meeting!"

Ignoring her demand, John replied, "I'll handle any future business dealings with Stone. I don't want you communicating with that scum. Stay away from him, you hear?"

"Why? Because he's unsuitable?" she mocked.

"Correct."

"What determines suitability? Land? Money? Social status?" Her voice raised fractionally. "He's rich! He can buy Texas Proud and have plenty of money left over to pay twenty times the price for that tract of land!"

"Don't be coarse, daughter," John rebuked. "I have never objected to any decent young man you dated because of their financial statement."

"Are you calling Waco indecent?"

"He's an opportunist. He grabbed for the brass ring and broke your heart." Slowly, nodding his head, he continued up the steps. "That was a hard lesson you learned, one you should remember. I do. If Stone shows up on our front porch, I'll gladly shoot the bastard!"

Her father was bluffing; he abhorred violence. He didn't own a gun, much less know how to shoot one. Deciding it was time to call his bluff, she steeled her nerves and said, "Since you're determined to be unreasonable, you leave me no choice. I don't want you shooting anyone you disapprove of, so I'll move. I should have found my own place after I graduated from college."

"Dixie Lee Mayson," he snapped icily, "you're my daughter, my only child. Until you've met and married a respectable man, who is as strong-willed as you are, you'll live under my roof."

Despite his angry tone, she sensed his wariness. "You just described Waco Stone. Respectable. Strong-willed. And you know it, don't you?"

"He's weak. He couldn't stand up to me, so he deserted you."

"No, Waco left because he didn't want to go to jail, thanks to your influence with the sheriff's department."

John gave a short, scathing laugh and derided, "Is that what Stone told you?"

"Yes."

"Well, he's spun you a tall tale that Paul Bunyan would have been proud of." John turned toward the master suite. "Who are you going to believe? Your father, the man who has always loved and looked out for your best interests, or the man who took advantage of you and then left you?"

Hours later, Dixie stared blindly at the ceiling, unable to answer her father's question.

Who did she believe?

John never out-and-out lied, but she had known him to cast a favorable light on a half-truth. Like today, she mused, as she bunched her pillow under her head. Against her will, he'd ordered her to meet with Waco to discuss buying waterfront property. The whole truth was that John really wanted Waco's lots. And, if Waco had agreed, John would have been pleased. But, and this was a real butt-kicker, John had an alternate plan in process that would prevent anyone from profitably developing that land. Without new waterfront lots available, the ones Texas Proud owned on Galveston Bay would increase in value.

Win-win. Either way, her father came out the winner.

He hadn't lied to her; he just hadn't fully informed her.

Half-truths.

She loved her father dearly, but she wondered how many other half-truths had he told her? Or worse, how many times had he shut her completely in the dark?

John had not denied sending the sheriff after Waco; he'd accused Waco of exaggerating the truth. Deep in her heart, she knew that her father disliked Waco because they were like two oak planks hewn and milled from the same tree. Both of them were shrewd businessmen who would do whatever it took to achieve their goals.

"I'm caught in the middle," she whispered as she rolled to her side.

Her gaze automatically fell on the telephone. She'd meant it when she'd told Waco that she wasn't interested in sneaking around behind her father's back to be with him. This time, his job wasn't at stake.

Mine might be, she added with a low groan. Consorting with the sworn enemy had to be a major rule violation in Texas Proud's policy handbook. If the rule was not carved in stone, it was implied. She'd threatened to move out of her father's house. What about the family business? Was she willing to leave it, too?

Finding another place to live would be elementary; finding an executive position in the male-dominated construction industry would be difficult. The building trades were the last stronghold for anti-feminists. Unfortunately, she lacked the one qualification that automatically made her eligible for membership in the Good-Ole-Boys' Club: a penis. She couldn't earn one, buy one, or grow one.

Instead of despairing, Dixie grinned at the thought of buying a package of penis seeds, planting them, and watching them sprout up in the backyard, then pinning one to the lapel of her suit jacket when she went to business meetings or job interviews.

She had to be exhausted to come up with that outrageous idea!

Closing her eyes, she willed herself to follow the only good advice her father had given her: Get some sleep. Tomorrow would be a busy day.

With the first rays of sunlight bursting into her bedroom, she awoke with the solution to her problem. Let John and Waco feud. She could circumvent being caught in the middle by avoiding both of them. They could make her life chaotic, but only if she let them. Until the Mayson-Stone feud ended, she'd work from dawn to dusk.

In the week that followed, Dixie rigorously focused her energy solely on locating other waterfront properties, kept a sharp eye on the houses in progress, and supervised the ground work at Mayson Manor. She delayed foundation work on the elaborate barn; authorized Kate to start the interior design plans; delegated Paul Getz to film each phase of construction for advertising purposes. Before the concrete trucks poured yards and yards of concrete into the manor's wooden forms, she went over the plumber's measurements and his installation of PVC pipe. Two to three inches out of a wall could make the difference between having a sink in a bathroom or a living area. While the concrete cured, the first loads of lumber were delivered, unloaded, and covered with a tarpaulin until the framers needed it to erect the wooden skeleton. Her evenings were spent at headquarters, comparing cost analysis printouts with suppliers' bills and labor expenses.

She switched from business suit to hard hat with the furious pace of a runway model at a Paris fashion show. Each day, she had Sara type a note to remind John to contact the men who'd voted against raising the bridge at Mud Gully Lake. A duplicate copy was mailed to the corporate offices of Tumbleweed. She'd promised Waco she'd do everything within her power to change the association's recommendation. She wanted him to have written proof that she'd kept her promise.

Her intention of being too busy, too exhausted to think of Waco Stone should have worked, but there were those odd moments in her day when she was hung up at a stoplight in her drive from the office to a job site, or when she was waiting for an elevator, or like now, standing beside her truck, filling her gas tank, wondering what Waco was doing at ten o'clock on a Friday night.

Thoughts of him caused a sick hollow feeling in her stomach. With the least bit of encouragement on her part, she could have been with him. She had the perfect excuse to call him. Today, John had left a message on her desk saying that "because of her stubborn insistence, he would use his influence to reverse the decision of the businessmen's association to block efforts to have the bridge raised."

On the surface, her father's change of heart appeared benevolent. Dixie knew better. Texas Proud still needed waterfront lots. Since John hadn't bothered to brief her on what tactic he planned to use to get them, she'd merely faxed a copy of John's note to Waco's office without a personal note. Mentally, while she'd watched the slip of paper being fed into the fax machine, she'd marked her debt to Waco paid in full.

Let Waco draw his own conclusion and react accordingly, she mused, clicking the handle of the gas pump until she'd rounded the amount she owed to a tidy dollar amount. After replacing the handle, she scrounged into the front pocket of her jeans for cash as she strode toward the cashier's window and paid her tab.

Since the gas station was less than a mile from her house, within minutes she drove down Pearwood Boulevard. When she turned on her street, she couldn't help noticing the cars and trucks lining both sides of the street.

Vaguely Dixie recalled Sara mentioning a get-together of the planning committee for the class reunion. From the number of parked cars, it appeared as though everyone still living in Pearwood was on the committee, with Dixie being the only exception.

Silently, she scolded herself as old feelings of being the odd-man-out insidiously began to accompany the strains of music and laughter coming from the house next door. She inhaled a deep breath of sultry night air, held it, and let the fragrance of hyacinths planted along the front porch of the house refresh her thoughts. She could be at Sara's, if that was what she wanted. She exhaled quietly. It wasn't. Listening to reminiscences about the glorious, carefree high school days would bore her stiff.

Impulsively, she bent at the waist and picked a fragile stalk of blooms. She cupped it in her hands as she slowly mounted the front steps.

Waco sat motionless on the porch swing, deep in the shadows of the porch, watching Dixie as she pulled her thick braid of hair over one shoulder and tucked the flowers behind her ear. Observing her graceful movements, he finally understood why his powers of concentration had been derailed by obsessive thoughts of Dixie Mayson. She was such a bundle of contradictions—sweet and sassy, virginal and provocative, naive and smart. It was no wonder she intrigued him as no other woman had.

He lifted his feet, letting the rusty chain that secured the wooden swing to the rafters creak to announce his presence. Dixie turned and looked at him, her eyes wide and bright.

"I got your notes and your fax," he said, motioning for her to join him on the wide swing. When she remained at the door like a doe caught in the bright headlights of a truck, he added, "Friday night must still be your father's poker night."

"Yeah," she breathed huskily, wondering if she'd conjured him up from her imagination. From the faint light coming through the front window, she could see the lines of strain in his face, how his forelock appeared as though he'd been running his fingers through his hair while he'd waited for her. The past week had been hard on him, too. The urge to sit beside him and stroke his hair back in place had her feet moving toward the swing of their own accord. "I wanted to keep you posted on the latest developments."

As she took the last step to close the distance between them, he held his hand out, palm upward. The unwonted feelings that tore through her as she lightly placed her hand in his were too strong to hold back. The longing and loneliness she'd held in check seemed to vanish when his fingers curled around the palm of her hand and he laced their fingers together.

Damn his soulful black eyes to hell, he must have known the effect his slightest touch had on her because she could see the lines beside them radiate upward, even though his lips weren't smiling at her.

He tugged her hand until she collapsed beside him on the swing. Automatically his arm circled her shoulders. "Truce?"

"It's not my feud," she replied simply.

"I'm glad to hear that, because I plan on asking outrageous prices for those lots."

"By the time you've invested a fortune in clearing the land, making the roads, and putting in the water services, you'll need buyers to recoup your capital."

Waco nodded. "I just want you to know my dealings with Texas Proud are strictly business, nothing personal."

"Nobody has to duck when they see you coming?" she teased, grinning at him as she reiterated his threat.

"All John has to do is pay the asking price." He applied light pressure to her hand to seal the truce. "Friends?"

She tilted her head back to allow the faint light that spilled through the lacy curtains to highlight the hard planes of his face. Every key element of his personality was etched there—his pride, his integrity, his ruthlessness, his vulnerability. Twin lines creased his brow like grooves in a hardwood floor. His nose was straight, utilitarian, not one that stopped to smell the roses. His jaw was strong, rock hard, like his last name. And yet, the scant light pooled in the centers of his dark eyes, making them iridescent and soft, almost wistful.

"You didn't come here to talk about your business or our friendship, did you, Stone?"

A hint of a smile tugged at the corners of his mouth. "I might have had one or two ulterior motives," he confessed, hugging her closer to his side.

"Such as?"

"This," he whispered while his hand dropped to her waist and he pulled her on his lap. His lips hovered over hers momentarily, then brushed against them. "And this."

His kisses were light, not demanding, as though he was uncertain of her reaction. For a man so big and tough and dangerous, he could be unbelievably gentle with those he cared for.

He did care for her. His caring made her feel vulnerable and fragile. Tears burned her eyes. Should she open her heart to him and risk being hurt? Her heart quickened, as though startled awake. Would he walk away from her again, without a backward glance?

What she needed was passion, passion so hot and intense that it would defy reason and stop her inner turmoil.

Wrapping her arms around his broad shoulders, she held the back of his head with one hand and kissed him hungrily, with a wildness she hadn't realized she possessed. Waco pulled her against him, bending her back over his arm, opening her mouth with his, matching her aggression as his tongue thrust deeper and deeper. His hand slipped between them, kneading, fondling, nipping her. The snap, snap, snap of his own shirt opening beneath her fingers gave him the impetus to pinch the hooks and eyes of her flimsy bra. A yank later, her breasts were against his hot, feverish skin.

Dixie groaned as she swayed with enticement against him. His hands were big and broad, but no longer did he have the calluses. His thumb rubbed across the aching point of her nipple until the pure pleasure of it drew her legs up until her body curled next to him. She loved touching him, feeling the fire just beneath his skin as her hands glided up his chest to the thick mat of masculine hair.

And still he kissed her as though her lips contained a magical elixir, one that could extend time until he reached that special place he'd named *someday.*

When their mouths parted, she gulped a breath of air and whispered, "The front door is unlocked. My room is at the top of the steps, on the right."

She felt giddy and slightly dizzy as he lifted her up. The flower she'd tucked behind her ear lay crushed between them; its heady fragrance had the potent effect of a powerful aphrodisiac, exciting her sexual desire. She closed her eyes, seizing this moment of supreme rapture with all her strength of will.

"Not here," Waco said firmly. He held her cradled tightly against him as his long legs ate the distance between the porch and his car.

Beyond caring where he took her, she consented with a dreamy, passion-ridden expression in her eyes. His kisses had made her forget everything that stood between them—his abandonment, her father, the feud—everything. No whole truths, half-truths or anything in between. She only felt a deep immutable need to be with Waco.

The short trip to the Hilton at Clear Lake could have lasted minutes, hours or decades. When he solicitously placed her on the front seat beside him, it was as though she'd stepped into a mental time warp. Moonlight, shadows, stoplights and blaring horns became part of a virtual reality kaleidoscope.

None of it seemed real.

Her mind was attuned only to the touch of his hand, the deep timbre of his voice, and the love song humming in her heart.

She wanted him and wasn't ashamed to tell him exactly how much when he unlocked the door to the suite, swept her up and carried her across the threshold to the king-sized bed. He knelt beside the bed as though it was an altar and she was the woman he worshipped from afar.

Flattered, but dissatisfied with that image, she reached for the front of his shirt, pulling him toward her. Humbleness didn't suit him. Maybe there was a time when she'd wanted him down on his knees begging forgiveness, but this wasn't it. She wanted the strong, confident, swaggering carpenter, the man who'd stolen her heart and taken it with him when he'd left her.

His ardor equaled her own because he quickly dispensed with his clothes, then hers. Buttons, zippers, hooks and eyes, none of them posed a problem, until he reached her sheer lacy panties. Unable to peel them off her or slide them down her hips, he used the strength of his powerful hands to rip them off, shredding them, tossing them aside.

Spurred like a wild stallion by her womanly scent, he buried his face against the source of her heat. He heard her gasp; he could have, would have stopped after one flick of his tongue against her moistness, but she lifted her hips and twined her fingers into his hair. Her knees tightened next to his torso, signaling that this was new to her. Hungrily, he parted the petals of feminine flesh and kissed her, feeling her shudder and melt as his tongue darted, licked, and delved into her.

Dixie clenched her eyes shut. She'd heard women giggle and twitter about it on television talk-shows, and deny ever doing it in their bedrooms. She'd nodded, believing herself too modest to ever allow it to take place.

How wrong she'd been!

This gave her far more pleasure than she could possibly have imagined. As the black blobs dancing on the backs of her eyelids became radiant with pure color, she felt her insides involuntarily clench and the desire to feel him inside of her intensified.

"Waco," she cried, her fingers tugging his hair, "Please, I want you inside of me."

His massive chest heaved as he rose up on his arms, panting, swiftly entering her. For several long seconds he held himself deep within her, fearing the white heat of his climax would erupt abruptly. His mind forced the muscles in his buttocks to relax. He sucked air into his lungs to quench the explosive heat. Slowly, he allowed himself to move against her. With every stroke he felt his haunches reflexively tighten, building the tension, until he pumped against her, mindlessly exploding, draining his manhood as his seed spilled inside her.

Afterward, he sank beside her, kissing her neck, ears, cheeks, and finally her lips. And then he held her, his heart continuing to race a mile a minute. He'd wanted it to last longer, forever, far beyond eternity. Nothing made a man feel stronger, or weaker in the aftermath.

"You okay?" he murmured, feeling more like a Neanderthal than a civilized man.

Dixie cuddled against him and smiled. "I don't want to sound like a braggart, but personally I think I was better than just okay."

"How was I?"

Pretending to give his question grave thought, she paused, circled the lobe of his ear with the tip of her tongue, and whispered, "Marvelous."

"Spectacular?"

"Stupendous," she said, topping his adjective in their game of one-upmanship.

"You'll spend the night with me, won't you?"

One night, she reiterated silently. Long ago, she'd hoped and dreamed for more than one night; now, she couldn't take less. She wanted more time than he was willing to offer, a lifetime. Refusing to set a time limit, she draped her arm around his middle and hung on to him for dear life.

"I know you're expected at home by your father . . ."

She shushed him, then sealed his lips closed with a brief, smiling kiss. "You couldn't pry me out of here with a crowbar."

Sixteen

The first sun rays of morning barely entered the hotel room when Waco woke. Dixie was snuggled up to his side closer than paint to wood. He turned his head slightly to inhale the pleasant scent of her hair.

Better than waking to the smell of coffee, he thought, smiling for no apparent reason.

In thoughtful silence, he feasted his eyes on the woman who had haunted every step he'd taken since returning to Houston. *Liar!* he castigated silently. Since the day he'd pulled up beside her in his wreck of a truck, she'd always been in the back of his mind. There had been hundreds of occasions when he'd glanced at the empty passenger seat of his vehicle, wishing Dixie were there to share his minor triumphs over adversity. He'd never admit it to another living soul because they'd think his elevator didn't reach the top floor, but he'd actually had imaginary midnight conversations with her. Fear had kept him from actually picking up the phone and calling her long distance.

In his worst nightmares, he'd pictured her happily married with a passel of kids.

Inwardly he cringed at the blasphemous thought as his lips lightly caressed her hair. He stared down at the top of her head as she stirred restlessly against him. He couldn't look at her without wanting her, couldn't have her without wanting more. And yet, he feared she was less attainable now than she'd been ten years ago.

He'd left one factor out of the equation stored in his warehouse of memories: her determination to be independent. He'd witnessed her teenage rebellion against her domineering father. Hell, he'd been a major part of it. From asking around, he'd learned that Dixie was as independent as a hog on ice.

Sure, she'd created the illusion of an impenetrable, consolidated front at Texas Proud. But judging from what he'd heard, it had been Dixie who'd put the brakes on building Mayson Manor during the recession. A visionary, she'd also been the one who'd wisely made the jump from building upscale tract homes, which had been sold to corporate middle managers, to contracting custom-built mansions, designed and paid for by the owners of successful companies. In an economic crunch, it was the middle managers who were squeezed out of the corporate structure, not the top dogs.

Smiling, he figured John rationalized those changes as merely allowing his daughter to make little decisions. In his mind, Waco felt certain her old man believed he wasn't merely a figurehead; John believed that he made all the big, earthshaking decisions.

*Like keeping outsiders off TP's turf or erecting
a mausoleum as homage to his success.*

In spite of his cynical thoughts concerning
Mayson, he did have a certain admiration for him.
In an uncertain economic climate it didn't take
much for a sure-footed builder to skid off a shake-
shingle roof and land on the ground, with only
splinters in his ass to show for his years of hard
work.

Mentally, Waco ran his hand down his own
rump. No splinters, yet. That didn't mean he was
immune to John's push. He'd sunk a king's ransom
into undeveloped property. He'd have to work like
hell to make a sound return on his investment.

*Which doesn't allow for reducing the price on
those lots, much less giving them away.*

As though his dark thoughts had traveled along
a mental telepathy line straight to Dixie, he watched
her lashes flutter upward. His brow puckering, he
felt a slipping sensation when he gazed into the
depths of her dark blue eyes.

"Am I crowding you off the edge of the bed?"
she asked in a husky voice. She made a feeble
attempt to scoot over; his arm locked around her
back like a steel band. Pleased by his quick reflexes, she reached up and ran a finger across the
stubble on his jaw and inquired, "Do you always
wake up with a scowl on your face?"

He nibbled the fleshy pad of her finger, sucking
it into his mouth. "You're in danger of getting a
severe whisker burn if you rub your tootsies down
my leg one more time."

"Oh yeah?" Her toe had trekked up his shin until her knee was against his taut abdomen. "Will a whisker burn be harder to conceal than a sunburn?"

"Nobody'll notice it." He chuckled, ran his hand down her throat and tormented her by adding, "Not when they see the trail of passion marks. Here. Here. And here."

"Hickeys!" she squealed. "You vampire!"

She scrambled off the bed, scooped his shirt off the floor, and as she started toward the mirror she pushed her arms through the sleeves. Before she'd taken two steps, she heard a low rumble of laughter. Spinning on her heel, she lunged for him, aiming for his midsection. She locked her lips on him, sucking hard. She'd teach him a thing or two about tormenting a half-awake woman before she'd had coffee!

What Dixie had started as wholesome fun, was quickly transformed. She hadn't intended to arouse him, but with her breasts intimately massaging him, her sharp teeth nipping him, she became aware that her play graduated to *foreplay,* instantaneously. As inevitable as the sun rising in the east, she felt him rise long and hard, until the velvet tip of his penis stroked the underside of her chin.

The smirk he saw when she looked up at him could have been caused by his immediate response to her touch. But then again, he thought silently, the shine in those bright blue eyes and the gleam of her teeth indicated she had something very, very wicked in mind for him.

Or something very, very delightful!

"Careful," he warned, just in case it was the former and not the latter. "You've already ruined me. I'll never be able to make love to another woman. Don't make it permanent."

Dixie cocked her head to one side. "Was that a compliment?"

"Hmmmmm," he hummed.

With his teeth clenched in anticipation, he was unable to slide even a monosyllabic word through his lips as her hot breath caressed him.

"How long does it take for hickeys to go away?" she crooned, her voice lilting upward.

The tormentor had become the tormented. When her lips touched him, gently sipping his manhood, rational thought was beyond his capacity. He closed his eyes and let the myriad sensations wash over him.

Somewhere in the dark recesses of his mind he knew a passion mark would fade; this he would never forget.

Sunday at noon, they surfaced from their lover's cocoon. Room service had been their only contact with the outside world. In addition to food and drink, the hotel had provided fluffy terrycloth robes while their clothes had been sent to the dry cleaners.

Dixie had almost been embarrassed by the gratuity Waco had casually given the hotel's concierge. Those panties he'd bought had cost almost more than it took to feed a small, war-torn nation!

Being only a rock's hop-skip-and-a-jump from the land Tumbleweed had purchased, Dixie suggested they drive by it. Wanting to give her project equal time, he countered by asking to see what progress she'd made on Mayson Manor.

Neither of them mentioned taking her home. It was as though a page had been torn from time and space by benevolent gods and bestowed on them as a reward for services rendered and hardships endured. If either of them had been superstitious, they'd have hidden the glow surrounding them, for fear the same gods would have been jealous and snatched back their blessings.

"What are your plans for the old mansion at the front of the property?" Dixie inquired as he drove slowly in front of the massive stone structure. Spanish moss draped from the huge white oaks like grey ghosts protecting the structure from prying eyes. For as long as she could remember, it had stood vacant. "Restore it or demolish it?"

"Good question. I'm a builder at heart. I hate the idea of destroying what was once a showplace."

She empathized with him by lightly squeezing his leg.

"Last Wednesday a local movie producer contacted me. He'd like to see it and the building behind it made into a combination sound studio-slash-office building."

"The *Chronicle* said you had Hollywood connections."

Waco chuckled. "I'm not going to get naked and sing dirty ditties, if that still worries you."

"You'd better not," she forewarned, laughing gaily. "I'd have to buy all the tickets to make certain I had the only front-row seat in an empty theater!"

After he'd driven across the troublesome bridge he wanted raised, he made an illegal U-turn—called a Texas U-eee—and traveled back up NASA Road One toward the Space Center.

"It's a shame you'll have to bulldoze those trees," she commented, mentally weighing practicality against aesthetic beauty.

Slightly repelled by the notion, he glanced from the road to Dixie and shook his head. "I'm no tree-hugging environmentalist by any means, but my plans don't include scarring the land for convenience sake or to save a few bucks. One day you'll have to drive down to my headquarters and take a peek at the architect's rendition of how the land will be developed."

"I'd love to," she replied eagerly. "When?"

"Anytime. Just call me before you come."

"Why? So you can shoo the builders out of your office so I won't know what they're paying for your lots?" she teased, nudging him in the ribs.

"Nope," he drawled, giving her a sexy wink. "I want to make certain my desk is cleared."

"Ahhhh. That's certainly a provocative idea."

"It will be," he promised. "With you living at home, and Zeke and Crystal at the condo, I have to start thinking of places that are conducive to being private."

"I imagine your office would be about as private as the ferryboat between Galveston and Pelican Island," she replied drily.

"Good idea. I hadn't thought of that possibility. I should have. Every man has fantasies about making love to a gorgeous woman aboard a yacht."

"I don't think a ferry is what those men had in mind."

"Anything over fifty feet long is considered a yacht. Isn't it?"

Dixie muffled a laugh behind her hand. He could be incorrigible, without her encouragement.

"It was your idea, sweetheart. I'm just trying to be amicable." Slanting her a smile, he asked, "Open the glove compartment, would you?"

Her mind rang out with joy when she saw a square jewelry box covered with black velvet. Only a moron could mistake it for anything other than a ring box. Perplexed, she glanced at him; his eyes were on the road, unreadable.

She folded her hands in her lap, leaving the box untouched. Not wanting to jump to a conclusion, she asked gravely, "Is this what I think it is?"

"Looks like a ring box to me. Why don't you open it?"

She reached inside the compartment, halted, then let the tips of her fingers touch the velvet's soft nap. Pensively, she worried her bottom lip with her front teeth.

Back while they'd been sitting on her porch

swing, she'd made a conscious decision to seize the moment, to take what Waco offered—sex—and enjoy it. She hadn't asked questions or made demands. She'd left their problems behind them, unresolved. If there was an engagement ring in there, what the hell was she going to do?

"It's yours. Take it," Waco urged. "I've been carrying it around with me for years."

Dixie licked the lip she'd chewed raw while she retrieved the box from the compartment. "Nice box," she commented inanely, slowly turning it end over end.

"I scrounged it from Crystal. She's a charter member of the Home Shopping Club."

She flipped the lid open. The ring nestled in the bed of white velvet was as blue as her eyes, set in a wide band of scrolled silver. She instantly recognized it as the one she'd worn the day she helped Waco trim out the house at Bayou Oaks.

"I'd completely forgotten that I'd given this to you for safekeeping," she crowed, relieved, laughing at her mistake. She slipped the ring on her finger, pleased to know he'd had it all these years. She leaned across the console and gave him a peck on the cheek. "Thanks."

"You're welcome."

Intent on making Dixie happy, he didn't hear the siren from the fire truck until it was practically on his rear bumper. Swerving to the side, he let it pass. He pointed to the column of black smoke coming from a stand of trees about a mile up the road.

"Step on it," Dixie ordered loudly over the wail of the blaring siren. Her smile flattened to a grim scowl. "Mayson Manor is in that direction."

The wheels spit road gravel as Waco careened back on the road and followed the Pearwood volunteer fire truck. "It's probably a small brush fire."

"Let's hope so." She leaned forward anxiously. Her seat belt cut into the thin fabric of her blouse; she unbuckled the clasp. Her face was scant inches from the windshield as she said, "There's a mountain of lumber stacked there. The framers start this week."

Trying to comfort her, he patted the back of her hand. "It's probably a small brush fire. Easily extinguished. Doing little damage."

"With the afternoon thundershowers we've had? The underbrush would be too wet."

"You're insured, aren't you?"

"Yeah, but you must know what it means when a claim is filed—the premium skyrockets."

A couple of hundred yards ahead of them the fire truck slowed and turned.

"Is that your lane?"

"Yes," she groaned, her fears justified when she saw orange flames coming from where the land had been cleared. "How could a fire start out here in the middle of nowhere?"

Windblown cinders showered the hood of the car like lit fireflies, flickering, then leaving a grey ash. Dixie pitched forward as Waco veered off the road and parked beside a silver-grey truck. Without glancing at the logo painted on the side she knew it was Texas Proud's. The tailgate was down; the ten-gallon water jug was missing.

Good Lord! Surely Dad isn't hauling water from the lake to put out this inferno!

In a flash she was out of the car running toward the fire, scanning the perimeter, searching for John. From the corner of her eye, she saw Waco sprinting toward the back of the towering flames.

"Hey, lady! Stop!" a firefighter shouted, hurriedly uncoiling a length of grey hose.

Shorter than Dixie, younger, with wiry blond hair sticking out from under his helmet and a gleam of excitement burning in his eyes, she could picture this kid playing with a book of matches more than she could envision him as a firefighter.

"Have you seen the man who reported the fire?" she yelled. "He's over six feet tall, white-headed . . ."

A man stepped around the backside of the truck. He appeared to be in charge. "Where's the god-damned hydrant?"

"There isn't one," Dixie screamed, recognizing the captain. She'd gone to school with his daughter. "Use the lake."

"Lady, this ain't no pumper truck!" the kid derided, mocking her ignorance.

"Get on the squawk-box," Captain Aspenwald thundered as he stalked toward the blaze. "Call Alvin. They've got one."

"You mean you can't put it out!" The concept

of a fire truck unequipped to put out fires was incredible to Dixie. "What are you going to do?"

"Well," the kid drawled, after squirting a foul stream of tobacco juice from the side of his mouth, "I reckon this here bonfire is jest turned into a weenie roast, iffen you brought the makin's."

Just what I· need, she fumed silently, a red-necked, tobacco-dipping, smart-ass!

Not waiting for his permission, she circled the front of the useless fire truck and darted in the direction Waco had gone. Maybe he'd seen something she'd missed.

"Waco!" she shouted, skirting dangerously close to the scarlet boundary of charred prairie grass. Sweat beaded on her face. A thick layer of black smoke began to blanket the entire clearing. The wind had died, which was a blessing and a curse. The fire wouldn't spread to the nearby trees, but the smoke had settled until it seemed thick enough to cut with a knife. She could barely see ten feet in front of her. "Waco!"

"Over here! Backside of the slab. Get a fireman up here with some oxygen. Radio for an ambulance!"

She heard the urgency in his voice. At the same time, her foot tangled in an orange mesh barrier. Instinctively, she knew she was dangerously close to an open ditch. Probably the sewer line, she deduced. It would lead her straight to the concrete slab or back toward the fire truck.

She turned, following a direct route away from Waco.

"Hurry!" He counted silently as his hands pumped rhythmically against John Mayson's chest. He pinched John's nose, held his jaw, took a short, deep breath, and exhaled between the victim's flaccid lips.

Damn your ornery hide! Breathe!

He had justifiable reason to hate John Mayson. The night Mayson had tried to pulverize him flashed in his memory. Fear. Guilt. Shame. Anger. And humiliation. He'd felt a wide range of emotions. Hate Mayson? Hell, yes! But none of his reasons were sufficient cause to stand by and do nothing while the man died from smoke inhalation, or a heart attack.

Dixie would never forgive him.

Desperate, close to panic, Waco knew John would cancel a nonreturnable ticket through heaven's gates if it meant preventing Dixie from enjoying a life with him.

"Your daughter was with me this weekend, old man. What are you going to do about it?"

Hatred had medicinal value.

Waco heard a weak cough and saw movement behind John's eyelids.

Encouraged, he leaned closer to John's ear, panted loudly and said, "You die and she's mine. She'll inherit Texas Proud and get your company, too!" *Breathe, damn you!* "Your signs go down. Tumbleweed's signs go up." He inwardly cringed as he put voice to every man's worst fear. "You'll be dead. Forgotten. What's yours will belong to the low-life scum you kicked off your front porch!"

He pinched John's nostrils in preparation to give another kiss of life, when he saw John's lips move.

"Bastard," John mouthed, his throat too raw to give adequate volume to his claim. Too weak to open his eyes, he whispered, "No lying . . . son-of-a-bitch . . . shit-bum . . . will get what's . . . mine!"

Waco sat back on his heels feeling so damned grateful he wanted to fiercely hug his enemy. But, beneath the film of soot coating John's face, he could see the grey pallor hadn't changed. Although his bluish-tinged lips had spouted a foul epitaph, Mayson's breathing remained shallow. He was still in danger.

"Yeah, well, what's that gonna make your grand-kids?" Waco gibed. "Think about it. Me and Dixie making babies while you're rotting six feet underground."

A seizure of coughing and spitting and John rolling to his side was Waco's answer. Bending forward, Waco watched moisture flow down John's face, not realizing tears had left tracks down his own until he wiped the back of his hands across his cheeks.

Tears? For Mayson? His sworn enemy? Couldn't be! He scrubbed his shirtsleeve across his face. Must have been caused by the smoke in his eyes. He sure as shit wouldn't cry over John Mayson!

* * *

Dixie's heart lurched. Through the grey haze she could see her father struggling to catch his breath and Waco kneeling beside him doing nothing to help!

"Dad!" she screamed as a rush of adrenaline made her legs churn faster. She'd made the wrong choice. She should have gotten to her father's side and helped him, and sent Waco to the truck!

The three firemen who'd been following her, bolted past her, blocking her view. They were beside John, starting to strap an oxygen mask on his face and lifting him on the stretcher by the time she reached his side.

One part of her brain told her to stay back, to let the firemen do their job; the irrational side had her elbowing between the firemen, dropping to her knees. Her hands shook with fear as they grabbed the front of his stained shirt. Above the plastic inhalator and elastic straps, his eyes were closed.

"Dad! Be okay!" she pleaded, feeling totally helpless. "Please, please, *please* . . ."

"Lady!" one fireman protested. He started to take vital signs. "Move aside, will you? Let us do our job! He's gonna be all right."

She felt familiar strong hands gently settle on her shoulders, pulling her away from her father. She wrenched loose from them and jumped to her feet. Whirling around, she pushed against Waco's chest.

"Don't touch me, you sonovabitch!" she screamed hysterically. "Don't ever touch me again!"

Stunned, Waco's hands dropped to his side as though she'd struck his gut with a brickbat.

"Don't pretend you cared what happened to him," she screamed. "I saw you sitting there like a bump on a log while he was choking to death!"

"Dixie, I did the best I could," Waco protested calmly.

"Deny that you hate him!" she huffed, tears streaming down her face as she vented her spleen on Waco. "Deny that you'd be better off with him dead!"

Waco opened his mouth to defend himself from her recriminations, but snapped it shut. Her eyes were wild. She was scared, too distraught to hear a word he said. He stepped away from her when he wanted to hold her close to him.

Experience had taught him there was a time to fight and a time to walk away. He chose the latter, turning away and striding toward the distant sounds of sirens.

When the air had cleared and her emotions weren't riding high, she'd listen to reason. He'd done his level best to save Mayson. By his standards that didn't make him a hero, but he was a long way from being the villain.

Smoke quickly enveloped Waco's retreating form before Dixie could comply with the urge to pick up a chunk of concrete and hurl it at him.

"Okay, let's get him to the ambulance," she heard the fireman say through a red haze of anger.

"I'm going with you," she announced firmly, taking her father's limp hand.

When there was no argument, she concentrated on keeping pace with their slow trot. She was purposely blocking out thoughts of Waco's perfidy. Once her father was safe, she'd sort through her feelings.

Lack of fresh air, fear, and overexertion began to take their toll on her reserves. Her legs ached; her knees felt weak. She felt nauseous and dizzy, but she kept running until the blood pounded loudly in her ears. What took minutes, seemed like hours, days.

Exhausted, she barely noticed the additional emergency truck, or the hoses that stretched from the pond across the drive, or the shafts of water dousing the fire. Her father's fingers had to be peeled from her hand before he was lifted into the ambulance. A stranger's helping hand boosted her into the emergency vehicle.

As the back doors closed, she saw Waco standing beside his car. His arms were locked together across his filthy shirt. His shoulders slumped. He looked utterly forlorn. Beaten. Defeated.

Completely the opposite of how she'd remembered him the night he'd encountered her father and stumbled down their front porch steps. Her entire being had been tormented by the image imprinted in her memory of Waco straightening his shoulders, holding his head high as he'd walked away from her.

This image caused her agony that doubled her over at the waist.

"She's gonna fall," Dixie heard the paramedic call as she crumpled.

A merciful, impenetrable wave of blackness encompassed her.

Seventeen

"You look like you've been trampled by a horse, mauled by a dog, and dragged in by a cat," Crystal observed blithely when she heard the front door slam and came in from off the balcony where she'd been sunbathing. When her brother didn't have a snappy comeback, her tone changed to concern. "Where've you been? What happened?"

"With Dixie. There was a fire out at Mayson Manor." He unbuttoned his shirt and tugged it from his slacks as he crossed to the kitchen. After he'd turned on the faucet and dribbled liquid soap on his hands, he said, "John Mayson tried to put it out single-handedly and half-killed himself."

Zeke, who'd followed Crystal and was sliding the balcony door closed, beamed a smile at Waco. "I hope you did the right thing and finished the bastard off."

"Mayson is on his way to the hospital. Dixie went with him."

His succinct version of what happened purposely deleted everything other than the bare facts. Waco splashed water on his face, scrubbed it hard with both hands, then rinsed. His eyes stung as he watched the black-flecked foam whirl in the sink before slithering down the drain.

Crystal handed Waco a dishtowel. "You didn't go with them?"

"Hell no," Zeke chortled. "Somebody had to stay there and fan the flames!"

"Not funny, Zeke," Crystal reprimanded, shooting her uncle a dirty look. "How'd you like it if your house burned down and you lost everything you owned?"

"There you go, shooting off your mouth when you're only half-cocked." Zeke flopped into the armchair in front of the television. "Mayson's house is under construction. The wood ain't even erected yet."

Waco lowered the towel from his face. "How did you know that?"

"Saw Mayson's straw boss over at the lumber yard yesterday." Zeke picked up the television's remote control and flicked the "on" button. "Hey, look here. It made the local news."

". . . arson is suspected," the newscaster finished. The cameraman widened the lens to encompass a panoramic view of the smoldering remains and firemen slogging hoses back to the trucks. "Back to you, Bill."

"Cops never catch barn burners," Zeke gloated, flicking rapidly through the channels, searching for the complete coverage of the story, but to no avail. He punched the "off" button with his thumb. "Damn, I'd have liked to have seen that. Would've made my day."

Biting his tongue, Waco held back his suspicions. Zeke was family. He had an-eye-for-an-eye, a-tooth-for-a-tooth mentality, but he wouldn't burn down a pile of lumber to get revenge on John Mayson. A dull pain stabbed behind his eyes. Waco couldn't bear the thought of his uncle being like a kid harboring a grudge, with a box of matches in his hands.

Zeke was his responsibility. Had been since he'd grown strong enough to carry a carpenter's toolbox. Before that, he'd been responsible for food on the table and clean sheets on the beds. His entire damn life, in one way or another, he'd been responsible for Zeke's actions. The weight of his worries pressed heavily across his shoulders.

"What did the two of you do today?" he asked casually.

"I lazed around the pool. Zeke went house-hunting," Crystal said, answering for both of them.

"Find anything?"

"Nuthin' worth you lookin' at."

Concerned by the desolate expression on Waco's face, Crystal shooed Waco out of the kitchen. "You go take a shower while I whip up some dinner."

"Thanks." His feet felt as though he'd waded through concrete as he moved toward his bedroom. "I restocked the freezer with dinners. You all go ahead and eat. I'll nuke mine in the microwave after I've showered."

"No more MRE's," Zeke objected strenuously.

Crystal planted her hands on her bare hips. "What the devil are MRE's?"

"The stuff the army serves the troops! M-R-E stands for Meals Rejected in Ethiopia!"

Laughing, Crystal said, "How about chicken, mashed potatoes, red-eye gravy . . ."

"No more KFC, either! How come I keep buying you cookbooks and you keep servin' me food that tastes like the book covers?"

Waco closed his door, shutting out the friendly family squabble. Automatically his hand went to the back of his neck to assuage the pain. He strode past the bed, though he was tempted to simply crash and pull the covers over his head. Fastidious by nature, he nixed the impulse.

Minutes later, as hot water peppered his skin, he leaned against the cool tile and wondered if Zeke's alibi would hold water. He told himself it didn't matter. There wasn't a doubt in his mind that Mayson could probably fill a thick telephone book with the names of people he'd slighted. If the fire marshal investigated the case alphabetically, it could take months for him to get to the S's.

Not that he didn't want the miscreant to be found and prosecuted.

Waco frowned as he lathered shampoo into his hair. From what Dixie had told him about her dawn-to-dark work schedule, she often checked on the various subcontractors' progress with an early morning or late evening drive-by inspection. The thought of her alone on an isolated job site, unprotected, with an arsonist on the loose, made chills run up his spine.

Maybe nobody started it, he mused, dropping his

head to let the spray rinse his hair. Lightning and accidents caused as many fires as arsonists. There had been a storm Saturday night. Could a bolt have struck the pile of lumber and ignited it? Or, maybe some kids from the nearby subdivision had ridden their bikes over there. This wouldn't be the first time kids playing with matches or teenage smokers had started a fire.

Waco prayed to God the fire had been an act of nature or a freak accident. Thoughts of Dixie being in danger, or, of Zeke being the perpetrator of the crime, tied his stomach in knots. He had two eyes, but it would be impossible to keep one on Dixie and one on Zeke without going permanently cross-eyed.

"Your eyes are bloodshot," Mayson observed, waking from a restless nap to find his daughter hovering over the rail of the hospital bed. "Have you been crying?"

"A little," she admitted solemnly.

She twisted the turquoise ring around and around on her finger. Earlier, the emergency room doctor had examined her father and decided to be on the side of caution to keep him overnight. While she watched him slowly recover, she worried about Waco.

Common decency demanded at the very least a small attempt on his part to help a man who was suffocating. Disappointment and fright combined with exhaustion, had ignited her temper. Spitefully, she'd lashed out at Waco, wanting him to suffer for his doing nothing to help John.

Judging from the desolated look on his face, she'd succeeded. What she hadn't expected was for the barb she'd hurled at Waco to bounce back and smack her, with twice the force.

"Smoke get in your eyes?" He started to smile, but winced. He coughed, wiped his mouth, and scowled as he suddenly remembered Stone forcing air into his lungs. The memory made him want to puke. "Don't think this changes anything between us."

"Us? You and me?"

John shook his head.

"Who?"

"Stone and me. My guess is that he started the fire. When the smoke asphyxiated me, he got scared, maybe felt a little guilty, so he came out of hiding and . . ."

John strangled as he swallowed; his saliva tasted like charcoal.

She handed him a tissue. The first part of what he'd said had to be a figment of her father's imagination. Unless Waco could be at two places at once, he couldn't have started the fire. "And?"

"And he showed me what kind of man he is. He's a sexual pervert!" John spat, with a vile grimace. "A man does not lock lips with another man."

Her eyes widened in stark disbelief. "He resuscitated you?"

"The nurse called it CPR. I call it disgusting."

His face turned red. "Worse than sucking rattle-snake poison from a man fanged in the butt!"

"He could have let you choke to death."

"Better dead than . . ."

"Beholden?" Dixie prompted when he paused.

"Red . . . faced. *Mortified!*"

Dixie gave him a hard look. "Your pride will recover. I thought you were dying. I gave Waco a terrible tongue-lashing."

"Good," he huffed. "That's the best news I've had since he returned to Texas."

She stepped back from the bed, fuming, wanting to teach her father a few lessons in gratitude. "Why can't you give the man credit for saving your life?"

"Because the sonovabitch wanted to kick me while I was down. When he couldn't steal the breath right out of my body, he said obscene things. Things that made me want to clean the tracks of his trencher with a stick of dynamite."

"I'm not listening." Childishly, Dixie wanted to cover her ears to protect her heart.

"He isn't interested in you. Never has been. Stone wants to get even with me for humiliating him. You are the weak link in the chain. He plans to use you to steal Texas Proud right out from under my nose!"

"I don't believe you." Her voice quavered with doubt when she wanted to be composed. Her father wanted to vilify Waco; he'd say or do anything to meet his objective. "Waco doesn't need me to get Texas Proud."

The vein on John's forehead throbbed furiously as he hacked and coughed. "Ask him!"

"I will." As the nurse on night duty entered the room to check on her patient, Dixie recovered her composure and said calmly, "I'll be back in the morning."

"I'll take good care of your father, Miss Mayson," the stout, grey-haired nurse assured, placing the tray she carried on the nightstand. "A couple of these pills and he'll sleep like a baby."

John pushed the button that raised the head of his bed. "No pills."

"The doctor ordered them."

Knowing how difficult her father could be, Dixie approached the side of the bed. "Dad, you have to do what the doctor says."

"I don't give a damn what he ordered." After the nurse had slipped a digital thermometer between his lips, he mumbled, "Let her take 'em if they have to get rid of them to run the bill up."

Stoically, the nurse checked his pulse. "Can't take pills? Are you having difficulty swallowing?"

"Hell, no," John roared once his mouth was empty. "You get your fanny out of here and take those pills with you."

The elderly woman lifted one shoulder in resignation as she flipped back the folded cloth on the tray, revealing a syringe. A professional smile curved her mouth as she said to Dixie, "Would you excuse us for a moment?" Her voice changed to the tone of a construction superintendent as she turned to John and ordered, "Roll over on your side, Mr. Mayson. This will only sting for a second or two."

"Okay, okay!" John relented, holding up his hands to stop her. "I'll take the pills."

"I thought you might change your mind," the nurse replied sweetly.

"Where do you think you're going?" John demanded when he saw Dixie take the cash from his trousers and head for the door.

"To talk to Waco." Purseless, she had no cash, no keys, and no car. Over her shoulder she added, "Before you pick up the phone and have the sheriff escort him out of town."

John laughed harshly. He glared at the nurse, but took the glass of water she offered, and the pills that appeared big enough to choke a horse.

"Believe you me, daughter, I would if I could. I've known from the get-go that Stone was a bad influence on you. Once a shit-bum, always a shit-bum."

"Do you eat with that toilet-tongue?" the nurse scolded. "If you do, it must leave a dirty brown taste in your mouth. You'd best empty that water glass, to flush down your foul language."

Dixie slipped from the hospital room, certain the nurse could take care of any medical problem her father caused. As to the loathsome accusations John had made on Waco's character, she doubted every single word he'd uttered.

Waco fought hard, but he fought fair.

Eager to apologize for her behavior, she tapped her toe impatiently while she waited for the elevator. She'd turned toward the exit sign, deciding to take the flight of steps, when she heard a ding.

Kate charged from the elevator, bumping into Dixie, then fiercely hugging her.

"Thank God you're here!" Kate babbled, distraught with anxiety. "I saw the fire on the six o'clock news. How badly is John hurt?"

"He's fine"

"He is?" Kate sniffed, then blew her nose on the handkerchief wadded in her hand.

Dixie made a mental note of the interior designer's disheveled appearance. Wisps of hair had come loose from the coil at her nape; her eyes were watery and red-rimmed. In place of the fashionable suit she normally wore, Kate had on a rumpled pair of slacks and gingham shirt. Frankly, she looked in worse shape than her father when he'd been admitted into the emergency room.

Kate's shoulders sagged as she sighed with relief. "The reporter made it sound as though he was dying."

"Hardly. He just raised hell with me and the nurse."

"Do you think it would be all right for me to go sit with him? I promise I won't say anything to upset him."

"I'm certain the nurse would appreciate a calming influence on her patient. She had to threaten him with a needle to get him to take his pills."

"Poor John," Kate commiserated, blinking to keep back a fresh bout of tears. "Strong men get crotchety when they're ill. He deserves a medal for trying to put out that fire all by himself."

The elevator bell alerted Dixie that she'd better cut short Kate's sympathy unless she wanted to run down eight flights of steps. She stuck her foot in the door when it opened.

"I've got to go, Kate. Thanks for being here when John needs you. I'll see you at the office tomorrow."

The elevator lowered slowly, as though hand cranked. To curb claustrophobic feelings she'd never previously experienced, Dixie directed her thoughts toward what she'd say to Waco. First, she'd tell him how sorry she was for believing . . . what, that he wouldn't help the man he had every reason to hate? Scratch that. Or that seeing was believing and she'd believed what she'd seen with her own eyes? Scratch that, too!

How was she supposed to know he'd given John CPR? Dammit, why hadn't Waco told her he'd performed CPR?

Why?

Because she wouldn't have listened to him, a small voice inside her replied. She'd been like a strip of silver solder sucked into a heated copper fitting; circumstances had been beyond her control. She hadn't been thinking rationally, just reacting to the chaos that had surrounded her.

The elevator reached the ground floor. Hoping there would be a cab stand at the entrance, she crossed the main lobby. She'd forgotten how disreputable she looked until she noticed several people openly staring at her.

She'd washed her face and hands, but her clothes looked as though they'd been the main course at a barbecue picnic—soot-stained, with tiny holes peppered across the yoke of her shirt. Briefly, she considered going home to change clothes and get her car, then driving to Galveston. One glance at her wristwatch and she rejected the idea. It was nearly nine o'clock. If she wanted to arrive at a respectable hour, she had to forgo a quick shower and a change of clothing.

Outside, beneath the garish golden glow of the parking lot lights, she spotted two cabs parked beside the curb. "Cabbie!"

"Whaddayawant," Zeke demanded, pissed off at having to answer the door and miss the final shoot-out of the movie he'd been watching. Crystal and Waco had gone for their nightly stroll along the beach. Why weren't they back? Nobody came knocking on the door looking for him. They ought to be here to answer it when people came calling, looking for them.

Dixie gawked at the short, scrawny man who'd opened the door. She'd lived in Texas all her life, but never had she seen a man wearing cowboy boots and a skimpy Speed-O swimsuit.

"Is this the Stones' condo?" she asked cautiously, uncertain the man at the desk had given her the correct number.

"Yeah. What of it?"

Her memory jarred, allowing her to identify Waco's relative. "You must be Zeke?"

"Must be. That's the name I answer to when the dinner bell rings." His eyes squinted up at the bedraggled woman. "Who in tarnation are you?"

"Dixie Mayson." For a second, she thought Zeke would slam the door in her face. Quicker than a door-to-door vacuum cleaner salesman, she wedged her toe in the open space by the doorjamb. "Is Waco here?"

"Nope." Zeke hitched up his swimsuit as though it was a pair of jeans. One bony finger stabbed the air between them as he accused, "I suppose you'll be sendin' the sheriff after him, again? Or have the Maysons started doin' their own dirty work for a change?"

The hostility Zeke radiated was palpable. A red tide of anger climbed from his neck to his forehead, as if he were a mercury gauge she'd pumped up on a gas main. At any second she expected the old man to explode.

Her own tolerance level was at minus ten. She'd been through a fire, the hospital, and a hellacious fight with her father. Staring down at the dark strands of hair Zeke had brushed to one side to cover the bald spot on the top of his head, Dixie was in no mood to swap insults.

"I'm not responsible for my father's actions in the past," she replied calmly, although her fists were clenched at her side.

Zeke goaded, "You just stir shit and wait for the

flies to buzz? You probably struck a match to that lumber so's you could blame us. Well, girlie, that fly don't buzz around here no more. Hit the road."

"I'm not here to accuse anybody of anything."

"Liar," Zeke spat. "I saw the news. Waco didn't have nothin' to do with that fire."

"I know he didn't. Waco was with me."

"You're his alibi?" Zeke grinned, exposing his stubby, tobacco-stained teeth. "Bet that sticks like a chicken bone in your old man's craw."

"John doesn't know. He's recovering from smoke inhalation at the hospital."

Zeke's smile widened. "More good news. Two birds with one stone."

"Was that a confession, Mr. *Stone?*"

She caught the door with her forearm as Zeke gave a hoot of laughter and started to close it. His small, black eyes raked her from head to foot, wanting to make her feel ten feet tall with size fourteen, double-wide shoes. Years ago, that look would have decimated her. She'd have slouched her shoulders and slunk off to the nearest corner.

Dixie stood tall, stubbornly keeping eye contact. "I'm not leaving here until I tell Waco I'm sorry."

"That ain't necessary. I told him that years ago. You Maysons are sorry folks."

Dixie bristled at how he'd twisted the meaning of her apology into an insult; her back stiffened with family pride. Her father had treated the Stones shamefully, but John had believed he'd been protecting her from Waco's bad influence.

With no doubt in her mind that Zeke thought

he was protecting a member of his family, she said, "If Waco isn't home, I'd appreciate your lending me a pad of paper and a pencil. I'll leave him a note."

"You'd have to tack it to my dead carcass. That's the only way I'd deliver your message to him."

Reduced to begging for a favor, Dixie whispered, "Please . . . I have to let Waco know that I was wrong. Would you have him call me?"

Zeke felt himself weakening. She wasn't snooty and haughty, the way he'd always pictured her. But, she was John Mayson's daughter, the man who'd wanted him and Waco locked up in the county jail and the key thrown away.

The acorn never falls far from the tree, he reminded himself silently.

Not wanting to be a sappy old fool tricked by feminine wiles, he pointed toward the parking lot and ordered vehemently, "Git off my property, Miz Mayson, or I'll be the one doing the callin'—the cops! You stay away from me and my kinfolks!"

For a moment or two, Dixie thought Zeke would relent. When his eyes hardened like black pebbles and he began shaking his finger at her, she knew he'd spoken his final words. He would get great pleasure out of having her arrested.

Turning toward the steps, she murmured, "I never meant to hurt you or Waco. It's a habit I'm bound and determined to break."

She didn't hear the door close or see Zeke lean against it as he scratched his belly thoughtfully. He'd heard her. Grudgingly, he had to admit that the woman had spunk. He'd been as obnoxious as a polecat poked with a plumber's helper, but she hadn't looked down her uppity nose at him. Well, maybe, 'cuz she was such a long drink of water she'd had to do a lot of lookin' down, but she hadn't done it in an unkindly manner.

Zeke pushed away from the door. Her being nice didn't change how he felt about her old man. He'd been checking around, talking to Texas Proud's suppliers and subcontractors. Mayson was about to get his comeuppance. His credit was stretched thinner than a bead of caulking.

Grinning, he flopped into the chair and picked up the remote control. One more fire would burn Mayson right out of the building business, Zeke gloated, as he turned on the television set. The sweet flavor of revenge for past wrongs flooded his mouth.

A spray of bullets blasted from Clint Eastwood's six-shooter. The guys wearing black hats fell from their saddles, sprawling on the ground. The lonesome wail of a harmonica matched the sorrowful expression on the cowboy's face as he dropped to his knees. He cradled the bullet-riddled body of his ladylove against his chest.

As the credits began to roll across the screen, Zeke felt his conscience being tweaked. In the movies the good guys won, the bad guys lost, and sometimes innocent bystanders got caught in the crossfire. Justice was served, no matter what the price.

He glanced over his shoulder at the closed door and scowled.

Nothin' wrong with wanting justice. That's all he craved. No matter what price Dixie Mayson had to pay. Self-righteously he decided that it would be a cold day in Tombstone, Arizona before he informed Waco that he'd had a visitor.

Eighteen

"Good morning," Sara greeted, with her usual bright smile. "I heard about the fire, so I've placed a phone call to the insurance agent. Kate called from the hospital . . ."

"I talked to her." Dixie waited for the remainder of the Monday morning messages, then departed for her office. When Sara's nose for gossip began to twitch, Dixie cut her off by saying, "She's taking John home from the hospital. He's supposed to rest at home for a couple of days."

"Oh? Is talking to Kate what made you arrive late at the office?"

Dixie sat at her desk, propped her elbows on it and rubbed her forehead. Late once in her entire career and Sara, who acted as though she didn't own a watch, wanted to glue a gold star on the calendar to mark the date. One more cheerful, chipper word out of her mouth and Dixie swore she'd pull every curly blond hair out of her head by their dark roots.

Realizing she was treating Sara unfairly, Dixie said, "You'll have to forgive my abruptness. I have

the mother of all headaches. Do you have a couple
of aspirins stashed in your desk?"

"A king-sized bottle. Do you want me to get
you a Coke, too?"

"Coffee. No cream or sugar this morning."
Dixie eyed the telephone. "Any other messages?"

"Scads. John's calls were routed to your phone."

"Great," Dixie grumbled, closing her eyes.
"Would you bring the whole bottle of aspirins? It
sounds like I'm going to need them."

"Most of them were from people concerned
about the fire. I accepted their condolences on
your behalf and told them you'd get back to them
later today."

"Good." Her eyes felt like two eggs, fried crispy
around the edges of the whites. That's what too
much smoke and too little sleep did for her. As Sara
left her office she murmured a belated, "Thanks."

She waited until long after midnight for Waco
to call her. When the phone did not ring, she'd
tried to sleep, but the entire weekend flashed in
her mind like a nightmare. Starting with her irrational decision to set aside old grievances and
blindly follow Waco's lead, she saw images of their
making love. No, she corrected silently, having
sex. Great sex.

Her mind had played heartless tricks on her.
Sharp images of Waco gazing at her after they'd
had sex, as though she was the Christmas angel
who'd fallen off the tree and landed in his bed. If
she'd been smart, her overly active brain would

have counted his kisses, like sheep, and fallen asleep.

But no, her mind had been cruel. She saw the fire, heard herself make wild accusations, and then quarrel with her father, all fast-played through her mental projector. As though those disasters weren't enough, she'd capped off her memorable weekend by running up a huge taxicab bill to talk to a half-naked cowboy who hated her.

Her intentions were good; her mistakes seemed insurmountable. The whole world hated her, with the exception of Sara, and she was working on her.

"Here's your coffee," Sara said, carrying a mug, aspirins, and her phone-message record book. "I put the important one on top."

"Waco called?" she gasped, reading his name and noting the hearts and flowers Sara had doodled around it. "When?"

"Actually, he left his name and number on the recorder."

Dixie popped the pills in her mouth and took a swallow of scalding hot coffee. "Oh!"

"Was that oh, as in, ouch? Or oh, as in aaaahhhhh!" Sara arched one carefully plucked eyebrow. "You didn't come to the reunion meeting Friday night. And I just happened to notice you weren't home all weekend. Does that oh mean you're hiding something from me?"

"That oh means it's none of your business," Dixie replied blandly.

Sara's smile sagged. "There was a time when we shared all our secrets."

"Like your ex-husband's car parked at your house Friday night? Or like Todd asking Texas Proud to bid on a quarter-of-a-million-dollar house he plans to build? Is there some secret behind him wanting such a big house?"

"Oh," Sara quoted, shooting Dixie a sly wink before she scooted toward the door. "Did I forget to mention that I've been meeting Todd for lunch?"

"No, but that does explain those long lunch hours. Should I send my bridesmaid's dress to the cleaners?"

Sara giggled with delight, then slanted her finger across her lips. "I'm not supposed to say anything."

"But?"

"I think I might be going to Vegas one weekend," she whispered. "Soon. Don't tell anybody."

Dixie leaned back in her chair. Either the aspirin had taken effect or Sara's secret had raised her spirits. She crossed her heart with her finger, the way she'd always done when they were youngsters, and asked, "Why go out of town? I hear the room service at the Hilton is excellent."

"Great view, too. Lots of lovely ceilings," Sara said, with a faint smile.

"Gossip," Waco derided, staring out the window at the oppressive grey clouds hanging low over the gulf. "Mayson wouldn't be interested in buying lots if he was broke."

"I'm telling you, Texas Proud is out on a financial limb," Zeke roared, tossing a yellow pad of paper on Waco's desk. "The concrete mason says they're pinchin' pennies to the point of removin' reinforcement rods after their ground inspections pass. The plumber I talked to admitted to cutting corners to the point of paintin' steel screws with copper-colored paint, just to save three cents a screw. And Mayson's framer is usin' green wood. I seen it for myself yesterday morning when I walked their buildings. I'd bet my last bottom dollar that the suppliers are gonna buzz-saw that limb by cutting off their credit."

Waco spun around. "You walked their buildings?"

"Don't worry. Nobody saw me."

His uncle being seen at Texas Proud's job sites was only part of Waco's worry. Yesterday, Zeke hadn't appeared the least bit surprised by the newscast that covered the fire at Mayson Manor. Zeke had made no bones about hating John Mayson and wanting revenge. What etched deep lines across Waco's forehead was the possibility that Zeke had discovered Mayson was in financial trouble and had pulled the cord to start the buzz saw.

Waco was reluctant to start checking Zeke's pockets for a lighter. Zeke hated Mayson, but that didn't make him an arsonist. He ripped off the top sheet of the pad, wadded it into a tight ball, and lobbed it into the trash can. "I don't want you sneaking around on Mayson's property."

"Why?" Zeke's eyes narrowed to slits. " 'Cuz you think they'll blame me for startin' that fire?"

"Nobody is blaming you." *Yet.* Waco eased into his chair and looked up at his uncle. "We're the new kid on the block, a threat to the old regime. We have to keep our nose clean."

Zeke chuckled. "You savin' Mayson's life ought to make you a hero." He held his thumb and forefinger two inches apart, and swept them to the right as though reading the morning paper's headline. "CINDERFELLA SAVES FOE FROM FIRE."

"We don't need publicity, either."

Zeke strutted to the side of Waco's desk, braced one arm on the corner and said softly, "It'd be a smart move for them to blame us if they're doin' what I think they're doin'."

"Which is?"

"Robbin' Peter to pay Paul. Burnin' material to collect the insurance and usin' the money to pay their suppliers. If they can shift the blame to us, it'd be a sure-fire way to get their cash flow movin' while hurtin' our reputation."

Waco physically recoiled from the idea, pushing his chair away from Zeke.

"Mayson could've used his daughter as a decoy, again," Zeke said, reminding his nephew of the dirty trick Mayson had played at the businessmen's meeting. "She distracts you from what's goin' on by making you think you're stud of the year. Meanwhile, Mayson is dealin' off the bottom of the deck to get the winnin' hand."

"You've overlooked an important detail. I couldn't have started the fire. I was with Dixie."

Zeke gave a snort. "She probably doesn't know

that he's playin' both ends against the middle. Mayson is counting on her keepin' her mouth shut, just like she did when he had us packin' our bags the last time. Dixie doesn't want her father to know she spent the weekend shacked up with you, does she?"

Avoiding the question, Waco responded wearily, "You're letting your feud with Mayson distort what happened."

"And you're letting Mayson set you up for another hit. I also heard two of TP's contracts on houses fell through because the rumor is out about your opening up bay-front lots. You're taking business away from Mayson."

"That's ridiculous. If I wanted Texas Proud, I'd make Mayson an offer. We're *developers* in the Bay area. The only building we'll be doing is beach homes, here on Galveston Island."

"What's to stop us from developing the land and building the houses? We don't have a cash-flow problem." Zeke scratched his beard thoughtfully. "Waco, you may think I'm a crazy old coot, but I'm tellin' you this for your own good. Mayson ain't gonna tolerate you steppin' into his boots. You ain't gonna get his business or his daughter. Not as long as Mayson can draw a breath of fresh air." Determined to have the last word, Zeke hitched up his britches and strode to the door. He stopped only long enough to say, "That's how it's been, and that's how it's gonna be. Amen."

"You stay away from Mayson and his job sites," Waco warned before Zeke shut the door.

Much as Waco wanted to disregard Zeke's condemnation of John Mayson and only concentrate on the golden days he'd shared with Dixie at the Hilton, he had to give due consideration to key points Zeke had made. The information on Texas Proud's financial situation bothered him. Was Mayson between a rock and a hard place? If so, the fire could have been an act of desperation. Texas Proud wouldn't be the first builder to use arson as a means to get money in the bank.

Deciding there was only one way to verify or discredit Zeke's claims, he pressed the intercom button. "Liz, get Scott Michaels on the phone, would you, please?"

Liz glared at Zeke, who'd dared to sit in the chair across from her, put his glue-stained boots on the corner of her desk, and began unabashedly to eavesdrop on her conversation with her boss.

"Yes, sir," she replied. "He's the investigator in California. Correct?"

"Yes."

"Scott'll show you two who knows his butt from a hole in the ground," Zeke said, with a wide, sly grin. Swinging his feet to the plush carpet, he made a thumbs-up sign, and ambled out of Liz's office.

"Excuse me, Mr. Stone," Liz said, flustered by Zeke's comment. "What did you say?"

"When I get off the phone with Scott, call Texas Proud and ask for Dixie Mayson, again."

"I was just about to put her call through to you.

Shall I tell Miss Mayson you'll return her call later?"

"No. What line?"

"Three."

"Good morning, Dixie," Waco said, after he'd touched the blinking button. Worried about the aftereffects of the smoke she'd inhaled, he asked, "I almost called last night, but I thought you'd be at the hospital with John. How are you feeling?"

"Better than when you last saw me. Actually, after I left the hospital last night, I stopped by your condo," Dixie said, anxious to let him know she'd tried to make amends earlier.

"You did?"

"Your uncle said you were out for the evening."

Waco glanced at the door Liz had closed. Damn your interfering, ornery hide, Zeke Stone! "I must have been with Crystal. We usually go for a walk along the beach in the evening. Zeke conveniently forgot to tell me that you'd been here."

She wasn't surprised, not after Zeke had treated her as though he was a tin roof and she was a hailstorm.

"I want to apologize for what I said yesterday." Nervously, she curled the corners of the calendar on her desk. "I know you did everything within your power to help John."

And then some. "Apology accepted. It was a stress situation. None of us were thinking clearly."

"You did." She put a smile in her voice as she said, "Dad grumbled about you giving him CPR."

"When CPR didn't work, I said some things that had him gasping for air."

"Such as?"

Waco opened his mouth to repeat what he'd said, then clamped it shut. Without smoke burning his eyes and clogging his nasal passages, and fear pumping adrenaline through him, the threats he'd made would sound inordinately harsh. Dixie would think he was a presumptuous, first-class jerk!

"Nothing that I meant," he alleged. "I hope your father doesn't remember a word I said."

"Waco," her voice dropped to a hushed level, filled with misery. Without being specific, Waco had admitted to doing what her father had accused him of. "He does remember. Everything. John believes you haven't changed over the past ten years. That you're an opportunist who's using me to get your hands on Texas Proud."

"Do you believe him?" Waco asked starkly.

Confused, Dixie paused. She wanted to trust her instincts, to trust Waco, but he'd just proven her female intuition was faulty.

"I didn't believe John when he made vile accusations against you. I defended you."

"I appreciate your vote of confidence."

"But now, you've admitted that you did threaten him. I was wrong. Who should I believe?"

"I'd have said anything to get him breathing on his own." Trying to inject levity into the grave circumstances, he added, "I guess I should have kept my mouth shut, twiddled my thumbs, and let John asphyxiate himself?"

Startled, Dixie realized she'd put Waco in a no-win situation. "You're damned if you do and damned if you don't?"

"That pretty well sums it up, unless . . ."

Waco plowed his fingers through his hair as an idea began to form. If Zeke's information was correct, and Texas Proud was in financial straits, John would welcome an infusion of capital from a silent partner. Not having solid financial information on Texas Proud, he decided not to share his thoughts with her. That, and he couldn't think of a polite way to broach TP's cash-flow problem without sounding crass. Once Scott uncovered the facts, he'd broach the subject.

"Unless I can convince my father you aren't interested in his company, only in me," Dixie finished for him when the silence became prolonged.

"Did you tell John we spent the weekend together?"

"No. As angry as John was over what you'd said, he'd have gone into cardiac arrest."

Waco tried to put Zeke's theory out of his mind, but he needed to know if John was using her as a decoy without her knowledge. "Are you going to tell him?"

"We arrived at the fire together, remember? John is a smart man who doesn't believe in coincidence. I don't have to draw him a diagram for him to realize we were together."

"Openly? No clandestine relationship?"

"Definitely."

Waco smiled. "When did you make that decision?"

"My father is long overdue in realizing that I'm his daughter, but I'm not his little girl. I make my own decisions at work. The same should apply at home. Usually I come and go as I please, without asking permission. Why should there be anything different now?"

"I'm the difference," Waco answered pointedly. "You didn't feel that way the first night we went to dinner."

Dixie sighed, "I know. I despise arguing with John." She realized she'd had a significant change of heart. She was willing to do anything, no matter how disagreeable, to be with Waco. "He expects unquestioning loyalty and devotion. I've been predisposed to give it."

"Been?"

"I'm beginning to ask questions instead of accepting every word he says as the gospel truth. That isn't easy for me."

"It's always easier to go with the flow than swim upstream against a strong current."

Chuckling, Dixie said drily, "John is more like a riptide than a strong current."

"Can I be your safety line?"

"Safe is not the word I'd choose to describe how you make me feel."

"What word would you use?"

It was Dixie's turn to laugh. "When you start fishing for compliments, I'd say it's time for me to get out of the water, dry off, and get back to work."

Reluctant to end their conversation, Waco asked, "Have you contacted the insurance company?"

"That's exclusively John's department. Since he'll be in the office tomorrow, I can't see any reason to step on his toes by filing the paperwork."

"It should be interesting to read the fire inspector's report. He'll ask for a list of suspects. Have you compiled one?"

"How can I make a list when I can't think of anyone who'd deliberately start a fire?"

"No disgruntled employees?"

"At Texas Proud? We all love our jobs," she answered with her tongue in her cheek. "We're happy campers that whistle while we work."

"Point made. It isn't called work because it's fun and games. You and I are lucky. We do love our work."

Dixie grinned. "I guess that puts me above suspicion."

"You were with me. Has TP received any threats?"

"None I've heard."

"What about John? Or your job superintendents?"

"No one has mentioned being threatened."

"Have you fired a subcontractor or hourly employee recently?"

"I'd have to check the personnel records." She jotted a reminder on a note pad as she said, "Most of the men have worked for TP for years. We pay top wages for quality workmanship."

"C'mon, Dixie, that fire didn't start by itself. Somebody went out of their way to go up that lane to torch a pile of lumber. Material bought to be used building your house." They were getting nowhere fast. "What about customers?"

"We get a few complaints, but they're taken care of immediately."

"Do you or John have any personal enemies?"

"I'm sure we've both stepped on some toes, but . . ." She thought of Waco's uncle. Zeke certainly wasn't a member of the Mayson Fan Club. Dixie shifted uncomfortably in her chair. She bit her lip to stop from tossing out Zeke's name. Instinctively she knew that Waco would be as protective of his family members as she was of John. ". . . I can't think of anyone who'd start a fire to get revenge."

Waco exhausted the mental list he'd thought of during the night. It scared him spitless to know Dixie had an enemy, someone crazy enough to start a fire in broad daylight. "I want you to be careful," he said, his voice husky with fear. "Don't go alone to a job site after your men have left. Lock your doors. Watch your rear-view mirror to see if you're being followed. Don't . . ."

"Waco! Stop! You're making me paranoid."

"Good!"

"It was a fire, not a sniper on a rooftop with a grudge."

"Whoever lit that match has a screw loose. I

don't want you to be in his vicinity when he comes completely apart."

Flattered by his concern, she promised, "I won't take any risks. The fire could have started accidentally or by an act of vandalism."

"Maybe. I had thought of that possibility." Waco softened his tone as though by doing so he would make his question less offensive: "Could this have been an inside job?"

"You mean someone here at headquarters?" Dixie gave the idea a moment's thought and rejected it. "John trusts these people, implicitly. What motive could they possibly have?"

"Money."

"They each get a share of the profits."

His voice lowered another notch as he said, "Jealousy? Did your coming into headquarters and taking charge cause any problems?"

"A few," she admitted reluctantly. Texas Proud presented a united front to outsiders; they might destroy the walls from within, but heaven help anyone who transgressed against the company. Generalizing, she said, "There are men in the construction business who resent a woman who knows how to read blueprints as well as pour concrete and wield a hammer and saw."

"Who would John promote if you resigned?"

"Each officer has a specialty." Mentally she went down the row of doors at headquarters. "Blake Jergins knows computers inside and out, but he doesn't know the difference between a drill bit and a pipe cutter. Tom Thorpe, being an architect, has a broader picture of what takes place in the field. He did work his way through college as a framer."

As she spoke, Waco jotted notes. "He'd be a likely candidate."

"Tom's qualifications are good, but quite frankly, he's more interested in being with his wife and four sons than putting in a sixty-hour work week. Little League Baseball would never be the same in the bay area if he took my job."

"Who's your project manager?"

"Walter Block. He'd be a good choice, but he hates paperwork. His weekly reports look like a hen scratched them. But then again, he does have great leadership qualities and knows how to put a building together. I work closely with him."

"Is he in charge of building Mayson Manor?"

"Yes."

"Keep an eye on him." Waco put a star by his name.

Dixie chuckled. "He's the man I'd vote least likely to be an arsonist.

"Aside from being a deacon in the Baptist church, he was my mentor for years. I'd bet my life it isn't him."

"Don't."

"Don't what?"

"Don't trust anyone."

"Yourself included? Or how about my father? Do you think he might be a pyromaniac?" Her small joke fell flat when Waco did not respond. A worried expression creased her brow. "Do you?"

Her question gave him the perfect opportunity to ask if Texas Proud was in financial difficulty. Money motivated most crimes. That, and passion. Using those criteria, neither he nor John were above suspicion.

Certain she'd be offended by an affirmative reply, he said, "Let's stick to the other officers. Who else would be in line for your job?"

"Paul Getz, advertising. Dirk Stallman, financial adviser and material procurement. Gil Albertson, land procurement and sales."

"That's it?"

"Yes, other than Kate Williams, the design coordinator. She heard the news broadcast and rushed to the hospital to be at John's bedside. She's the least likely."

"Is she emotionally involved with your father?"

"I asked myself that same question."

"And?"

"I don't know." Out of habit, Dixie pulled her long braid over her shoulder and curled the loose ends around her finger. "I can't imagine John in bed with Kate, or with any woman for that matter. It's difficult to think of one's parent as being . . . sexually active."

Waco grinned at Dixie's naïveté. Did she believe John had been celibate since her mother had died? With a fair amount of certainty, Waco believed most men in John's situation would place an order for their tombstone if they thought their sex life had ended.

On the other hand, he mused, wouldn't it be

ironic if John had been involved in a clandestine affair ten years ago? An office romance that John had hidden from his daughter? He wondered what Kate's father would have done if John had been caught at her front door.

"Waco?" She twisted her braid until it coiled at her nape, like on an old-fashioned schoolmarm. "Are you there?"

"I'm here. I was just contemplating what you'd told me."

"As an adult, realistically, I know my father isn't a candidate for priesthood, but he's been discreet. *Very* discreet." She let the coil unwind and let it fall. "We should have taken lessons from him."

Waco chuckled. "Our thoughts are on the same wavelength."

"Don't you think I would have noticed something? Like lipstick on his collar? Or a woman's perfume on his shirt? Or his arriving home at the crack of dawn?"

"You said you both come and go as you please. At this late date, I don't think I'd be too concerned about his love life."

"But what if Kate is jealous of me? A woman is capable of striking a match." She worried her bottom lip for a couple of seconds, thinking what she'd do. "Then again, speaking as a woman, I'd be more likely to set his bed on fire than stacks of lumber."

Laughing, Waco said, "Remind me to buy a couple of fire retardant blankets, would you?"

"You're safe. I was just kidding." Recalling the

scene of the fire and her urge to hurl a piece of concrete at him when he'd walked away from her, she blurted, "I won't be responsible for my actions if you turn your back on me and walk away without a word of explanation."

She quickly covered her mouth with her hand, as though by doing so she could capture what she'd said before it crossed the telephone lines. Her fear of Waco abandoning her without a trace was her deepest vulnerability, a bruise on her soul that hadn't healed. She didn't want to think about how Waco had hurt her, much less reveal it during a phone conversation.

Waco heard her sharp intake of breath. At the fire, with her father's health in jeopardy, he'd walked rather than fight with Dixie. But, his gut instincts told him she wasn't referring to what happened yesterday. No, she'd meant years ago.

"What would you do?" he asked, wondering if he could ever live down his callous, ruthless past.

"I'd come after you." She said it with such aplomb that Waco could take it as a threat he should fear, or as a promise he could cherish. Deep in her heart, Dixie didn't know how she'd meant it. "I have a million items on my agenda for today. Can we continue our discussion later?"

"I'll call you."

"Bye."

Slowly, Dixie returned the receiver to its cradle. One day at a time, she chastised herself silently, no expectations, no promises, no recriminations.

No love?

Self-preservation instincts made her hand move protectively to cover her heart. She should have practiced the litany sooner. More often. With conviction.

She glanced down at the turquoise ring Waco had kept tucked away for her. She didn't know how or why or when, but somehow, someway, she'd fallen in love with Waco Stone, again. And, she didn't know whether it was appropriate to jump for joy . . . or kick herself in the butt.

Nineteen

"Stop fussing over me," John growled. He resented Kate's treating him as though he was completely incapacitated, and yet, he secretly relished having her undivided attention. "I am not an invalid, for crissake!"

Kate, who'd bent to fluff his pillow for the third time in ten minutes, resisted the compelling urge to stroke the side of his unshaven face. Years ago, when she'd ended their impassioned affair, there had only been a smattering of white stubble mixed in with the dark whiskers. Now, his facial hair was as pure white as the hair on his head. Her hand moved down his throat to the mat of equally white, curly hair on his chest.

"My shaving cream and razor are at home," he grumbled, half-apologetically. The feel of her hand lightly skimming across his skin reminded him of the many times he'd shared her four-poster bed. "I guess you should have driven me to my house instead of insisting that I recuperate at your condo . . ."

"And have you staying by yourself? I heard you on the telephone, insisting that Dixie man the fort at TP. Who'd look after you?"

"Me." His chin rose slightly as he met her troubled brown eyes. "I can take care of myself."

Kate removed her hand from his chest. Old arguments should have lost their sting with age, but this one hadn't. His self-reliance and invulnerability had always been a bone of contention between them. Strong men weren't allowed to show weakness. As she straightened and gracefully moved to the chintz-covered chair near the bed, she placated him soothingly, "Of course you can. Humor me, would you? Just this once?"

"Only if you'll humor me," he bargained.

"How?"

"Tell me why you removed your key from my keychain."

Kate removed her shoes and curled her legs on the chair, tucking her feet under the cushion. This was the closest she could come to holding herself together while she considered how to give him a straightforward answer.

How could she explain that she needed more than he was willing to offer? That it hurt to love a man who considered her a good romp in the sack and a loyal employee, but unworthy of sharing his name? That she couldn't compete with the cherished memory of his wife or live with the fear of him walking out on her when he finally realized she could never stand tall while balanced precariously on a pedestal made of clay?

Impatient with her unresponsiveness, John flipped back the top sheet and coverlet. "I'm going home."

"Wait!"

"For what?" He stood shakily. "Other than my being your boss, you don't give a damn about me. I won't make you sit there and dream up some polite excuse for getting rid of me."

She unfurled her legs, stood, and pushed both of her hands against his chest, which propelled him back on her mattress. *Polite excuses!* Is that what you think I've been doing all these years?"

"Hell, no," John roared, feeling more himself as he grabbed her arm and catapulted her into the bed. She toppled against him. Holding her face between his hands, he blustered, "You didn't say one damned word. You just cut me off!"

"Why wouldn't I?" Repressed tears of anger blurred her vision while he pinned her writhing legs and arms to the bed. "I'm not your sex toy!"

She could have slapped him in the face and it would have had the same effect. He reeled backward, flopping against the pillows, taking her with him, holding her tightly against his chest to keep from shaking some sense into her.

"I never treated you like a . . . a . . ."

While he futilely searched for the appropriate word, she spat, "Bimbo!"

"Precisely."

She squirmed to get loose from his hold. To her utter exasperation, she felt him growing hard against her. "All you wanted from me was sex. Deny it if you can!"

"I do. Dammit, do you think I made you a vicepresident because you're the best lay in Houston!"

"You ought to know." Her hands pushed against his chest as she tried to leverage some space between them. "After I retrieved my key, you interviewed every big-busted, hip-swaying, bleached blonde you laid your eyes on."

She felt rather than heard a low rumble that started in his chest and burst through his lips. Aghast at having admitted she'd noticed, and that she'd been jealous, she poked him in the ribs.

"Ouch!" he crowed loudly. "You just hit a sick man!"

"You deserve it . . . and more!"

John caught her wrists and raised them over her head. "I didn't deserve watching you make goo-goo eyes at Dirk Stallman."

"For your information, your trusted right-hand man made a pass at me *before* I took my key back from you."

With her lips only a breath from his, he whispered, "Why, Kate? You said you loved me. Why?"

"We wanted different things out of life," she confessed in abysmal misery, shutting her eyes when she couldn't turn her head away from him.

"What did you want that I didn't give you? I gave you only the best money could buy."

"You treated me like a Barbie doll—buying clothes and jewelry, and flowers."

Drily, he jeered, "I can understand why you'd hate me for that. I should have shopped for you at Kmart?"

"Thank you, Mr. Moneybags!" Her eyelids lifted. She stared straight into his eyes. "Dammit, John, you can't buy love. Not mine, not Dixie's, not anybody's."

"Kate, sweetheart, you aren't making sense. You broke off with me because I bought you nice gifts? That's ridiculous."

"You're the one who was being ridiculous! What makes you think love and money are synonymous."

"Everyone knows a man worth his salt is supposed to provide nice things for his loved ones. That's what separates a man from being a rutting animal!"

"Where did you hear that piece of malarkey? In a Flintstone cartoon?" She jerked her wrists, but couldn't free them. "The same place you learned these caveman tactics you're using on me?"

"I wish I could have banged you on the head and dragged you to my cave," he retorted grimly.

"I do, too," she agreed under her breath. "Not once did you take me to your home. Why do you think I insisted you come here today? I knew you wouldn't let me stay if I took you to your house."

John eased her hands down until his lips whispered across the backs of her hands. Totally mystified, he asked, "Is that what you wanted? A key for a key?"

"Symbolically, yes."

"It's only a housekey."

"True, but it unlocks more than a door."

"For instance?"

"Behind the door to your house is your daughter. Do you realize that to this very day, Dixie doesn't know that we were intimate?"

"Of course she doesn't," he agreed heartily, seeing nothing wrong with his love life being separated from his family life. "She was a teenager. I'm her only role model. What kind of example would I have been setting for her?"

"Dixie would probably have thought you had a normal relationship with a woman." One who loved you, she added mentally. "I wouldn't have flaunted the intimate side of our relationship."

"And what would I say when she brought a boy home and wanted to do what you and I were doing?"

"What did you say?" she posed.

John snorted with derision. "What any father says when he sees a horny male sniffing around his daughter—get the hell off my property!"

Kate shook her head sadly. "Funny, but I recall my parents being cordial to you. Are you saying my father should have made the same response when you met him?"

"That's different."

"How?"

"We were consenting adults."

"Oh? Age makes the difference? Your daughter is what . . . twenty-eight? Almost the same age I was when we began our affair. What happens if Dixie brings Waco Stone home?"

Feeling as though he'd been caught in a trap of his own making, John sputtered, "That's different, too. Stone wants to get even with me for . . ."

"The nurse said Stone probably saved your life."

John cleared his throat noisily; he swiped the

back of his hand across his mouth. "Waco probably had ulterior motives for that, too. I seriously doubt Stone is capable of having honorable intentions."

Kate laughed harshly, without humor. "And you did?"

When his reply was a fierce scowl, Kate rolled to the far side of the bed. As she sat up and slipped on her shoes, she said quietly, "You can keep your key, John. Mistakenly, I thought you were locking me outside your life. I've come to find out, you've locked yourself inside—emotionally." She walked across the width of the bedroom. "What are you afraid of?"

"Zeke authorized you to do what?" Before Scott Michaels could repeat that Zeke had ordered an investigation of Texas Proud ahead of the date the Stones had left California, Waco ordered, "Hold on. Let me get Zeke in here."

Waco activated the speaker on the phone, crossed his office and yanked open the door.

Startled, Liz flattened the oval curve of the fingernail she'd been filing with an emery board. "Yes, sir?" she hiccuped guiltily, glancing at the lit button on the phone.

"Did Zeke leave the building?"

"Yes, sir." She dropped the file in her middle drawer, shut it, and jumped to her feet.

"Do you know where he went?"

"No, sir. Do you want me to page him?"

"No. Go to his office, rummage through his desk and see if you can locate a financial report on Texas Proud. Bring it to me when you find it."

Irritated by Zeke's audacity, Waco returned to his desk and he wondered what other sorts of activities his uncle had hidden from him other than Dixie's visit and the investigative report. He raked both hands through his hair. The fire? Was the damned fool out to ruin Mayson and Texas Proud?

"Scott, I don't have the report in front of me." He collapsed in his chair and hit the two-way record button on the telephone. "I'm recording this. Enlighten me on what you found out, would you?"

"Texas Proud was incorporated in 1975 by John Lee Mayson," Scott droned. "Six years ago he signed over twenty percent of the stock to Dixie Lee Mayson, his daughter."

"Skip the history lesson. Get to the pertinent facts. What's TP's financial situation?"

"About the time Mayson signed over part of the stock, he had major problems. The bank he did business with was riddled with scandals; it merged with a group out of Atlanta, who tightened the lending policies. Same time frame as the oil market bust that rippled through the economy. TP struggled through the real estate crash, barely. Miss Mayson must have had some moxie. She consolidated their debt, sold off speculation lots to repay it, and cut expenditures throughout the company, top to bottom. Heads rolled like they were royalists under the guillotine's blade during the French Revolution."

"Could you get a list of men she fired?" Waco requested, thinking that might be a good place to start the fire investigation. Out-of-work employees tended to blame the head honchos for their problems.

"Yeah, I could, but listen to this." Scott's usual monotonous tone held a trace of admiration as he said, "She placed the men she was forced to lay off with Texas builders doing work in Florida, D.C., Maryland and California."

Impressed, Waco said, "No kidding?"

"From what I found out, the last couple of years she's been rehiring the ones who want to return to Texas."

"In other words, TP's back on its feet."

Scott hesitated; Waco heard pages of the report being turned.

"Overall, they're in fairly good shape."

"Fairly good?"

"Well, there's nothing I can specifically put my finger on, but I do have some reservations. They aren't in hock up to their eyeballs, but a little ready cash wouldn't hurt TP. Lately, they've changed several of their suppliers."

"Could it be they switched to get better prices or deeper discounts?" Waco suggested.

"Could have," Scott agreed with reluctance. "What about the fire Zeke told me about? Accidental or arsonists?"

"Arson is suspected."

"Uh-oh. That's a risk factor. Vandalism of any magnitude cuts into the profit ratio. TP is insured, but with any type of builder's insurance, the deductibles are high and the rates go up with each incident. If Zeke is thinking about investing money in Texas Proud, he might want to reconsider."

Waco almost laughed aloud. "Is that the impression Zeke gave you when he requested the report?"

"Zeke came to the office, said you were transferring your headquarters to Galveston and wanted the dirt on the Maysons and Texas Proud. He said, and I quote, if you can't lick 'em, join 'em, and if you can't do either, buy 'em out. Unquote. Last night when Zeke called, he seemed more interested in the personal lives of John and Dixie than the money aspects of their company. He belly-laughed over John Mayson conducting a secret liaison with a female employee."

"Kate Somebody-er-other?" Waco guessed.

"Yeah. How'd you know?"

"Simple deduction. Kate is the only female executive at headquarters."

"Could have been a woman of means he'd met socially, like his first wife," Scott remarked. "Or a secretary."

Waco stored the first bit of information and commented on the second piece, "Not John Mayson. He's status conscious. He'd never look at a woman beneath him to share his bed."

"Strictly a missionary position kind of guy, huh?" Scott bantered. "I'll make note of that."

A part of Waco wanted to ask about Dixie. He'd been the first man she'd slept with, and the most recent, but what about in between? Were there other men in her life?

Ignorance is bliss, he decided.

"He must have a chastity belt on his daughter," Scott commented drily. "From all reports, she's a workaholic with no love life. I can understand why none of TP's execs resent being accountable to her. She's the brains behind the operation. Maybe the guts, too. Zeke didn't like it when I told him to approach her with an offer, before he contacted John Mayson. He's a figurehead; she wields the power—fairly, I might add."

It pleased Waco to know Scott had been unable to find any men in Dixie's past, himself included. His pride in her reputation inflated more than his male ego. Somehow, she'd managed to waltz around her domineering father and become all a professional woman could be: independent, decisive, and trustworthy.

"Do me a favor?"

"It'll cost you," Scott joked.

"Fair enough."

"Okay. Shoot."

"The next time Zeke contacts you, tell him you don't have any further information."

Scott groaned. "Did I say it would cost you? Hell, you're officially closing the files. Zeke told me to bill Tumbleweed for my services."

"I don't want Zeke to know they're closed. If you can uncover information on the fire at Mayson Manor, you can double your fee."

"That's a tall order, but I'll give it the old college try." Scott chuckled as he added, "You might want to check out Mayson's daughter for yourself."

"Did anybody ever tell you to mind your own damned business?" Waco asked, mild rancor giving a sharp edge to his voice.

"Daily." Realizing Waco had misunderstood what he'd meant, Scott said, "But this business I'm in makes me too cynical to recommend a fairy-tale solution to any problem. One kiss from a prince isn't likely to wake up Miss Mayson's libido." He paused, waiting to hear Waco laugh. When his client didn't share his humor, to avoid the risk of losing a customer, he said bluntly, "What I meant is, Dixie Mayson could be an asset to Tumbleweed. And, as a by-product, you'd be ripping the heart and brains out of Texas Proud, which would make Zeke ecstatic. Why don't you consider hiring her?"

"I made her a substantial offer. She rejected it because she's loyal to TP and her father."

"Go refigure your offer," Scott suggested. "Dicker. I have yet to meet a person who can't be bought for the right price. After all, money's what makes the world go around."

"Believe me, Dixie's loyalty isn't for sale at any price. It's earned," Waco responded firmly. Ending their conversation on a lighter note, he added, "I'll expect your bill to reflect your cynical philosophy of greed and avarice."

"Hey, just send me a round-trip ticket to Houston," Scott jested. "If this Dixie-bird is the paragon of virtue that you say she is, she'd restore my faith in humanity. I'll think up an offer she can't refuse and maybe she'll fly home with me."

Waco laughed cordially, but he wasn't amused. "Call me if you discover who the arsonist is."

"Will do."

He hung up the phone and glanced at his calendar, which was booked solid with appointments. He laid his palm across the page to block those pressing engagements from his view.

Scott hadn't told him anything he hadn't known, or at least suspected, but his back-alley instincts nagged at him, warning that he was overlooking some small detail regarding the fire. Or, he mused, he'd overlooked the obvious.

He glanced at the list of names he'd pried out of Dixie. Maybe some of Scott's cynicism had rubbed off on him, but he doubted John's ability to endear himself to all his employees. The man had to have more than one enemy; someone other than . . .

Zeke!

His uncle had sworn to get revenge.

He said he didn't start the fire.

He had the opportunity. He'd been there.

Trust him. He's family. He wouldn't betray you to get even with John Mayson.

"Mr. Stone, call for you on line one," he heard over the intercom. "It's the man who owns the earth-moving equipment. He wants a date to start breaking ground in Clear Lake."

* * *

"Water is dripping from the light fixture in the great room," Walter Block said, reporting the damage to Dixie. "I found the problem."

"A fitting blew apart?"

"Hell no. The plumber has had two hundred pounds of pressure on the water lines for a week. Looks to me like the air conditioning man forgot to hook into the drain line. I'm going to have to pull out the insulation, remove the damaged drywall, and have the carpet vacuumed. Back charge the a.c. man."

Dixie entered the data on her computer. "The owners are supposed to do a final walk through tomorrow. They close on Friday."

"No way. I'll be lucky to get this mess cleaned up by Wednesday. Change their inspection to Thursday, late afternoon."

"What about the manufacturer's representative from G.E.? Has he been out to 4511?"

"Yeah. He said the scratches on the stove aren't a manufacturer's defect. Said it looked like vandals ran a key across it."

"That's bull-roar."

"He brought a replacement, but he's charging TP for it."

She made a note to call the rep. "What about the chandelier at 6412? Mr. Schwartz said it was shipped from Germany a month ago. Did it arrive?"

"In two huge wooden crates. Damned thing must weigh a ton." Walter laughed. "And the directions for assembly are written in German. The electrician said there's going to be an extra."

"How much?"

"He's going to have to reinforce the beams because of the weight and find a translator. Spanish he can do, but there isn't a German on any of his crews."

"I'll have Schwartz translate them. For a man who buys light fixtures from a castle in the fatherland, he's tight as duct tape on a hose when it comes to paying for extras. Anything else?"

"The new superintendent over at Scenic Point said the framers should finish today. Dammit, I wanted them to swing over to Mayson Manor, but Stallman hasn't had the shipment of lumber delivered. Jump his ass, would you?"

"Yeah. Is it a mess out there?"

"Not too bad, considering the fire department drained the lake. I can't get it cleaned up until the fire inspector gets out of there. No telling how long he'll be there. You want me to temporarily swing the road around the back side of the pond?"

"I'll check with Thorpe. If he gives the okay, I'll order the sand to make certain it's delivered immediately."

"Speaking of the architect, what about those idiot drywallers at 5887?"

Dixie grinned. "The ones you saw climbing out the second-story window onto the porch roof?"

"Yeah," Walter chuckled. "I've heard of painters painting themselves into a corner, but putting drywall up and covering the door opening was a new one on me. You'd think they'd have noticed something was wrong when they couldn't get out of the room they'd finished, wouldn't you?"

"You can't blame them. They did follow Thorpe's architectural plan."

Walter laughed. "Is the blame still being passed around headquarters?"

"Fingers are pointing in every direction. Tom Thorpe swears he had a door in the original plan. Jergins says it wasn't a computer screw-up. Jerkins says Kate must have . . ."

"Stop! It's your fault, right?"

"How'd you guess?"

"Same song, hundredth verse. I wouldn't have your job for a million dollars."

After Walter hung up, Dixie started killing snakes. On days like this, it seemed as though she'd get rid of one problem and three more would raise their ugly heads, fangs bared, ready to strike.

She worked straight through lunch without stopping long enough to take a deep breath. Her stomach growled, but she ignored it until Sara entered her office carrying a hot pastrami sandwich in one hand and a bouquet of yellow roses in the other.

"Waco had these delivered," Sara said, grinning widely at the surprised look on her friend's face. "Is the way to your heart through your stomach or nose?"

"Both," Dixie replied emphatically, rising from her chair and stretching the kinks from her neck and back. She took the vase and placed the roses on her desk. "They're gorgeous!"

"That's what he says you are. Aren't you going to read the card? It's handwritten."

"How would you know what he wrote?"

"I peeked," Sara admitted, without a hint of remorse. "He's going to pick you up here, around six o'clock."

Dixie cupped the petals of one rose between her hands and inhaled. It wasn't as fragrant as the hyacinth he'd picked from the yard at the display house and given to her, but she considered it every bit as sweet a gesture.

"I won't be finished that early."

"The flip side of the card says . . ."

"Sara!" Dixie protested. "Let me read it!"

"I'm supposed to open all your mail," she teased. "I'm just doing my job."

Dixie stared at the sealed notecard envelope in blank confusion, then across the desk at Sara. "It's unopened."

"Black ink. Nice, legible handwriting," Sara explained glibly, but slowly she began retreating to her office. "Press hard on the envelope and you won't have to open it either."

Hopeless, Dixie mused, as she peeled the flap open. After she'd read Waco's note, she momentarily hugged the note to her chest, then picked up the phone. Much as she appreciated his concern for her safety, she couldn't let him waste his time by sitting in the lobby waiting for her to finish her work. She would have liked to plan on a leisurely dinner at a fine restaurant, too, but by the time she cleared her desk only the burger-doodles would be open.

"Waco, the yellow roses are lovely," she answered softly when she recognized his voice. "Thank you for them, and for the sandwich."

"You're welcome. Where should I make reservations for dinner?"

On the spur of the moment, she came up with the only plausible idea. "My house."

"Crystal came in the office. Could you excuse me for just a second?"

Dixie heard a squeal of delight and imagined Waco getting a hug from his sister.

"Sorry, Waco, but I couldn't wait to tell you. Can you believe it?" Crystal babbled excitedly. "Me, auditioning for a feature-length movie starring Mel Gibson! Of course, it's a bit part, but . . ."

"Congratulations," Dixie called, hoping Crystal could hear her.

Waco picked up the phone, laughing at Crystal as she spun around as though looking for a ghost. "Dixie says congratulations."

"Tell her I'm catching the next flight for L.A."

Knowing he'd be caught relaying messages back and forth, he touched the speaker button. "Go ahead, both of you."

"It's a Western," Crystal said, clapping her hands together. "Since they requested me, my agent said I've got a real good chance at this one!"

"That's wonderful, Crystal! Did I hear you say you're leaving tonight?"

"Yeah. I've already arranged to stay with friends."

"Who?" Waco asked.

"The McMillens. You'd love them, Dixie. And their house. It's magnificent. It overlooks the Pacific, with a pool and tennis courts and . . . a small recording studio. Matthew, their son, is a guitarist-slash-composer. Well, last year, Matt wrote this country song and sold the rights to this other guy, who wasn't anybody at the time, but his father knows Garth Brook's sister, and . . ."

Dixie heard Crystal's voice being muffled; she assumed by her brother's hand.

"Crystal," Waco interrupted. "You're rambling. Say good-bye to Dixie. She's at work."

"Good-bye, Dixie!"

"Bye, Crystal. Have a safe trip. Break a leg!"

She heard Waco tell Crystal to go home and start getting packed, that he'd be there shortly.

A round of giggles and a squeal later, Waco said to her, "I don't know about Crystal setting off on her own. With her streak of wildness, she's like a magnet that draws trouble from out of nowhere." Waco chuckled. "Must be a hereditary trait, huh?"

"Could be," she agreed. "Crystal is definitely a risk-taker."

"Did I detect a note of admiration in your voice?"

"You'll have to admit, I do tend to sit back, take notes, analyze them, then take action." She recalled standing at the porch rail, sobbing, wanting to call out to Waco to take her with him. She'd been too cautious, too scared to take a big risk. "Sometimes, I'm a day late and a dollar short because I hesitate too long."

"A leap of faith can be damned scary," Waco replied, from his vast warehouse of experience. "Take that from a person who has learned how to splat."

"And rebound."

"Isn't there a physics theory about the harder you hit, the higher you bounce back?"

"Yeah, but you have to be made of the right stuff. Like you are."

Waco grinned, pleased by her cajolery. "Remind me to send you foliage more often."

"I wasn't flattering you. I meant it. You leap tall buildings, while I watch, like a couch potato."

"Someday you'll find somebody worthy of making you risk everything." Feeling daring, but not wanting to frighten her, he said, "Since Crystal is going back to California and I won't have to keep an eye on her, and you've said you'd considered moving out of your father's house . . ." He took a deep breath before plunging in, headfirst, ". . . would you move in with me?"

Disappointed by the practicality of his offer, she pulled her braid across her shoulder and fiddled with the blunt ends. This wasn't the "I'm madly in love with you, let's cohabitate" or "Let's elope" proposal that she'd dreamed of. No passion declaration of undying love. Just, "I need a roommate. You'll do."

"Why don't we discuss it tonight?" she hedged,

uncertain she wanted to lose her hard-won independence for such a lukewarm, tepid arrangement.

Waco winced. "Tonight," he agreed, wondering if he'd ever be good enough for her to love. He'd worked his fingers to the bone to earn a fortune, but evidently it wasn't enough. Resigned to crawling inches to cover miles, he said, "I'll pick you up at your office."

Wishing he'd not let her postpone the issue, she said, "It's out of your way."

I want you with me. Don't you know I'd go to hell and back to get you? He bit the inside of his cheek to quiet his brash tongue. If she was going to take what she'd called a leap of faith, it wouldn't mean anything if he was bulldozing her from behind.

"I don't mind. Is six o'clock too early? We can pick up carry-out for dinner."

"I'll pick up something on my way home."

"Is something wrong?" he asked, picking up on her clipped reply, worrying that he'd leaped before looking for a safe landing.

"No." She flung the braid over her shoulder. "Crystal is waiting for you. I'll see you later. Bye."

"Bye, gorgeous."

Dixie hung up before she could change her mind and take Waco up on his offer. While she could silently admit to wanting him on any terms, she felt . . . short-changed. Greedy for his love, she couldn't allow *practicality* to be the reason they lived together.

"There's only one letter's difference between living and loving together," she whispered aloud, writing the two words on her pad. "The *i* as in inept, incompetent, and worst of all, insignificant. For twenty years I was a lowercase *i*."

She extended the size of the *i,* and made a line at the top and bottom.

"This I, as in me, won't settle for living together," she said with fierce determination. *I know how love can be and I know how love should be. Dammit, I'll die a shriveled up old maid in size twelve boots before* I *settle for less than how love* ought *to be!*

Twenty

She'd started for her office door, keys in hand, when the phone rang. She hesitated, letting it ring. The entire day she'd felt like a juggler juggling heavy buckets filled with nails; it required strength, timing and balance to maintain them in a circular motion over her head. One goof-up and she'd be nailed to the wall!

Let the recorder answer it, she decided, glancing at her watch. As it was, she'd allowed time for five-o'clock traffic, but unless she departed immediately, she'd have to drive like a maniac to get to her house before Waco arrived. Waco would understand her tardiness, but a mental picture of John answering the doorbell caused her reflexes to tighten her hold on her car keys. The phone recorder stopped the ringing. She listened for the caller's voice.

"Dixie! Are you there? Pick up!"

Her father's voice booming through the speaker left her without a choice. She darted back to her desk phone.

"Got it."

"I'm glad I caught you before you made your

rounds of the houses. I don't want you out there with a flashlight after dark."

"I won't be." Belatedly feeling guilty for not checking on him, she asked, "How are you feeling?"

"Fit as a fiddle. Kate's been taking good care of me."

"She's been at the house all day?" Dixie inquired, mildly surprised. Rarely ill, John sniped and snarled at anyone who dared to come near him when he wasn't feeling well.

"I'm at her place."

Curious, very curious, Dixie mused. "Will you be spending the night there?"

"I didn't ask you where you spent the weekend," John replied drolly. "Fair is fair."

Dixie grinned. "Okay, I won't ask questions . . ."

"And I won't lie to you. But my sleeping arrangement isn't the reason I called. I checked with the fire department inspector. He tells me a stranger has been seen sneaking around our job sites."

"Any idea who?"

"Not yet. The guy was described as being of medium height and thin."

"That description fits half of Houston's male population!" Dixie disparaged.

"And, he knows his way around construction sites. That's what one witness told the inspector."

"Which narrows it down to two-thirds of the men who work in the trades."

"How do you figure?"

"Only a third of them carry excess weight, especially in the summer heat."

"Whoever it is, he's out to get Texas Proud. There haven't been any other reports of vandalism in the bay area. And one more thing you ought to know, a third party contacted Dirk Stallman late this afternoon, wanting to know if Texas Proud needed a silent partner."

A spray of goosebumps pimpled the flesh on Dixie's arms. She hugged herself and glanced around the empty office. "Who?"

"An attorney . . . out of Galveston. He wouldn't reveal his client's name. I thought the fire and the rash of problems we've had were accidental. Now, I'm not so certain. Somebody has a vendetta against us. I want you to go straight home. Lock the doors behind you and don't let anybody inside, no matter how harmless they look or whether you know them or not. Until this arsonist is caught and put behind bars, you can't trust anybody."

"I hear you." *Waco being the exception. He'd been with her the day of the fire. He was above suspicion.* "I'll see you at the office tomorrow."

"I'll be there. Lock up the office. Above all else, be careful."

"I will be. You, too."

"See you."

"Bye."

It was closer to seven o'clock than six when she left the office building. She looked over her shoulder every two seconds to make certain no one was following her. A short, bald man with a forty-two-inch waist said hi to her and received a chilling glare in response.

Good Lord, she thought, climbing into her truck, I'm getting paranoid! She'd never dealt with fear; she hated having to watch every step she took. But, as she drove from the underground parking lot, she repeatedly glanced in her rear-view mirror.

She traveled Interstate 610 that looped the city and turned south onto I-45. The highways were filled with other workers returning to the bedroom communities that surrounded the city. Half of them seemed to be following her. When she weaved between lanes, other vehicles switched lanes. By the time she reached her turn-off, she was a nervous wreck.

Five miles later, she was dead certain a red truck was following her. The sleek, black sedan following it could have been the arsonist's accomplice. She wasn't about to lead either of them to her front door! The police department was only one block out of the way.

Heart pumping, she decided to make a quick right. Her tires screeched. With her eyes glued to the rear-view mirror, she jumped the curve, flattening a bedraggled bed of petunias. She slowed down by the police department parking lot, then sped up when neither the truck nor car followed her.

Feeling decidedly foolish and cowardly, she circled the block and took a shortcut to her house. *Wimp!* She wasn't some frail ninety-pound weakling who was afraid of her own shadow!

Dixie pulled into her driveway and turned off the motor. Momentarily, she folded her arms across the steering wheel and rested her forehead on them. She was home. Safe. Ten minutes early according to the clock on the dashboard. She could almost feel the fear ebbing from her body, replaced by a sense of security.

"Dixie?"

She jumped.

"It's me," Waco said, opening her door for her. "I didn't mean to scare you."

She tumbled out of the truck, into his open arms. Over his shoulder, she saw the dark sedan. "Did you follow me home from the office?"

"Guilty," Waco admitted, hugging her close. "I didn't think you saw me until I watched you demolish the flower bed in front of the insurance agency," he teased.

"You could have beeped . . . or something to let me know it was you." She'd paused to receive the brush of his lips against her mouth.

"And have you take your redheaded temper out on me in front of the police department?" Chuckling, he lithely swung her around, then deposited her feet on the ground. "Once the chief recognized me, he would have handcuffed me and thrown me in jail."

"I wouldn't let them do that to you."

"Wish I'd have been certain of that ten years ago," he joked, taking her hand and leading her to his car.

"Don't remind me of that night."

He squeezed her fingertips. The past had to be put to rest before they could get on with the future. "I'd have spent my one telephone call on you," he said solemnly. "What would you have done?"

"Rescued you."

He leaned against his car; his arms slipped around her waist and he hauled her tightly against him. "And I'd have saved you from wondering what happened to me. I can't change the mistakes I made, but I want to do right by you. Did you think about moving in with me?"

Her heart skipped a beat as she nodded. "I did."

"And?"

"I don't want to be your roommate," she answered clearly, concisely.

Astutely aware of how her body had stiffened and her turquoise eyes blazed up at him, he instantly deduced the depth of her disfavor. Several inches taller than her, she couldn't look down at him. But he felt lower than a snake's belly.

"What do I have to do? Buy Texas Proud to be good enough for you, Miss Mayson?"

Stung by the bitterness she heard in his voice, and that he believed he could buy her, she rebuffed, "You couldn't afford Texas Proud."

"How much is it worth?" he asked rhetorically. He knew. Scott had made an inquiry through a local lawyer. "One million? Ten?"

She wiggled from his arms. Pivoting on her heels, she started toward the house as she said, "Pride isn't for sale around here. Try Kmart, the blue-light special ought to have something in your size."

He caught her arm and propelled her back into his arms, holding her face in the crook of his neck and shoulder. He felt the hot wetness of her tears against his skin. "What I have to offer is of more value than Texas Proud," he promised rashly. "Me."

He waited for her to move, to stir in his arms, to recoil from him in disbelief.

When she remained close, he dared to tilt her face up toward him. His confidence grew. There was no laughter in her eyes, no derision, only profound wistfulness.

"I can't hand you the world on a silver platter, sweetheart. I can't even promise you financial security. But this I can promise." His dark eyes melted the stone hard blueness of hers. "I'll never leave you again. I won't draw a breath without thinking of you. My heart won't beat unless I know you'll be near me. You are my ultimate strength and my greatest weakness. I love you, gorgeous. My . . . *someday* depends on you."

His mouth slanted across hers, sealing his promises with a wild, intense kiss. She parted her lips, kissing him back with the aching love in her heart. His hands moved to her hips, her back, the sides of her breasts, then sweeping back again, holding her against him as though he could absorb her body into his—never being without her.

Time stood still, like a wonderful, glorious moment of triumph captured on film for the yearbook.

Her heart and soul opened to him as willingly as her parted lips. His promises obliterated her silent fear of abandonment and replaced it with her sweet yearnings of yesteryear.

"I love you, Waco Stone." Her voice shook with emotion; she was so happy. She wound one arm tightly around his muscular shoulders; her other hand smoothed back his unruly, dark lock of hair. "I've always been dazzled by you. I fell for you, hard, like a ton of bricks off a twenty-story scaffold. That's why I couldn't move in with you for . . . for *practical* reasons."

"Practical?" Waco hooted, tossing his head back and laughing with pure delight. He hugged her mightily, then let his arm slip to her waist as they strolled up the sidewalk. "One smile, one kiss, or merely hearing your voice causes the circuit breaker to shut down the rational side of my brain."

"Same here. Each problem that cropped up today did not get my undivided attention, the way they should have."

"Do you want to talk about them?"

Dixie shot him a sappy grin. "Broken pipes? Sagging drywall? Soggy carpet? Is that what you want to talk about while I fix dinner?"

He had one foot on the bottom steps and stopped, suddenly remembering the takeout order he'd left in his car, and the box in the glove compartment. Feeling incredibly young and lighthearted, he poked his finger in his ear as though it was a gauge, and read his palm. "Brain temporarily malfunctioned. Be right back."

Laughing at his antics, Dixie watched him sprint to his car. Her laughter changed to a broad smile as she was struck anew by his masculine athletic grace. Dressed in dark slacks and a white shirt, with the cuffs rolled up to his elbows and his collar open at the throat, he was sexier than the long, lanky carpenter she'd first fallen in love with.

And he loves me.

He thinks of me with each breath he takes, with each beat of his heart. I give him strength.

He loves me!

"Food," he shouted, holding up the white sacks as though he'd prepared it with his own hands. He carried it toward her saying, "I called Sara to find out what was your favorite. Sandwiches and blueberry cheesecake from Frenchy's. I've heard the way to a man's heart is through his stomach. Same way to a woman's heart?"

Dixie gave him a decidedly wicked wink, licked her lips, put one hand on her hip, and drawled, "Not if the man has a silver tongue."

A hot surge of lust slowed Waco from bounding up the porch steps. Hell, he nearly stumbled when she made a low groan in the back of her throat.

"Behave yourself," he warned, boldly letting his eyes roam up her silk stockings.

Her knees weakened. She had to hug the post as she watched him undress her with his eyes, sensually hesitating at each erogenous hollow and curve until those sinfully black eyes challenged hers.

"I'll be good," she said breathlessly, not intending her response to sound like a double entendre, but it did.

"No," Waco contradicted, stalking up the steps. When he stood inches apart from her, he whispered, "You'll be wonderful. You always are."

Her hand trembled so badly that it took a conscious effort on Dixie's part to find the right key to unlock the door.

"John isn't home?" Although his voice lifted upward from a gravelly bass to a sexy tenor, it was a statement of fact, not a question.

Dixie nodded. "He's with Kate."

"Hmmmm."

"Hmmmm?"

His eyes danced with amusement. "Hmmmm."

Dixie sensed that his ardor had cooled at the mention of her father's name. "So?"

"I was just visualizing how ridiculous I'm going to look, wearing only a silly, satisfied grin on my face, buck naked, dodging your father's fists." He knotted his fist and gently clipped her on the chin. "Not a pretty picture. Do you think history repeats itself?"

"Only if we don't learn from it." She relieved him of one sack and marched toward the kitchen. "As for me? I'm a quick learner. It's after eight and I'm starved."

Waco remained in the foyer. He began to wonder what it must have been like to grow up in this quaint Victorian house, with gingerbread trim on the outside and lacy curtains at the inside of the windows. Brightly colored chintz-covered over-stuffed furniture fairly begged to be bounced upon by small feet.

"Waco?"

When she heard no answer, she emptied her arms, and crossed from the kitchen back into the hallway. Waco Stone, tough, ruthless, invincible businessman that he was, stared earnestly at the curved banister at the foot of the steps with the longing of an eight-year-old boy.

"Our boys will slide down a banister like that one," he said, coveting for his son the joys he'd been denied. "You mark my words."

A loud beeping noise made Waco remove the pager from his belt, look at the message on it, and give a hearty groan.

"It's Zeke. He puts 666 after his cellular phone number for a good reason," Waco joked. "He has devilish poor timing."

"There's a phone in the kitchen. I'll set the table while you call him."

She had the sandwiches on plates when she heard Waco explode, "I told you not to go near TP's property!"

His dark eyebrows furrowed together in a straight line as he listened intently. "Did you call 911?"

Dixie swiftly crossed to be at his side. "What's wrong?"

"I'm on way. Don't take any chances." Waco hung up the phone. He moved toward the front door. "Zeke is over at the house you're building near Taylor Lake. Something suspicious is going on there. You stay here. I'll be back as quickly as I can."

"I'm going with you."

"You're staying here, where you're safe. Don't argue."

"I won't." She grabbed the keys in his hand and darted in front of him. "I know the shortcuts to get there. You don't. Did Zeke call the police?"

Waco clenched his jaw and nodded. Short of tackling her and locking her in a closet, she'd given him no choice. She was in the driver's seat and starting the engine as he slammed the passenger's door shut.

Streetlights flickered to life as she gunned the gas and roared toward the highway.

"What else did Zeke say?"

"There are piles of gasoline-soaked clothes distributed around the building," he replied starkly.

As she rounded a corner, she saw her father's truck. She laid her hand on the horn and braked Waco's car. John stopped beside her. "There's trouble at Creekview."

"Who's that with you?" John roared, poking his head through the opened window.

"Waco Stone."

"It's goddamned suspicious him being with you when there's trouble!" John blustered, wrenching the steering wheel to make a sharp U-turn. "I'll take care of it. You go back to the house."

Without replying, she moved her foot from the brake to the gas pedal and muttered, "He's the invalid and I'm the one who is supposed to go home."

She had no intention of wearing out the floorboards of the front porch, chewing her fingernails to the knuckle while she worried about Waco and John. To hell with being a pampered female!

Glancing sideways, she wondered if Waco had heard John's accusation.

"Watch out! You're going to rear end . . ."

Waco braced his hands on the dashboard as Dixie swerved; she passed the slow-moving truck on the right side of the road. The rear wheels spit loose gravel in their wake. "Buckle up."

"Keep your eyes on the road!" Waco snapped.

"I got my driver's license out of a Cracker Jack box," she said drily. "You're safe."

"This is a hell of a time to make jokes!" Hunched over the wheel, Dixie drove as though she was trying out for the Indy 500, taking risks that would have made A.J. Foyt shudder with fright.

"Nervous reaction." The rear end skidded as she turned on a back road. "Sorry."

Dixie bit the inside of her cheek to keep from apologizing for her father's allegation. In her mind, their being together should have exonerated Waco! Didn't saving her father by giving him mouth-to-mouth count for anything? Thoroughly annoyed at having Waco blamed, when she knew he was completely innocent of wrongdoing, she hit every pothole in the road with brutal vengeance.

Waco ground his back molars to keep from

barking out orders. Good thing, he decided, as his head hit the headliner. He'd have severed his tongue!

"It'll be completely dark by the time we get there. I'm going in the back entrance."

"Don't turn on your headlights. How far is it from the entrance to the house?"

"Fourth of a mile up the lane. Maybe less. It's a construction road that leads to the cul-de-sac."

"Block it."

Dixie nodded, noticing that John hadn't turned on his lights, either. For once, the two men were on the same mental wavelength. She braked suddenly, to avoid ramming into the side of the truck already blocking the drive.

Before she'd completely stopped, Waco spotted his uncle crouched down beside his truck. He jumped from the car, hunkered down and ran to Zeke's side.

" 'Bout time," Zeke grumbled, pointing toward the trees. "He be skulkin' back an' forth from the trees over there to the house."

"Where is he now?"

"Can't rightly say. The sun sank into the lake and it got darker than a coal digger's ass around here."

"You didn't see who it is?" Waco asked in a hushed voice.

"Nope. Didn't recognize him."

Dixie and John crouched low to the ground as they rushed to join Waco and Zeke.

"You the night watchman Dirk hired?" John asked Zeke.

"Nope." Zeke spat tobacco juice on the ground and wiped his lips on his arm. "I'm Waco's uncle—the one you tried to get throwed in the slammer."

"Not now," Dixie implored, watching her father's face tighten with anger.

"I'll circle . . ."

"You take your uncle . . ."

"Dixie, you stay . . ."

The three men simultaneously began to quietly issue orders. "Shhhh," Dixie commanded, shushing them by slicing her hand through the air between them. "What we don't need is three chiefs and no Indians!"

"It's my construction site!" John countered fiercely. "I'm the boss around here!"

"Suits me," Zeke snorted. "Guess I'll be moseyin' on down the road."

"Shut up, Zeke, and come around here" came from Waco, who'd moved to the side of the truck and peered over the truck's bed. "I'm going to swing over to the north side of the house. We crossed a culvert on the road. Does that drainage ditch lead to the house?"

"Yes," John whispered. "I'll take the east side, swinging wide of the clump of trees."

"Okay," Waco agreed. "Who wants to wait here, in case the police arrive? We don't want them shooting one of us."

Zeke looked at Dixie, who returned his glare without a blink.

"I'll stay," Zeke said, resigned to being left behind. "This might be his escape route."

"I'll circle to the far side," Dixie volunteered, giving Zeke a grateful pat on the arm.

"Don't take any chances of getting hurt," John commanded urgently. "The element of surprise is on our side. Everybody know how to make the whippoorwill whistle?"

Waco was shoulder-to-shoulder with John. "Good idea. When we start closing in, use it to signal your position. Anybody sees him start to run, just give a yell."

Single file, they departed from behind the truck: Waco, John, then Dixie. When John skirted to the right, Waco grabbed Dixie's wrist, silently urging her to follow him through the underbrush.

He held the branches back until she ducked through them. Low-growing briars scraped against Waco's slacks and snagged in Dixie's nylons. Intent on making as little noise as possible, she swallowed small whimpers of pain that the painful nicks caused.

Slivers of moonlight pierced faintly through the clouds rolling in off the gulf. Humidity saturated the air. She pinched the small beads of perspiration dotting her upper lip between her thumb and forefinger.

They'd traveled a hundred yards when Waco held out his arm and signaled her to stop. "There's the ditch."

"I'll keep going straight."

"You'd be safer coming with me," he coaxed, throwing a quick glance at the wooden framework of the house before he gave her a swift hug. She looked tense, but composed, not the least bit panicky. "Go on. For my sake, please be careful."

"You, too."

From her vantage point, she watched him slide down the bank and disappear into the darkness, as the ditch veered toward the house. She darted behind a mass of brush that grew where a fence must have lined the property.

Not for a moment did she allow herself to believe the arsonist would have a chance to do his dirty work. This house was in the embryo stage of completion, but it meant as much to her as the one she lived in. This house was a part of her dream, her future. She'd be damned before she'd scrape charred lumber off the concrete slab!

"We'll get him," she panted, running as fast as she could to block the arsonist from escaping from the back of the house.

She had almost flanked the back of the building when a flicker of flame, no bigger than a matchlight, caught her attention. The next instant, a ball of fire plumed upward.

"No!"

She clamped her hand over her mouth, but instinctively her legs churned, taking her toward the flames as though drawn to them like a moth. Shrill whippoorwill calls warned her to stop, to stick to the plan.

She couldn't. Wouldn't.

Flames lit the structure's interior. She could see a figure dressed completely in black dodging through the openings that led to the wall of studs nearest to her. In an instant, she knew the arsonist's destination: Discarded lumber had been piled in one corner.

Her eyes widened in horror as he flung what must have been a book of matches toward the pile . . . and charged directly toward her!

With an anger born from pure hatred, she bared her teeth, half-demented. She stormed onward. He lunged at her. Her reflexes saved her from the full brunt of his weight, but his arms wrapped around her ribs like a vise; his momentum propelled her to the hard ground. Pain rocketed through her as the wind whooshed from her lungs.

"You stupid bitch!" she heard as her fists struck his backside, with all her ebbing strength.

In a tangle of flailing arms and legs, she felt herself rolling down a short incline. Her bones jarred; her head reeled dizzily. She scratched and clawed, sometimes feeling flesh beneath her fingers, most often grabbing air. She elbowed him and had the satisfaction of hearing him grunt. Without realizing it, she'd snatched the skier's mask off his face, along with a handful of brown hair.

She screamed when he grabbed her around the throat with his arm, almost choking her.

"Shut up!"

She knew that voice! This wasn't the first time

Dirk Stallman had told her to shut up. Infrared dots swam in front of her eyes. Her chest heaved, laboring for precious air.

"You'll never get away with this," she wheezed. "I'm not alone."

"You think you're so goddamned smart!" he hissed, close to her ear, slightly easing his hold on her. He wound the braid trailing down her back around his hand and gave a sharp tug. "You thought you'd trick me by bringing your old man along, didn't you? I've already taken care of big, bad John," he sneered.

Physically, they were the same height. He out-weighed her by a hundred pounds. Soft flab, not hard muscle. Pushing a pencil did not require physical exercise. He had the advantage of not being winded, but that was balanced by the adrenaline screaming through her body.

Her eyes frantically swept the area. What had he done to John? Oh God, she prayed, be alive. Be well!

From behind, she felt herself being yanked to her feet. Dixie winced, rising on her toes to alleviate the pull on her hair. Panting, she kicked; he sidestepped.

Don't give up! Never give up! She gulped back a nagging scream from the past. *Where are you, Waco?*

Slightly turning, she shoved against his chest with her shoulder, wrestling for control. His fingers scratched her neck, parting the thick coils of twisted hair as he jerked it, like a noose, then pulled it down until all she could see was the black, starless sky. Tears spurted from her eyes.

"Do you want your brains splattered on the slab of your precious house?" he grunted ominously. He gouged her temple with the barrel of a stainless-steel Smith and Wesson .357 pistol. "Nobody would suspect I did it."

Air sliced in and out of her lungs. Through a shimmer of tears, a million images and feelings clamored through her head—yearnings, unfulfilled promises, a young, arrogant Waco sexily sauntering toward her, a hyacinth, yellow roses, a long-forgotten turquoise ring, her heart brimming with joy when Waco told her he loved her. She wanted to build on the strong foundation of their love. A home, yes, the home he'd never known. And children. Boys sliding down the banister. Girls with dark pigtails and shiny dark eyes. And love, love, love!

She was going to die, and all she could think of was how much she loved Waco Stone.

No! her heart shrieked. The fates had kindly given them a second chance; she couldn't allow Dirk Stallman to snuff it out. But she knew that regardless of how close Waco and Zeke were, they couldn't run faster than a bullet traveled. Dirk could kill all of them and escape unscathed while the media morbidly speculated on how rival companies had feuded over a land deal.

She had to stop Dirk! Divert his attention!

"You won't kill me," she bluffed, choking back her fear. The taste of black bile threatened to gag her. "The records at the office will point directly to you." Grasping at mental straws, she added, "Jergins uncovered your scam."

"Bullshit!" Dirk snarled. "That pipsqueak oughta to be designing computer games." The gun he held slid to her cheek; his hold on her hair fractionally loosened. "He didn't even notice the price change when I switched suppliers."

"They were lower."

Dirk chuckled, an odd nasal sound. "So was the quality."

"The lumber was green."

"As was the superintendent on this job," he replied snidely. "Hand-picked by me."

She swallowed another sob and twisted her head so she could see the slow-burning fire. "You torched the stacked lumber and pocketed the difference. It's in Jergins' report. You'll never get away with it."

The gun moved to her ear when a timber crashed. Dirk swung her around in time to see John weaving through the wooden skeleton as though drunk. Dixie gasped and struggled to be free when she saw blood smeared across the side of his face.

"Let her go," John called, tripping, grabbing hold of an upright brace, until he slid painfully to his knees. "She's done nothing to you."

"Nothing? She owns part of Texas Proud. My part! I earned it, but you gave it away! You'd be nothing without me, you scum sucking low-life bastard!" His voice rose higher and higher until it became a plaintive whine. "I'm the one who deserves Texas Proud and Kate. I'm the one who should live in a mansion!"

He's insane, Dixie thought, with revulsion. An uncontrollable shudder ran down her spine. Cold sweat dampened her clothing. Her nerves jerked beneath her skin like live electrical wires as her eyes frantically circled the perimeter of the clearing.

Don't come out of hiding, Waco. He's crazy. He'll kill you, too!

The tip of the barrel swung toward John; then made a wide arc as the undergrowth behind them rustled sharply, then burst apart.

Wild-eyed with fear, Dixie chopped her hand against Dirk's wrist to deflect his aim and she simultaneously screamed, "Waco!"

A bullet exploded from the barrel, deafening Dixie from the sounds of Waco's savage bellow, and the wail of police-car sirens. Spotlights blinded her. Reflexively, her arms covered her eyes.

She couldn't see or hear!

Did the bullet hit Waco?

Dirk's hand snapped her head violently, as he tried to free his fingers from her hair. Then she felt both his hands frantically claw down her back as he was tackled from the side. Stumbling, falling, she didn't know if she'd been pushed by the impact or struck by the butt of the gun.

Dazed, her eyes glassy, she blinked, once, twice. As her vision slowly cleared, everything appeared in black and white. Dirk swung wildly at Waco, who returned a bone-racking jab to the stomach. When Dirk started to cave in, Waco upended him with a right hook.

Dixie struggled to get up. She noticed that the fire Dirk had started had burned itself out. Green wood and concrete weren't combustible without gasoline, her mind slowly registered. Her arms and legs reacted lethargically. She got as far as her hands and knees, when Zeke and John helped her to her feet.

She could see Zeke's mouth moving, but heard only a dull ringing in her ears. Was this some sort of macabre joke he was playing on her?

"Get him out of here before I kill him," Waco yelled angrily, as four men in uniforms wrestled with his arms, restraining him from finishing Dirk off, permanently.

His face was a mask of tortured anguish, pale and gaunt, as he turned toward Dixie. Six long strides and she was in his trembling arms, fiercely holding on to him, while her father and Zeke stared proudly at him.

Unashamed of his emotions, Waco said breathlessly, "Oh, Dixie-love, I couldn't believe it when you started running toward him. I'd have died if anything had happened to you."

The ditch he'd been trudging through snaked through the property. He'd come to a fork and been disoriented. Choosing to go right, he'd been unnerved when the ditch abruptly ended, sinking into a drainage pipe. He'd hurriedly retraced his steps and started down the other branch when he'd heard Dixie scream.

Fearing the worst, he'd scratched and scrambled from the ditch, cutting across to a low growth of brush. His blood had run cold when he'd parted the branches. That maniac had a gun pointed at her.

Paralyzed with horror, unable to move forward or backward without risking her life, he'd waited for an opportunity to rush Dirk. Each yank on Dixie's hair caused his skin to crawl. He wanted to punish Dirk for each hair he'd pulled from her head.

Like most egotistical maniacs, Dirk wanted the Maysons to know how brilliantly he'd duped them. He'd nickeled and dimed them for years, waiting for a chance to stick it to Texas Proud. While he talked, Waco had inched forward, careful, so careful not to break a twig or move a branch. All the while, he listened intently.

When he felt certain Dirk was going to shoot John and then Dixie, a red haze of fury came over him. He'd gone mad. He'd looked down the barrel of that .357 pistol and not cared whether he lived or died. Death was preferable to living without her.

Without a second thought, Dixie had put herself at risk to save him.

"Don't ever put yourself in danger like that again," he pleaded ferociously. "I love you so much. I don't know how I'd have lived without you!"

"She can't hear you," John said, clapping Waco on the back. "Dirk fired the gun by her ear."

"You can," Waco growled, his dark eyes earnest. In a voice that should have shaken the rafters he declared, "I'm going to marry your daughter, Mr. Mayson."

John blotted the cut above his eye with the handkerchief Zeke had lent him, delaying approval or disapproval. Unlike his daughter, he made instantaneous decisions. Sometimes he was wrong, but what the hell—that's what made life interesting, wasn't it? He was damned seldom wrong, and never bored.

Today was a record-breaker, he mused drily. Kate, Dirk, and Waco had proven him wrong. He'd admitted to Kate that he'd been afraid of unconditional love. He'd loved Dixie's mother to distraction. When she'd died, he'd vowed never to go through living hell again. He'd enjoyed Kate, but he'd held back a small piece of his soul that required another total commitment.

Looking at Waco, he saw a younger version of himself. Ambitious, determined, and very, very much in love. Deep inside, he resigned himself to sharing the gift of love his wife had presented him with for safekeeping.

Poker-faced John looked straight in Waco's eyes and drawled, "You're fickle-hearted. You love 'em and leave 'em."

"Once, never again," Waco vowed, loudly. "There isn't a jail cell in Texas with bars strong enough to hold me inside them. Nothing will keep us apart. We belong together."

Grinning, Zeke played straight man. "When I helped John up off the slab, he asked me if the two of us were related. When I told him I was your uncle, he clamped his hand over his mouth." He winked at Waco. "Wonder why?"

" 'Cause Cinderfella kissed me first," John declared, grinning at his future son-in-law.

Zeke slapped John on the back, "He is kind of affectionate, like a puppy dawg. Breathin' in your face, wantin' to play kissy-mouth."

Dixie chuckled silently. It had taken several minutes for her hearing to recover, but she'd gotten the gist of the minor feud taking place.

"You did kiss Dad," she teased, nipping the lobe of his ear. "And now you want to marry me?"

"I do," he answered, smiling his special smile, only for her.

John wrapped his arm around Zeke's scrawny shoulders and ambled down the drive. "What do you think, Zeke? A big Texas blow-out or something small and informal?"

"My niece, Crystal, she'll be expectin' to be a bridesmaid. As for me?" He hiked up his britches, stuck his thumbs under his belt buckle and said, "I've always wanted to be the best man. I think that's kinda befittin'."

John glanced over his shoulder and saw his daughter locked in the arms of the man he'd always known was the one man he considered a worthy adversary. Strangely contented, he mused,

Waco wouldn't be the best man at his own wedding, but he could be when Kate set the date for their wedding.

Dear Reader,

I began my writing career fifteen years ago with the desire to become the Erma Brombeck of romance novels. Isn't laughter what keeps us all sane? I hope the characters in *Someday* make you grin and chuckle, and have your husband or loved ones asking, "What's so funny?"

Many thanks to those of you who took the time out of your busy schedules to stop and drop me a letter. Unlike most jobs, a writer doesn't get immediate feedback. Frankly, one of the things I miss about those days when I was teaching is when I saw a student's face light up with comprehension or when they'd smile at me and ask, "Are you going to tell stories today?" Of course, I sternly replied, "Yes. I will be lecturing on . . ." I guess I've always been a storyteller. Like most of you, I appreciate a pat on the head or a friendly letter in the mailbox.

My next book, *The Brides,* comes from a special place in my heart. It is about three women who go to extremes to fulfill their romantic dreams. Miranda, Stacy and Holly should have listened to the old saying: Be careful what you wish for . . . or you might get it!

'Til next time, be happy and keep smiling.

Anna Hudson